Lazar – after the murder of a Russian soldier drives them from their homeland to London's turbulent East End, he learns the bitter cost of their preservation – and determines to pay it.

Shmuel – the younger brother whose physical prowess leads him into the boxing ring and, unwittingly, the grip of corruption, until a new-found inner strength becomes the courage to fight his way out.

Leah – devoted sister, lured by wealth and charm to the marriage bed of a man deeply – and deceptively – violent, she can free herself only by risking the love of her brothers . . . for her, and for each other.

HERITAGE is a magnificent story of the struggle for independence and survival-as-family, in a city where the streets teem with temptation, where ambition, money and violence challenge the legacy of a world left behind but never forgotten.

Heritage

Lewis Orde

CORGI BOOKS

HERITAGE

A CORGI BOOK   0 552 12704 3

Originally published in 1981 in the United States of America
by Arbor House Publishing Company and in Canada by
Fitzhenry & Whiteside Ltd. First publication in Great Britain
by Judy Piatkus (Publishers) Limited of London.

PRINTING HISTORY

Judy Piatkus edition published 1985
Corgi edition published 1986

This book is set in 10/11pt Plantin.

Corgi Books are published by Transworld Publishers Ltd.,
61-63 Uxbridge Road, Ealing, London W5 5SA,
in Australia by Transworld Publishers (Aust.) Pty. Ltd.,
26 Harley Crescent, Condell Park, NSW 2200, and in
New Zealand by Transworld Publishers (N.Z.) Ltd., Cnr. Moselle
and Waipareira Avenues, Henderson, Auckland.

Made and printed in Great Britain by
Hunt Barnard Printing Ltd., Aylesbury, Bucks.

To Don Fine

1934

CHAPTER ONE

Winter came early and abruptly to Cologne. In the middle of November when the city's residents expected heavy soaking rain to be their biggest blight a blizzard struck with sudden ferocity. Overnight Cologne was blanketed with a dense layer of snow. The temperature plummeted. People ventured out cautiously onto streets devoid of vehicles, wearing the thick woollen clothing and high fur-lined boots they normally reserved for December, January and February when winter raged at its fiercest. Autumn, with its magical carpet of leaves and pine needles, became a nostalgic memory; spring was far too distant to even think about.

A roaring wood fire blazed out welcome warmth in the living room of a two-storey house on Koenigstrasse, close to the center of town. Around the fire sat three men and a woman, faces solemn in the flickering light as they sipped black tea from glasses cupped in silver holders. No one seemed ready to speak; it was as if they could communicate wordlessly.

Over the top of his glass Aron Boruchowicz regarded his three children thoughtfully. The advice he had to offer them was painful, and he was grateful that his wife, Sophie, was out of the room. Knowing what her husband wanted to tell his children, she had retired early.

Aron's eyes went to the youngest member of the family, his twenty-year-old daughter Leah. Leah was his favorite. Not because she was the only girl, although Aron knew that entered into his thinking. It was Leah's idealism that Aron found so endearing, her love of others, her sense of caring. She had a passion for fairness that glowed in her dark brown eyes and lent stature to her slender figure. Even as a young

9

girl she had been no different, always seeking a cause to champion. At school, her teachers had described it as a rebellious spirit. To Aron, with a father's understandably prejudiced view, Leah's idealism was an intrinsic part of her charm.

From Leah, Aron turned his attention to Shmuel, amazed as always how his younger son could be so differently proportioned from the rest of the family. Broad-shouldered, tall with a barrel chest and powerful arms, Shmuel was a giant whose awesome size contradicted his gentle nature. The havoc he could create by merely swinging a fist was compensated for by his easygoing nature. It was a wonderful example of God's wisdom, Aron had decided. Shmuel's gentleness in a weak body would have been the delight of any bully . . . just as a fiery nature would have been catastrophic in a man of his size and strength. Knowledge of the power he possessed also made Shmuel secure, slow to anger. But when aroused he could be fearsome.

Aron knew he would never be able to forget the previous year, even before Hitler had come to power, when Brownshirts had attacked Jewish-owned shops and houses in Cologne. Shmuel had stood guard outside the house, a heavy wooden club swinging almost nonchalantly from his ham-like hands as he dared anyone to come close. A rock had been thrown, missing Shmuel but breaking a window. With a speed that defied his size, Shmuel had gone after the rock thrower, scattering others who tried to stop him. One swing of the club had shattered the man's right arm, the arm that had thrown the missile. Shmuel had returned to his post, ready to challenge anyone else. The crowd had swiftly dispersed.

Aron now considered Lazar, at twenty-seven his older son. Lazar was an enigma his father could never completely understand. Most every family had its black sheep, but that didn't make it any easier for Aron to accept what his own son was. He was dishonest. A thief. What compounded the pain was that Lazar had the mental ability to be anything he wanted to be. He was brilliant with figures, with commerce . . . and also stupid enough to steal. Only because Aron knew the officers of the bank where Lazar had worked as an accountant before being exposed as an embezzler was he able to have the affair hushed up. As a personal favor to Aron the bank's chairman had accepted the return of the embezzled funds, and Lazar's resignation. Lazar's only regret was that he'd been caught milking accounts that had been dormant for more than five years. After the bank he had found work at a lumber mill, and there, as if to show up in glaring light the folly of his dishonesty, he had been appointed head of the accounting department within two years.

But perhaps Aron did know the driving force behind his older son's action. Lazar's childhood – until Shmuel had become strong enough to defend him from the spite and vicious taunts of other children – had been a miserable one. It was a mystery that no doctor could explain to Aron's satisfaction . . . how Lazar had hair so blond that he could be mistaken for an albino. The white hair, together with a capacity for learning that placed him high above other children of his age, had made Lazar an obvious target. The other kids had ganged up on him, made fun of him, pulled his beautiful platinum hair to see if it was real. They had made him into an outcast, a feeling no amount of love at home could offset. By the time Shmuel – two years younger than Lazar – had started to take his brother's part, it was too late . . . something inside Lazar had turned. A bitter hostility had blossomed, driving him on, forcing him to prove that he was better than anyone else. The embezzlement was his way of showing how much smarter he was than the bank. That he had been caught was a lesson to him that he had to be smarter still.

Aron sighed, turned to face the fire, then began to speak in a quiet, unemotional voice. "The three of you have to leave Germany. This is no country for young people to stay. Make plans to get out while you can."

"What about you and mother?" Leah asked. The girl seemed shocked by the abruptness of her father's words. "Do you want us to leave you?"

"Of course not. But we're too old to be pioneers. Perhaps when the three of you are settled we will follow. For the time being, though, it's better that we stay here where we've built

11

our lives." As he spoke Aron wished he would have listened to the same advice two or three years earlier, when he should have been sensible enough to judge which way the political winds were shifting. Hitler and his mouthpiece, that crippled lunatic Goebbels, had made it pointedly clear that there was little the Jews could hope for once the National Socialists came to power. So far they hadn't touched Jewish commerce . . . that would harm the country economically. But there would come a time, Aron knew, when Hitler would feel strong enough to carry out his threats against Germany's Jews.

"If you're staying I will too," Leah said defiantly. "You'll see . . . they'll realize that we are Germans first and foremost. We belong here as much as they do."

A burst of sardonic laughter came from Lazar .. . "Was that what they thought when they stoned the house? That they were throwing bricks because there were Germans inside?"

"Those people weren't real Germans," Leah shot back. "They were thugs. Animals."

"What do you think they are at the top?" Lazar persisted. "Angels? Didn't you listen to a thing Hitler's said these last five years?"

Before Leah could answer, Shmuel came to her defense. "We *are* Germans," he said quietly. "Our roots are here. Father fought for the Kaiser in the last war. He was a captain."

As Shmuel spoke Aron gave himself the luxury of remembering those days . . . As an engineer his skills had been sought by the army. He glanced up at the mantelpiece, at the photograph of himself taken nineteen years earlier, standing proudly in uniform. Two other men were with him, fellow officers. What were they doing now? Advising their children to run off . . . or praising the new government, like so many others, and all it stood for? "Lower your voices," he told his children. "Your mother is asleep upstairs. Have some respect for her if not for each other."

Shmuel and Leah did, but Lazar went to the other side of the room. Climbing an imaginary podium, he started to harangue his listeners. "Jews to the slaughter! Let's all sit around and wait for Hitler to show us that he's not a liar.

12

We'll even make it easier by standing outside the house in a straight line while we chant that we're Germans first. They'll be able to kill us so much more efficiently. Don't you ever absorb anything from history?" Lazar's voice acquired a spiteful, biting tone as he aimed the question at his sister. "What about Russia under the czars? One third of our Jews we'll convert. One third we'll drive out. And the other third we'll kill! What about Poland? The same will happen here. At least Hitler warns us in advance. Can't you get it into your head, Leah, that to the Nazis we were never Germans? Only *Jews*?"

Leah's anger showed in her reddening cheeks. Her body tensed and she started to get up from the chair. Shmuel reached out quickly and placed a hand on her. Realizing how close he was to overstepping the mark, Lazar turned around to face the wall. He fumbled in his jacket pocket and then moved his hands swiftly to his face. Moments later, when he swung around again, he was wearing a false moustache. It made no difference that the moustache was jet black and clashed violently with his own coloring. Everyone watching knew who he was impersonating.

"Little Leah Boruchowicz has made me see the light!" he barked in an uncannily accurate imitation of Hitler. "Our Jews *are* Germans first! They are heroes to our country! To our party! I retract everything I ever said about them. Mainly because" — Lazar dropped his voice and winked conspiratorially — "I think my great-grandfather might have been one."

Watching his son's antics Aron couldn't resist a slight smile. If only Lazar would put his talents to a worthwhile use. No question that his older son was talented, head and shoulders above his brother and sister when it came to academic subjects. He had a natural aptitude for languages, had picked up English and Dutch as well as the German and Yiddish the others spoke. He also worked with his head while his brother and sister labored with their hands, Shmuel at a furniture factory and Leah as a seamstress.

They should all listen to him, Aron decided, and leave Germany. Leah could open her own dress shop. Shmuel could start his own furniture factory. And Lazar? Lazar could become anything he wanted . . . *if* he put his mind to it.

"One day," Shmuel told his brother in an ominously soft voice, "the wrong people will see you do your Adolf act. And we'll be rid of you at last." He grinned and drew his index finger across his throat.

"Don't talk like that, not even as a joke," Aron said, frightened that Shmuel's words might somehow tempt fate.

"But he asks for trouble," Shmuel said.

"I only ask for trouble where no one can hear my question," Lazar pointed out. "I'm not like little Leah, safe in my delusion that we're Germans first and Jews second while I wait for a bullet in my empty head."

Shmuel slapped his knees with his hands. "Well, finally you at least admit that your head is empty...you are no better than the rest of us . . ."

Lazar ripped off the black moustache, looked disparagingly at the theatrical prop before tossing it to the floor. "And how else, might I ask, would you expect my head to be when I'm impersonating our beloved leader?"

Even Leah joined in the laughter, and the tension aroused by Lazar's earlier taunting of his sister was forgotten as the four of them joined to deride the common enemy. They were together, at least for the moment.

The train to Aachen was almost empty. Lazar settled himself into a corner seat and pulled his heavy coat tightly around himself. His breath hung in icy clouds across the compartment and he longed for the journey to begin.

The short trip west to Aachen – on the border with Belgium and Holland – was the second Lazar had made in less than two weeks. The company in Cologne that he worked for was buying a lumber mill in Aachen and it was Lazar's responsibility to check the books. He would be away for two days, staying overnight in a hotel at the company's expense.

Lazar looked forward to the trip. The last time in Aachen he had met Rachel, a clerk at the mill, a pretty hazel-eyed girl who had laughed at his jokes, appreciated his wit. He knew what had attracted her initially, his pure blondness. She'd been fascinated by it, and her fascination had intrigued him. What had once, in childhood, been an embarrassing curse was turning into an advantage.

The girl had invited him home to meet her parents, who owned a large clothing store in the town. They had welcomed him graciously, knowing he held a responsible position in Cologne, letting him know that he was the kind of man they felt their daughter should bring home. Lazar still remembered the warmth of Rachel's goodnight kiss as he stood on the front step of her home before walking back to the hotel. It was a memory he wanted to live again.

The train pulled into Aachen. From the station Lazar went directly to the mill, carrying his overnight case; he'd check into the hotel after work. The mill owner greeted him with a stiff courtesy. The accountant from the firm that was buying his own company was a man to be respected. The price had been agreed upon subject to an exhaustive inspection of the books. Lazar's quick eyes could spot a discrepancy; they could cost the selling company money. Lazar relished the respect given him by the older, more affluent man.

It was chilly in the office so he kept on his coat while he sat at a desk and began to examine the books that had been set out. Rachel was seated only a few feet away, head bent low over her work. Every so often she would look up and catch Lazar gazing at her and they'd both smile. A couple of times during the afternoon Lazar called the mill owner over to ask a question about the books, each time noting how the girl would look in his direction.

When closing time came Lazar slammed the books shut with an exaggerated gesture of finality. A fine cloud of dust sprang up which he blew away, smiling through it at Rachel. He picked up his small case and got ready to walk to the hotel three blocks away. When he had gone a hundred yards he stopped. A minute later, Rachel was beside him, the fur collar of her coat pulled up around her neck to hide her face.

"My parents have instructed me to ask you for dinner tonight, Herr Boruchowicz."

The girl's formality amused Lazar. A very proper girl.

"Thank you. I would be delighted. But first . . . can we maybe steal a few minutes to ourselves? To talk?"

Rachel nodded. She knew Lazar was in Aachen for only one night and wanted to spend as much time alone with him as possible. Arm-in-arm they walked to the hotel, where Lazar registered and left his case at the desk. Then they chose a tearoom close to the hotel. Lazar held open the door for Rachel to enter the steamy, comfortable warmth.

Once inside the tearoom Lazar knew their choice had been a mistake. Seated close to the entrance were two *Sturm Abteilung*, SA Brownshirts, talking loudly, laughing. One banged heavy boots on the wooden floor as his companion said something funny. Lazar guessed they were drunk. Other people in the tearoom pretended not to notice; no one looked around.

Rachel reached out and pressed Lazar's hand. "Let's go somewhere else."

But to enter and then leave would be to invite dangerous attention, Lazar decided. He let the door swing closed, a defiant gesture. "We'll do like everyone else and pretend they're not here."

Rachel led the way into the tearoom, heading toward an empty table in the corner furthest from the two Brownshirts. As she passed by their table she looked away. Lazar was not so tactful. Walking by the men, fur hat clutched tightly in his hand, he gave them a lingering gaze. The disgrace of Germany, the scum of the earth; the thugs who formed the backbone of the damned Nazi Party.

One of the Brownshirts glanced up, a huge beefy man with red hair and an aggressively flourishing moustache. His eyes met with Lazar's, then moved upward to take in the white hair. A grin spread slowly across the Brownshirt's face.

"Blondie!" he roared, banging his fist on the table. "Blondie! Come over here!"

"Ignore them," begged Rachel. "Make believe you don't hear."

Lazar nodded, recognizing the wisdom of her advice. Reaching the table, he helped Rachel into a chair and sat down himself. But before he could get comfortable a shadow loomed across the table. Lazar stared straight ahead at the wide leather belt that separated shirt from trousers, at the swastika armband. Slowly his gaze rose to the man's bristling red moustache.

"Blondie, I called you. Don't you speak German?"

"Please leave us alone," Rachel said quietly. "We aren't bothering you."

The Brownshirt looked from Lazar to Rachel, smiled. "The rustle of your pretty clothes bothers me. The smell of your perfume bothers me. Why would anyone as attractive as you waste time with this . . . this freak of nature, a Jew who tries to look like an Aryan . . . when you could be the guest of real men?" He turned back to Lazar and ran thick, stubby fingers through his hair, insultingly blew him kisses. Lazar flinched at the man's touch but did nothing, willed himself to stare into space.

Rachel was terrified. Why hadn't Lazar listened to her? They should never have come into the tearoom once they'd spotted the Brownshirts. "You speak as a gentleman would speak," she said, struggling to conquer her fear. "Would a gentleman interfere with a lady and her friend?"

The red-haired man laughed. "As a gentleman I make you this offer. When you've gotten tired of the company of this blond *untermensch*, leave him and join us." He turned around to rejoin his comrade, pleased with himself.

Lazar glared after him, face burning, jaw tightening. The owner of the lumber mill had given him respect. Rachel's parents would treat him with respect. What right did this illiterate Nazi bully have to insult him? Rachel reached out a hand to steady Lazar. When the explosion came, though, nothing could control it. Lazar swung around on the seat and called out across the dead-silent tearoom:

"When hell freezes over she'll sit with pigs like you."

The red-haired man stopped walking. He shook his head, and in half a dozen strides was back at the table. Out-size hands reached down to lift Lazar bodily from the chair. He could feel the Brownshirt's hot breath on his face.

"So, Blondie *does* have a tongue, he can speak for himself..."

Lazar swung impotent fists at the face in front of him. The man laughed and shook him like a dog worrying a rat.

"*Please*, leave him alone . . ." Rachel was getting up from her chair. "He meant no harm . . ."

The Brownshirt, turning to look at her, momentarily relaxed his grip and Lazar stumbled backward, colliding with the edge of the table, reaching out blindly for support. His right hand skipped across the linen tablecloth, scattered china and cutlery. Fingers touched the blade of a knife, moved downward until they rested on the bone handle, gripped it tightly.

The Brownshirt sensed something was wrong, looked away from Rachel and grabbed at Lazar. The knife in his hand gave Lazar strength, and confidence. With a speed and ferocity he never knew he was capable of Lazar lifted the sharp knife straight up and plunged it into the man's stomach.

The Brownshirt's red face collapsed in surprise. He staggered back a few steps, both hands feeling in numb confusion the knife handle that protruded from his belly. Blood stained the front of his shirt, seeped out between his clutching hands to drip onto the floor. His mouth opened and closed without giving out a sound, his eyes merely stared at Lazar.

Rachel screamed. A single, high-pitched scream. The noise acted on Lazar like adrenalin. He forced himself to look away from the stricken Brownshirt, grabbed Rachel by the hand and ran toward the door. The second Brownshirt stood up slowly, stunned. His attempt to stop the two fugitives was half-hearted. Lazar slammed into him, shoulder first, sending him spinning into a table.

"Where to?" Lazar yelled when they were out on the street. From inside the tearoom he could hear men shouting, women screaming.

"Down *here* . . ." Rachel led the way, cutting left down a narrow alley which opened onto another street. The bitter cold hurt their lungs, made them fight for every breath. The darkness tricked them into stumbling over unseen objects, but they didn't stop running. Twisting and turning down a labyrinth of streets and alleyways that were foreign to Lazar,

18

doubling back on themselves and cutting across streets they had already covered, they reached the offices of the lumber mill. Rachel opened the door with her key, they slipped inside. Only then, surrounded by the security of almost total darkness, did they dare to relax.

"I think I killed him." Lazar tried to control his frantic breathing. His chest heaved, threatening to explode.

"They'll arrest you."

"If they can catch me. I'll be wearing a Nazi necktie if they ever get their hands on me . . . You'll have to go back to the hotel," Lazar told her. "To get my case."

"But—"

"You'll be all right, no one in that tearoom got a good look at you. They were all too busy watching me." It was the truth. With the target of his platinum hair who would have eyes for anything else? He moved away from Rachel and began to open desk drawers, peering inside.

"What are you doing?"

"What does it look like I'm doing?" Any money he found he stuffed into his coat pocket. If he found a couple of hundred marks he'd consider himself fortunate.

"You're *stealing*."

The absurdity of Rachel's accusation made Lazar throw his hands into the air. "Stealing? My God, Rachel, I've just killed an SA man. Stuck a knife clean through him. What difference do you think taking a few miserable marks makes? Any more money in the office?"

Rachel said nothing, not able to accept the transformation in this man who only minutes earlier had been talking about spending a few precious minutes with her —

"Do they?" Lazar gripped her by the shoulders and raised his voice, only lowering it when he realized he might be heard outside.

"In there." Rachel pointed to a locked closet.

"Where's the key?"

"I don't have it." Reality suddenly caught up with Rachel. She began to cry, her head dropping onto her chest as the truth of the evening fought its way past the initial shock.

19

Leaving her alone, Lazar searched the office, holding up lit matches to clear the darkness. A cupboard revealed a toolbox; inside was a crowbar.

"Wipe your eyes and go back to the hotel," he told Rachel. "Bring my case back here, then go back to your family."

She hesitated; Lazar gently turned her around and pushed her toward the door, "Go, run, there's no time . . ." As the door closed behind her he gave his full attention to the locked closet that held the money. Jamming the crowbar behind the door's hinges, he shoved as hard as he could. Wood splintered. The door popped back. Fumbling inside he found a locked strongbox. He forced it open. By the light from a match he counted quickly, breathing easier when he saw how much there was . . .

Rachel came back a few minutes later. "Police are at the hotel, I couldn't get through."

"Well, thanks for trying." He managed to force a smile. "Go home now. And please convey my deepest apologies to your parents that I cannot accept their invitation to dinner after all. Another matter has forced my cancellation."

She saw through his forced irony and shook her head. "Good luck," she whispered as she held his hands for a long moment. "I'm sorry we didn't meet earlier . . ."

"So am I."

As she turned to leave, Lazar forced himself to concentrate on his situation . . . Police were at the hotel. They were checking premises next to the tearoom. The case containing a change of clothing didn't matter . . . but something else did. His description – and what a description – must have been put out. The clerk at the hotel would be able to identify him. They would get his name from the register. *And* . . . his home address in Cologne.

"Wait," Lazar called after Rachel. "Would you . . . go to Cologne for me?"

"What? Why?"

"To warn my family, Rachel. I don't dare go to the station."

". . . But what should I tell them?"

"Exactly what happened, and that I'm running for the border."

20

"How will they know where to find you?"

"Tell them I'll be in Maastricht, across the Dutch border. I'll wait there for two weeks. And," he added, reluctantly foreseeing possible trouble, "if they get there before me, they should wait two weeks for me."

Rachel repeated the message, and left.

Lazar stood by the door long after it had closed behind her. Finally he pulled out a chair and sat down heavily, his mind in turmoil as he tried to sort out the events of the past thirty minutes and plan his next move. He had only the clothes he stood in and the money he had taken from the strongbox and desk drawers . . . he'd been lucky and found more than three thousand marks, a handsome start. But what about his family? If Rachel managed to warn them in time, what would they be able to bring? Would they even leave? Would his father give up the house, all he had worked for, because of the foolish — yes, Lazar forced himself to admit it — actions of his son? Damn it, why had he taken hold of that knife like his life depended on it? Why had he even called out after the man? He should have left him alone. The red-haired oaf was walking back to his own table anyway, his moment of fun at Lazar's expense over . . . Stop it . . . no point in these recriminations now . . .

He waited an hour before venturing outside. Snow had started to fall again, a welcome cover. No one was on the street. Lazar began to feel a little better. Head down, bending into the blowing snow, he began to trudge toward the western edge of the city. Beyond that was the border, where he could slip across at any one of a dozen places; and from there he could reach Maastricht.

As he walked on he thought about his family. What would be their reaction when they learned the news? They would leave, of course they would . . . It would be crazy to stay put when your son, your brother, had killed a Brownshirt. Just let them be warned in time, he prayed silently . . . and he'd spend the rest of his life making up to them what they'd lost . . .

He thought about the Brownshirt . . . the surprised face, the hands clutching at the handle of the knife. It had all

21

happened so quickly that he hadn't had time to think, not even to be really afraid. But he also knew that if he were sitting in that damn tearoom now he'd do exactly the same thing. It was as if he'd suddenly exorcised a whole lifetime of fear. At school other children had ganged up on him, only letting up when Shmuel had taken his part. Tonight, there had been no Shmuel. He had helped himself. That one thrust with the knife had seemed to purge the fear from his body, told him he never needed to fear another man again . . .

Inside his glove his right hand tightened around an imaginary knife. In front of his eyes appeared the Brownshirt's face. And Lazar felt a deep joy that he had killed the man.

It was a start.

Aron Boruchowicz heard the hammering on the front door of the house and shook himself fully awake. Lazar already back from Aachen? At this hour? It must be after eleven.

The long white nightshirt flapped around his legs as Aron climbed out of bed. The cold bit into his body and made him shiver. He struggled into a heavy woollen dressing gown, tied up the belt and went downstairs. When he pulled open the door he saw a young woman with her coat collar pulled up around her face.

"I am a friend of your son Lazar," she said breathlessly. "My name is Rachel –"

"Come in." Aron made a sweeping gesture with his hand. "What brings you here so late?" He couldn't remember seeing the girl around Cologne, nor had Lazar ever mentioned her.

"I've just travelled from Aachen. I was with Lazar earlier this evening when he killed an SA man during an argument –"

"He did *what*?" Aron heard footsteps on the stairs. Looking around, he saw Shmuel.

"He stabbed a Brownshirt during a fight –"

"What *happened*, did they catch him?" Shmuel asked.

"No. He got away. He took money from the lumber mill office in Aachen. Now he's trying to get to the border. He sent me here to warn you, and to say he'll wait in Maastricht . . ."

"Do the police know who he is?" Shmuel asked.

The girl nodded weakly. "I think so. They were checking the hotel where he was staying. I went back there for his case but I couldn't get through." Briefly she explained what had happened in the tearoom, stressing again Lazar's message to his family.

"We all must leave," Shmuel decided. He ran up the stairs to wake his sister and mother. Aron sat down in a daze, not able to believe that his son could have done such a thing.

The girl's voice intruded on his thoughts. "I have to get back to Aachen . . . my parents will be worried −"

"Of course," Aron said to her without even seeing her.

When the door closed behind her, he stood up and began to pace the living room, hands clasped behind his back. Was the Brownshirt indeed dead? Could Lazar have struck with enough force and hate to *kill* a man?

"What happened, father?" Leah asked as she came downstairs. She was already dressed; her heavy boots sounded loud as she walked across the floor.

"Your brother . . . killed a Brownshirt in Aachen, he's run for the Dutch border. We all must do the same −"

"Lazar did *what*?" Like her father, Leah was unable to take in that Lazar could have committed such violence.

Aron nodded grimly. "You heard me. We all have to leave now, before the police come." He went to a corner of the room, pushed back a heavy wooden chest and lifted a loose floorboard. Underneath was a wooden box. Inside was a little more than twelve hundred marks. "Take everything from the cupboards," he ordered Leah. "*Hurry . . .*"

More steps sounded as Sophie Boruchowicz came downstairs. A short, heavy woman, she took the stairs slowly, still half-asleep, unable to comprehend the commotion that had suddenly torn her house apart. "What's all this about Lazar?"

"He killed an SA man in Aachen during an argument," Aron told her as he put the twelve hundred marks on the table. "We're to meet him in Maastricht."

Sophie looked about the room, confused by all the action. "What's Leah doing?"

"Taking everything that's valuable," Leah told her. "Do you want to leave it for the Nazis?" She put silver wine goblets next to the money on the table, following them with candlesticks. She looked around for other silverware.

"Make some food," Aron told Sophie.

Sleep departed from Sophie's brain, and she took charge of her domain, the kitchen. The sounds of pots and pans being moved rang through the lower part of the house; soon an appetizing aroma of food wafted from the kitchen.

As Sophie worked it crossed her mind that this would be the last time she would ever prepare food in this house. And there was not even enough time to make a proper meal . . . haste was no way to end an association with a house that had lasted from the day of her marriage to Aron thirty years ago. She wiped a tear from her eyes. Embarrassed, she looked around quickly to see if anyone was watching. No one was there. Sophie straightened her back and returned to her work. She would cry only when her family was together again. Then at least they would be tears not of sadness, but of joy . . .

By two in the morning they were ready to leave. Everything of value was packed carefully into a large suitcase now held by Shmuel. Another two cases, carried by Aron and Leah, contained clothing, while Sophie carried the food in a covered basket. They stood in the center of the living room, taking a final look at the house that had been their home for so long. Leah and Shmuel had been born there; they had never known anywhere else. Lazar, too; and he had been denied the opportunity even to say good-by.

"What will happen to the house?" Sophie asked the question on all their minds.

"The government will confiscate it, I suppose," Aron said, shaking his head. All he had worked for would go to a government he despised. It didn't seem fair. He looked at his son, at his daughter. "Should we leave it for them?"

Shmuel needed no time to think. He went quickly into the kitchen and returned moments later with a large container of lamp oil. While the others watched, he spread a wide pool of oil over the highly varnished floor, ran trails to the walls, the furniture, the drapes. At the center of the oil he placed two short candles. He lit them carefully and stepped back. "Let's go," was all he said.

Aron was the last to leave. He gave a last look at the inside of the house. He closed the door gently to avoid creating a draft that might blow out the candles. In an hour, the candles would burn down and ignite the oil. The house would be gutted. The Nazis were welcome to that.

Shmuel sensed trouble as the train pulled into Aachen. It had not been so smart, he decided, to travel there, even if it did offer an easier escape route. A Brownshirt had been killed only a few hours earlier. By a Jew. Jews would be fair game... especially if they had the same surname as the man wanted for the killing.

As the train slowed down Shmuel rubbed the window clear of condensation. Snow was falling heavily, but he could see the patrol of armed police waiting on the poorly illuminated platform. Passengers who got off were being made to stand in line, waiting their turn to produce identity documents. Aron began to step down, but Shmuel pulled him back.

"Out the other side," he whispered. Leah went down first, stepping carefully into the darkness. Aron was next, followed by Sophie who needed help from her husband. Lastly Shmuel dropped down onto the snow. Holding the cases, they made their way along the length of the train, hidden from the platform.

A hiss of steam belched out and the train began to move. Above the noise of steam escaping under pressure and the clanking of wheels and connecting rods could be heard the yells of police as they spotted the shadowy figures in the snow.

"*Run*," Shmuel called out. Lugging the heavy case containing the silverware, he shepherded his family away from the track. They ran only thirty yards before warning shots from the platform made them stop. Three policemen carrying rifles dropped down from the platform and ran through the snow. Shmuel set down his case and held up both hands. The men approached cautiously. Shmuel waited for the lead policeman to get close enough, then jumped at him, slamming a tightly clenched fist down on his head. Before the man could fall to the ground Shmuel lifted him high in the air and threw him at the other two.

A rifle sounded. A woman screamed in pain. Shmuel swung around to see Aron and Leah bending over the form of his mother, lying on the snow. Blood made a crimson stain on the white snow where her head rested.

More shots came from the platform as police opened fire into the snow-laden darkness, sensing rather than seeing their targets. Shmuel and Leah tried to lift their father away from the body of his wife, but Aron refused to budge, holding Sophie's body in his arms. A bullet kicked up snow inches from him.

"Come *on*," Shmuel said. "You can't do anything for her." He hated himself for his forced callousness, but if they didn't run they'd all join her. It was time to think of survival . . . grief could be indulged later.

"*Father*," Leah called out now, "let's go, you've got to leave her . . ."

"You go, you leave . . . I stay . . ."

Shmuel glanced up to see more figures running across the track toward them. He tried again to pry his father from his mother's body. For the first time since reaching manhood Shmuel found that his strength did not equal his father's. He could not budge him.

Aron would go nowhere, he would stay with his wife even if it meant dying with her. Especially if it meant that. Shaking off Shmuel's hands, he stood up and took hold of one of the fallen rifles. Swinging it like a club, he moved toward the approaching policemen. They fired at him from point-blank range, but the bullets that slammed into his body seemed to have little effect. Around and around went the rifle as Aron laid about him. Three men went down under the swinging rifle until at last the bullets had their way. Aron collapsed slowly, falling to his knees, using the rifle to prop himself up. And then that too gave way, and he fell face down into the snow.

26

Shmuel watched, horrified. Only when Leah grabbed his hand and pulled as hard as she could did he force his eyes away. Tears mixed with snow on his face as he picked up the case of silverware and joined his sister, running just ahead of him . . .

Shmuel and Leah met up with Lazar two days later in the Dutch town of Maastricht. Lazar was easy to trace. Questions about a young man with white hair brought them to a small inn where they found their brother in a room on the ground floor.

"Thank God," Lazar said when he opened the door to find the disheveled figures of his sister and brother standing outside . . . "Where are mother and father?"

"Dead." Shmuel spat it out. His wildly swung punch grazed Lazar's cheek and knocked him back into the room. "Because of you." Shmuel dived after his brother, wanting to kill him. Leah jumped onto his back, arms locked around his neck as she tried to stop him.

"Leave him alone, isn't it bad enough that we've lost our parents already? It's not Lazar's fault – "

"Why the hell are you starting on me?" Lazar yelled. "Do you think I wanted this?" Another punch slammed into his shoulder and sent him to the floor.

"Lazar didn't plan for this to happen," Leah said from her uneasy perch on Shmuel's back. "Leave him *alone* . . . we're all on the same damned side, you idiot . . ."

Shmuel stopped. His enormous body seemed to shrink in on itself as he understood what he was doing, why he was doing it. He needed someone to blame for his parents' death, for the craziness that had made the family nomads.

"I'm sorry." He reached down and helped Lazar to his feet. At the same time he felt Leah climb off his back, saw her move to help Lazar. Lazar stood up and felt his face. He knew he had to put himself in charge. Shmuel had strength. Leah had fire, her idealism. Neither of them, though, had the reasoning ability, the capacity for planning that he did. As the oldest member of the family it was his responsibility to lead them . . .

"What do you have in the case?" he asked Shmuel.

"Silverware. Father made us take it all. We gutted the house to leave the Nazis nothing. And" – he pulled money from his pocket – "twelve hundred marks."

"No clothes?"

"We had clothing," Leah told him, "but we left it in Aachen when the police tried to stop us. When . . . when mother and father were killed." In a sudden, unstoppable flood of words she told Lazar how their father had refused to leave Sophie, how he had attacked the police with the rifle. Lazar listened quietly, imagining the scene. The final act of a gentle man driven to violence. A man who had spent his whole life without harming a soul snapping at the sight of his wife shot down before his eyes. Lazar could understand his father's rage. Before he'd been provoked by the Brownshirt in the tearoom Lazar, too, had avoided violence. Well, there came a time in a man's life when he had to stand up and fight –

"Where do we go from here?" Shmuel broke into his thoughts.

"I say we go to England," Lazar told him. "Start again over there. I have more than three thousand marks. We buy new clothing for the trip so we don't turn up there looking like tramps. When we arrive we liquidate whatever's in the case to give us capital."

"England's fine for you," Leah said. "You speak the language."

"Are you too old to learn? Where would you like to go with the language you already speak? Back to Germany? We all have trades. We'll find work. We'll start again and build something . . ."

Shmuel and Leah looked at each other. A new country. A new language. A new way of life . . . would they be able to adjust?

"Come on," Lazar said impatiently. "Do you think I waited here for you so I could be turned down? I could have run anywhere. I didn't have to wait."

Leah was the first to accept her brother's decision . . . they could not go back, they could only go forward. Lazar was offering to show them the way.

"And you?" Lazar asked Shmuel.

"All right." Shmuel placed a heavy hand on Lazar's shoulder, exhausted by the running and hiding of the past two days. "I'm sorry I lost my temper before."

Lazar let Shmuel's hand remain on his shoulder for several seconds. "That's all right, you were entitled."

No question, Leah thought, Lazar had changed. He was a man who had direction. Her brother, for better or worse, had grown up.

CHAPTER TWO

Lazar, Leah and Shmuel arrived in London's East End looking and feeling like three frightened, insecure refugees. The miserable, wintry voyage from the Hook of Holland to Tilbury Dock on a Dutch boat where cargo came first and passengers second had shattered them. The new clothes they had bought for their journey were now stained and torn. They were hungry, frozen, tired.

A tender ferried them from the ship to a flight of steps leading up to the wharf. Dockworkers carried on their business around them, adding to the confusion. Brawny Irishmen with ruddy cheeks shouted to each other in a strange, incomprehensible tongue. Even Lazar, who understood English, could make little sense of the language the Irish spoke.

Beyond the dockers were immigration officials, stiff-lipped men who asked their questions with no expression on their faces. Lazar spoke for the entire family. They had money to pay their way; they all had trades; they were refugees. The immigration officials, satisfied, passed them through.

Lazar asked a dock official about accommodations. The man pointed north, to Whitechapel. They began to walk, tired limbs encouraged by the knowledge that soon they would sleep in proper beds, live again like human beings.

The first view of Whitechapel and the area to which immigrants had been drawn throughout British history came as a bitter shock. Once they had passed the wide expanse of Commercial Road they entered dark, narrow streets, hemmed in by rows of cramped, grubby buildings, sheltered from the sky by huge viaducts over which steam trains rumbled to add their own sooty layer. Laundry hung from open windows.

Barrows lined the streets. Rows of tiny shops sold everything from buttons and thread to used furniture. And everywhere there were people . . . children running and shouting, poorly dressed men, old before their time, married women . . . crowded in doorways, standing in groups on the sidewalk, talking, watching suspiciously what went on around them. The noise was unbelievable, an unintelligible babble of voices speaking half a dozen different tongues in a dozen different dialects, and somehow each making itself understood.

"Lazar, we need shelter," Leah reminded her brother as she caught him gazing around in bewildered fascination. "It's six o'clock. We don't want to sleep in the gutter."

"I know, I know." He didn't, of course, have the first idea where to begin looking. The East End was not what he'd expected. He'd thought of London and imagined a big city . . . hotels, inns, elegant shops and buildings. What surrounded him now was a warren of activity, a neighborhood of dirt, the entire Jewish community of Middle and Eastern Europe transported to another corner of the globe and crammed into a shoebox.

In Yiddish they asked people where they could find a place to sleep. Leah stopped one woman and explained that they had just arrived; did she know where they could stay? The woman replied that her own family had room for tenants. Relieved, they followed her through the dingy entrance of a building on Wentworth Street.

"Here," the woman said, showing them a room that contained a rickety double bed. "My son and daughter-in-law have just moved away. One of you will have to sleep on the floor."

Lazar choked back nausea from the smells. "Thank you," he managed to say, "but we don't wish to impose on you." Quickly he led his brother and sister out of the house, gratefully breathing in the dank air of the street as if it were the sweetest oxygen.

They stopped to eat at a small restaurant where the smell of frying fish was strong enough to cling to their clothing. They continued their search, but now it was late. Eventually they entered a Christian mission in Whitechapel Road that was dedicated to the good work of proselytizing Jews. They were offered cots for the night, which they accepted gratefully. In return they had to listen to a sermon in English that neither Leah nor Shmuel understood; Lazar did not bother to translate for them.

Early the following morning they continued their hunt, knocking on doors, asking in shops. Finally, they were offered furnished accommodation in Brick Lane, next to Shaffzics steam baths and close to the Maziche Adas synagogue. The accommodation comprised one large room with three beds, a dresser, wardrobe, table and three chairs. In one corner of the room was a cold-water sink and gas ring. The only toilet was located in the hallway and was used by all eight tenants of the building. Bathing was done at the public baths half a mile away.

"Well?" Shmuel asked, standing in the center of the room, hands on his hips. "Do we take it, or do we keep on looking?"

Leah slumped down onto one of the beds. "I'd take anything right now. Even . . . this." She bent down and traced a pattern in the dust that covered the floor. "You know what? There's nothing wrong with this place that a good scrub wouldn't cure."

Lazar walked to the window and looked down onto Brick Lane. Like every other street it was lined with barrows. Noisy vendors yelled at customers, at their helpers, at each other. "There's a shop selling sheets and blankets," he said. His sister and brother joined him at the window. "We can spend the rest of the day cleaning this place up."

"And making a screen for me," Leah added. "If I have to sleep in the same room with you two I want a partition."

"What about finding work?" Shmuel asked. Much of their money had gone, used for transportation and clothing. They still had the case full of silverware but they were reluctant to part with it, representing as it did their last tangible link with the house in Cologne.

"Today we'll clean," Lazar replied. "Tomorrow we'll find work."

From shops in Brick Lane they purchased bedding and the

basic necessities of a household. Then they set about cleaning the room. Shmuel washed the grimy windows, dusted, erected a screen to give Leah's bed a bit of privacy. Leah sewed together covers to disguise the stained mattresses, fashioned cheap drapes to cover the windows and brighten the room. And Lazar, remembering with a touch of whimsy how he had once derided manual workers, got down on his hands and knees to scrub the floor.

When they were finished it was a different room, crowded but livable. They had a home in their new country. They had put down roots.

Together they went out to search for work. It took only an hour for Shmuel to find a job as a cabinet maker with a small workshop in Hanbury Street, close to where they lived. Leah kissed him and Lazar solemnly shook his hand for good luck. Then they left him to find work of their own.

"I prefer you like this," Leah said to Lazar as they walked along the crowded streets, stopping to look in every doorway, hoping to see another scrawled sign like the one that had advertised Shmuel's job. Despite the fact that her parents' violent death was still painfully fresh in her memory, Leah felt happy. Their first day in London had been a disaster, sleeping in a Christian mission because they had nowhere else to go. Now they had a place of their own. Shmuel had a job. She and Lazar would soon find work. She would learn the language and settle into English life as if she had been born into it. "Do you realize how much you've changed?"

Lazar wasn't sure how to reply. He knew he'd changed. All because of an SA man with a bristling red moustache. "I suppose I grew up," he said. "I just wish I'd done it earlier."

Leah squeezed his arm affectionately. "I was hoping you'd say that. You know, there were times when I wanted to kill you, the way you used to poke fun at us. It was like you were ashamed of us, we weren't good enough for you."

"I'm sorry," was all he could say.

"You apologized a long time ago," she told him. "When you waited for us in Maastricht. When you led us here. That was apology enough." She turned onto Middlesex Street, pulling Lazar with her. Tacked to a door was a sign that attracted her attention. Written in English and Yiddish was the message: "Goldstein's Coats is hiring. Apply Mr. Goldstein, second floor."

"I'll go up with you," Lazar offered.

"Thanks." Leah clutched his hand tightly. She had only ever held one job in her life, and there her employers had been friends of her own family. For the first time in her life she was trying to establish herself in her own right.

They walked up a narrow stairway which opened onto the factory of Goldstein's Coats. To their left twenty women worked at sewing machines, heads bowed, fingers flying as the needles buzzed up and down like silver streaks of lightning. To their right, cutters and pressers worked. A young woman walked quickly from one group to another, distributing work, collecting finished pieces. Clouds of steam wafted up from the pressing tables to cover everything with condensation.

Overseeing the whole operation from the center of the floor was a short, chubby, balding man with a gold watch chain stretched across the front of his vest. Holding Leah's hand, Lazar removed his hat and approached the man.

"Are you Mr. Goldstein?" he asked in English.

"I am." Saul Goldstein's attention was taken immediately by Lazar's startlingly white hair. "How can I help you?"

"We saw your notice downstairs. I'm Lazar Boruchowicz. My sister, Leah, is looking for work as a seamstress."

Goldstein glanced quickly at Leah, then back to Lazar's hair. "Where did she work before?".

"In Cologne. Germany. We only arrived two days ago."

"Just off the boat, are you?" Although he laughed at his own description of the newcomers, Goldstein was immediately sympathetic. Almost thirty years had passed since he had come to London, from Kiev in Russia, but he still remembered his own first impressions . . . the confusion, the certainty that he would never belong. Whenever he saw obviously new arrivals wandering through the East End, looking like lost children, he felt touched by them. "Where

34

did you learn to speak English?"

"In Germany."

"What was your work there?"

"I was head of the accounting department for a timber company."

Goldstein was impressed. In his eyes, the platinum hair had already marked Lazar as unusual. Somehow it seemed only right that he should have held a responsible position. "I'd prefer it if you were a good cutter instead of an accountant but I've got room for your sister." He turned to Leah and asked in English when she could start. When he saw she didn't understand, he repeated the question in Yiddish.

"Right away," she said quickly, "just show me where to sit." She had felt lost while Goldstein and her brother had spoken in English but she'd sensed a warmth in the factory owner.

Goldstein called over the young woman who was distributing work. "This is my daughter, Katya. She'll show you where to sit and give you work."

"Thank you." Leah paused to kiss Lazar on the cheek before following Katya Goldstein to a vacant machine.

"How many of you came over?" Goldstein asked Lazar.

"Three. My younger brother Shmuel just started work as a cabinet maker."

"You don't believe in wasting time. What about yourself?"

"I'm looking."

"Are you really an accountant?"

"I really am."

"Come over here." Goldstein led the way to a small office tucked away into one corner of the factory. A table and chair took up most of the available space. From the walls hung sheets of orders, scraps of correspondence, patterns. "I don't need an accountant, I need a commercial genius." Goldstein laughed. "Someone who can run the entire administrative side of this factory. I'm a tailor . . . that's how I started. But I've never been a businessman. My daughter will tell you that."

Uninvited, Lazar began to sift through the orders. There was no doubt that Goldstein was busy, but there seemed to be little routine to the way he conducted his operation.

Orders from the previous week had been already completed; earlier orders were still outstanding. "Are you offering me a job, Mr. Goldstein?"

Goldstein nodded. Lazar was the first man he'd ever seen get off the boat with a high degree of education. Goldstein's contemporaries had been farmers, folk from small villages, cobblers, tradesmen. Lazar signaled a new breed of immigrant. "I'll take you and your sister. You'll save me enough to pay you both." He put his hand into his pocket and pulled out some money. "How are you off for funds? Do you have enough to last until Friday?"

Lazar declined the offer, at the same time moved by this stranger's generosity, which was such a contrast to what they'd found their first day in London. "We have some money. And valuables. Our father made us take them."

"Your father stayed behind?"

Lazar recounted the nightmare of Aachen, the Brownshirt, the escape and the death of his parents. Goldstein listened quietly, then said, "If you and your sister couldn't do a thing I'd have given you both jobs. I read what's going on over there. At least you paid one of the *mumzerim* back."

Lazar spent his first hour at Goldstein's Coats by going through the orders, pushing up or relegating work according to date received. Next, he turned to the factory's accounts. The entire system was a shambles. It was a mystery how Goldstein managed to stay in business. For the rest of the day until the factory closed at seven o'clock he copied all of Goldstein's poorly handwritten information into new ledgers, which he had been out to buy. When he left with Leah he was satisfied that the next day he'd be able to start afresh with legible books.

"Are you tired?" he asked his sister.

"A little. I don't think I finished as much work as I was supposed to, but Katya Goldstein was very kind. She credited me with more work than I actually did."

Lazar told how Saul Goldstein had said he'd have given them jobs no matter what, and Leah understood even more his daughter's kindness.

"Katya was born here, you know," Leah said suddenly. "She's English."

Lazar smiled at that, finding it funny how she put so much importance on someone being *born* in England. He guessed it was Katya — young as she was — who ran the business. He'd watched her from the office, a scarf around her head to protect her long auburn hair from the dampness as she welded the efforts of cutters, pressers and seamstresses into one fluid operation. "Katya's his only child. Mr. Goldstein told me his wife died soon after she was born."

"That's sad," Leah said. Then, affecting a casual manner, she added, "Katya asked about you. I think she was fascinated by your hair."

"Everyone seems to be." Lazar realized he was embarrassed hearing his sister talk about a girl's interest in him and tried to change the subject. "Come on . . . we'd better hurry, Shmuel will wonder what's happened to us."

Leah decided to buy food. She would make dinner that night, she declared proudly . . . her first cooking in her new country. Even if it was over a single burner and would make their communal bedroom smell like a kitchen. Caught up in her enthusiasm, Lazar bought a small bottle of whisky. They would follow Leah's meal with a toast to their future.

As they reached their building on Brick Lane Lazar pointed at the entrance to Shaffzics steam baths. "Come Friday, I'm going to use that place. I haven't felt clean since we left Germany."

"And I'll do something with my hair." The hours at work had made Leah feel a part of something useful again. And the knowledge that her brother was nearby brought extra comfort. Soon, when they'd managed to save money from their wages, they'd be able to move to a better area. Like Hackney, to the north, where Saul Goldstein lived . . . wherever Hackney was.

"A toast!" Lazar shouted when he entered the room and saw Shmuel sitting at the table with his back to the door. "Scottish whisky for a toast to England."

Shmuel turned slowly around, his mouth set in a grim line. He looked at the bottle in Lazar's hand. "You'd have done better to save the money it cost you. The case has gone."

"*What*?" Leah let the shopping bag fall to the floor, ran to the corner of the room where the case of silverware had been left. The sheet that had hidden the case was screwed up into a bundle.

"Someone stole it while we were out," Shmuel said.

"How did anyone get in?" Lazar asked. There were only two keys. He had one, Shmuel the other.

Shmuel pointed to the splintered wood of the doorframe. "The door was open when I came back from work. I thought one of you were home –"

"Did you speak to anyone?"

"The landlord. He said he wasn't responsible for tenants' property."

Leaving the bottle of whisky on the table, Lazar ran downstairs to the street. A barrow vendor gave directions to the closest police station on Commercial Street. Lazar ran all the way.

"We've been robbed," he burst out to the first policeman he saw inside the station, a sergeant.

"Where did it happen?"

"Our house. Our room. In Brick Lane." Lazar realized he didn't even know the number of the building. "By the steam baths."

"What was taken?"

"A case full of silver. Candlesticks. Goblets. Plates –"

"Really?" The sergeant took more notice of Lazar's accent, the torn clothing that was so obviously European. "What's your name?" Lazar told him, and the sergeant said, "Where would someone living in Brick Lane get silver plates and candlesticks?"

"What business is it of yours where I got them? The crime is that they have been stolen."

"Where did *you* nick them from in the first place?"

Lazar had never heard the slang the sergeant used, but he had no doubt of its meaning. "I didn't steal them from

38

anywhere. I brought them with me from Germany . . ."

Other police officers appeared, constables attracted by Lazar's furious shouting. He didn't see them. All he had eyes for was the sergeant. What kind of police were these? English versions of the ones he'd left behind in Germany.

The sergeant decided to give Lazar at least the benefit of the doubt. "I'll come back with you."

Lazar forced down his animosity toward the sergeant as he led the way back to Brick Lane. When they entered the room the sergeant looked with undisguised contempt at the three beds. "Couldn't you squeeze any more in?" Seeing Leah and Shmuel, he asked, "Who are you two? What are your names?"

"Neither my sister nor brother speaks English," Lazar cut in. "Only me."

"Oh, so you're the smart Yiddisher, are you. Where did you leave all this silver you're supposed to have lost?"

Lazar felt his anger rise again as he showed the sergeant the sheet. "Here. The sheet covered it."

"You can say good-bye to that. One of your own kind's robbed you. They're the only ones who do any thieving around these parts." The sergeant turned to leave, not even bothering to take a description of the stolen silver. If these Yids were stupid enough to leave valuables in a room like this they deserved whatever happened to them.

"That's all you're going to do?" Lazar said in disbelief. "Don't you even want to know what was stolen?" He grabbed the sergeant's shoulder, tried to turn him around. "You're supposed to be helping us. We've been robbed and you're the police."

"Don't tell me how to do my job." The sergeant shook off Lazar's hand and took a step toward him. A figure moved in swiftly between the two men, solid, immovable. Shmuel placed a warning hand on the sergeant's chest, smiled down at him and shook his head. The sergeant glanced into Shmuel's eyes, retreated. At the door he swung around to say he'd be back, then ran down the stairs.

The mood of celebration had been transformed. Leah hardly felt like cooking. She picked the groceries up from the floor and suggested they find a restaurant. There was no point, even, in getting the door lock repaired, she pointed out. Nothing was left in the room worth stealing . . . any money they had was in their pockets.

When they came back an hour later the police sergeant was waiting for them. And with him were four burly constables. Neither Shmuel nor Lazar put up a struggle as they were marched away to Commercial Street police station to be charged with assaulting a police officer, and locked in the cells overnight.

Frantic, Leah followed her brothers to the station. Unable to make herself understood, she refused to leave the building until a Yiddish-speaking interpreter was found to explain the situation to her. The interpreter was an inspector in his early thirties who took Leah into a bare, green-painted room. He told her gently that her brothers had been charged with a criminal offense. They would be tried. If found guilty they faced not only imprisonment — and here even the inspector's compassion could not shield Leah from sudden terror — but deportation.

"*Deportation?* Back to Germany?"

"If that's where they're from, yes. Look, why don't you go home, try to get some rest? You're not helping them at all by getting yourself into a state." He led her back to the main entrance and smiled down at her. "Maybe it won't come to that."

She hardly heard his words. All she could think of was her brothers being returned to Germany. The theft of the silverware paled into insignificance when compared with the threat of her brothers being deported. And herself staying in a country where she was a total stranger. She had to find help. But where? Only the Goldsteins came to mind, Saul and his daughter Katya. People she'd known for less than a day.

When Goldstein and his daughter arrived at Middlesex Street to open the factory the following morning they found Leah waiting. Mistaking her early arrival for enthusiasm, they were surprised to notice her red-rimmed eyes and the dried tear stains on her face.

"What happened?" Goldstein asked. "Is something wrong?"

40

"My brothers were taken away by the police. Last night. They're going to send them back to Germany — "

"Lazar?" Katya asked quickly.

"And Shmuel." Tears started to flow again as Leah blurted out the story, how Shmuel had discovered the theft of the silverware to the confrontation with the police sergeant and the double arrest.

Katya put a comforting arm around Leah's shoulders. "Don't worry, my father will find out what's happening."

Goldstein nodded, he knew people to contact. They took Leah inside, made her clean up and drink a cup of sweet tea, then Goldstein escorted her to the police station. He could leave the operation of the factory to his daughter.

The sergeant Lazar and Shmuel were alleged to have assaulted was no longer on duty. Another sergeant asked Goldstein what he wanted. Goldstein told him he wanted to speak to Inspector Davies.

Inspector Ivor Davies was a tall, brooding Welshman with jet black hair and a sallow complexion. When he saw Leah he smiled. "I spoke to you last night, remember?" he said in Yiddish. "I told you to go home and get some rest. It doesn't look like you did — "

"Would you have done in the same situation?" Goldstein broke in.

"I suppose not."

They seemed to know each other well and Leah began to feel a little better. Goldstein explained that one of the arrested men was an employee of his, the entire family were his friends, he would vouch for any of them. Every so often Davies nodded, as if he knew that Goldstein was pledging character references for people he hardly knew.

"They're due to appear at Old Street Magistrates Court this morning. Find someone to represent them."

"I will." Goldstein shook hands with the inspector and led Leah from the station. "Don't worry about a thing. Tonight your brothers will be home with you. That sergeant, the one Shmuel and Lazar had a fight with, he's the exception to the police here. My friend Inspector Davies . . . he's the rule." Or so he hoped

Shortly before eleven o'clock Goldstein accompanied Leah to Old Street Magistrates Court. Waiting there for the factory owner was a solicitor who explained that he had spoken with Lazar and Shmuel, had heard their side of the story and was convinced that the magistrate would dismiss the case.

Leah entered the court with Goldstein and sat down in the public gallery. Another case was being heard. Leah understood nothing of it, although everyone seemed to be very polite. She looked around, awed by the solemn atmosphere, the solitary magistrate on the bench, the clerk of the court sitting in front of him, the defendant in the dock.

The case was quickly dispensed with. Goldstein told Leah that the prisoner had been committed for trial by a higher court, explaining that a magistrate was empowered only to pass judgment on minor cases; for major crimes his function was to supervise committal proceedings. Leah was wondering which category her brothers fell into − major or minor − when she heard their names being called. Lazar and Shmuel were each led in by a police constable and made to stand together in the dock. When they looked in Leah's direction she forgot where she was. She waved and called out their names. The clerk of the court warned that any more such demonstrations would result in Leah's removal from the court. Goldstein translated the caution and Leah was quickly silent.

Lazar, in English, and Shmuel through a court-appointed interpreter, entered pleas of not guilty. The police sergeant who had come to the room in Brick Lane was the only witness for the prosecution. Very gravely he testified how he had been called to the premises to investigate a theft. While taking details from the two defendants, he had been threatened by them.

"He" − the sergeant indicated the hulking figure of Shmuel in the dock − "raised his hand in a threatening manner and then attempted to push me down the stairs leading from the room to the street."

Lazar glared at the sergeant. But when the interpreter

42

translated for Shmuel's benefit, Shmuel shook his head vehemently and gabbled a string of German in denial.

"Please inform the defendant that his turn will come to present his own evidence," the clerk instructed the defense counsel. The message went through the interpreter.

Lazar took the witness stand and described how the police sergeant had insulted him. His brother, he testified, had done nothing more than step in between himself and the sergeant. Shmuel repeated Lazar's story in German, stopping after every sentence while the interpreter translated.

A short cross-examination by the prosecution followed, after which the magistrate retired with the clerk to discuss the case. When they returned the magistrate acquitted them and lectured the sergeant about allowing personal prejudices to interfere with his work. When Goldstein explained the verdict to Leah she forgot about the clerk's earlier warning and shrieked with joy, covering her mouth and looking apologetically toward the bench only afterward. The clerk gave her a weary smile but said nothing.

"How much do we owe you for the lawyer's services?" was Lazar's first question when they emerged from the court.

"My treat," Goldstein insisted. "Sort out my factory and you'll have paid me back a thousandfold. And you . . ." He glanced up at Shmuel, whom he had never seen before the court appearance, and wagged a stern finger in his face . . . "never, ever try to knock a policeman's head off again."

"I didn't hit him," Shmuel protested. "I held him back from Lazar, that's all."

"If you raised your hand it can be legally construed as assault," another voice said. They turned around to see Inspector Ivor Davies. "You've all got a lot to learn, and no one expects you to learn it in just a couple of days. Just put this lesson at the top of the list . . . the police here are on your side as long as you respect the law."

"We'll remember."

Davies gave a little smile which grew broader as he switched his attention to Leah. He wasn't sure whether to reprimand the sergeant or commend him – certainly his behavior deserved a reprimand but if he hadn't provoked Lazar and Shmuel, Davies knew he might never have met Leah . . . he had purposely come to Old Street so he could see her again.

To Leah's surprise Davies drew her aside and asked her out for dinner. And, to her even greater surprise, she accepted.

Saul Goldstein broke tradition the following Friday night by inviting Lazar and Leah to his home in Hackney, and telling them to bring their brother. Never before had he socialized with his employees. He maintained a warm relationship with factory staff but always drew a firm line at off-hours fraternizing. Leah and Lazar made him think differently. Not only had they just lost their parents, they were strangers in a new country, and during the few days they'd been there they'd been robbed of all the wealth they possessed. Instead of falling back on self-pity, though, they'd adopted a positive attitude, determined to succeed. He liked and respected that.

Besides, Katya had also made the suggestion. And what his only daughter wanted, Goldstein could never refuse. It would be nice, she'd said, to have guests for a Friday night dinner; a nice change from the somber meal they normally shared. Her father was not a man who socialized much. His life centered around his business. It would also be nice – but Katya did not share this particular thought with her father – to have Lazar around to the house, to be able to meet him outside of work.

Like her father, Katya was impressed with Lazar. Not only had he straightened out accounts and work priorities, he'd brought her father's attention to discrepancies in the buying – differences in cost from one trimmings merchant to the next for the same quality merchandise. True to his confession of being a tailor and not a businessman, Goldstein had simply paid all bills on presentation; he'd never thought to check whether one trimmings supplier was cheaper than another.

Katya's interest in Lazar did not stop with his business sense. He was different from other men she had met, a level above. Despite the patched-up clothes he would continue to wear until he could afford new ones, he was more sophisticated,

44

educated. And ambitious. There was no doubt in Katya's mind that Lazar wouldn't stay with her father one hour longer than he needed to . . .

To three people sharing a single room, Goldstein's modest home in Hackney was a palace. Although it was at the center of a long row of attached houses it boasted three bedrooms, small gardens front and back, and two toilets — one indoors, the other in the back yard. While her father changed from his working clothes into his Friday night best, Katya showed the visitors around the house. The way she directed most of her comments to Lazar was not lost on Leah and Shmuel.

"Do you feel like I do that Katya wouldn't miss us if we left?" Shmuel whispered to his sister.

"She'd never notice we were gone." Katya's undisguised interest in Lazar amused Leah. Since that first day in the factory, when Katya had asked about Lazar, she had made excuses to visit the small office where he worked. Sometimes she stayed for as long as five minutes, neglecting her own duties until her father rapped discreetly on the door.

"We'd better stay," Shmuel decided. "I don't know the way home." He supposed he was a little jealous of his brother's ability to mix so well with other people. He'd never been able to relate easily to strangers.

The candles were already lit. Goldstein made the blessings over wine and bread and Katya served the meal. Leah spoke for them all when she complimented Katya by saying it was the finest meal they had eaten since leaving Germany. Her words, reminding them that the last time they had eaten together in Germany had been with their parents, brought an awkward silence.

"Why don't we sit inside by the fire?" Katya suggested, sensing the unease and guessing the reason for it. "It's more comfortable in there."

In the living room Goldstein sank contentedly into what was obviously his favorite spot, a shabby leather armchair close to the fire. Katya pointed out seats for Shmuel and Leah. Lazar she guided to a narrow couch that she shared with him.

"How much English have you learned in your first week here?" Goldstein asked.

Proudly, Shmuel replied in English. "Policeman. Not guilty. Court. And" – he raised a hand in the air – "assault." His words made everyone laugh.

"And you?" Katya asked Leah.

"Needle. Thread. Middlesex Street. Brick Lane."

Goldstein then became serious. "Your priority is to learn English and learn it well. Without English you'll never fit in over here. All your life you'll remain German Jews."

"How does one learn a new language?" Shmuel asked. It seemed a reasonable question. Children could learn a new language easily; he and his sister weren't exactly children.

"You can attend classes. And good advice is that you stop talking in German or Yiddish, even among yourselves. Lazar speaks English . . . better than I do. Make him speak it for you. And you . . ." He looked at Leah. "You can tell Ivor Davies for me that he isn't doing you any favors speaking Yiddish to you. Tell him you want to hear English when you see him again, even if he does speak it with a funny accent."

Leah smiled, partly in recognition of what Goldstein was saying, mostly at the memory of her dinner with the police inspector. She'd never heard Yiddish spoken with a Welsh accent. Nor could she at first understand why Davies even spoke it. He wasn't Jewish, he was a Protestant. He'd told her he was from a coal-mining town in north Wales and had joined the police there before being switched to London's East End. He'd learned Yiddish because he wanted to work closely with the people he came in daily contact with. Friends like Saul Goldstein had gone out of their way to help him, appreciating his interest in their lives . . .

Almost unrecognizable in a dark gray suit Davies had called for Leah in a five-year-old Austin to take her for her first look at the West End. She had been waiting outside the building, hoping that he would not want to come upstairs. When he drove up and saw her waiting he asked if she was ashamed of letting him see where she lived. Red-faced, she'd taken him upstairs. He'd looked around and told her that in

46

no time she and her brothers would be out of there. "Plenty of people started out even more cramped than this. At least you've got some privacy."

After dinner he had shown her the sights. Eros at Piccadilly Circus, Trafalgar Square and Nelson's Column, then down The Mall to look at Buckingham Palace. When they had returned to Brick Lane she'd shown no hesitation in inviting him upstairs. Shmuel and Lazar were there, and Davies had spent almost half an hour with the three of them, talking about the East End, about London. He'd left with the promise to Leah that he would be in touch when his duty gave him a chance. She hoped it would be soon . . .

"How long did it take you to learn English?" Shmuel asked Goldstein.

"Maybe six months before I was able to carry on a long conversation. You know . . ." Goldstein began to digress as he recalled his own early days in London. "This is a very funny country. Who knows how many foreigners have been washed up on its shores as refugees, but none has aroused as much feeling – for and against – as we have." He started to tell the history of the Jews in England from their expulsion in 1290 and their readmittance under Cromwell in 1656. He moved onto other groups of immigrants. The Huguenots who had come to the East End in Elizabethan times to practice their weaving skills. The Irish during the previous century. When the East European Jews had followed the Irish, however, the English had sat up and taken notice.

"You see, the Huguenots were fine because they were Protestant refugees coming to a Protestant country. The Irish, while mostly Catholic, spoke the same language." Goldstein paused as Lazar smiled, remembering the Irish dockworkers whose English he had been unable to understand. "What's funny?" he asked.

"The way the Irish speak," Lazar told him. He found himself becoming fascinated by Saul Goldstein. On the surface the man was a harried little tailor; underneath lurked a scholar. "I couldn't understand a word they said." He could feel the steady warmth of Katya's thigh pressing against his own and he responded, reasonably confident that it would go unnoticed in the dimness of the room.

"A geographical difference," Goldstein said. "Even in London people speak with different accents." He swung back to his original topic. "After the Irish, the East European Jews began to arrive in force. We, unfortunately, were like nothing the English had ever seen before. Strange mannerisms, strange clothing, different language, religion, everything. To the English who were used to Sephardic Jews, the *Ashkenazim* came as quite a shock."

Lazar glanced at his brother and sister, sitting comfortably, lulled by Goldstein's voice and the warmth from the fire. He wondered if they were thinking as he was . . . that to move forward in this new country there was only one way – be like their hosts. Well, he had a head start, knowing the language. He'd try to be sure that Leah and Shmuel followed along. They'd better . . . the stakes were survival . . .

"She loves you. She loves you not."

Shmuel sat on the edge of his bed and pretended to pick petals from a flower while he teased his brother. He laughed when Lazar's skin reddened. "I think she loves you. What about you, Leah?"

"He's unlovable, why should a girl as attractive as Katya even look at him?"

"Laugh all you want," Lazar said. "It was me she sat next to on the couch."

"True," Shmuel said. "And it was your leg she was pressing against the entire evening. Didn't think we saw, did you?"

"Jealous?"

"No," Shmuel said a little too quickly, as if he had been expecting the question and was ready to refute it. He wasn't jealous of Lazar because of Katya. It was just . . . just the same old envy of his brother's easy ability to socialize that gnawed at him, in spite of himself.

Long after the others had fallen asleep Lazar lay in bed, eyes staring at the dark ceiling. From time to time he could hear noise from the street, a car bumping over the cobblestones, the discordant singing of a drunk on the way home. He thought about what Goldstein had said . . . nothing like the English had ever seen before. So much reason for distrust in that sentence. To act like the British, to live in a house even finer than Goldstein's took money. More money than Lazar would ever make by fixing Goldstein's sloppy business techniques. More money than he'd ever make by working in any clothing factory or timber mill.

And he thought about Katya. Green eyes, like a cat. He'd never been with a green-eyed girl before. Green eyes, and auburn hair. What a marvelous combination. Coloring as unusual as his own. And, he sensed, a strong-willed girl, with an ambition to rise as powerfully strong as his own.

His hand reached down to his thigh, touched where Katya had touched.

CHAPTER THREE

The steam that filtered from the main baths into the side rooms made the cards damp and slippery, awkward to hold and spread into a fan. Lazar didn't mind, not when he was holding the five, six, eight, nine and ten of spades, trump masters to win his bid. With a flourish he couldn't resist, he slapped his cards onto the table, face up.

"You learn quick," grumbled Manny Goodman, the player on Lazar's right, as he tossed his own cards into the middle of the table. "Quickly . . . and too bloody well for my liking."

Lazar laughed. "Maybe," he said slowly, trying hard to mimic Manny Goodman's East London speech, "you taught me . . . too . . . bloody . . . well . . ." He scooped up his winnings and turned to grin at Manny, bare-chested like himself, with only a long white towel wrapped around his waist.

"I didn't teach you nothing about winning week in and week out. There's such a thing as gratitude, right?" Manny asked the other two men at the table.

Jerry Jacobs and Harry Sherman nodded. The four men had been regular partners in the Saturday night game of Solo for almost three months, playing from midnight – when Lazar came back from seeing Katya Goldstein – until four or five in the morning. Then Lazar would tiptoe his way to the room he still shared with Leah and Shmuel. Most nights he won, enough to add the occasional luxury to the bare necessities their careful budgeting allowed. In spite of saving a little each week they were still a long way from accumulating the capital they would need to find a better home.

The very first time Lazar had visited Shaffzics steam baths he had felt a psychological as well as a physical lift. He'd cleansed not only his body, but his mind, sluicing away more of the pain and grief of Germany. It was a miracle, he'd told Shmuel and Leah after returning upstairs, what a little steam, a little *shivtz*, could do for one's morale. After that he became a regular visitor; the Saturday *shivtz* was one of the few indulgences he allowed himself.

At first Shmuel had gone with Lazar. The two brothers had sat with towels around their waists, bodies streaming with sweat while they watched and listened to other men. There always seemed to be at least one card game in progress. Most popular was a game Lazar learned was called Solo, where one man bid for a certain number of tricks and the other players combined to try to defeat him. Lazar quickly picked up the basics of the game, became fascinated with it, the skill needed to play appealing to his agile mind. Shmuel, however, could work up little enthusiasm for either the game or the regular visits to the baths.

So it was something of a relief to Lazar when Shmuel met a girl at the Maziche Adas synagogue in Brick Lane, where he attended services every Saturday morning; neither Leah nor Lazar felt a similar urge to pray. Shmuel gave up visiting the steam baths in favor of seeing the girl, leaving Lazar to go by himself. It was then that Manny Goodman, noticing Lazar's steady interest in the game, had invited him to sit in, to take the place of a player who hadn't showed up. "Oy, Whitey," he'd called out, "you want to play instead of sitting there like Almighty God passing judgment on the rest of us?"

Lazar had not been offended at the name Manny called him. He'd been in London long enough to know that nicknames were tossed about without any special malice intended. Usually it was the opposite. So he'd joined in, and within a couple of weeks he'd come to look on it as a ritual. On Saturday evening he would go out with Katya and then he'd return to Brick Lane and Shaffzics for the weekly game. The post-mortems of each hand taught him far more than he'd ever learned by merely watching. The criticism if he'd played a hand badly bit deep, but at the end of the game there was never any bitterness. Playing cards was a good way to end the week, Lazar had decided . . . after going home a winner for the first time . . .

"This had better be my last hand," Jerry Jacobs said. "If I don't get home soon my wife's going to be waiting behind the door with a rolling pin."

"Mine, too," Harry Sherman agreed. "Manny and Lazar don't know how lucky they are, being single."

Manny picked up the cards, shuffled with difficulty because of the dampness, and began to deal. Lazar waited until all thirteen cards were in front of him before picking them up, sorting them into suits. "A hand like a foot," he muttered.

The time-worn joke met with an automatic chuckle from the other players. While he waited for a bid from someone else Lazar concentrated on Manny Goodman. Jacobs and Sherman didn't interest Lazar nearly as much as Manny did. The other two men were married with families, solid citizens, shopkeepers. Manny was only a year or two older than Lazar, with a greengrocer's shop in Booth Street that he'd inherited from his father, who had died a few years earlier. Lazar could never figure out the relationship between the three men. Jacobs and Sherman were in their forties, yet Manny was the dominant personality. When he laughed, they laughed. When he showed a glimpse of anger over a misplayed hand, they kept silent. From the occasional hints he picked up by listening, Lazar guessed the three men were loosely involved in business, and Manny was the boss.

After the final hand Jacobs and Sherman dressed quickly and left. Lazar took his time, knowing Manny was in no hurry. "Why doesn't your brother come down here anymore?" Manny asked as he slipped into his jacket.

"He's more interested in some girl he met at the Maziche Adas than in cards and a *shvitz*."

Manny laughed. "At least that means he's normal." Fully dressed, he looked a totally different person from the man wearing only a towel. The shoulders of his jacket were padded, adding bulk to his narrow frame. His light brown hair, combed off his face instead of being plastered flat against his forehead by the steam, made him appear taller.

Lazar had some trouble imagining Manny as a greengrocer, weighing potatoes and onions all day long. The man facing him now was too dapper, even if the suit could not completely disguise the rough, wiry energy that went through his body like a tight coiled spring.

That was another thing that set Manny apart from Jacobs and Sherman, the way he kept himself in shape, cared about how he looked. Jerry Jacobs was grossly overweight. When he sat with just a towel to cover himself the steam and sweat collected in folds of skin above his stomach. Harry Sherman was also heavy, muscle turning to fat. His skin the palest, most unhealthy color Lazar had ever seen, and his head was as free of hair as if he shaved it daily. Lazar found it strange that a young man like Manny Goodman would associate with them, even if there were business ties.

"Is your brother Shmuel as strong as he looks?" Manny asked conversationally as he gave his appearance a final check in the mirror.

"Stronger."

"Did he ever box? You know, fight?"

"In Germany. Youth clubs. Why?"

"Just wondering, that's all. Tell you what. Come along with me on Saturday afternoon to Hoxton Baths. There might even be some money in it for you."

The atmosphere at Hoxton Baths was as steamy and heavy as it was at Shaffzics. Lazar felt his clothes begin to wilt the moment he walked in behind Manny Goodman and took his seat close to the ring.

Lazar had never been to a professional boxing match. At first he was put off by men trying to maim each other for purses that could be no larger than a few pounds. He was close enough to hear the sound of every blow, to see in detail eyes become puffed, noses and mouths split, made to pump out blood. He'd killed, yes – he could still see that Brownshirt's face – but not for money. That had been for revenge, out of anger, fear, all mixed up in one. As the card progressed, though, he began to take a different view. He knew Manny was enjoying the spectacle, his fists clenched and unclenched as if he were delivering every blow himself, whether it was the the quick fists of the feather-weights or the more ponderous, sledge-hammer blows of the heavies.

By afternoon's end Lazar was into it too, shouting encouragement, banging his feet on the floor, echoing the referee as he counted a fighter out.

"What do you reckon?" Manny asked as they made their way out.

"About what?"

"About your brother, Shmuel. Could he stand up on his own two feet in that ring?"

"He's strong enough to destroy any of the men we saw today."

"But can he box? Being a strong slab of meat's one thing. Does he know how to use these?" Manny waved his fists in the air.

Lazar shrugged. "He hasn't fought for a long time. And he never fought for money . . . not to hurt anyone, like the men in there."

"Would he be interested?"

". . . For how much?"

"I can probably get him five quid for his first fight. But that's only the start." Manny grinned, showing perfectly even teeth.

"What do you get out of it, Manny?"

"Only what's coming to me, Whitey . . ."

Lazar had to be content with that. Five pounds in the family's savings was enough to stop him worrying about Manny's angle.

Shmuel and Leah were struggling for sole possession of the space in front of the mirror when Lazar returned from Hoxton Baths. They were so intent on seeing how they looked they didn't even hear him come in.

He watched for a few seconds, then: "Big dates tonight?"

Startled by his voice, they swung around like two marionettes controlled by the same set of strings. "Ivor's calling for me in half an hour," Leah said, turning back to the mirror. She gave a final touch to her hair, seemed satisfied.

"And you?" Lazar asked his brother. "Are you seeing Lottie?"

"We're going out for dinner."

Leah turned to look at Shmuel. "When are we going to meet this girl? You talk about her all the time but we never get to see her."

"You will. When I'm ready to show her to you."

"Katya's been up here," Lazar pointed out. "So has Ivor Davies. Surely you can't be ashamed of bringing your Lottie up here?"

The smile on Shmuel's face became self-conscious and Lazar changed the subject, describing his visit to Hoxton Baths and the chance for them to earn money from boxing.

Leah was dead set against the idea. "Shmuel doesn't know how to fight like that, he boxed for sport in Cologne, not for a purse. Where did you get this craziness from?" In her excitement she'd switched back to German, forgetting every English word Lazar and Ivor Davies had taught her.

"From Manny Goodman, one of the men I play cards with in Shaffzics —"

"One of *those* men. I should have guessed." Although Lazar had spoken of them, Leah had never met any of the card players from Shaffzics. Nonetheless she'd already drawn a mental picture of the kind of man who would stay up all night to play cards. She didn't approve of Lazar spending every Saturday night with them, though the winnings he brought home helped blunt her displeasure.

"One of those men — as you call him — says Shmuel can earn as much as five pounds from just one fight. And much more if he's any good."

"What if he isn't any good?" Leah wanted to know. "Is five pounds worth getting his brains knocked out, his face disfigured?"

Shmuel decided it was time to speak up for himself. "Tell me something, Lazar. You saw these men fight. Would I stand a chance?"

Lazar knew he had to be honest with his brother. "I really

don't know. You're strong enough to flatten the biggest, but boxing isn't all-out brawling." He knew he could have told Shmuel yes . . . you'll win easily. That's what Manny Goodman would have done, what he would have wanted Lazar to do. But what if Shmuel got into the ring with that kind of false confidence and was seriously injured? Lazar would never be able to forgive himself. "Manny says you'll train at a proper gymnasium. Experts there will know how good you are."

Shmuel chewed his lips. As a teenager he'd enjoyed boxing as a sport, at school, in youth clubs, but he'd never imagined that one day he might put on gloves for money – even desperately needed money. Now it was the thought of that money, how it would benefit his family, that made up his mind. "Tell your friend Manny that for five pounds I'll fight." He walked to the wall and threw punches at his shadow. "See?" he called out for Leah's benefit, "I'll knock them to Berlin. To the *moon* . . ."

Lazar smiled and patted him on the back. On the way to Hackney, to pick up Katya, he would visit Manny, who lived in a flat above the greengrocer's shop. With luck the little Cockney might even have news when Lazar met up with him later at Shaffzics.

Shmuel wouldn't get hurt. It would be money – as Manny would say in his inimitable manner – for bloody old rope.

When he saw Katya that evening, Lazar mentioned the possibility of Shmuel earning money from boxing. She was interested. So was Saul Goldstein . . . until Lazar mentioned whose idea it was. His friend, Manny Goodman.

"How did you ever get to meet a man like that?"

"At Shaffzics. We play Solo every Saturday night –"

"Do you ever win?" Goldstein managed to make the question sound redundant. When Lazar said that he did win most nights, Goldstein's response was: "Your good fortune amazes me. Manny Goodman does not come out of many ventures with a loss."

Katya turned away as if she didn't want to listen again to something she'd heard many times before. Lazar asked

Goldstein what he meant.

"Manny Goodman inherited the greengrocer's shop on Booth Street from his father. At the same time he took over every dirty little racket that went with it. You want to know what happened to that silver you brought over from Germany? Ask Manny Goodman. Most probably it passed through his hands –"

"He stole it?" Lazar could no more imagine Manny breaking into a room than he could see him selling vegetables.

"No. He's too clever to do it himself. He handles stolen goods. What the police call a receiver. He passes them on to other people who sell them." As Goldstein spoke, Lazar thought about Jerry Jacobs and Harry Sherman. And suddenly he could see where they fitted in.

"And he also has a very good business – please God, I should have such a money-making business – with, with . . ." Goldstein glanced nervously at Katya, knowing she was listening in spite of her apparent disinterest, "with prostitutes."

"Daddy –"

"What's the matter? You don't think Jews are involved in things like that? You don't think there are Jewish prostitutes? There are. All thanks to scum like Lazar's friend Manny Goodman."

"How do you know all this?" Lazar asked.

"From Ivor Davies."

"Why doesn't he do something about it?"

"Knowing and proving are two different things. No one will speak out against Manny Goodman. They're scared of him."

Lazar could never remember seeing Goldstein so upset. "For a man like this, what interest would he have in getting Shmuel to box?"

"I don't know, but you can be damn sure his interests aren't your brother's. Boxing's run by crooks anyway. Managers in each other's pockets, sometimes one manager for both boxers in the same fight." He lowered his voice and laid a fatherly hand on Lazar's shoulder. "Look, I can't tell you what to do. I've got no right. But you'd be doing both of us a big favor – and your brother – if you didn't see this man anymore. Wash your hands of him.''

A wet blanket had been thrown over the evening for Lazar and Katya. They ate dinner and then walked aimlessly around the West End. Remembering the claim that Manny was a conduit for stolen merchandise, Lazar and Katya looked in windows of jewellery shops. They saw nothing that resembled the stolen silver. In spite of badly wanting the silver back, their failure to see anything pleased Lazar. Maybe Goldstein had painted a blacker picture of Manny than was true. Lazar hoped so, because, to tell the truth, the greengrocer's intelligent, brash personality attracted him . . .

''My father upset you – ''

''I like to think I'm a pretty good judge of people,'' Lazar said. ''I can't help feeling your father exaggerated.'' The more he thought about it, the more exaggerated Goldstein's allegations sounded. Receiving and being involved in prostitution were acts of common, brainless criminals. Even if Manny wasn't straight, Lazar gave him more credit than to be involved in such operations. If you were going to be a thief, you should work with some . . . style. Like what he'd carried off in the Cologne bank. What would be Goldstein's reaction if he knew about *that*?

''My father's reasoning is always is-it-good-for-the-Jews-or-is-it-bad-for-the-Jews,'' Katya said. ''He brought it with him from Russia.''

''I understand,'' Lazar said. What he'd done in Aachen, knifing the Brownshirt, had been bad for the Jews, but maybe good too . . . at least in the long run. A Jew had stood up to a Nazi thug.

''Are you going to let your brother box?''

''Well, Shmuel wants to, and we can certainly use the money.''

''Who couldn't?'' Katya linked arms with Lazar and drew him closer. She had seen Manny Goodman a couple of times, had heard the stories about him. Perhaps you could find fault with the way he made his money, but you certainly couldn't argue with the money he made. If Manny wanted to put some money Shmuel's way, what was so wrong with that? There was nothing illegal about boxing. Shmuel should be able to fight for money if he was good. The times Katya had seen Lazar's younger brother he had seemed one of the biggest, strongest men she'd ever laid eyes on. Quiet. Perhaps a little slow. Certainly so when compared with Lazar.

But then, she thought fondly, holding Lazar's arm even tighter, so were most men.

Shmuel's girlfriend, Lottie Bloch, did not even come up to his shoulder. A delicate brunette with wide brown eyes, she was as tiny as he was large. And it was this physical contradiction that had attracted them to each other in the first place.

Lottie came not from the East End but from the comfortable North London suburb of Palmers Green, where her father practiced as a doctor and she worked as a teacher at a primary school. When she had met Shmuel at the Màziche Adas she'd been attending the *bar mitzvah* of a cousin who lived in the East End. Shmuel and Lottie had entered at the same time, becoming wedged like a comedy act in the narrow door, her head pressed into his chest, legs entangled. They had both laughed, apologized to each other and gone inside. During the service Shmuel had constantly glanced toward the women's section, trying to spot the girl. She had smiled, and once even given him a tiny wave of encouragement. Afterward he had waited outside, anxious to see her again. She'd come out with a small group of people, chattering brightly. When she'd spotted Shmuel, so obviously waiting for her, she'd walked right over to him.

"I was invited to bring a friend to the dinner-dance tonight. Would you like to be that friend?"

In stumbling English Shmuel had said that he would. He had rushed away to learn where he could hire a dinner suit at such short notice. The one he had managed to find would have better fitted Lazar. The trousers were tight and finished two inches shy of his shoes; the jacket refused to button; and the sleeves and shoulders were so constricting that they almost cut off circulation to his arms. He didn't mind a bit. He'd hogged the dance floor proudly, aware of only one thing.

For the first time since he'd come to London he felt like he belonged . . . Lottie's family made him welcome, and his visits to her parents' home in Palmers Green became as regular as Leah's and Lazar's trips to Saul Goldstein's house . . .

"Can you box?" Lottie asked Shmuel over dinner, after he had told her about Lazar's idea.

"Feel that." He flexed his arm. Lottie reached across the table to feel his biceps. The muscles stood up like small mountains. She knew he could lift her up with one hand; he'd done it enough times, showing off.

"That doesn't answer my question."

"I've boxed before. Clubs."

"Hoxton Baths won't be clubs. I don't think you *could* hurt anyone on purpose."

"I don't want to. It's just . . ."

"For the money." She finished the sentence for him. "Do you need money that badly?" The first time they'd been out together she had offered to help him pay. It was a mistake she had never made again.

"Extra money would help my family find a better place to live —"

"And you'd invite me up there?" she asked, grinning impishly. "You shouldn't be ashamed of where you live right now. Everyone starts off small —"

"There are three of us in one room."

"So? Ask my father how his parents lived when they first came to England." She toyed with her food, then said, "You could at least let me meet your brother and sister. If you fight I'll have to see it, I guess . . . and I want to meet Leah and Lazar."

Shmuel gave in. He took Lottie's hand in his own and squeezed gently. It felt like a toy. He hoped the fight would be an easy one, because he knew his pride would never recover if he were to lose and Lottie was there to see it.

"Your friend Manny's waiting for you in Shaffzics," Leah told Lazar when he came back from his date with Katya. "He came up here a few minutes ago, looking for you."

60

"Did he say what he wanted?"

"He's arranged a fight. Didn't waste any time, did he?"

"I dropped in to see him on the way out." Lazar looked around the room, expecting to see someone else. "Where's Ivor? Did he leave already?"

"He had to go back on duty," Leah said quickly. "Just brought me up here and ran off."

Lazar remembered Goldstein's mention of Ivor Davies during their conversation about Manny. "Did Manny and Ivor see each other?"

"Briefly. Manny came up as Ivor was leaving." Leah wondered if her brother could see through her lie . . . She'd been making tea for herself and Davies when Manny had knocked on the door. He'd asked if Lazar was in. Even when she'd told him no he'd invited himself inside. For some reason she hadn't been able to understand there'd been an instant moment of confrontation between the two men. They'd stared at each other, and then Davies had excused himself, saying he had to return to the station on Commercial Street to check on something. He'd kissed Leah on the cheek and gone right past Manny, who had turned around to look after the police inspector. Leah could swear she'd seen a spark of hatred flash across Manny's eyes. When he'd turned back to her it had gone, replaced by a warm smile. "Seems a shame to let a good cup of tea go to waste," he'd said brightly. "I take mine with two sugars."

Over the tea Manny had told her about the fight he'd arranged for Shmuel; how, if he was any good he could make a career for himself. When he'd left the room ten minutes later Leah was ashamed to realize that she had nearly forgotten about Ivor Davies. Mostly she was thinking about Manny Goodman . . .

"He's, uh . . ." Leah started to say something but changed her mind.

"He's what?" Lazar asked.

Leah made a face. "He's not what I imagined." What had she imagined? Some boor whose fingernails would be encrusted with grime from the vegetables he served all day? A layabout who spent his spare time sitting in a steambath while he played cards and talked about getting complete strangers five pounds for putting on a pair of boxing gloves?

"What did you think he'd be like?" Lazar was seriously interested, he wanted to see if Leah felt something of the same thing about Manny that he did.

"I don't really know," she said, becoming flustered. Seeking to hide her confusion, she switched to the reason for Manny's visit. "He said Shmuel would be fighting a man called Jackie O'Brien in four weeks' time. That he was to start training. Once he was fit he could take two fights a month."

Lazar hardly heard the last sentence. "O'Brien? An Irishman?" Lazar recalled the Irish dockworkers he had seen. Broad-shouldered, thick-armed giants who looked incapable of being hurt by a falling wall, let alone a human fist.

"Your friend Manny said it would be an easy fight. The Irishman has a glass jaw . . . is that the expression?"

"Never heard of it," Lazar said, although it sounded vaguely reassuring. "I'll go downstairs and see him. Find out more about this Jackie O'Brien."

He found Manny sitting on a bench in the steam room. "Did your skin and blister give you the good news?"

"My *what*?"

"Your sister. Leah. Did she tell you about the fight I'd made?"

Lazar stored away the slang expression, adding it to his vocabulary. "What's this O'Brien like?"

"Like an Irishman. *A shtickfleish mit zwei oigen.* A piece of meat with two eyes. Your brother should take him apart with one punch." Manny moved his position on the bench, swung around to face Lazar. "You should be ashamed of yourself, hiding your sister from me. I'm your friend, you're supposed to be nice to friends. Beautiful girl like that, letting her stay upstairs all by herself."

"She has friends – "

"Yeah, I saw one of her friends. He scarpered as soon as I showed up."

62

"You know Inspector Davies?"

"Like I know bubonic plague. Leah should stay away from the likes of him. You can catch all kinds of diseases from bluebottles."

"I hear he speaks highly of you too."

Manny's blue eyes flashed dangerously. "What did he say about me?"

"Nothing . . . What about this fight?"

Manny relaxed. "I told you. Five quid for doing nothing."

"I still want to know what you get out of it."

"I'm Shmuel's manager. I don't need a cut from a five-pound purse. But if things get good . . ."

"Manny, I want to ask a favor."

"Go ahead."

"When Leah and Shmuel and I first arrived from Germany we were robbed. Silverware, ornaments that belonged to my family in Cologne were stolen. Do you have any idea where we could find them?"

Manny regarded Lazar, blue eyes cold. "Why ask me, Whitey? I'm not the law. Why don't you ask Leah's friend Davies?"

Lazar no longer even noticed his nickname. "Someone told me you were better than the police, that you had more influence."

Manny gave a tight little smile, accepting the flattery, as his due. "Give me a description of the stuff. I'll ask around."

Lazar closed his eyes and thought about Saul Goldstein. Katya's father was probably right. Which was unfortunate, because every time he saw Manny he found himself being drawn to the brash little Cockney even more. The man was clearly no angel, but angels belonged in heaven, not here on earth, in London, where an innocent man could be arrested for reporting that his own possessions had been stolen. Sure, he and Shmuel had gotten off that time, but what about the next? Fine for Goldstein to moralize about Manny Goodman. He'd already made his mark, he could afford to pick and choose. Lazar was head of a family too . . . and he couldn't afford Goldstein's luxury of taking high moral positions.

Someday, maybe. But not now, not yet. It was his *duty* to look out for his family, to see that they survived and prospered. He wouldn't fail them, no matter what . . .

CHAPTER FOUR

When Lazar asked to borrow ten pounds Saul Goldstein wanted to know why. A business venture, Lazar told him. To do with Shmuel and his boxing match against the Irishman Jackie O'Brien. With an equal amount of his own money he'd have twenty pounds to bet on Shmuel. Manny had said O'Brien would be the favorite, so they would be able to get good odds on Shmuel.

Guessing what the loan was for, Goldstein looked sour but lent Lazar the ten pounds. Had he known that Lazar intended to take Katya to see the fight the following Saturday at Hoxton Baths, Goldstein no doubt would have turned down the request.

Lazar had been with Manny at a gym in Whitechapel Road to watch Shmuel train. Sharpened up by strenuous exercise, Shmuel had lost eight pounds and looked impressive, a solid, heavy body with barely any fat. Just rock-hard muscle. The way he hammered a bag and then sparred had brought glowing praise from both Manny and the trainer he'd appointed, an ex-heavyweight called Steve Josephson whose claim to boxing fame was a battered nose and cauliflower ear that testified to his own unsuccessful career fifteen years earlier.

"Steve'll be in your brother's corner," Manny had explained to Lazar. "He'll see to him, all right. Oh, one other thing. Your brother's getting a new name for the fight. Sammy Brooks, we're calling him. That's his ring name."

"Sammy Brooks?" Lazar had tried it out a couple of times, not certain whether or not he liked it. "Why?"

"Because some idiot *yok* announcer's going to get his tongue all in a twist trying to spit out Shmuel Boruchowicz, that's why. Over there . . . see?" Manny had pointed to a billboard pasted to the wall of the gym. In the middle, mention was made of a fifteen-round heavyweight contest between Dockland's favorite son, Jackie O'Brien, and introducing the Brick Lane Lion, Sammy Brooks. Next to Shmuel's ring name was Manny's name as manager . . .

Saul Goldstein counted out ten pounds in single notes and handed them to Lazar. "I'm upset you don't see fit to take my advice. You mix with scum like Manny Goodman and sooner or later you wind up in a lot of trouble."

"I'll get off his train when I see it headed for trouble," Lazar said. "I just think I can pick up some very much needed money on the trip." Lazar was still uncomfortable when Goldstein criticized his new friendship with Manny. There was little the factory owner could do about it, but it upset Lazar to go against the man who had been so kind to him and his family. And now Leah seemed to be looking forward with growing excitement to Saturday. Not, Lazar knew, because of the fight but because she would see Manny again. He'd been up to the room a few times, ostensibly to discuss the fight, but he had always made time to talk with Leah, to joke, to make her laugh. Without taking her out, without ever spending a farthing on her, he had apparently displaced Ivor Davies. Two totally opposite personalities, Lazar thought. A dour police officer, almost boringly responsible; and a light-hearted merchant with a dangerous, intriguing reputation, and a charisma to match. Lazar had not mentioned it to Goldstein, but since Manny and Davies had come face to face in the room, the police inspector had not come by. Lazar had seen him once on the street, had nodded and called out a good evening. Davies had inclined his head curtly and never said a word.

"One day you'll learn that real money is never *picked* up," Goldstein told Lazar. "When it comes to you that way, it means nothing. Ah . . ." He waved a hand. "What's the use of talking? Whatever I say won't make you see the sense." He turned and walked away, leaving Lazar feeling miserable.

But it was a festive group that met for the fight. Announcing that he was already spending the money he'd win on Shmuel, Manny took Lazar, Katya and Leah out for lunch, where he dominated the conversation by painting rosy pictures of Shmuel's future career as a boxer.

"The whole thing's in the managing. A poor boxer with a good manager will go further than a bloody fine fighter with a fool in his corner. The real skill is . . . well, not to over-match your boy . . ."

"This Jackie O'Brien, he's experienced?" Leah asked.

"Yes, but believe me, Shmuel can take him. I know it, but the punters don't, they have got to go with O'Brien. They haven't seen Shmuel in the gym."

Lazar began to feel how his brother and sister must have felt that first night at Saul Goldstein's, watching Katya monopolize him. From talking about the fight Manny turned his charm on Leah, never missing an opportunity to compliment her on her dress, her hair, her improving English. And as he watched, Lazar could see Leah becoming mesmerized. Her eyes followed Manny's every movement. Lazar had seen it before, when Manny came to the room. But he'd never seen it like this. Well, he couldn't really blame her . . . Manny had quite an effect on him too . . .

When they arrived at Hoxton Baths Shmuel was already in the dressing room he shared with other boxers, receiving final instructions from his trainer Steve Josephson as he waited nervously for the bell to ring on the start of his new career.

"I put your twenty quid on Shmuel," Manny told Lazar as they entered the arena.

"What odds?"

"Seven-to-two."

Lazar glanced sideways at Manny. "What happened to the four-to-one odds you talked about?"

Manny smiled and shrugged his shoulders. "After I put my hundred quid on Shmuel the price went down. Always does."

Clever, Lazar thought. If you'd put my twenty pounds on first, the price would have shortened on you. If a mere twenty pounds would do that. But Manny wasn't taking any chances. Saul Goldstein's face surfaced in Lazar's mind but he willed it away. Twenty pounds at seven-to-two was still good.

Lazar's thoughts must have shown on his face. Manny clapped him on the back. "Don't go thinking bad things about me. I'm minding you, protecting your interests."

They settled down to watch the first bouts, a featherweight bout followed by cruiserweights. Lazar held Katya's hand, feeling her fingers grab at him and then go slack as punches landed or missed. Her gasps provided a tense counterpoint to the action in the ring.

"Enjoying it?" he asked.

"I . . . am." She sounded surprised. "I'm ashamed to admit it —"

"I know, what would your father say if he knew you were here?"

"Please . . ." she whispered.

Lazar turned to look the other way, eager to find out how his sister was reacting. Leah was looking up at the ring, eyes riveted on the two boxers. Her right hand was on Manny's thigh, held there by his own hand.

"Ladies and gentlemen! The next contest on your pro-grame, a fifteen-round heavyweight bout . . ."

Lazar snapped alert at the sight and sound of the master of ceremonies in the center of the ring announcing Shmuel's fight. He had been so taken up by the sight of Leah and Manny that he'd been diverted from the ring.

". . . between, in the red corner, weighing in at thirteen stone, four pounds, the pride of Dockland, Jackie O'Brien!" Cheering soared up from the Irish heavyweight's contingent of supporters. Lazar looked around to see an ocean of waving arms. When he turned back to the ring, the fair-haired, red-faced O'Brien was lifting a gloved hand in acknowledgment.

"And in the blue corner, at thirteen stone, twelve pounds, introducing the Brick Lane Lion . . . Sammy Brooks!"

This time, Katya, Leah, Lazar and Manny jumped to their feet, applauding. Wearing navy blue shorts with a white Star of David embroidered on the left leg, Shmuel looked down through the ropes at the small legion of support. He grinned, somewhat embarrassed by the ovation, then quickly turned his head away and looked out over the crowd, as if searching for something.

Lazar sat down again, forgetting now all about Leah and Manny. The bell rang. Both fighters came out of their corners to meet in the middle of the ring. For the first half-minute they felt each other out. Then O'Brien shot out his left to land two swift jabs to Shmuel's face. Stung, Shmuel shook his head like a bull being teased and advanced on the Irishman. Whatever he lacked in style and grace, Shmuel made up for in force. He let loose a barrage of lefts and rights, thrown with less finesse than power. They landed on O'Brien's arms, his chest, his shoulders. And wherever they landed, they hurt. One grazed his jaw and he retreated quickly out of range, surprised by the power of his unknown opponent.

"Follow him!" Manny's voice made itself heard above the roar of the crowd as he sensed the opportunity for Shmuel to finish O'Brien off. "Get in after him, get it over with!"

"Go on, Shmuel!" Lazar yelled "Knock him out!"

Shmuel merely trailed his opponent, seemingly satisfied with the respect he'd earned from the older, more experienced boxer. The round ended with a chorus of jeers from hardened fight fans who felt they'd been cheated out of a first-round finish.

"What's the matter with that dope?" Manny yelled across Leah to Lazar. "Doesn't he know he's supposed to knock the stuffing out of O'Brien? He could have knocked him cold there and then."

"I'm not his trainer," Lazar shot back, suddenly angry. He felt Katya's restraining hand on his arm and lowered his voice. "Go tell that man in his corner what he's supposed to do. Not me."

"I will." Manny stood up and half-walked, half-ran to Shmuel's corner, where he spoke urgently to Steve Josephson and the seconds. Shmuel turned his head and listened to something the trainer told him.

"What did you say?" Lazar asked when Manny returned.

"I told him to finish off the bloke ; . . . otherwise he'd never get another fight in the East End.'' Shmuel came out slowly, guard up. He knew he'd hurt O'Brien in the first round and wasn't sure whether he liked the feeling. Rarely could he remember hurting a man deliberately. There had been the fool who'd broken the window of the house in Cologne . . . and the police in Aachen. But O'Brien hadn't done anything to him. Manny's words came to the front of his mind. He needed to win because his family needed the money. To win he had to batter O'Brien senseless, beat a man who was just trying to earn a few pounds in a time when a few pounds were very hard to come by . . .

O'Brien came close, jabbed out again and Shmuel felt the punches jar his head. He shook off the effect and closed with the Irishman. He felt arms wrapped around his body, tried to punch but couldn't, heard the referee call for them to break.

A bomb exploded over his right eye as the Irishman butted him. Instantly he felt O'Brien's arms release him. Through blurred vision, Shmuel saw his opponent step back a couple of paces. Shmuel wiped the back of his glove across his eyes. It came away covered with blood from his split eyebrow.

At ringside Leah and Katya screamed. Lazar gulped, not able to accept what he saw. This wasn't supposed to happen. O'Brien was a mug, Shmuel could take him apart with one good punch. Manny had privately assured him . . . He glared at the little Cockney, who was bent forward in his seat, fists clenched as if he were doing the fighting, blue eyes hard.

Suddenly all Shmuel could think of was the blood that now stained his glove, poured down his face to drip onto his chest. His family was watching. So was Lottie, somewhere out there. He'd told her he was fighting for the money. Well, if he lost this, there would be no more. Besides, the man had fought dirty . . . With a bellow of rage that could be heard clear across the hall Shmuel lowered his head and charged after the Irishman. A savage bombardment of punches whirled around O'Brien's head and upper body. Some missed, but those that got through sent O'Brien spinning back into the ropes, where he raised his arms in a futile gesture of defense. Shmuel gritted his teeth, fought down any remaining feelings of pity for the man on the ropes and told himself he was back in Germany. The man on the ropes was the Nazi who'd thrown the rock, he was the taunting Brownshirt Lazar had knifed. He was Hitler . . .

Under the pressure of Shmuel's relentless punching O'Brien's arms dropped. For a fraction of a second his jaw was exposed. Shmuel brought over his right. The punch travelled no more than a foot before it slammed into flesh and bone. O'Brien collapsed slowly, landing on his knees, toppling forward onto the side of his face, his buttocks raised in the air like a flag of surrender. The referee's count was a formality. Shmuel's hand was held aloft to a reception of cheers. He had won his first professional fight like a champion.

"What did I tell you, Whitey!" Manny jumped up and down, clapping his hands, applauding.

"What about that cut on his head?" Lazar had to shout to make himself heard above the din.

"It'll heal. In a couple of weeks he'll be able to fight again."

"If he wants to."

"He'll want to," Manny said confidently. "He's tasted success. It's a bloody hard drug to quit. You believe me. I know."

Lottie Bloch was waiting by the exit from the baths when Shmuel came out. His trunks, shoes, gloves and towel were in the bag he carried. A strip of plaster covered his split eyebrow. The official doctor had put in two stitches, telling Shmuel he'd be able to fight again in three to four weeks.

Manny's forecast had apparently been right. Shmuel had tasted success and wanted more of it. He was strong enough to take any man they put against him, and whatever skill he lacked he'd compensate for in sheer power. A few more victories like this one and he'd head the bill, not be just a makeweight. Maybe he'd be able to give up his work in Hanbury Street and concentrate on boxing.

"How did I look?" He stooped down to kiss Lottie, conscious of her perfume and how it contrasted with the sweat he'd just washed from his own body.

Her unexpected reply hurt him more than O'Brien's butt.

71

"Like a wild animal. Those last few seconds you were frightening. If I hadn't known it was you I would have thought it was somebody in a street brawl."

Some of the heady excitement drained from Shmuel. "Well, it was a fight, the man butted me, and the money – "

"Look what the money cost you." She fingered the strip of plaster tenderly. "How many times does this have to happen?"

"He *butted* me, it was a foul, Lottie . . ."

"And what you did to him? What happens when someone does that to you? You could be crippled for life."

Shmuel tried to wave away her protests. Right now he felt invincible and dearly wanted her to share in his enthusiasm. The Brick Lane Lion, they'd called him. After that fight, wasn't he indeed a lion?

"You don't need to box to make a decent living. You can do better than that. You're a skilled craftsman – "

"I can make extra money for my family . . ." Before he could say more, footsteps sounded behind him and a hand was slapped on his shoulder.

"Hey, champ! We've been looking for you in the dressing room!"

Shmuel swung around to see Manny. Behind him were Lazar, Leah and Katya.

"You were great! Marvelous!" Manny ducked and weaved and feinted.

"Thank you." Shmuel knew he sounded more subdued than was expected, but what Lottie had said had deflated him. Now, with the same self-consciousness he'd first shown in the ring, he finally introduced her.

"We thought Shmuel had dreamed you up," Lazar told Lottie. "We kept asking to meet you and he always put us off."

"You must be very proud of Shmuel," Leah cut in, wanting to make her brother's girlfriend feel welcome.

"I'm glad that he won," Lottie said quietly.

Manny laughed. "Hey, we all are. Now we can afford to eat dinner tonight. How about coming to join us?" He took hold of Leah's arm and began to lead her away, confident that his offer would be accepted.

72

"Thank you, but we have other plans," Lottie told him.

Manny frowned. "Suit yourself. And take care of that body," he told Shmuel. "Your manager's reminding you that you're an athlete in training." Laughing again, he led the others away.

"Is Manny your sister's boyfriend?" Lottie asked Shmuel.

"Just a friend. He's a bit on the loud side," he added, realizing Lottie's antagonism toward Manny. "But he's friendly, and generous. He's helped us out, Lottie. Remember, we're not like your family, we're new and — "

"And helped *himself* at the same time, I wouldn't doubt," Lottie said, looking after the group of four people. "I think he's a spiv. A loud-mouthed, flashy, East End spiv. Shmuel, watch out for him. Please . . . ?"

Shmuel nodded, put his arm through hers and walked toward the bus stop. He'd go back to the room in Brick Lane, drop off the bag. He'd let Lottie see the room. He was no longer ashamed of it because he knew with the money he was making — that they were all making as long as he continued to win — they wouldn't be in the single room for much longer.

Afterward they'd go up to the West End, to eat, to dance. He'd been blooded into his new career, prospects looked bright. He had every reason to celebrate, didn't he?

A car's horn sounded and Manny swept by in a new model Standard. Leah was next to him; Lazar and Katya were in the back. Shmuel waved and wondered how long he'd have to wait for the bus.

"Your manager has a car and you have to travel by bus," Lottie observed. "You might keep that in mind . . ."

After dinner Manny excused himself to the others, saying he had business to attend to. He gave Leah a hug and a boldly lingering kiss, told Lazar he'd see him at midnight in Shaffzics for the weekly Solo game and waved a cheerful farewell. Lazar held onto Katya's arm while Leah walked ahead by herself, happily swinging her handbag from side to side.

Later on, when he saw Katya home to Hackney, Lazar would return the ten pounds to Saul Goldstein. And tell him he'd won seventy. Then he'd see what the factory owner had to say about Manny Goodman. How bad was a man who put that much money into your pocket? Manny might come out on the debit side of Saul Goldstein's good-for-the-Jews-or-bad-for-the-Jews equation. He might not be educated in the formal sense of the word, the way Lazar was. He might not have the respectable family advantages that Saul Goldstein had. But he knew how to make things *happen*. He knew how to get the best out of people, to recognize their strengths and help them capitalize on them. So he profited in the process . . . what was wrong with that? Who else would have thought of arranging for Shmuel to box for money?

Still, there was one aspect of his relationship with Manny that troubled Lazar . . . "Leah," he called out to his sister. She turned around questioningly, her handbag maintaining its rhythmic swing. "You like Manny, don't you?"

"What do you think?" Her face widened into a smile. Manny's easygoing, self-assured manner appealed to her. In someone else she might have found it cocky, but Manny managed to temper it with a genuine-seeming charm. He was, in fact, like no one she'd ever met before. Certainly *not* like the men in Germany. He'd moved into her life in the most natural way in the world, from the moment he'd knocked on the door to announce Shmuel's fight and had interrupted her with Ivor Davies. She knew she should feel guilty . . . Davies was obviously such a good man . . . but, face it, she didn't even miss Ivor. She would, she suspected, have grown tired of him eventually. Manny, on the other hand, was the kind of man you weren't likely ever to grow tired of. He always seemed so . . . fresh, something new each time she saw him. She'd willed him to ask her out, always disappointed when he'd left without doing it. Then had come today, the way he'd taken her hand, pressed it against his leg. The long kiss that told her without words how much he wanted her. Needed her. Well, she felt the same way . . .

Lazar left Katya and hurried to draw alongside his sister. "Leah, don't get *too* fond of Manny. I don't think he's for you – "

A flash of annoyance shone in Leah's dark eyes, her mouth tightened. "Since when do you tell me who is and who is not for me?"

"Leah, he's a gambler. He bet a hundred pounds on Shmuel. What if he'd lost?"

"Are you jealous, dear brother?... Just because he can afford to bet a hundred pounds when most people are earning three pounds a week if they're earning at all..." She knew her words were hitting Lazar like slaps in the face, but her defensive feeling swept her along. "Do you believe in double standards... that Manny's good enough to be *your* friend but not mine?"

"He's getting to be more than a friend to you."

"Lazar, please don't give me an older-brother lecture in the middle of the street. I'm big enough and old enough to know what's right for me. You've changed since Cologne. Shmuel has. Would you ever have dreamed that he'd fight professionally? What about me?"

Lazar gave up the argument for now, returned to Katya and took her arm again. She asked him what had happened and he told her.

"Is it really your business, Lazar?"

"Of course it is. I'm responsible for Leah and Shmuel. I'm the oldest member of the family."

"Lazar, you let Shmuel get into that ring today. He could have been hurt —"

"But he wasn't. He won —"

"Yes. Because he knew how to take care of himself. He made a decision, you did, why shouldn't Leah? Besides, you're interested in money too. Most people are. Be honest about it."

He smiled and squeezed her arm, realizing she was right. Katya had the ability to see right through him, and still put up with him. Certainly he was concerned about Leah and Shmuel. But he was also concerned about his own welfare. He had profited from Shmuel. And from Manny.

Katya's green eyes were sharper than he'd realized. He should be grateful, even if a bit uneasy ...

Predictably, Saul Goldstein seemed surprised when Lazar

returned the ten pounds, and angry to learn that Katya had been taken to Hoxton Baths to watch Shmuel fight.

"I don't like *you* mixing with this Goodman. You think I like it any more when my daughter is with you −?"

"I wanted to see Shmuel fight," Katya cut in before Lazar could utter a word. "I'm glad I did."

Goldstein ignored his daughter. "I take it your brother won."

"He knocked out the Irishman in the second round."

"Was Shmuel hurt?"

"A cut above the eyebrow, from a head butt."

"What do you intend doing with your seventy pounds? Your . . . honest earnings?"

"Move from the room in Brick Lane. Find a better place to live."

Goldstein shook his head. "You haven't listened to a single word I said about Manny Goodman. Throwing in with the likes of him is like taking sides with the devil. Sooner or later you have to pay with your soul."

Lazar thought of his own warning to Leah, then pushed it aside. "Mr Goldstein, with all due respect to you, I'm not going to get rich working in your factory. I need additional income. My whole family does −"

"For what? Plenty of men raise a family on less than I'm paying you."

"I'm not plenty of other men, sir. I don't want to support your daughter on that kind of money." The words were out of Lazar's mouth before he even realized what he was saying. He couldn't even think of the precise moment he had made up his mind . . . was it when Katya had shown how well she understood him? And accepted him?

Katya was delighted, her father was not. "Not too long ago I thought you would have made a wonderful husband for my Katya," Goldstein said. "You're clever. You have an education. You want to get on in the world. But now . . . when you mix with scum like Manny Goodman. I could never allow it −"

"Father." Katya moved closer to Lazar and held his hand. "I'm of legal age."

Goldstein's shoulders sagged. "You are, you are." He turned to Lazar. "I ask you this . . . whatever your dealings are with Manny Goodman, please don't ever tell me. Don't ever speak of them in this house. I do not wish to know how you make money with such a man to support my daughter."

The regular Saturday night game of Solo started shortly after midnight. During the first hand Lazar casually mentioned that he was getting married, which announcement was greeted with a back-slapping round of congratulations.

"That bit of money gave you the confidence to pop the question, eh, Whitey?" Manny laughed. "Just goes to show what a little bit of *gelt* can do for a man. And there's more where that came from. Plenty more."

"Other fights for Shmuel?" Lazar said uneasily.

"Something else." Manny took no notice of Jerry Jacobs or Harry Sherman, speaking as if they were not even there. "How would you like to . . . work for me instead of Katya's old man? You shouldn't work for your in-laws anyway. Best way to make enemies of everyone, ruin a marriage."

"What would I be doing?" Feeling even more uneasy.

"You'd be bookkeeper, your trade, isn't it?"

"For a greengrocer's shop?"

"Come off it, Whitey, you weren't born yesterday: I run a firm with a lot of varied interests. Besides" — he picked up the cards that were scattered across the tabletop and started to shuffle — "I'm superstitious. I look on you as a good-luck charm. Things have gone well since I met you. I'm Moses, see . . . and your barnet's my burning bush leading me to the promised land of milk and honey."

"Barnet?"

"Barnet Fair, your hair! Christ, when are you going to learn the real English language?"

Lazar had to laugh at that one. English, he knew already; the Cockney rhyming slang patois that Manny frequently slipped into was a totally different language. "I'll let you know," he said, deciding to talk it over with Katya.

"You do that. By the way, Harry's got a little gift for you.

77

Turns out to be a wedding present." He motioned to the pale-faced, bald-headed man. Sherman pushed back his chair and left the table. He returned almost immediately, carrying a scruffy shopping bag he handed to Lazar.

"These were sold to me," Sherman said. "I bought them in good faith. Now Manny here tells me they might belong to you . . ."

Lazar glanced first at Sherman, then at Manny. Finally he looked inside the bag and recognized the six silver wine goblets from his parents' home in Cologne. "How did you get these?"

"He just told you," Manny said slowly. "Someone sold him a load of silverware. Harry's a dealer, he buys and sells. Same as Jerry here. Harry had no reason to suspect the stuff he bought might have been nicked. I asked around, just like you wanted me to, and this is what came up."

"Where's the rest? The candlesticks? The plates?"

"No idea, son," Sherman replied. "All I was offered is what's in that bag." He didn't have the heart to tell Lazar that he had sold everything else within a week of Manny's passing it to him. The goblets had refused to move, though. Their design was too distinctive, everyone had told him. He was about to have them melted down for scrap when Manny had passed the word that he wanted them back.

"Who sold them to you?"

Sherman scratched his head. "Strike me down but I can't remember his bloody name. And if I might be so bold, Whitey, maybe you ought not to look a gift horse in the mouth . . ."

CHAPTER FIVE

Lazar departed Saul Goldstein's factory in Middlesex Street and became a jack-of-all-trades for Manny Goodman.

He kept the books for three gambling clubs Manny owned, small premises where seven-card rummy was played. The house, of course, took in a percentage of the money that crossed the tables. The books were not for tax purposes – it was a strictly cash business – but once a month Manny took the books away for an evening. Twenty percent of the take, he explained, went to the man who . . . protected him . . . and that man, not unreasonably, liked to go over the books himself.

He kept track of stolen merchandise that passed through Manny's greengrocer's shop and a warehouse he operated off Whitechapel Road. Lazar, as he was by Manny himself, was simultaneously intrigued and put off. Consignments of goods – from boxes of cigarettes or crates of spirits to jewelry and clothing – were regularly picked up by supposedly reputable retailers for eventual resale. Manny covered himself by dealing only with people he knew on a long-term basis. Twice in as many months Lazar saw him agree to receive from an unknown source. Both times when the delivery was made to the warehouse, the police were waiting, tipped off by Manny that he suspected someone of trying to sell him stolen goods. "Rule number one in this business," he told Lazar . . . "You've got to live with old Bill. Now and again you have to give a body away. You give him a sacrifice and he's happy. It makes it look like he's doing his job and it keeps him off my back."

Lazar was also obliged to collect rents from the half-dozen rundown buildings Manny owned in Whitechapel. All exorbitant, it seemed. Supply and demand, Manny called it, "the secret of the real-estate business." The demand was always greater than the supply in the East End because of all the East European Jews who had come over twenty, thirty years ago and hadn't moved out. Now the new lot of refugees was moving in, all looking for accommodation, too much money chasing too few rooms. Lazar remembered his own first day in the East End, the room that had been offered in Wentworth Street. He did his best to numb himself to the memory, the old feeling. This was the real world, business. Who was he to make judgments? Soon he'd have a wife to support. He had obligations . . .

But the prostitutes that operated from a house Manny owned in Leman Street . . . well, prostitution was a business like anything else, the oldest profession, they called it. But he was worried because Leah was seeing even more of Manny. How could she help it — and how could he reasonably now object — when he was working for Manny? Leah must know about Manny's enterprises, the man rarely tried to dissemble with those close to him. Give him that . . .

Manny's father had bought up substandard property when he'd first arrived from Poland in 1902. From there it had been a natural step for his father to move into "houses". It made more sense, and more money, to give one house to prostitutes instead of tenants. The arrangement was benevolent . . . the women looked after their own affairs and cut Manny's father in for fifty percent of their take to cover accommodations and protection. All parties were satisfied. Then stolen goods had started to find their way to the greengrocer's shop on Booth Street. Before long Manny's father had set himself up in business . . . with thieves willing to let "the Grocer" — as he came to be known — take care of *their* business for them.

When the Grocer had died a few years ago from a heart attack, struck down while carrying hundredweight sacks of potatoes into the shop, Manny had taken over. Already well known in the area, Manny had projected a new image into his father's business. Manny liked to dress well, to patronize exclusive tailors in the West End, while his father had been content to wear the cheap clothes he had worn in Poland.

Manny loved to spend money, to entertain his friends. His father had begrudged parting with a single farthing unless he thought he could turn a profit from it.

"That's why he dropped dead from a heart attack," Manny once said, "because he was too tight to even hire some *shtarker* to do his *shlepping* for him. Richest bloke in Marlowe Road Cemetery, my old man. I'm making bloody sure I don't follow him."

"Why do you keep the store?" Lazar asked. "It doesn't make money." If anything, it lost money. Manny seemed to delight in charging considerably less for his produce than anyone else did. Often he sold it at cost and had women lining up outside to take advantage of the bargains. Lazar put it down as Manny seeing himself as a sort of Robin Hood, helping the needy, making restitution for his other activities. Did it really even out?

"Because it's a great meeting place," Manny answered. "Anyone who wants to see Manny Goodman, they know where they can find him."

One evening while Lazar and Manny were at the back of the shop four men entered. Their leader, a short, dark-skinned man with oily hair and piercing black eyes, strode toward Manny, one fist clenched tight at his side, the other hand hidden in his pocket.

"Goodman," he said quietly in an accent Lazar had difficulty identifying. "You and me are going to sort out territory, once and for all."

"Whitey." Manny gestured toward the swarthy man. "Take a good look at Davey Vanetti, the pride of Malta. But don't breathe too deep. He smells like the bloody garlic he stuffs his face with."

Lazar glanced nervously at Vanetti and at the three men escorting him, who had remained by the entrance.

Vanetti was king of a vice ring that stretched from Soho to the City. There was no similarity between Manny's operation and what Vanetti ran. Manny's attitude toward prostitutes was ambivalent; they ran their own business and cut him in. Vanetti pushed women into prostitution. And kept them there with the threat of a razor or a bottle of vitriol.

Vanetti scarcely looked at Lazar. He closed the distance between himself and Manny. "We had an agreement, Goodman. As long as your women stayed in Whitechapel there'd be no trouble between us. But you don't listen to me. Two of your women were in the Star and Garter pub in King's Cross last night."

"Maybe they were thirsty."

"Sure. For my money they were thirsty. I" – Vanetti pointed to himself – "with my own eyes, saw them pick up men and leave."

"So what?" A grin began to etch itself on Manny's face. Somehow it never reached his eyes, which stayed cold as glass.

"You keep them away from there. That's my ground."

"My girls will work wherever they bloody well choose," Manny said quietly. "The Malt's not crawled out from under a rock yet who's going to stop them." The grin remained, but under Manny's left eye a nervous tic appeared. Lazar had seen it once before, during the fight between Shmuel and Jackie O'Brien.

"Then they won't work for you. No woman will work for a man who's been marked by me." He moved a step closer. The hand in his pocket emerged with a razor, taped shut with the blade forced through the white handle to expose a quarter-inch of shining steel.

Instinctively Lazar stepped forward.

"Stay out of it, Whitey," Manny told him, then ducked under the blade as it swung toward his face and dived beneath the counter. A split second later he came up clutching a hollowed-out, lead-filled chair leg. Before Vanetti had a chance to recover his balance from the missed stroke Manny brought the chair leg down across his head.

Vanetti fell to the ground, blood pouring from his torn scalp. The three men who had accompanied him moved uncertainly. Manny ran at them with the chair leg. They turned around and ran off. He chased after them onto the street, still brandishing the weapon.

"Don't go without your guv'nor. What kind of people are

you anyway?" He threw the chair leg like a club at the Morris, into which all three men dove. It hit the roof and skidded off as the car accelerated away from the curb.

Inside the shop Vanetti writhed on the floor, groaning as he clutched his injured head. Manny, returning to the shop, told Lazar to help drag the Malt out to the alleyway in the back.

"You just learned a lesson, Whitey," Manny said, straining under Vanetti's dead weight. "Malts are like Paddies. Can't break their damn skulls unless you hit them with the Tower of London."

They dumped Vanetti in the alleyway and went back inside. Lazar picked up the chair leg Manny had retrieved from Booth Street and weighed it in his hand. Vanetti's thick head of hair had undoubtedly saved his life, which thought sent a shiver along Lazar's spine, until he remembered the red-faced SA man in the tearoom in Aachen, and the knife he had pushed into his stomach. By Manny's lights, was what he had done to the Malt so different from what Lazar had done? As for lessons, the one Lazar had gotten had little to do with the thickness of Irish or Maltese skulls. It was to watch out for the half-grin, and the nervous tic below Manny Goodman's left eye.

Within three months of leaving Saul Goldstein's factory Lazar's world had turned upside down. From the rented single room in Brick Lane he had bought a three-story house in Stoke Newington. The first two floors would be for himself and Katya; the third floor he gave over to Leah and Shmuel.

A week after buying the house Lazar married Katya. Manny expected to be the best man, telling Lazar not to forget who was responsible for his upturn of fortunes. Lazar chose Shmuel. It was difficult enough for Saul Goldstein to resign himself to seeing his only daughter marry a man who was associated with Manny Goodman. If Manny were best man, occupied a place of honor behind the wedding couple, Goldstein might not even turn up. As it was, the factory owner maintained a stiff mask throughout the ceremony and reception that followed. When Manny approached him to offer congratulations to the father of the bride, Goldstein presented him with a view of his back.

Manny turned to Lazar, shrugged, although he was hurt and angry. Lazar didn't explain to him that what especially upset Goldstein was that his daughter was not against Lazar's link with Manny. Not, Lazar knew, that Katya liked Manny personally. She mistrusted him . . . his charm, she felt, was like a snake's, mesmerizing victims like Leah until it was ready to strike . . . She went along with Lazar working for Manny because she saw the man as a means to an end. Katya, in her fashion, put them all to shame as a realist. People like Manny weren't likely to disappear from the earth because her father and "decent" people clucked disapproval of them. The rich customers for her father's goods were not exactly nature's noblemen. So if Manny was here to stay, why not use him? Surely better that than be used by him . . .

With Leah on his arm Manny wandered about the hall until he saw Shmuel sitting with Lottie Bloch. "Want to talk to your brother?" he asked Leah.

"You're not really angry, are you, I mean because Lazar picked Shmuel over you as best man?"

"No. I'd have probably palmed the ring anyway, replaced it with a cheap one. That's what old man Goldstein thinks I'd do." He laughed at his own joke and guided Leah to the table where Shmuel and Lottie sat. He held out a chair for Leah, then sat down to face Shmuel.

"That cut healed up nice."

Instinctively Shmuel raised a hand to his eyebrow. Other than a slight scar from the clumsy stitching of the ring doctor, he had nothing to remind him of O'Brien's head butt. "It made me more careful for the next time."

"I bet it did at that. Nothing like a Paddy butting you in the face to show you what it's all about."

Since that first fight Manny had arranged two more. A return with O'Brien at Hoxton Baths that Shmuel had won in the first round, followed a month later by a third-round knockout of a well-regarded Jamaican heavyweight at York Hall in Bethnal Green. Convinced that he had the real goods in Shmuel, Manny was no longer so concerned with the betting angle. The way Shmuel was going he'd soon be a favorite himself. Manny was thinking about the regional eliminators. The Southern Area heavyweight championships. And after that . . . ? Manny wasn't sure about the legal technicalities of a German citizen fighting for the British championship, but . . .

"You know you're banging your head against the wall in that Hanbury Street job, don't you?" he told Shmuel.

"Manny feels you'd be better off working for him," Leah put in.

"What kind of work?"

"At one of my clubs."

"The gambling clubs?"

"Social clubs," Manny corrected him. "A tea bar, a place for men to go. Billiards, snooker, rummy for a couple of coppers. I need a responsible doorman for my place in Dalston. Evenings only. Twenty quid a week."

Shmuel looked at Manny. Social clubs! Who was he trying to fool? "Social clubs don't pay a doorman that much, Manny. Only clubs that have eleven-to-four rummy at ten shillings or a pound a game."

"All right. Gambling clubs, if you want to split hairs. What about it?"

"I've *got* a job," Shmuel said, and reached out and held Lottie's hand. He knew what Manny wanted. He already had Lazar on his payroll. Leah would do anything for him. All he wanted now was Shmuel.

Manny held a hand in the air, palm facing Shmuel. "Before you rush into any hasty decisions, why don't you talk it over with Lottie?" He gave her a broad smile. If he could win her over, Shmuel would follow. "Maybe Lottie can understand the importance of money better than you can." He almost added that, after all, she had more of it than he did, or at least her family did.

Lottie smiled back just as sweetly and squeezed Shmuel's hand. "Why should he have to talk it over with me? If he doesn't want to work for you, I wouldn't want to persuade him to do otherwise." She was proud of Shmuel, of the way he had turned down the offer. Other men would kill for twenty pounds a week. Shmuel would rather earn less and know he was earning it decently. Even the money he made from fighting was earned honestly. Although Lottie continued to be unhappy about his ring career, she was willing to put up with it because he was fighting for a good reason . . . for money to open his own business. That she could understand, sympathize with, and she knew it included her. Manny's kind of money tied you to Manny. She knew it had taken courage to turn Manny's offer down, but she'd never doubted Shmuel had courage.

"You should think about it again," Manny said. "Think hard. Good jobs aren't so easy to come by these days. Read the newspapers about all the unemployed and then see how you feel." He got up from the table and walked off, taking Leah with him.

"Thank you," Lottie whispered. "I enjoyed watching you put him in his place."

"Just as long as he doesn't try to put me in mine."

"How could he do that?"

"I don't know." Shmuel wasn't even sure why he'd made the remark. Was it because he knew how powerful Manny was? And if something did happen, he wondered, on whose side would his brother be? Or his sister? They were both tied in with Manny . . . wouldn't they side with him against anyone? Even against their own brother?

"I think you should move out of your brother's house," Lottie said abruptly.

Shmuel understood, and was touched. "That's not necessary. We're a family. We've got to stay together." He wondered as he said it if Lazar and Leah felt the same way now . . .

"All families have to part eventually. It's part of life – "

"When I can afford to open my own business . . . when I can afford to get married – "

"You know my father would help you – "

"Lottie, I want to do it by myself. With money I *earn*."

"All right," she whispered, accepting and respecting his pride. "I shouldn't worry about you anyway. You're strong enough to stand up to your brother." She hoped . . .

"I won't have to," Shmuel said, "he'd never try to force me to do anything I didn't want to do –"

And just then the band struck up the opening waltz. Shmuel turned around to watch Lazar and Katya open the ball. They took a few steps, then other couples joined them on the dance floor. Shmuel stood up and helped Lottie to her feet.

"The best man and his girl should be out there too," he said.

"At least your suit fits you this time," Lottie told him, and they both laughed as they walked out onto the dance floor, the conversation with Leah and Manny pushed to the back of their minds.

But not forgotten.

CHAPTER SIX

Panic stories in the newspapers screamed that after fifty years Jack the Ripper had returned. When the headline "PROSTITUTE MURDERED! RIPPER STRIKES!" hit the streets, double locks went on doors at night. Women refused to walk alone. The pubs and dance halls became deserted.

Police investigating the vicious slaying of a prostitute whose body had been discovered in an abandoned building in Holborn could turn up no clues to either the murderer or the motive. The woman's throat had been slashed. Her body had been mutilated. Both ears had been severed. One was found lying a few feet from the body; the other was missing. The dead woman's name had been Henrietta Minsky.

Manny Goodman knew better than to let himself get worked up by sensationalized newspaper reports. He didn't believe for a moment that the murder had been the work of a mindless maniac. He had known Henrietta Minsky. She'd worked from the house he owned in Leman Street and her murder was a message for him. What he thought he had discouraged by cracking the lead-weighted chair leg across a Maltese skull was still very much alive.

The following morning's mail brought Manny a small parcel. Inside, he found a letter scribbled in thick black pencil promising a similar fate to any of the Leman Street women who strayed from Whitechapel. Accompanying the letter was the missing ear. Manny called an emergency meeting, ready to issue a declaration of war, ready to crack his chair leg over the head of every Malt in London.

Jerry Jacobs was the last to arrive at the flat above the greengrocer's shop. Manny, already waiting with Lazar and

Harry Sherman, wasted no time in reading out the letter's contents and displaying the severed, decomposing ear he had set out in the middle of the table, resting on a bone china saucer. Forcing himself to look at the ear, Lazar made a mental note never to have a cup of tea in the flat.

"Vanetti?" Sherman asked needlessly.

"You know any other nutty bastard who'd do a thing like that?" Manny said. "Only a Malt would even think of it."

"What are you going to do?" Jacobs asked. "Tell your women to get off the streets for a while, I mean until this thing blows over?"

"Are you crazy?" Manny's voice rose, his face went red. Lazar waited for the little tic to appear, and was not disappointed. Even before Manny began his next sentence the skin below his left eye commenced to jump. "If we give in to the Malts now there's no telling what they'll do next. They'll take it all."

"They're whoremongers, that's all," Sherman pointed out. "That's their main business." There was disapproval in his voice, as if he thought prostitution was below the level of a civilized man.

Manny ignored the rebuke in Sherman's tone. If Sherman didn't like that he ran tarts, tough. It was none of Sherman's business. "For now it's their only game. But if you show them you're weak, they'll want *whatever* you've got. How many men can you let me have?" Manny looked at the fat figure of Jacobs.

"Maybe half a dozen."

"And you?" he asked Sherman.

"Three or four."

"Good. I can arrange for another half-dozen. We know where Vanetti goes. I say we go down there and put the blag on him and his whole crew." He reached across the table to the saucer, picked up the severed ear and studied it, like he was seeing it for the first time. Lazar thought he was going to be sick.

"What's the matter, Whitey? Bit squeamish, are you?" Manny seemed to be enjoying the look on Lazar's face. "You think your part in my business is just adding up figures? Maybe it's about time you learned different."

"Will you please put that thing down?"

"Here, *you* put it down." With a quick underhand motion Manny flipped the ear toward Lazar, who looked on in disgust as it skipped across the tabletop to land in his lap. His legs twitched and the ear, mercifully, dropped to the floor. Manny gave a high-pitched giggle and looked around the table, unable to understand why no one else was sharing his amusement. Jacobs finally got out a laugh. Sherman sat stony-faced.

"There's nothing funny about a woman being killed and her body used for ghoulish games," Lazar snapped.

Manny's mouth dropped open. Jacobs was taken aback, while Sherman glanced at Lazar with new interest. He'd looked on Lazar as one of Manny's whims, someone he'd taken under his wing as an obedient henchman because he liked the color of his hair. Obedient henchmen didn't answer back, no matter what color their hair was.

"This Henrietta Minsky worked for you," Lazar said. "She made money for you. You were paid to protect her and she died. Is this all you care about her?"

"Of course I bloody care about her," Manny burst out. "That's why I'm going to get Vanetti. By the time I'm finished with him he'll wish he'd never left his dirty little shack in Malta —"

"And what will that solve? There'll be another Vanetti. And another woman. And you'll be sitting here again, deciding what to do."

"Listen, Whitey. One thing my old man taught me. When someone shoves you, you shove back. Only harder. Otherwise you're going to get shoved right off the pavement and under a flipping cart."

Sherman risked the gleam of annoyance in Manny's eyes to suggest: "Maybe Whitey has another idea."

"Oh? Do you?"

"I think so." Lazar bent down and using his handkerchief picked up Henrietta Minsky's ear and placed it in the saucer. "The last thing you want is a full-scale war that's sure to bring every policeman in London down on your neck. So . . ." He began to outline a plan, improvising as he went. In Jerry Jacobs' eyes Lazar could recognize disbelief that such an idea could even be considered. Sherman looked thoughtful. On Manny's face, though, Lazar saw excitement. No . . . not excitement, delight. Manny was like a small child, anticipating . . . And suddenly it occurred to Lazar that all too often Manny looked like a little child. His face was smooth, young; his emotions were never far below the surface . . .

"Christ," Manny murmured when Lazar had finished. "Can you imagine" – he turned to look at Jacobs and Sherman – "what that slimy Malt's going to have to live with for the rest of his life? And we'll make sure everyone knows what happened to him." He got up from the chair, walked around the table and rubbed his hands through Lazar's platinum hair. "A *leben* on your *kapele*, Whitey. You're a bloody *genius*."

Sherman coughed into his hand. And coughed again until Manny swung around. "You're going to have to clear it first with Joey Taylor."

"Yeah, Joey . . . I know." Manny's enthusiasm diminished some, and Lazar's interest rose at the mention of the name. So far he'd never met Joey Taylor, the man Manny took the books to once a month. Joey Taylor kept the peace. Arranged deals. Liaised with the police when something got out of hand, gave them the occasional body to keep them happy. He kept the underworld honest. The police let him stay in business because he was doing their job for them, was good business for them. Without him there would be anarchy. When someone got out of control the police came down on Joey Taylor first . . . and made damned certain that he came down hard on everyone else.

"Joey'll go for Whitey's idea more than he'd go for chopping Vanetti's head off," Jacobs said. "You know he doesn't like war."

"That's if he lets you do anything at all," Sherman pointed out. "Remember . . . he made up that agreement between you and Vanetti in the first place."

91

"So he did," Manny said. "But no one ever claimed that tarts were smart. How are they supposed to know where one district ends and another begins? They haven't gotten around to reading maps." He studied the ear in the bone china saucer. "I'll call him now and arrange a meeting. Whitey, you can come with me. Be as convincing with him as you were with me."

Lazar looked about the table. Jacobs and Sherman seemed thoughtful. Only Manny was outwardly *happy* at the idea.

And it was then that Lazar decided that Manny Goodman was quite mad.

Joey Taylor was a bookmaker who had become an organizer. When he'd started at the tracks thirty years earlier he'd witnessed and often participated in the violence between rival bookies as they fought for the choicest pitches. The scar he wore like a medal down the right side of his face was a reminder of the battle on Derby Day at Epsom when razor gangs had fought for the most desirable positions. People had scattered in panic as groups of men had attacked bookies' stalls. Forewarned, the police had waited patiently. The dead they buried. The wounded they ordered off to hospitals. Those with enough strength to keep standing they arrested.

It was almost a year before Taylor returned to the race track. But he didn't go to make book. He went to see the pitch committees at the various southern tracks, gentlemen who were still recovering from the reverberations of the previous year's Derby Day battle. Taylor had offered them professional services. He would handle the pitch allocations. For a price. And he guaranteed that there would never be trouble again at any track he minded. The pitch committees asked him how he would do it. He told them he'd use fear and if necessary force. He, and he alone, would be responsible for handing out pitches to the bookies. Anyone who gave him trouble wouldn't receive a pitch; they'd be out of business. And anyone who gave him further trouble would be taken care of by one of the hundred men he had on his payroll. It was a gamble on Taylor's part. If the pitch committees had turned him down he would have been bankrupt. Only they hadn't turned him down. Why reject the solution to a problem that might close their tracks.

After that Taylor had become an institution at the southern tracks. A tall bony man who perpetually wore a black bowler hat no matter what the weather, he would walk around the bookies' stalls acccompanied by two of his retainers. The bowler hat was not an ornament, it was protection. Lined with steel, it had saved his life at Brighton when a renegade bookie's thug had tried to split his head open with an iron bar and had only succeeded in making a vee-shaped dent in the crown of the hat. While he wondered why Taylor was merely dazed and not dead, one of Taylor's men had taken the iron bar away from the man and broken his arms and legs with it. After that there had been no more attempts on Joey Taylor.

From the race tracks Taylor had turned his peacemaking skills to London's gangs. In his view the gangs were the same as the bookies he'd once organized. They spent more time fighting each other than doing what they should be doing . . . making money. Most of the groups were small, involved in petty crime, robbing shops, stealing anything not nailed down. The larger ones were into protection, extorting money from publicans. All too often, because there were no distinct boundaries, war broke out between rival factions over claims of trespassing. Arbitrarily Taylor had decided which little fish had to be swallowed up by larger ones. When he got them together and explained that they should work as allies, respecting each other's territorial rights, they saw he made sense. The violence declined. The profits of each group increased. And, most importantly to Taylor, the police were happier . . .

Manny swung the Standard into the semicircular driveway of a house on The Bishop's Avenue in Hampstead Garden Suburb and turned off the engine. "Not bad, eh, Whitey?"

Lazar took in the house. It was like a castle. The outside lights bathed the grounds in brightness. Luxurious lawns rolled up to walls that were as white and clean as if the painters had just left. Even as Lazar watched, the solid oak front door opened and a uniformed butler stepped out.

"You'd like one just like it, wouldn't you?" Manny laughed. "See that?" He pointed to an illuminated fountain that sent streams of water gushing high into the air. "That's what I paid for, I reckon. Every crook in London has paid for a piece of this place."

"How long has he lived here?"

"What does it matter? All you've got to worry about is that he lives here, and you live in a tiny shack in Stoke Newington." Manny got out of the car, and as he walked toward the open door and the butler his face took on a fixed, blank expression.

"Manny Goodman. Mr Taylor's expecting me."

"Yes, sir. And the other gentleman?"

"My associate."

"I'll need his name to announce him, sir."

"Boruchowicz, Lazar Boruchowicz."

"Thank you, sir. Would you please wait here?" The butler showed them into a deeply carpeted parlor. Lazar started to lower himself into a leather wing chair. Manny told him to stand up.

The parlor door opened and the butler reappeared. "If you'll follow me, please. Mr Taylor will see you right away." He led them across the wide hall into a room on the opposite side. Lazar's eyes were immediately taken by the framed racing prints that covered the paneled walls . . . thoroughbreds, steeplechasers, signed paintings of famous jockeys. In one corner of the room was a highly polished saddle. In another was a hat rack; only one hook was taken . . . by a steel-lined bowler hat with a vee-shaped dent in the crown.

"Good evening, gentlemen. I'm pleased to see you."

Lazar turned from the dented bowler hat and looked at the man who was rising from behind the mahogany desk to greet them. Taylor was now in his fifties, a spare figure of a man with white hair parted in the center and slicked down. He wore a red silk dressing gown over his open-necked shirt and trousers, leather slippers. The scar on his right cheek had whitened with time until it was nothing more than a thin, faint line.

"Mr. Taylor." Manny shook the offered hand. "This is my associate, Lazar Boruchowicz."

"How do you do? Please sit down. A drink?"

Lazar opened his mouth to accept, closed it again when he saw Manny give a slight shake of the head.

"Now" – Taylor took his seat behind the desk again, picked up the cigar that lay smoking in the crystal ashtray and puffed contentedly – "what seems to be the trouble between you and Davey Vanetti?"

"He killed one of my women, Mr. Taylor."

"So I heard. I don't approve of killing, Goodman, you know that. Especially when it receives the amount of publicity that this unfortunate episode got. But as I understand it, that Minsky woman of yours had no business being where she was. Vanetti had warned you earlier."

Manny fidgeted on the chair. "He came by my shop a few weeks ago."

"And?"

"I threw him out."

Taylor removed the cigar from his mouth and consulted a notepad on the desk. "Vanetti claims you almost killed him."

"Self-defense. He came at me with a razor."

"I see. So what do you propose? Not more of the same, I trust. The police won't stand for it. To be honest" – he moved his head to include Lazar in the conversation for the first time – "neither will I. My friends at Scotland Yard have already been onto me about the late Miss Minsky. We've had no trouble for a long time. I don't want to see anything happen that might reverse that situation."

"Nothing violent," Manny said. Lazar could never remember seeing him so subdued, like he was in the presence of Almighty God.

"What do you intend?"

"Whitey, tell your idea to Mr. Taylor."

Lazar found his mouth was dry. Nervously he tried to spread moisture with his tongue, then outlined the plan he'd first put forward to Manny, Jacobs and Sherman. Taylor listened carefully.

"Almost poetic in its justice," Taylor commended Lazar when he had finished. "What do you think Vanetti will do in return?"

"Nothing. He'll be too embarrassed when the story gets around to ever tangle with me again."

"And you'll keep your women out of his territory?"

"Maybe."

Taylor frowned. "No maybes about it. I'll approve your plan, but it has to stop there. After you've carried it out I'll order Vanetti to stop. If he doesn't I'll have him chopped up and served to the police on a silver salver. The same goes for you." He stood up to signify the meeting was over.

"My congratulations to you," he said as he shook Lazar's hand. "You've shown imagination."

Taylor rang for the butler to show his visitors out.

In the car on the return trip to Stoke Newington, Manny was silent for a long time. Finally, when they stopped for a traffic light in Holloway Road, Manny said, "This is your show, Whitey. You arrange it. The women. Your team. Everything."

The women? Who could Lazar trust? Only Katya . . . and Leah . . . ? "I don't know where to get the men —"

"Then you shouldn't have opened your bloody big mouth to Joey Taylor. You wanted to show him how bloody clever you are. Well, go ahead."

"I never asked for credit, you told me to go ahead —"

"Yeah, I did. But I didn't tell you to put on a performance that belongs in the Old Vic. You did everything but take a fucking bow."

Lazar was quiet. Could it be that Manny was jealous? He remembered how Taylor had congratulated him. He'd said nothing to Manny.

The light changed and Manny sent the Standard surging forward. "Whitey . . . just because Taylor tells you what a clever little boy you are, don't you go getting ideas. This is still my firm. You work for me."

"Hey, Manny, I haven't said a thing. You're saying it all."

Manny looked at him, nodded. But he said nothing.

The rest of the journey to Stoke Newington was completed

in silence. Manny kept his eyes fixed on the road; his knuckles gleamed white as he gripped the wheel. Lazar watched the rows of shops and houses slide past.

"Are you coming in?" Lazar asked as they turned into his street. The way Manny was behaving, he hoped the answer would be no.

"Is Leah in?"

"I think so."

"All right." Manny swung the car to an abrupt halt, scraping the tires against the high curb. On the way into the house he said, "You get your brother Shmuel to help you, then I'll supply a couple of men."

"Shmuel? He'll never help with something like this." Lazar felt panicky as he understood Manny's condition.

"You get him. You ask him right now."

"Wait a minute." Lazar reached, grabbed Manny's arm. "Are you that sore because this thing is my idea? Because you didn't think of it or get credit for it?" He didn't need to wait for Manny's answer to know what it was. "Is insisting Shmuel be a part of it your way of getting back at me?"

"I just want to see how good an organizer you are," Manny said. 'Having an idea's one thing. Getting it off the ground's something else." He shook himself free of Lazar's grasp and walked into the house.

Only Katya and Leah were at home. Leah was happy to see Manny so unexpectedly.

"Where's Shmuel?" Lazar asked Katya.

"He went to the gym. Then he was going over to Palmers Green to see Lottie."

"What time will he be back?"

"Around midnight. What's the urgency?"

Lazar glanced at Manny, who stood watching him. "I have to talk to him. To all of you." He knew Manny was judging how he'd handle the situation, recruit the personnel he'd need for the action against Davey Vanetti.

Briefly Lazar explained about the woman who had been murdered, then outlined his plan, feeling less and less pleased with himself. My God, he would be involving his own sister, his wife . . . but he'd make sure there'd be no harm to them . . . and they *were*, after all, part of his life . . . Stop it, he told himself, it was *necessary*. Leah and Katya listened with the same sort of reaction Jerry Jacobs had shown.

"Katya and I are to be bait?" Leah asked slowly.

Lazar glanced at Manny, who stared back, face blank.

"What do you think, Katya?" Leah asked, wondering why Manny hadn't said anything.

"It's necessary," Katya said. She too wondered about Manny staying aloof. "A woman was murdered, horribly. Vanetti has to be paid back. Lazar's way avoids bloodshed —"

"And police involvement," Lazar quickly added.

Katya took a deep breath. "I'll do it." Lazar deserved her support . . . she'd helped, in a way, to bring him to this point. "Tell me what I'm supposed to do."

". . . Pretend to be a . . . a prostitute." He forced himself to go on . . . "We'll find out where Vanetti is, you go in there, he'll figure Manny hasn't learned his lesson . . ." Lazar tried to bring Manny into it. "He'll think Manny's not afraid of him."

Manny's face tightened. "Of course I'm not scared of that disgusting barbarian. I've got the okay to pay him back and I'm going to do it."

"Then I'll come too," Leah said. After all, this was her brother, and the man she'd given her love to . . . as strange as that might seem to Shmuel and some others . . . Well, they didn't really know Manny the way she did. Lying next to him in bed — yes, she'd done that — she'd found out what it was really like to be a woman, and what a man her Manny was beneath all that hard talk . . . he was gentle, loving, yes and even funny too with his Cockney stories that made her laugh. Nobody knew the real Manny Goodman as she did, which at first upset her but now pleased her. It made what they had together all the more special, private. All their own . . .

And Manny, a smart man, a versatile man, knew a bloody good deal when he saw one.

Lazar saw Manny out to the car. As he sat behind the wheel, Manny rolled down his window and looked up. "You've got the women. Now you've got to get your lump of a brother involved too. He thinks he's too damned good to work for me. He takes the money I get him through boxing . . . that's all right. But he won't bloody well work for me! Maybe he'll work for *you*." He started the engine, shoved the stick into first and sped away, leaving Lazar looking after him, feeling as though a cold wind had just passed over him.

Shmuel came home just before midnight, carrying the bag of equipment he'd taken on his date with Lottie. When he saw the light on in the front room he automatically thought the last person to bed hadn't turned it off. He was surprised to find Lazar waiting for him.

"How's Lottie?"

"Fine."

"Where did you go?"

"We stayed in. Listened to some music on the radio." Shmuel dropped the bag onto the floor and sat down. "You didn't stay up just to ask me where I went."

"Shmuel . . . I saw a beautiful house tonight. I was inside it. It was the kind of house you only read about." He started to describe Taylor's house, and Shmuel listened, unable to guess where his brother was leading, but feeling vaguely uneasy all the same.

"Shmuel, I want us all to live in houses like that, big houses with enough rooms for a dozen children and all their friends and —"

"Who lives there now, Lazar?"

"A man called Joey Taylor. A very rich man. I want us —"

"Us? You've got a house already. You'll get a bigger and better one, take your time. Lottie and I have our plans too . . ."

Lazar scarcely noticed Shmuel's hint that he might be getting married to the girl from Palmers Green. "Shmuel, the first step toward a house like that, a life like that, is a big one. I need your help because I can't take that step on my own."

"What do you want?" Shmuel felt tired and wanted to get to bed. In six hours he would be up, ready for the long trip to the East End and his job.

"You read about the woman who was killed?"

99

"Minsky?"

"She was one of Manny's women."

"So?" Shmuel said.

Lazar ignored his brother's obvious antagonism. "Shmuel, I work for Manny. Right now, I need him. You do too. Without him you'd have no future. He showed you how to make something of yourself. Now I've got the chance to make something of myself."

"How?" Shmuel asked dully.

"I've a plan to get even with the man who killed the Minsky woman. No bloodshed," he said quickly. "But I need your help."

"Why me? I'm sure Manny's got a dozen men he could use."

"Because he wants me to ask you."

"Is this his way of getting me to work for him? Through you?"

"No. It's my way of reaching for a life like Joey Taylor's. This is *my* chance. You're getting yours in the ring."

"I still don't understand why you need me."

"It seems Manny's jealous of me, of the way I got on with this Joey Taylor. Unless I get you involved, Manny won't help. And my plan, my opportunity . . . will be gone." Seeing his brother was still unconvinced, Lazar knew he had to try one final tactic. He wasn't proud of himself but . . . "Shmuel, I waited for you and Leah in Maastricht. I led you here. Remember that."

Shmuel closed his eyes and sighed. He should have listened to Lottie. He should have moved out, found a place of his own, not been dependent on his brother. Sooner or later he knew he'd have to pay him back. Lottie had said he was strong enough to defy Lazar. Not this time, not when it was put this way to him. "All right, but this is the only time, the last time . . . this wipes out my debt to you, *and* to Manny . . ."

"*Right.*" Lazar reached out to clasp his brother. He was not quick enough. Shmuel got up, grabbed his bag and went upstairs.

Manny parked the Standard under a light on Frith Street in Soho and turned off the engine. Next to him was Lazar. In the back of the car sat Leah and Katya, both had knives in their bags. Looking in the mirror, Manny saw another car pull in behind him. Harry Sherman's Austin, bringing Sherman, Jacobs and Shmuel.

"That's the Pied Piper," Manny said, pointing to a public house twenty yards along the road. "Vanetti's going to be there tonight. When we see him go in, you two girls give him five minutes and then follow. You know what to do after that."

"There he is now," Lazar said. A car had stopped directly in front of the pub. Three men had gotten out and now stood for a moment where the light shining through the pub's windows illuminated their faces. He turned in the seat and looked at the second car, waved to the figure behind the steering wheel that he knew was Harry Sherman.

Manny counted the minutes off out loud. When five had elapsed he reached back and opened the door for Leah and Katya. "See you in a moment," he called out.

Only Katya looked back. "You make sure you do," and then she hurried to catch up with Leah.

"Glad your brother decided to come," Manny said to Lazar as they watched the girls enter the Pied Piper. "Seems you've got a way with him."

"Only this one time."

"I wouldn't be too sure about that. I bet he never told his girl what he was up to. And I bet he'd do us any favor to keep his girl from knowing."

Before Lazar could say anything Manny had gotten out of the car. He signaled to the occupants of the second car and now all five men walked slowly toward a narrow courtyard that ran off Frith Street.

Leah and Katya entered the Pied Piper arm-in-arm. The noise of loud talk and laughter hit them like a physical force and they hesitated in the doorway, uncertain whether to continue. It was an atmosphere far removed from the world they knew.

"Come on," Katya whispered, gathering up all her courage. She moved a few steps, pulling Leah with her. Davey Vanetti was easy to spot from Lazar's description. Two other dark-

101

skinned men were seated with him at a corner table. Glasses of whiskey were in front of them. All three looked up as Leah and Katya walked with forced boldness across the floor and sat down at a nearby table.

Both women were heavily made up, gaudily dressed in bright reds and pinks. Katya wore a thin gold chain around her ankle which glinted when she provocatively moved her leg. Vanetti got up from his chair and approached their table.

"Buy you ladies a drink?" He sat down with them.

Leah exchanged a glance with Katya. Each tried to encourage the other. "Thank you very much," Leah said.

"I haven't seen you in here before," Vanetti said after he'd returned with the drinks. "Where are you from?"

"Whitechapel," Katya said, avoiding eye contact with Vanetti.

"Whitechapel?" Since Henrietta Minsky, Vanetti had expected some kind of reprisal from Manny Goodman. Especially after he'd mailed him the missing ear. But the last thing he'd expected was for the Jewboy to do this. Send his women right into Soho, his turf. Was Goodman that stupid he couldn't understand a message as plain as an ear in the mail?

"You work for Manny Goodman?" Vanetti asked, just to double check.

"Yes, do you know him?" Katya managed.

Vanetti grinned. "Manny and I go back a long time. Did Manny tell you to come here?"

"Oh, yes. He said business was very good in Soho."

"I bet he did." So Manny was poking fun at him, daring him to do a repeat performance. That little creep was even willing to sacrifice two more of his tarts. Good-looking ones too. Vanetti ran his hand through his hair, across the top of his scalp, feeling where the lead-weighted chair leg had crashed down. Well, if Manny Goodman had a fetish for getting ears through the mail, Vanetti vowed he'd keep obliging him. "Where do you ladies do your business? It's a long way from here to Whitechapel."

"We've got a room the other side of Shaftesbury Avenue, in Lisle Street."

The grin returned to Vanetti's face. "Have you got a friend? There's three of us, you know." He indicated the two men he'd been sitting with. He'd send all six ears back to Manny this time. If that spivvy Yid wanted to keep this up, he'd be able to make a necklace for himself.

Katya forced herself to smile at Vanetti. It seemed they had him, at least the bait had worked . . . "I think we can find a third girl for you." Her fingers darted inside her bag, came into contact with the handle of the knife. More than anything she wanted to plunge the blade into this smiling pig who she knew even now was contemplating doing to her and Leah what he'd done to Henrietta Minsky. She'd feel the satisfaction that Lazar must have known when he'd stabbed the Brownshirt. But she made herself seem calm, detached. Lazar had other plans for this man. Lazar wanted to teach him a lesson, not kill him. And at the same time Lazar wanted to show that he was the brains of Manny Goodman's East End firm.

"Dom. Rafe." Vanetti called out to his two henchmen. "We've got business to look after." He nodded at Leah and Katya. "Think you can handle all of us?"

"I wouldn't be a bit surprised, ducky." Katya got to her feet and straightened her skirt. "Shall we go?"

"We're right behind you."

Katya took Leah's arm, hoping to God the men were waiting. Arms linked, with the three Maltese following, Leah and Katya left the Pied Piper. The street outside was dark, uninviting. The nearest light was twenty yards away, shining dully over the two cars they had come in. Leah nervously began to whistle "Rozshinkes mit Mandlin," "Raisins with Almonds," a soft Yiddish melody she'd learned as a child in Germany. As hard as she tried she was unable to hold the tune, which told her how terrified she was.

"Another few yards," Katya whispered to Leah. Close behind she could hear the heavy footsteps of the three Maltese.

As they passed the shadowy entrance to the narrow courtyard, both women quickened their pace, and Vanetti and his two companions moved to keep up. From out of the courtyard darted five figures. Shmuel reached out, grabbed Vanetti's

103

companions by the shoulders and slammed their heads together with a crunch. They sagged in Shmuel's arms as he dragged them into the darkness of the courtyard. Vanetti spun around to find himself surrounded by Manny, Lazar, Jacobs and Sherman. He charged at the nearest man – Jacobs.

Fists and feet whirling . . . Vanetti pounded the heavy body of Jacobs, who gasped in shock, then screamed as Vanetti put a shoe into his groin. Manny moved forward, slapped a hand over Vanetti's mouth, an arm around his neck and dragged him to the ground. Jacobs collapsed to his knees, struggling for breath, eyes turning glassy as they dragged the squirming body of Davey Vanetti into the gloom of the courtyard, past the bodies of the two unconscious Malts. Leah and Katya stayed behind, holding onto each other for support . . . in a state of near-shock.

"This is far enough," Manny decided. "Shmuel. Open his mouth."

Shmuel, disgusted, reached down, forced Vanetti's mouth wide open. Vanetti tried to bite down on Shmuel's thick fingers but his jaw muscles were no match for the strength in those hands.

"You know what my old man always told his customers?" Manny crooned as he knelt on the concrete beside Vanetti. "He said if they touched his vegetables they had to buy them." Manny could still see his father, shouting in any one of half a dozen languages at customers who insisted on prodding the merchandise to see how fresh it was. "Now I'm telling you the same thing, Vanetti. You touched my merchandise" – he began to laugh, the same high-pitched, unnerving giggle Lazar remembered when the ear had been thrown across the table – "and now you've bloody well got to eat it."

Manny pulled a rag from his pocket. Inside was the severed ear of Henrietta Minsky. Lazar turned away. Shmuel, eyes shut, tugged at Vanetti's mouth. At the last moment, as Manny dangled the ear between finger and thumb, Sherman turned away too.

"Feeding time, Davey." Manny opened his fingers and the ear dropped into Vanetti's gaping mouth. Shmuel released his grip immediately. Vanetti was choking on his unwanted meal.

"Stuck in your throat, is it? What a shame. Want something to wash it down with?" Manny opened his trousers and urinated over Vanetti's face. "*Bon appétit.*"

Manny did up his fly and walked, to the mouth of the courtyard. The other men followed, all trying to blank from their memories what had just happened.

"Is it over?" Leah asked nervously, knowing only about the ear. Which was more than enough.

"All over. It'll be a while before we hear from the likes of Davey Vanetti again," Manny told her. "Especially after this story gets around." He put his arms around Lazar's shoulders. "A genius."

Lazar didn't hear, he was pointing to the figure of Jerry Jacobs, sitting against the wall like a man overcome by exhaustion. "What about him?"

Manny looked at Jacobs, tapped him with the toe of his shoe. "Come on, Jerry. Time to go home."

When Jacobs made no move Shmuel and Lazar knelt down beside him. Lazar felt the fat man's pulse. Nothing. "I think he's dead —"

Manny swore. "I told him a million times he was too bloody fat for his own good. We can't stay here and we can't take him with us. Leave him. The rozzers'll find him."

"We can't leave him," Sherman argued.

"Do *you* want to carry that lump to the car? The rozzers'll know what to do. They'll think he got done over here. They might even go looking for a few Malts on a murder charge once they see what Vanetti done to him. Come *on.*" He took Leah by the arm and pulled her along toward where they'd left the cars. The others followed, not able to look back to where Jerry Jacobs still sat slumped against the wall.

Lazar managed to wait until he reached his own house before being sick. Making Vanetti eat the ear hadn't done it. That was a way to teach the man a hard lesson. What revolted him was Manny's obvious enjoyment, the gratuitous act of urinating over the helpless Vanetti. And the way he'd abandoned

Jacobs' body at the scene.

Sherman hadn't said anything after his token complaint about leaving Jacobs, but Lazar knew it was burning him up inside. And Shmuel . . . he'd closed his eyes, his ears, his senses to Manny's crazy giggling.

It was time, Lazar knew, to face the reality of Manny, time to start thinking about himself. Manny Goodman was a baby-faced nut who shouldn't be on the streets without a leash. What Vanetti had done with the woman's ear had been child's play to what plagued Manny.

That night in bed he told Katya that he'd worked for Manny too long, it was time he was his own boss.

Katya cautioned him. "Learn everything you can from him. Only when you're strong enough can you afford to strike out on your own. And *never* let Leah know what your intentions are . . ."

"But she's my sister — "

"She's also in love with Manny, that's the point. She only sees his good side, his so-called charm."

She should have been down in that courtyard with us, Lazar thought. Then she'd know what kind of person Manny Goodman really was.

Shmuel's next fight was on a Saturday night card at Hackney Baths. He won it by a knockout in the fourth round against another Jewish heavyweight who dropped to the canvas from a chopping right hook. It was a tribute to Shmuel's growing reputation that the odds for the fight were the closest they had ever been . . . Shmuel only a six-five underdog. By the time Manny had got down his two-hundred-pound bet, Lazar was left with eleven-to-ten.

Lottie was there to watch, digging her fingernails into her palms each time Shmuel was tagged with a punch. But the spectacle of Shmuel fighting, the possibility of his being hurt no longer upset her the way it once had. She shared Shmuel's confidence, but she still felt each punch Shmuel absorbed.

After the fight Manny took everyone to the Corner House for a celebration dinner, and there was no resemblance whatever to the man who'd done what he'd done to Davey Vanetti. Here was the jubilant, witty charmer who made sure everyone enjoyed themselves at his expense. Knowing that Lottie disliked him, Manny went out of his way to make her feel welcome. Actually, it was almost a repeat of the performance he'd put on for Leah, now making Lottie the center of attention, her and Shmuel. Lazar, in spite of his feelings, could see why Leah might be so taken with Manny, why he himself had been so attracted to the little Cockney. It was Manny's captivating side that was on public display . . . the dark side mostly was kept hidden. He could be so generous, flattering, a man who seemed really to care about the lives of those lucky enough to be his friends . . .

Katya's pronouncement that Leah was so attracted to Manny, maybe even in love, had come as a shock. Of course Lazar knew his sister liked Manny . . . they went out together often enough, but he didn't realize – didn't let himself – that it had gone this far. Manny, never mind his damnable charm, was the man who'd forced Shmuel to participate in the Vanetti business, had hinted he could and would blackmail Shmuel with the threat of telling Lottie about Vanetti –

"A toast!" Manny suddenly called out, lifting his glass of wine. "To the next fight. Your health, Shmuel!"

Shmuel looked at him, barely inclined his head . . . But he was thinking that if he won the next fight he'd qualify for the Southern Area regional championships at Holborn Stadium. The going would be rougher, but the purse would be that much bigger. Tougher opponents didn't bother him, he was sure he could take them. One reporter had described Shmuel as having the style of a runaway truck careening down a steep hill. Clumsy and obvious, but lethal for anyone who couldn't get out of the way.

When they left the Corner House Leah went with Manny while Lazar – showing off the new Morris he'd just bought – took Shmuel and Lottie to Palmers Green before driving home to Stoke Newington. Tired, Katya went to bed immediately. Lazar stayed up. He wanted to see what time Leah came in. He'd never bothered about it before, had just sort of assumed Manny brought her home at a decent hour. Suddenly, he was interested. Worried . . .

That night the front door opened only once – to admit Shmuel just after one o'clock. Shmuel went straight upstairs to the top floor, having no idea that his brother was waiting up in the living room . . .

Shortly before seven in the morning Lazar jerked awake in the armchair when he heard a car door close. Half a minute later Leah entered the house.

"Where have you been?" Lazar asked quietly as his sister walked past the open door of the living room.

Startled by his voice, Leah stopped and turned around. "Where have I been? With Manny. Why?"

"What were you doing?"

"Dancing . . . not that it's any business of yours."

He looked through the window to see the slowly lightening sky. Birds were singing. He stood up and turned on the light. When he studied his sister's face, he saw her lipstick was so smudged that in places it had rubbed off. The dress she'd worn the night before looked scruffy. "Did you spend the night with him?"

"How dare you ask a question like that –?"

"It wasn't the first time, was it?"

"No, it *wasn't* the first time. And it won't be the last –"

"Do you love him?"

The look of anger on her face slowly gave way to a half-smile as she relived the feeling of Manny's arms around her, his hard body pressed against hers, his mouth on hers, tongue gently pushing its way past her lips –

"Does he love you?"

"Why don't you ask him yourself?"

"Leah, I'm no censor. You do what you do, but I worry about who you do it with –"

"I told you once before, Lazar, we are survivors. Each in his own way. If Manny is my way of surviving, what right do you have to question it –?"

"Leah, you saw the way Manny left Jerry Jacobs in Soho that night."

"No." She waved a finger in his face. "No, not Manny, *all* of you left him — "

"All right, we all left him, but you never saw what happened down in that courtyard with Davey Vanetti. Manny *enjoyed* what he did. Do you understand me? He actually giggled when he made Vanetti eat the ear, and then . . ." He forced himself to tell her the rest of it.

Leah literally jumped back, eyes on fire. "Manny wouldn't do a thing like that."

"Except he did," another voice said.

Leah and Lazar turned around to see Katya and Shmuel standing in the doorway, awakened by the argument. "Manny did just what Lazar said." Shmuel said it quietly.

"You're both *lying*, you're in this together, you don't want me to see Manny. Why? Do you begrudge me a little happiness?"

It was obviously pointless to argue, Lazar decided, turning away. Leah had been mesmerized, had helped the process by mesmerizing herself, convincing herself that her senses made more sense that her head. Facts were only a challenge now, making her defensiveness only worse . . .

So *what* action of Manny Goodman, Lazar wondered, would it take to break the spell for Leah? If any . . .

CHAPTER SEVEN

When Katya discovered she was pregnant Lazar's first bizarre thought was a wish that the child would not physically resemble its father. The painful memories of his own childhood, when he was teased on account of his blondness, still were with him. His life had been made a constant misery. And yet, in a way, he should be grateful for those experiences . . . weren't they what had driven him on, molded his ambition? No one laughed at the color of his hair now. Manny had nicknamed him Whitey and the name had stuck. Everyone called him that . . . with respect in their voices. Whitey had squared accounts with Vanetti . . .

"Do you want a boy or a girl?" Katya asked.

"As long as it's healthy."

"I want a boy," Katya said, "so that when you go into your own business you'll have a partner and then an heir."

Katya was building castles in the air again, planning for the day when he would leave Manny Goodman . . . it was good that she never dreamed out loud when Leah was around. His sister's relationship with Manny had become even stronger. Half the time now she didn't even bother to come back to Stoke Newington to sleep. She'd left Saul Goldstein's factory in Middlesex Street and didn't work at all . . . whatever she wanted was paid for by Manny. She had, in a word, become Manny's mistress, and Lazar strongly doubted Manny would ever make her his wife.

Shmuel found out about Katya's pregnancy the next morning, and thought how his father and mother would have loved to hear of their first grandchild. Clasping Lazar around the shoulders, he hugged him tightly, kissed him. Whatever had happened between the two brothers in the past was in this moment pushed aside by the joyous news. And Lazar felt momentarily ashamed of the way he'd persuaded Shmuel to be a part of the Vanetti business.

"If it's a boy, I want to be the godfather," Shmuel demanded.

"What choice does the child have?" Katya wanted to know. "You'll be the only uncle. Except, of course, for you-know-who . . . if they ever decide to make it legal," she added quietly. "But he wouldn't be a blood relative—"

"Good!" Shmuel said. "So the job's mine, no arguments."

Lazar was going to the greengrocer's early and offered Shmuel a ride to the East End. In high spirits the two brothers left the house. Lazar was stopping in Hanbury Street to let Shmuel out when he saw a familiar figure walking toward them.

"Well, well, if it isn't Manny Goodman's errand boy and the Brick Lane Lion," Ivor Davies said. "You two have come a long way."

"Inspector Davies, good morning to you," Lazar said uneasily. "How are you?"

"I'm well. So, apparently, are you," Davies said, looking at the new Morris, Lazar's expensive suit. "And to think I knew the pair of you when you were just a couple of poor foreigners who got picked on by a wicked police sergeant. My, my . . . the weak really have inherited the earth. Going to Manny's shop now, are you?" he asked Lazar.

"I have to work for a living, Inspector Davies, just like you. So does my brother."

"How's your sister getting on these days? She seems to have got very friendly with your governor."

"Why don't you ask her yourself." Lazar's voice rose.

"Oh, struck a nerve, have I?" Davies was glad he wasn't the only one upset by Leah's involvement with Manny Goodman. The first time he'd met Leah — when she'd rushed to Commercial Street police station after her brothers had been arrested — Davies had thought he'd seen something in her, a special quality . . . she'd seemed, well, soft, gentle . . . at

111

least too gentle to be mixed up with a piece of filth like Manny Goodman. Davies still wasn't sure he'd been wrong. He didn't want to be . . .

"Lazar, I've got to go," Shmuel said, starting to walk away. "I'll see you tonight."

"No . . . don't go yet," Davies called out. "I want to talk to you." He rocked back and forth, heels and toes. "Nasty little caper that, with the Minsky woman."

"Who?"

"Henrietta Minsky. The woman they found in Holborn with her throat slashed and her ears cut off. She worked for your Manny, she did. In his house on Leman Street. Oh, I forgot . . . it wouldn't mean a thing to you." He said this to Lazar. "You just wear that whistle and flute to work in Manny's shop, selling spuds and cabbages . . ." He fondled the lapel of Lazar's suit. "Nice, very nice. And I bet you didn't know anything about Davey Vanetti changing his diet to ears, or leaving Jerry Jacobs dead of a heart seizure."

Lazar felt his face begin to burn.

"I know it all," Davies told him. "About how Joey Taylor gave you his royal go-ahead to whack Vanetti. Nothing works without Joey saying so. It didn't happen on my turf so there's nothing I can do about it. And the people on whose turf it did happen were only too glad that you sorted it out between yourselves. But there's one thing I'll tell you, and you'd better listen up . . . your damn Manny Goodman's nuttier than a fruitcake at Christmas. Vicious little bastard with it. Always has been."

"What's all this to me?" Lazar said, hearing in the back of his head Manny's awful giggling over Vanetti.

"Because I want to know how you like working for such a man. I want to know how you feel about your sister being his mistress. And you . . ." Davies pointed a bony finger at Shmuel. "How do you like having your boxing career handled by a loony?"

"You've seen me?"

"I've seen you, all right. At Hoxton. You're not bad. But I'd watch out for your own corner if I were you." Davies cut them off then with a wave and strolled away.

Maybe, Davies thought, he hadn't got through to Lazar . . . the man was another tough one, like Manny. But at least he hoped he'd stirred up Shmuel.

Shmuel found it impossible to concentrate, his normally skillful work deteriorated as he thought about what Davies had said. The police inspector knew about what they'd done to Vanetti. Everyone must know about it. Since that night in Frith Street Shmuel had done everything he could to block out the image of Vanetti's struggle . . . the rest of it . . . Lazar had brought it up once during his argument with Leah about Manny and now Davies . . .

Pretending sickness, he left work early and went to the gym in Whitechapel Road. It didn't help. Hard workouts under Steve Josephson sharpened his memory instead of dulling it. All he could see as he pounded the bag was Manny. All he could feel as he sparred were Vanetti's teeth while he held the Malt's mouth open.

Finally he called Lottie from the gym, arranged to see her that night. She'd help, somehow . . .

They were walking, hand in hand, Shmuel unusually silent.

"What's wrong?"

"Why should something be wrong?"

"You said you had to see me, now you act like you can't be bothered to talk to me. What is it?"

He stopped under a streetlight, turned to face her. "It's Manny Goodman," he said quietly. "There's a whole lot of trouble with him – "

"What kind of trouble? Leah?"

"Yes . . . and she's only part of it . . ."

"What else is there?"

Shmuel took a deep breath. Lottie was the only person he really trusted, felt closest to. But if he told her everything he'd hardly be able to blame her if she walked away, and right out of his life. Still . . . "Do you remember reading about a woman called Henrietta Minsky?"

"The prostitute who was murdered?"

Shmuel nodded. "She worked for Manny."

"She—?"

"Let me finish. You can ask me questions afterwards." And he told her about Lazar's plan, how he'd been coerced into joining. All of it.

"My God, couldn't you say no, even if it was your brother asking for help?" She felt sick to her stomach that the gentle, decent man she knew had been involved in such a filthy business. But reaching above that shock was her deeper love for him, and with it a determination to get him out of that house, away from his too-ambitious brother and helplessly entangled sister, away from the whole damned crowd as quick as she could . . .

"I couldn't refuse him, Lottie. I just owe him too much—"

"You owe him *nothing*. If anything he owes you. He's used you, Shmuel, your boxing skill to make money for himself, and he used you to make himself a big man with that filth Manny Goodman. Do you know what's going to happen if you stay there, Shmuel? You'll finish up like Manny and his crowd. Please . . ." She gripped his hand and started to pull him back toward her parents' house.

"We'll see my father, you can tell him everything you told me. Remember, he offered you help once before, help to open your own shop. I don't give a damn about false pride anymore, Shmuel Boruchowicz. You're going to let my father help. And I don't care whether you marry me now or not. I'm not letting you stay with those people one minute longer."

Shmuel looked at her, and was grateful for once in his life to let somebody else strong-arm him. Especially since it was a woman he was crazy about and . . . miracles of miracles . . . who seemed to feel the same way about him.

He arrived back at the house in Stoke Newington after midnight, keeping a taxi waiting with its meter running. He went up to his room on the third floor, cleared everything from his wardrobe and dresser, and threw things into a case. When he came out of the room he noticed Leah's door was closed. She was home for once. He debated whether to knock and say

114

good-by. Not now, he decided. Outside the door to Lazar's and Katya's bedroom he stopped again. This time he did knock. Loudly.

"What is it?" Lazar called out sleepily.

"I'm leaving, I'm saying good-by—"

The door opened almost immediately. Lazar stood there, blond hair ruffled. "What did you say? What's that for?" He pointed to the case in Shmuel's hand.

"Where in the world are you going this time of night?" Katya had joined her husband at the door.

"To Lottie's. I'm staying there until I find my own place—"

"You're crazy."

"No, I think I've just come to my senses. I've had a talk with Lottie and her parents. They're waiting in Palmers Green for me to come back. Her father's going to loan me the money to open my own shop—"

"Shmuel, does all this have anything to do with Inspector Davies this morning? It doesn't matter what he knows, he can't do anything—"

"It matters to *me*. I have to live with it. And when you see friend Manny in the morning you can tell him he's fired, I'm getting a new manager . . ."

As the cab pulled away Shmuel looked back at the house, feeling less righteous than he'd sounded. Yes . . . what he was doing was right, damn it, he had to get away, make his own life with Lottie, but knowing he was right didn't make it any easier to leave, didn't stop the ache. They were his only family, his brother, his sister. He turned around and stared straight ahead.

As Lazar drove slowly to the East End the following morning the confrontation with Shmuel was still too much in his mind. He hadn't been able to go back to sleep. Neither had Katya.

All right, face it, he couldn't really blame Shmuel for leaving. Better blame himself. And Manny. Shmuel should never have been pulled into the Vanetti business. Manny's life . . . and Lazar had involved himself in it . . . was too much for a man with Shmuel's sensitivities. And Shmuel should be grateful for that . . .

Lazar parked the car in Booth Street. Instead of going into the shop he went upstairs to Manny's flat. The front door was open.

"Manny?"

"In the kitchen, Whitey."

Lazar walked through the flat, stopping to look at the sepia prints of Manny's parents, the Grocer and his wife. Manny must have inherited his baby-faced looks from his mother. There was hardly a line on her face and Lazar guessed the picture must have been made when she was at least forty. His father looked like a stereotype Pole. Short-cropped hair, a square, solid face, pale eyes. A strong-looking man who appeared hostile, aggressive.

He passed Manny's bedroom, glanced inside. The bed was unmade, sheets and blankets thrown back in disarray, both pillows on one side. Which side did Leah sleep on when she stayed overnight? he couldn't help wondering.

In the kitchen he found Manny in trousers and undershirt, shaving. The sink was filled to the brim with water, topped by a frothy lather. Manny held a razor. Half of his face was clean-shaven, the other half covered with lather. Propped above the sink was a mirror.

"Shmuel's gone," Manny said.

The razor continued to skim over Manny's face, held in a rock-steady grip. The shining blade held Lazar. He could well imagine it being put to other uses. "So . . . what happened?"

"He's left the house. Came back last night, packed up and went to live with Lottie's parents—"

"Did he say why?"

"Vanetti. And—"

"And what, Whitey?" The razor stopped moving as Manny twisted about to look directly at Lazar.

'He doesn't want you managing him anymore. Fact is, he doesn't want anything to do with any of us and I can't blame—"

Manny exploded. "Who the bloody hell does he think he is?"

"He's my brother, Manny, that's who he is—"

"Well you don't seem so terribly upset about it, Whitey.

You were more so when I told you to get Shmuel involved in the first place." He wiped the razor clean and held it in front of him, blade still open. "Look, you had nothing to do with him leaving, did you?"

Lazar couldn't take his eyes off the razor.

"I'll tell you something, Whitey. I'm getting nervous about you. Things are making me edgy."

"What *things*?"

"Like the way you showed off to Joey Taylor. Now Shmuel leaving after all I've done for him. And I hear Harry Sherman's thoughts, Whitey. What a bright boy you are, he's thinking." Now the razor definitely looked like a weapon. Lazar tried to back away; the edge of the stove stopped him.

"It's all right for me to say you're a bright boy, Whitey. You *work* for me. But I get troubled when I know someone else is thinking the same thing." He laughed and flipped the razor closed. "It's just that flattery can sometimes go to a man's head. I'd hate for it to go to yours. Know what I mean?"

Lazar wanted to kill him, but for the moment only nodded.

"Good." Manny set the razor down on a ledge beside the sink.

"I always like to know where I stand with my people."

What he thought was that he didn't trust Lazar further than he could see his head of platinum-blond hair on a dark night. Losing Shmuel and the money he represented if he got to the championships didn't bother Manny nearly as much as the ambition, and broken love, he knew Lazar still had. He'd taken Lazar into the firm because he was clever. Too bloody clever, as it now turned out.

Well, Manny knew a way out. Leah. He'd only paid attention to her in the first place because he knew Ivor Davies was interested in her. He'd stopped Davies cold, just like he'd planned. Spoiled it for that rotter by getting Leah for himself. Now, she was in love with him. Good. Love solves all, the books say.

Simple. He would marry her. No matter how Lazar felt he'd think twice before he went up against his precious sister's husband. Especially if he had any interest in her going on living. Love, sweet love . . .

Three months later Manny and Leah were married. They sent an invitation, on Leah's urging, to Shmuel and Lottie, who declined. By coincidence both couples had circled the same Sunday for their own weddings. Shmuel read the invitation, showed it to Lottie, and felt a kind of relief. Although he hadn't been in contact since leaving his brother's house, at least the bridge between himself and the rest of his family was still open.

The break with his family, while still painful, had been eased by having so many other things on his mind. With money borrowed from Lottie's father he'd leased a shop on Stamford Hill, redecorated it and filled it with furniture samples obtained from workshops in the East End. He would be middleman, take orders at the retail level, farm them out to specialist suppliers.

On the day before the shop was to open Shmuel added a final touch. In the front window he pasted a montage of photographs showing the Brick Lane Lion in action. Lottie laughed, called him conceited, but she'd try to love him anyway.

The loss of Manny as manager hadn't hurt Shmuel's career. He'd telephoned Steve Josephson, his trainer, at the gym in Whitechapel Road, and told him he'd left Manny and was looking for a new manager. Of the three men interested in handling Shmuel, Josephson recommended Ben Kosky, a former middleweight who had held the British, European and Commonwealth titles. When Kosky had quit the ring he'd gone into managing and now had a string of moderately successful boxers in his stable.

Shmuel met with Kosky at the gym.

Kosky was in his late forties but his body was still trim, his face unmarked. The only signs of age were the wisps of gray that flecked his brown hair. A burned-out cigar jutted from the side of his mouth as he talked. He watched Shmuel work out, promptly signed him on.

Three weeks later Shmuel had his first fight under Kosky, another impressive victory in a Saturday evening card at

Hackney Baths.

"You've qualified for the Southern Area championships. You think you're ready for them?" Kosky asked Shmuel in the dressing room afterward.

"What do you think?" Shmuel's question took in both Kosky and Josephson. He was glad the trainer was still in his corner; there was something comforting about the battered face, a link with the past.

"I think you're good enough," Kosky said. "Just make sure you don't wear yourself out on your honeymoon."

"Good thing they start after your wedding," Josephson said. "I'd hate to see you standing under the *chuppah* with two black eyes."

Shmuel laughed, then realized he didn't have a best man. A month ago he would have asked Lazar. He couldn't do it now. Besides, Lazar would be at Leah's wedding that day. He asked Kosky, and his new manager accepted. *New* was more and more what was going on in his life.

In contrast to Shmuel's wedding, which was followed by a reception in a local hall, Manny Goodman's and Leah's was a magnificent affair. From the synagogue — where Leah insisted on being married even if Manny could not care less — a gilded carriage drawn by four white horses took the newlyweds to a banquet suite for a dinner-dance attended by more than a hundred couples.

Leah, in a gown of white silk and lace, looked more beautiful than Lazar had ever seen her. The frame of white gave her an air of serene happiness Lazar had never noticed before. In spite of his own feelings about Manny, Lazar had to admit that in their fashion they made a rather impressive couple. In white tie and tails Manny was in top Manny form . . . laughing, accepting congratulations, never letting go of Leah, telling his guests this was the greatest day of his life. Who knew . . . maybe he even meant it. At least at that moment. The little spiv was so damned convincing when he put his charm to it that he could even fool himself.

During the reception before dinner, Lazar wandered about

119

the hall with Katya on his arm. Pregnancy suited her. Almost six months now, her auburn hair was lustrous, her green eyes fairly shone. Wherever they stopped, guests told Katya how marvelous she looked. As for himself Lazar felt uncomfortable in the stiff-collared dress shirt and tightly fitting tailcoat. The collar stud seemed to be choking him, and his trousers kept riding up.

Across the hall, he spotted Joey Taylor talking with Manny and Leah. The first invitation that had been sent out had Taylor's name on it . . . Manny's mark of respect. During the reception, Taylor had nodded once to Lazar as they came face-to-face but no words had been spoken. Lazar had to admit he'd expected some recognition beyond a courteous nod. Maybe Taylor didn't want to upset Manny on his wedding day by any further acknowledgment of Lazar . . .

"Only on *simchas,* Whitey," a voice behind Lazar said. He turned around to see Harry Sherman, a champagne glass in each chubby hand.

"Only on *simchas,*" Lazar agreed. "Are they both for you?"

Sherman glanced at the glasses, as though surprised to see them. He lifted one to his lips, emptied it. "Got lots of nice things to say about your new brother-in-law when you toast the bride and groom?"

"He's marrying my sister, Harry." Lazar studied Sherman's eyes. Was Sherman looking for an opening to talk about Manny? He'd never mentioned the confrontation in Manny's kitchen to anyone but he'd wondered about those thoughts of Sherman's that Manny claimed he knew about.

"Manny's been saying how you gave your approval to this *shidduch,*" Sherman said. His words came fuzzily, obviously he was drunk. "Was a bit surprised when I heard that, I can tell you. Working for him's one thing. I just thought you had a smarter head on your shoulders than" — Sherman glanced nervously around to make sure no one except Lazar and Katya could hear; drunk as he was, he knew he'd already said too much but now he found it impossible to stop — "to let your only sister marry a certifiable crazy."

You should only know how much I was in favor of it, Lazar

thought bitterly. Except he couldn't have stopped Leah with an army. At least she'd insisted he give his approval as the oldest member of the family. A straw . . . ? "I think you've had enough to drink," he said quietly to Sherman, smiled and tried to walk away.

Sherman pulled him back. "I drink to kill the pain. The same as you should be doing, letting your sister marry him —"

"Harry . . ."

"Don't Harry me. Just listen. I've known him longer than you." He took Lazar's arm and guided him and Katya to an empty table in the corner of the hall. "His father was okay, but he's a little bastard. Sure, the Grocer was a rogue, but he was good to work with, if you understand me."

Lazar glanced at Katya, who was listening to the bald man with careful attention.

"The Grocer didn't carve up his own mates, for one thing. And he would never have done what Manny did to Vanetti. Oh, he'd have made him eat the ear, all right. He'd have loved that idea. But he'd have left him with a little dignity. He wouldn't have done the other thing."

A nice distinction, Lazar couldn't help thinking.

"What happened to Jerry Jacobs is another thing. Tragedy, him getting a heart attack just like that. Manny's father at least would have given Jerry's widow some money. Not Manny, didn't give her sweet Fanny Adams. I did . . . out of my own pocket . . ."

Sherman took a swig from the remaining glass, then launched into a story about how he'd first met Manny's father just after the Great War . . . After coming out of the Army Sherman had started working from a barrow in Wentworth Street, selling cheap fabric by the yard to the immigrant women who thronged the area. Manny's father had approached him with a dozen bolts of heavyweight woollen cloth of a much better quality than Sherman normally sold. The price Goodman wanted was markedly less than what Sherman paid for his cheap goods.

"I never asked the Grocer where the stuff came from," Sherman told Lazar and Katya. "Who does? Anyway, it started moving off the barrow like hotcakes. Next thing I know I've got the rozzers crawling all over me. The goods had been pinched the week before from some posh cloth merchant in the West End who dealt with the Savile Row tailors. That's what I was selling cheap . . . the kind of cloth that the King, God bless him, gets his suits made from. Old Bill couldn't nail me for pinching the goods so they had to be satisfied with doing me for receiving. They wanted to know where I got the stuff from. Of course I wouldn't tell."

"What happened?" Lazar looked around the hall, relieved when he saw Taylor still talking to Manny and Leah.

"Half a stretch in Pentonville. Six months. When I got out and picked up the barrow again the Grocer showed me he didn't forget. He paid me off for keeping my mouth shut. And then he started to pass me stuff he knew I could get rid of with no trouble. Gold. Silver. Either I could flog it myself or I could get it melted down. That's the difference between father and son. Manny would have let me rot and never tried to make it up to me."

"But you still work with him?"

"I do."

"Why?"

"Because I'm scared witless of the little sod. The same as . . ." He looked from Lazar to Katya. "Well, at least your brother's got the good sense to stay clear . . ."

Sherman picked up the glass, was disappointed to find it empty. "So long as Manny's got Leah none of you can do anything, right? You're all in his palm." He got up from the table and walked unsteadily away. Watching him go, Lazar decided that Manny Goodman knew less than he thought . . . if he'd really known what was on Harry Sherman's mind Harry would have been at the bottom of the Thames a long time ago . . .

Toward the end of the evening, while the dance floor was still full, Manny and Leah searched out Lazar. They were ready to leave, spending the night in a West End hotel before taking the train to Southampton, where they would board a liner for New York and their honeymoon.

"You're in charge now, Whitey. Anyone gives you any trouble, you write it down so's you don't forget it. I'll break heads when I get back."

Lazar watched them walk toward the exit and their waiting car, stopping by the door for one final photograph for the wedding album. He turned back to the floor and saw Joey Taylor alone for a moment. He went over to him.

"The happy couple just left?"

"They're sailing for New York tomorrow afternoon."

"New York? Ah yes, they'll enjoy themselves there. From the look of your wife you're in for an exciting time yourself. When is the happy day?"

"Another three months –"

"And Manny's away for two. Looks like you'll have your hands full. You need any help, any advice, you know where I am."

His smile was as warm as an arctic blast.

CHAPTER EIGHT

Lazar knew all about Shmuel's furniture shop in Stamford Hill. Only a mile from the house in Stoke Newington, he had driven past it often enough, had watched the work going on, the new name being put up. He'd thought about going in. Something had always held him back. This time he made up his mind to enter. With Manny away, there was no one he had to justify his actions to.

A cardboard box under one arm, he entered the shop, head jerking back involuntarily as a bell jangled above him. A smooth-cheeked youth approached, the professional welcoming smile of a salesman springing automatically to his face.

"Can I help you?"

"Mr Boruchowicz, please. Sammy Brooks." Lazar pointed to the montage of photographs in the window. "I'm his brother."

The youth disappeared into the back of the shop. Moments later Shmuel came out, his expression tentative.

"Congratulations," Lazar said. "The shop looks nice."

"Thank you."

"How's Lottie?"

"She's fine."

"Where'd you go for your honeymoon?" Lazar felt stuck in banal questions, a feeling of awkwardness. This was, after all, the first time he'd spoken to his brother since the night he'd left the house.

"Blackpool, for a week," Shmuel said. "Not as grand as Leah and Manny but −"

"I hear you're working with Ben Kosky now. How is he as a manager?"

"All right." Shmuel didn't bother asking his brother how

he knew about Kosky. The boxing world was so small that everybody seemed in everybody's pockets. "You minding the store now that Manny's away?"

"It minds itself, I pick up the money and bank it."

"That's what you always wanted to do."

"Only if it was my money." Lazar began to wish he'd never come into the shop. What had he hoped to prove? Then he remembered the box he held. "I forgot your wedding present."

"You and Katya sent us a tea service."

"This was more important." He handed Shmuel the box. Inside were two silver wine goblets. "Leah has two and I have two."

"You mean Manny has two. You know" – Shmuel seemed to soften a bit as he looked at the goblets, remembered what they represented – "I think maybe it's better our parents are dead. If they could see what Leah married . . ."

"And what I work for?"

Shmuel shook his head. "Lazar . . . I don't blame you, you did what you thought you had to do and you got trapped by a snake. But can you see now why I had to get away? I can't breathe in that kind of life." He picked up one of the goblets and looked closely at it. "How much longer will Manny and Leah be gone?"

"Another six weeks."

"Would you and Katya like to come over for dinner one night?"

"I don't even know where you live."

"That's right," Shmuel said, suddenly grinning. "You don't." He pointed at the ceiling. "In the flat above."

"Hadn't you better ask Lottie first?"

"You can ask her for yourself." Shmuel nodded toward the door. "Here she comes."

Carrying a briefcase heavy with homework to be marked, Lottie pushed back the door and entered the shop. When she recognized Lazar, she stood quite still. "Hello, Lazar."

"Lottie, I . . . I came to drop off the rest of your wedding present."

"These belonged to our parents." Shmuel held up the goblets.

"They're very nice, thank you. How's Katya?"

Lazar held both hands in front of his stomach to signify how big she was getting, and was relieved when he saw Lottie smile just a bit. "She can't sit close to the table anymore, maybe she's carrying twins." He turned to Shmuel. "We're still expecting you to be godfather."

"Maybe you'd better ask Manny instead."

"And have him responsible for my child's *spiritual* well-being? Look, Shmuel . . . Lottie . . . it took a lot for me to come in here, but I came because Shmuel's my brother. No matter what's happened between us, I still love him. You wanted to make the break, now you've done it. You've got your own lives. Can't we be friends now?"

"I asked Lazar and Katya over for dinner," Shmuel told Lottie.

"That's fine," Lottie said, and meant it. She believed Lazar's words were sincere, and she knew how much Shmuel had been upset by the freeze between himself and his brother. No matter how brave he acted, how happy he was with her, his small business and his continuing success in the ring, he missed his family. Well, he had nothing to fear from them anymore . . . he was away from them. "Why don't you come over this Thursday? Maybe we'll invite some other people and have a belated wedding party."

Lazar smiled. "Sounds good. Takes a lot to break up *this* family."

Katya eyed herself in the mirror, feeling the bulge that was steadily destroying her figure. She could swear she grew larger by the day. God alone knew what she'd be like at full term; she could hardly get into the car as it was. Still, she decided, pregnancy had its advantages too. Her eyes were a richer green than she'd ever seen them before, full of life, and her copper hair shone with a healthy gloss.

Lazar called out that he was going to start the car and Katya speeded up. This evening was important to Lazar. She was glad he'd taken the step, gone to Shmuel's shop. Brothers shouldn't be apart; life was too short to indulge bad feelings between them . . .

Three other people were present in Shmuel's flat when Lazar and Katya arrived, a married couple who were friends of Lottie, and a quietly dressed man with a burned-out cigar sticking out of the side of his mouth. Shmuel introduced him as Ben Kosky, his new manager.

"Your loss was my gain," Kosky told Lazar after removing the dead cigar from his mouth and placing it in an ashtray. "Your brother's got everything it takes to be a top-class heavyweight."

Lazar nodded. "What are your plans for him?"

"We'll take it step by step. The Southern Area championship first. That'll give him a taste of really good opposition, much better than what he's met so far."

"What are his chances?"

"I think he'll walk all over them . . . otherwise I wouldn't be wasting my time managing him." Kosky picked up the cigar again, stuck it in his mouth so that it pointed upward and looked over the end at Lazar. "At least, now he's got a real chance . . . know what I mean?"

"He didn't before?"

"I know Goodman. People like him get involved with boxers for the same reason they get involved with everything. A quick profit. Mark my words, there would have come a day when the bigger profit was in getting Shmuel to lose."

Lazar suspected Shmuel's new manager was probably right. Sooner or later Shmuel would have been asked to take a dive to make a killing on the odds. Manny would have expected him to obey to show his loyalty, to pay back the favors. Would Shmuel have gone along? For Lazar, maybe . . . for Manny, never . . . He would have refused or crossed up Manny and there would have been hell to pay . . .

The announcement from Shmuel that dinner was ready brought a welcome relief to Lazar from such thoughts.

"Katya looks wonderful," Lottie said as she sat down next to Lazar after serving the meal. "You must be very happy."

"More nervous than happy, I think. What about you and Shmuel?"

"We've only been married for a couple of weeks. Give us a chance — or are you so desperate to be an uncle?"

Her warm chattiness was so obviously genuine that Lazar found it difficult to see her as the fierce young woman who had literally ordered Shmuel to move out of the house in Stoke Newington.

"Just desperate to be a father," he said. "And selfish enough to want to see someone else share the feeling."

"Shmuel was touched you still want him to be the godfather if it's a boy."

Lazar glanced across the table to his brother, who was talking to Katya. "He didn't seem very keen on the idea when I asked him."

"He was a little shaken when you came into the shop, but I know he wants to do it."

"Would you let him?"

Lottie raised her eyebrows at the question. "I'm his wife, Lazar, not his keeper. Of course I'd let him . . . I'd want him to be godfather." She was silent for a long moment, eyes fixed on the table as she tried to find the right words. "Lazar . . . you have to understand why I did what I did."

"I think I do."

"You can't imagine how upset Shmuel was over what happened. When he came back to my parents' home after collecting his clothes he had tears in his eyes. It broke my heart . . . it still does . . . when I think of it. But he had to get away from that house. From your association with . . . with that little—"

"You don't have to explain," Lazar cut it.

"I *do*. I'd love nothing more than to see you and Shmuel close again. After all, you're flesh and blood. But for his sake, *and* mine, he just can't have anything to do with . . . with your sort of life. Neither of us wants to know about it, or be involved in it." Lazar remembered Saul Goldstein saying the same thing. "You have to swear to me that whatever you do, you'll never try to involve Shmuel." Lottie felt she needed the promise, she understood Shmuel, the loyalty he would

128

always feel to his brother and sister . . . if Lazar was in trouble and asked for his help, she knew Shmuel would not be able to refuse.

Lazar nodded solemnly, believing at that moment in his promise.

"Thank you." She allowed a smile. "You know . . . it's nice to have a brother-in-law after all this time." . . .

The evening broke up shortly after ten when Katya admitted that she felt tired. Shmuel walked down to the street with them and, after helping Katya into the car, stood alone with Lazar. He asked about Leah's wedding, whether Lazar had heard from them yet.

"Just a postcard mailed from the boat before they left."

"Do whatever you can to break them up," Shmuel said quietly.

"I couldn't stop her before, what makes you think I could do it now that they're married?"

"He'll get tired of her. He's not a man to stay married—"

"Leah has got to find that out for herself. There's nothing I can do—"

"Then be there for when she does find out." Shmuel clasped his brother around the shoulders, leaned forward and kissed him on the cheek.

During the short drive home from Stamford Hill Katya snuggled sleepily against Lazar's shoulder and murmured how happy she was that he had taken the initiative in renewing contact with his brother. Lazar told Katya about the promise Lottie had extracted from him, and they both agreed that Shmuel would probably never know that his wife had made Lazar take such an oath.

By the time they reached home Lazar was feeling very satisfied with the evening. He was speaking to his brother again. And he knew now that Shmuel had married a woman who was worthy of him. His parents would have been horrified by Leah's choice . . . but most certainly they'd have approved of Shmuel's. And of him, and his life . . . ? Don't even think about it, he instructed himself.

Katya went straight to bed. Lazar stayed up, his mind too

full of the evening. He tried listening to the radio, reading. Nothing worked. When midnight struck and he was more alert than ever he quietly left the house. Manny was away, he was in charge. He'd make a late-night check on the gambling clubs, the spielers.

Two of Manny's spielers were in the East End, close to the greengrocer's shop. The third and most profitable – where Manny had offered Shmuel a job – was in Dalston. Called Pearl's after Manny's mother, the club took in more than two hundred pounds on a good week. Lazar visited the two East End clubs first, had a cup of tea in one, stood around to watch a few hands of rummy and left. He made Pearl's his last stop, calling in on the way back to Stoke Newington.

Pearl's was next to Dalston Junction railway station and only a hundred yards from the local police station. Lazar parked the car and walked along a narrow alley, picking his way carefully between puddles as he headed toward the chink of light showing from a slightly open door. A blast of warm air – spiced with cigarette smoke and sweat – greeted him as he pushed back the door. All ten card tables were full. Men not able to get into a game sat watching as they waited for an empty seat, for a player to go broke. Two billiard tables in the centre of the club were in use. The quiet talk of card players was interspersed with the clicking of billiard balls, the solid thud of a shot hitting the pocket.

As Lazar entered, a tall, heavy man wearing a suit and tie detached himself from the crowd of onlookers at one table and came over to him. The pockets of the man's jacket bulged from the half-dozen packs of cards he carried. "Up late, aren't you, Whitey?"

"Goris." Lazar acknowledged the bodyguard. "Couldn't sleep." Lazar realized he didn't know if Goris was the man's first or last name – he allowed himself a smile – maybe both. Goris Goris. "Been this busy all night?"

"Pretty much."

"Any trouble?"

Goris' square face creased into a slight smile. "Here? With old Bill only a few yards away?" Even as he spoke the door

130

opened again and a uniformed constable walked in. He looked around, nodded to Goris and went directly to the tea bar. The woman working behind the counter handed him a cup of tea and a cheese sandwich. "We must make better tea than they do down the station," Goris commented.

The first time Lazar had been in a spieler and had seen a policeman enter he'd been shocked. Now he was used to it. The police allowed the spielers to keep open because it suited their purpose . . . that way, they at least knew where everyone *was*.

Balancing the tea and the sandwich, the constable stood next to Goris and Lazar, watching a game of eleven-to-four rummy. A bookmaker operated each table, playing seven-card rummy against three other men. If they won, they were paid out at eleven-to-four and the bookmaker kept the other quarter of a point. If the bookmaker won, he kept everything. Out of his takings over the night, he paid four percent to the house.

"You heard from Manny yet?" Goris asked.

"Postcard. Having a nice time . . . wish you were here."

"Like hell he does." Both laughed. "You must feel pretty set up now. I mean . . . with Manny your brother-in-law . . ."

Lazar didn't answer.

The constable finished the sandwich, gulped down the tea and handed the crockery to Goris. "Goodnight," he said, and walked toward the door. Goris muttered something about "bloody cheek" and returned the plate, cup and saucer to the woman behind the counter.

A minute later the door opened again. Three men walked in. Solid men in raincoats, hats low over their foreheads. They stood by the door for a few seconds, looked around, knowing they were the reason for the abrupt hush that came over the club. Goris hurried over to them.

"I'm sorry, gentlemen, but this is a private club. Members only."

One of the men turned to look at him. "That's all right. I've got my membership card right here." His hand came out of his pocket holding a cut-throat razor. The handle was inside his fist, the blade doubled back across his fingers like a set of brass knuckles. Without warning, he jabbed Goris in

131

the face with the blade.

Goris' scream filled every space of the club. The men at the tables stared downward, at the walls, at the ceiling, anywhere but at Goris, who staggered backward, both hands to his face, his mouth elongated grotesquely by a deep gash that spilled blood down his front. He spat something out with the blood. Lazar was sick as he recognized the tip of the man's tongue.

The man with the razor didn't give Goris a second glance. He motioned to the two men with him. They pulled lengths of iron pipe from their pockets and advanced into the club. Lazar rushed to Goris, kneeled down, tried to staunch the flow of blood with his handkerchief.

"Leave him there," the man with the razor said. When Lazar was too slow in getting up, he kicked him. "Get over by the bar or you're going to look like his twin." Lazar retreated until he felt the counter against his back.

"Money in the center of the table," the man with the razor ordered. "We're going to pass the hat." One of the men with the iron pipes took off his hat and went from table to table, waiting while money was thrown into it. After passing the money to the man with the razor, the other two men approached the bar. One picked up a bottle of HP sauce and threw it at a pile of crockery. The other man leaped over the counter, shoved the woman aside and systematically began to wreck everything in reach. Within half a minute, broken china littered the floor like sawdust.

"Thank you, gentlemen, for your cooperation." The man with the razor signaled to his men. They joined him by the door. "We've got another man waiting outside. No one put his face out there for five minutes." They turned around, and were gone.

Lazar, shouting for someone to call the police and an ambulance, ran through the door into the night. A footstep sounded close by. He turned his head to look, saw a shadowy figure, arm raised. The next moment his head exploded as an iron pipe crashed into his temple, and he toppled forward into a puddle.

Lazar came to inside the club. Men in navy blue uniforms

filled his sight as they asked questions of club members, took down notes.

"Are you all right?" a voice asked.

"I'm . . . fine." He tried to get up and his legs gave way to brand him a liar. Two men helped him to a chair. The woman who operated the tea bar somehow found an unbroken cup and brought him hot, sweet tea, held it to his lips so he could drink. "Where's Goris?"

"Hospital," a policeman said. Lazar recognized him as the constable who'd left the club only a minute before the three men had entered. "They're finding a tailor to sew up his face."

A sergeant pushed his way through. "Did you recognize any of them?"

Lazar licked his lips, forced himself to concentrate before answering firmly, "No."

The telephone behind the counter rang. One of the policemen answered it. He spoke a few words, put back the receiver and came over to where Lazar sat. "Your man's not going to be very pleased with you," he said.

"What do you mean?"

"Your other two places just got done. Fire-bombed."

"Fire-bombed?"

The policeman nodded. "Firemen have dragged two bodies out of one place so far. Both burned up beyond recognition."

He said something else but Lazar didn't hear. All three clubs hit at once . . . he was just lucky he'd been at Pearl's . . . all he'd got was a whack in the head. If he'd still been in the East End, at one of the other clubs . . . his brain went cold at the thought of it.

"You feel well enough to make a statement?" the sergeant asked.

"I've already told you all I know. I . . . did . . . not . . . recognize . . . anyone." But he had. The man with the razor. The man who'd put Goris in hospital was one of the three men who'd been with Davey Vanetti at the greengrocer's shop in Booth Street that evening. When Manny had chased them out with the chair leg after crowning Vanetti. The man hadn't remembered him . . . Lazar had been too insignificant that evening in Booth Street, they'd all only had eyes for the madman with the chair leg.

"Have it your own way," the sergeant said. "Go on home."

Lazar stayed in the wrecked club for another fifteen minutes. He watched the woman try to clear up some of the debris. He listened to rummy players complain about what they'd lost. If players weren't protected, he knew, they'd find somewhere else to play. He called the hospital to ask about Goris. Goris, he learned, had been injured badly enough to permanently disfigure him and probably impair his speech. At three-thirty Lazar drove home.

Katya heard him come in. When he entered the bedroom the light was on and she cried out at the sight of the ugly purple swelling over his right eye. She asked what had happened, he told her. Three clubs had been hit, two had been burned out, two men were dead.

The following morning – head still throbbing in spite of the cold compress Katya had made for him – Lazar visited Goris in hospital. He lay in bed, his face a patchwork of stitches, unable to speak, eyes following Lazar as he left a vase of flowers on the bedside table. Lazar could think of nothing to say, as if speech itself would be a mockery of a man who probably would not be able to speak normally again. After a minute of silence he patted Goris on the shoulder and left, glad to be out of the ward.

He drove slowly to the East End, inspected the two burned-out clubs. At Booth Street he found Ivor Davies waiting for him.

"Manny's not going to be too pleased with you," Davies said. "When he finds out what happened, it won't help a bit that you're his brother-in-law."

Lazar knew the police inspector was right. Vanetti had chosen this moment because he knew Manny was away.

"Of course, it might make it easier if we could get some help for a change," Davies said. "You know who did it to you. What about letting us in on the big secret?" He looked closely at Lazar, wondering if he'd unbend. "I don't give a damn about what happened down at Pearl's. That's not my patch. But we've got two dead bodies here."

"If you find out, you'll tell me," Lazar said. "Then we'll both know."

"God . . . I thought you had more brains than Manny . . . All right, but I promise you, if one innocent person on my patch gets even a bruise while you lot are going at it, I'll come down so hard you'll wish you'd never left Germany . . . Well, at least your brother had the brains to get away from all of you."

Lazar watched the police inspector leave the shop, waited five minutes and then went to a public telephone booth and called Harry Sherman. And then Joey Taylor. It was time to take him up on the offer he'd made at Leah's wedding.

The road narrowed to single-vehicle width by the toll house that had once marked the boundary of London. Lazar waited for a car coming from the opposite direction before guiding his own car through the narrow gap and bringing it to a halt by the Spaniards Inn. Dusk was falling quickly as he got out of the car. Hampstead Heath was disappearing in the darkness. The only light came from inside the public house.

Harry Sherman was waiting at a table, an untouched glass of whiskey in front of him, his head shining dully as it reflected the glare of the light above. He looked at the swollen bruise on Lazar's head and silently thanked God he'd not been at Pearl's the night before. What happened to Goris might have happened to him. Crippled for life. And what would Manny care? Nothing.

Lazar brought a drink from the bar to the table and sat down, wondering how smart it was to meet Sherman at the Spaniards before they both went to Joey Taylor's house. Sherman had been drunk at the wedding. He needed to be cold stone sober now. Then he noticed that Sherman hadn't touched the drink and felt better.

"How's Goris?" Sherman asked. Lazar shook his head, and Sherman said, "You're lucky they didn't fix you up as well."

"I don't think they remembered me. They just wanted to make an example of Goris."

"But why burn the other two clubs and not touch Pearl's?"

135

Lazar had thought about that too and had come up with an answer. "Pearl's is the biggest, the most profitable. Maybe Vanetti thinks that once he moves in he doesn't want the trouble of getting Pearl's back on its feet again."

"What did you tell Joey Taylor?"

"Exactly what happened." The story of the attack on the three clubs had been in the afternoon edition of the newspapers. Lazar's name had not appeared, but Manny's had, as the owner. A gang war, the papers called it; editorials demanded that the police crack down on the elements that were endangering the lives of ordinary citizens . . . After the first story had appeared Shmuel had called the house, wanting to know if his brother was all right. Lazar had been out and Katya had taken the call. She reassured her brother-in-law by saying that Lazar had been home asleep at the time of the attacks.

"When I went with Manny the last time," Lazar said, "Taylor approved our plan and said he'd make sure Vanetti didn't come back at us again. He did come back . . . and I think I'm entitled to know why."

"Maybe Taylor even knew Vanetti was coming," Sherman said. "That means he must have given him the go-ahead. Which also means that we aren't going to be very welcome."

Which possibility had also occurred to Lazar. When he'd spoken to Taylor that morning the man hadn't sounded especially angry. If anything, he sounded very calm, resigned . . . as though he had no control over what would happen.

Lazar finished his own whiskey and told Sherman to drink up. The bald man pushed away the glass; he didn't want it. They went outside to their cars and, with Lazar leading the way, drove to The Bishop's Avenue in Hampstead Garden Suburb.

The butler greeted them, took their coats and showed them through immediately to Joey Taylor in the study. As Lazar had done, Sherman glanced around the room with interest, taking in the prints, the saddle, and finally the hat rack and its solitary article . . . the steel-lined bowler hat with the vee-shaped dent.

Taylor got up from behind the mahogany desk and held

out a hand to Lazar and Sherman. "A drink?"

Sherman looked to Lazar for guidance. Lazar accepted, and Taylor pulled at one of the wall panels. It swung back to reveal a well-stocked bar.

"You picked the wrong time to be in Pearl's last night, eh?" Taylor said as he poured whiskey into heavy crystal glasses.

Lazar took the glass. "I don't think you were very surprised when I told you who was behind it."

"No . . . I wasn't. I knew it was going to happen."

"And you *approved*?" Sherman couldn't help blurting it out.

"No. But I think we should wait for a few minutes before we continue with this discussion. I'm expecting another guest." Taylor set out a fourth glass and perched himself on the corner of the desk, leaving Lazar and Sherman to wonder about the missing guest.

The front door bell rang. Quick footsteps followed as the butler answered the summons. A gentle murmur of voices. The door to the study opened.

"Mr Withers, sir," the butler announced to Taylor as he showed in a middle-aged man with a red face, dark brown hair that was streaked with grey, bushy eyebrows and moustache. Taylor stood up to greet him, shook his hand warmly and introduced him to Lazar and Sherman as Alan Withers.

"An associate of mine," Taylor explained after pouring Withers a drink.

Withers nodded as he sat down in a leather wing chair. He eased his heavy body carefully into the seat, undoing the buttons of his waistcoat to give his ample stomach breathing room.

"Now," Taylor said to Lazar, "would you please go over exactly what happened at Pearl's last night, and the reports you received from the two other clubs. I know already, but Mr. Withers hasn't as yet heard your version."

Lazar began to relate the events of the previous night.

"By the way," Taylor interrupted, "what were you doing at Pearl's in the first place? It isn't your habit to visit the clubs in the early hours of the morning, is it? Even with Goodman away."

"I couldn't sleep." Knowing Taylor and the newcomer

137

wanted to hear everything, Lazar talked briefly about the reunion with his brother.

"I hear he's doing very well in the ring," Taylor said.

"Uh, yes, he is." Lazar was surprised at Taylor's interest. He switched back to Pearl's. This time, no one interrupted him until he'd finished his story. He looked around expectantly. Withers kept looking at him. Taylor stood up and began to pace the study.

"I knew this was going to happen. And do you know why it happened?" The question was directed at Lazar. "Because Goodman thinks *he* knows best. He doesn't listen to me." Pausing by the hat rack, he lifted the dented bowler and gazed thoughtfully at it, as if remembering the days when he'd fought other people instead of controlling them. Finally he put it back and swung around to face Lazar.

"You were here, in this very room, when I told Goodman to keep his women out of Vanetti's hair. Vanetti only has one business . . . his women. He's scum who lives off his women. Terrorizes them. Just like he'll terrorize anyone he sees as a threat to his firm. Goodman doesn't have the brains to realize that if Vanetti's left alone, he'll leave everyone else alone. He's too stupid to back off. Or perhaps it's misplaced pride . . . I don't know. Even after you got back at the Malt, Goodman wasn't satisfied. He wasn't going to let any Malt tell *him* how he should run his business. So he sent his women right back into Vanetti's territory."

"I didn't know about that," Lazar said. "I thought he'd agreed to end it. Didn't you?" he asked Sherman.

Sherman nodded.

"He lied to all of us," Taylor said. "And because of him we now have an all-out war on our hands. Vanetti's sworn to wipe Goodman out. To take him over." He looked at Withers.

"I won't tolerate a situation like that." Withers spoke in a slow, deep voice that seemed to rumble its way up from his stomach. "Vanetti's got to be taken care of. Two people are dead. The newspapers – and now the public – want blood. Whack Vanetti. And then . . . give a body away."

"Whose?" Sherman asked.

138

"Need you ask?" Taylor looked at him closely.

"The police will be satisfied with only one body," Withers said. "Goodman. He's your brother-in-law, isn't he?" he said to Lazar.

"As of a few weeks ago."

"How do you feel about stitching up your own brother-in-law for Vanetti's murder?"

Lazar considered it. What Withers — whoever he was and wherever he fitted into Joey Taylor's organisation — was proposing could only have one ending. Manny Goodman, his brother-in-law, dancing at the end of a rope in one of His Majesty's prisons. Leah would be free of him . . . "I'd like to make everyone happy," he said, "including myself, but I've got a question."

"Tell our young friend," Withers told Taylor, "what's in it for him."

"Goodman's operation," Taylor said immediately. "You'll have your own firm. Good enough?"

Lazar's imagination went to work. How would he run it . . . ? For starters he'd get rid of the women . . . prostitution, living off women, was work for scum like the Malts. He'd sell off the houses too. He didn't need to make money from the misfortune of immigrants, people who'd been refugees like himself. There were better ways . . .

Withers said, "We of course need the public to see justice being dispensed. We need Manny alive and kicking . . ."

Taylor put in. "Work out whatever you're going to do," he told Lazar. "When you're satisfied with it, brief me. I'll tell Mr. Withers. Just so we know what to expect."

"Knowing Goodman," Withers said, "he'll go crazy when he comes back and learns his spielers are closed. He might even make it easier for you."

Lazar could well picture Manny's reaction when he came back from New York to find the clubs closed. He glanced at Sherman, silently asking if he was in. Sherman nodded.

"There's one thing," Lazar said. "The two clubs in the East End that were burned out. I'm getting problems about them from an inspector at Commercial Street police station."

139

"Davies?" Withers asked. "Ivor Davies?"

"You know him?"

"We've met. What kind of problems?"

Lazar told about the conversation he'd had with Davies that morning, expanded on it to bring in earlier confrontations with the Welsh police inspector.

"Don't worry about him anymore," Withers said. "As long as you do a good job with Vanetti and Goodman, I'll keep Davies off your back."

"Thank you—"

"Don't be too quick with your gratitude," Taylor said. "We're doing you favors. Sometimes favors have to be paid back."

Lazar could not even begin to guess how Withers would take care of Davies, knew it was none of his business but asked anyway.

Taylor's cool amiability changed instantly to anger. "You do your job and we'll do ours."

Withers raised a pudgy hand in the air. "There's no harm in letting him know. If he's going to run the firm after Goodman's taken care of he might as well know what's going on." Withers pushed himself out of the chair, reached into his jacket pocket and pulled out a leather wallet. From it, he extracted a card he handed to Lazar.

Lazar had to read the card twice before its impact finally hit home. He passed it to Sherman, and then looked up at Withers.

"Superintendent Alan Withers?"

"That's what it says there, sonny." Withers retrieved the card from Sherman. "I'm with the Yard . . . C.I.D."

CHAPTER NINE

The following week Lazar was too preoccupied with Manny's return from New York to concentrate on anything else. Even Katya, who had swollen to alarming proportions as she approached the final month of her pregnancy, couldn't divert him. He'd worked out a plan with Sherman to take care of Vanetti and point the finger at Manny, had presented it to Taylor and gotten it accepted. So he was only a single step away from taking over the firm, from freeing Leah . . .

Still, Manny was very unpredictable. No way of knowing which direction his fury would take. The spielers were closed down. The house on Leman Street was empty . . . Lazar had let the women go. The only money coming in was from the rented houses. Manny had left Lazar in charge, and he'd return to find a debacle. It would be at Lazar's throat he'd go first. Or . . . Leah's . . . Above all else, Lazar knew he had to protect his sister . . .

"You'd better get yourself ready or you'll miss half of it," Katya said, nudging Lazar's leg as he sat in a chair in the living room after dinner.

He glanced up, startled by the break into his thoughts. "What time is it?"

"Almost seven."

He got up slowly. Shmuel's fight at Holborn Stadium was on the second half of the card. He didn't need to see the earlier bouts. Under Ben Kosky's management Sammy Brooks – the Brick Lane Lion – was taking his first real step toward the Southern Area heavyweight title. The preview in that morning's newspaper had favored Shmuel over his opponent, a heavyweight from South London named Tim Fredericks.

The winner of the bout would advance into the semi-finals of the Southern Area championships.

"Are you sure you don't want to come?" Lazar asked as he slipped into his coat. "I've got a ticket for you."

"I'm certain. The way I look right now I don't have to see any more heavyweights. Besides" – she leaned forward and kissed him – "looking like this, they might throw *me* in the ring with someone."

Lazar laughed and returned the kiss, glad of the opportunity to forget, even for a moment, that Manny would be home the following week.

He drove leisurely to Holborn, parked the car and met Harry Sherman as arranged by the underground station. The bald man had become his constant companion. In Sherman's eyes Lazar already ran the firm . . . or what was left of it. Removing Manny, taking his place, was a technicality. They knew already what they'd do once he was out of the way. The spielers would open again. New sites would be found. And then, once they had a firm base in the East End, they'd start to look at the West End . . . where the real action was.

Together they walked to the stadium and made their way down to the dressing room. Shmuel was there, warming up under Steve Josephson's watchful eyes. Ben Kosky was giving his fighter final instructions.

"Lottie upstairs?" Lazar asked. It was the first time he had seen his brother since the attack on Pearl's. The bruise on his head had disappeared.

"She's there," Shmuel said. "And wishes she wasn't." He paused while Josephson tied up the laces on one glove. "She doesn't want to see me fight anymore." He held out his other hand, watched as the trainer tied the laces. "I suppose I'm selfish but I want her here. I've never lost a fight that she's watched."

"You've never lost a fight at all," Lazar said.

"Leave him alone," Kosky cut in. "Every boxer's allowed a superstition."

"Go up there and keep her company," Shmuel told Lazar. "Good luck." As he and Sherman walked away, Lazar wondered what Shmuel's reaction would be if he asked him to help in bringing down Manny . . . getting rid of Vanetti and then offering up Manny to the police. Sherman had mentioned the possibility and Lazar had rejected it . . . Shmuel was totally straight, and Lazar respected him for it. Of course . . . if he stressed to Shmuel how it was a way of getting Leah free of Manny . . . it just might be a different story.

Reaching his ringside seat, he found Lottie watching a middleweight bout with fixed attention. Lazar guessed she wasn't really *seeing* anything . . . what passed in front of her eyes was blotted out of her mind. She probably wouldn't even see what happened to Shmuel. She refused to watch but she went along because Shmuel needed her to be there.

"Hello, Lottie."

The blank look disappeared from her eyes as she turned to look at Lazar. "Have you seen Shmuel? How is he?"

"Confident, I wish I were so confident."

"What about? You're not fighting."

He smiled, trying to put her at her ease. "About Katya, I mean. She's getting so big I think she's carrying triplets."

Lottie made a face. "I don't think Shmuel's figured on being godfather to three children. He's only got two knees to balance them on."

"They'll take turns."

Lottie looked back to the ring. One of the boxers had blood coming from cuts about and below his eyes. Lottie shuddered. "Don't watch," Lazar said.

"I keep thinking it could be Shmuel," she whispered, clutching hold of Lazar's hand. "This could happen to Shmuel—"

"No, he's too good." The grip on his hand continued, and he said, "Do you want to come outside with me? Until Shmuel's ready?"

"I think so." She stood up and followed him along the row until they reached the aisle. A roar from the crowd made them both turn; they were in time to see the bleeding middleweight hammered to the canvas under a succession of blows.

They stayed outside for a half-hour until Harry Sherman came looking for them with the news that Shmuel's bout against Tim Fredericks was next. They re-entered the hall and took their seats. Shmuel was already in the ring, raising an arm in acknowledgment of the cheers that greeted his introduction. Fredericks was next, shorter than Shmuel and two years older. He danced up and down in his corner, anticipating the most important moment of his life. Unlike Shmuel, Fredericks had no other job. Everything he owned, all his hopes were concentrated in the gloves that covered his taped hands.

The two fighters met in the middle of the ring, touched gloves, listened to the referee's instructions. Fredericks attacked from the bell. Aware of Shmuel's power the South Londoner was determined to get in the first punches. He couldn't afford to give Shmuel time to settle down. Surprised by the opening assault, Shmuel backpedaled, tried to stay out of range. Fredericks threw himself after the retreating figure. A flurry of punches stung Shmuel's face, raised angry red blotches on his chest. Lottie covered her mouth with her hands, not wanting to let out her screams, afraid they'd distract Shmuel. He'd recognize them, look around, leave himself open for the one punch from Fredericks that might end the fight.

"Cover up!" Lazar heard himself yelling. "Cover up and box him!"

Shmuel brought his gloves up in front of his face, trying to weather the opening flurry. Punches landed like hammer blows on his arms as Fredericks attempted to wear him down. Shmuel retreated to his own corner and Josephson yelled at him to get out into the middle of the ring. Shmuel fought back, slowly finding his own rhythm. Twice he rocked Fredericks with straight lefts but the burly South Londoner continued to bore in, shaking his head to clear it, looking for the target the bigger Shmuel represented.

When the bell rang, Lazar slumped back in the seat. He knew his brother had lost the first round . . . by a mile. Eleven rounds to reverse the situation. Shmuel had never been that distance, he had to go for the knockout.

"What's the matter with you?" Josephson rasped as he held the bottle out to Shmuel. "You're letting a pub brawler walk all over you."

Shmuel fought for breath as Josephson toweled him off. He was in a different league here. The fights in the baths hadn't prepared him for this. Fredericks had no respect for the Brick Lane Lion. Shmuel knew he'd have to go out and earn that respect all over again.

Kosky appeared next to Josephson. Shmuel leaned over to listen to what the manager had to say. "Don't let him make you fight his way. He'll tear you to pieces. Box him. Stay away from him until you wear him down. Use some skill, for God's sake . . ."

"Seconds out."

Shmuel got off the stool and advanced slowly toward the center of the ring. Fredericks was on him, leaping out of his own corner. Shmuel tied him up, pinned his arms. The referee told them to break. Shmuel let go and jumped back just in time to avoid a roundhouse right thrown on the break. The missed punch overbalanced Fredericks. Shmuel saw his chance and banged him on the side of the head with two sharp chopping rights. The crowd roared in anticipation as Fredericks fell to the canvas. Shmuel refused to let himself be taken in by the crowd. He knew he hadn't hurt his opponent. Fredericks had been off-balance when he hit him.

Fredericks was up almost immediately, lunging forward. Shmuel blocked the frenzied punches, using every trick he'd learned at the gym. Then he changed his tactics. He took one punch to land two, three of his own. Fredericks was solid, tougher than anyone Shmuel had faced before. He refused to go down.

At the end of the fifth round Shmuel sat back in his corner, heart pumping wildly. His right eye was swollen, a trickle of blood showed from his nose and his body felt like it had passed through a thresher. It was no consolation to look across the ring at Fredericks, who was bleeding freely from a cut below a left eye that was almost closed. With both eyes closed, Fredericks would still fight.

He glanced down at Lottie and Lazar, saw the worry on their faces. He was sure he was ahead on points now, fighting back after that disastrous first round. But Lottie wouldn't know that. All she'd see was the blood on his face.

By the eighth round Shmuel was tiring badly. The only thing that gave him strength was the knowledge that Fredericks was even more exhausted. Both of the South Londoner's eyes were closing. His legs were wobbly and his punches were nowhere near as crisp as they had been. Now he flailed away, hoping for a lucky punch, knowing that with each minute that passed the odds were shifting more heavily in Shmuel's favor. Tired as he was, Shmuel felt he could finish it now.

Fredericks came out of his corner slowly at the start of the ninth round. He'd never fought a man like Shmuel before, a rock who wouldn't wilt under his best shots. Fredericks felt little comfort in knowing that Shmuel had never met anyone like him either . . . They closed at the center of the ring, punches sliding off each other's sweat. Fredericks feinted with his left, brought up his right. Shmuel read the punch, moved inside it and let go with a murderous right hook to his opponent's body. Fredericks gasped. Shmuel stepped back, straightened his man out with two jabs. Fredericks' hands went up to protect his face. Shmuel attacked his midsection. As the hands dropped again, Shmuel set himself for the final punch.

It was a right uppercut. A crisp, smooth arc of a punch that lifted Fredericks six inches into the air. And dropped him unconscious to the canvas.

The crowd went wild. Programs were thrown into the ring as Shmuel lifted his arm. He looked down to where his wife and brother sat. Lazar was on his feet, clapping with Harry Sherman. Lottie was still in her seat, her face covered by her hands, crying . . .

Shmuel's attention returned to the prone figure of Tim Fredericks as the official doctor entered the ring. A hurried discussion took place between the doctor, the referee and Fredericks' seconds. The doctor knelt down beside the stricken boxer and Shmuel tried to get closer. Kosky and Josephson leaped into the ring and pulled him back, dragged him away.

"I want to see what happened to him," Shmuel yelled.

"*Later*," Kosky said. He'd known the moment that final punch had connected with Fredericks' jaw that serious damage had been done. The man had been helpless, his jaw completely exposed, and Shmuel had been desperate to finish the fight. Desperate enough to pack every ounce of strength he possessed into that one punch.

Back in the dressing room Kosky found the strength to force Shmuel into a chair, holding him there while Josephson went to work on his swollen eye and bloody nose. They'd know soon enough what had happened to Fredericks. All that mattered now was that Shmuel was in the semi-finals.

At ringside Lazar craned his neck for a better view of the commotion in the ring. He'd seen Shmuel dragged away by Kosky and Josephson, guessed that something was seriously wrong with Fredericks. Lottie tugged his arm, asked what had happened. Lazar shrugged his shoulders. He looked to Harry Sherman. The bald man muttered something about Fredericks getting caught flat-footed and turned to leave, he'd had enough. Lazar and Lottie followed him, trying to push their way down to the dressing room.

They waited outside the dressing room until Shmuel in street clothes emerged with Kosky and Josephson. The swelling over his right eye shone dully from the dressing the trainer had applied. As Lottie rushed forward to hold him, a man pushed his way between them. Tim Fredericks, he said, had been taken to the Middlesex Hospital with a broken jaw and concussion.

They left the stadium in a somber group, stopping at a nearby restaurant for a snack. No one felt like talking about the fight, about the future. Even when Shmuel was recognized by two diners he accepted their congratulations lethargically.

"Shall we go to the hospital?" Shmuel asked Kosky.

"No point. I'll telephone tomorrow, first thing in the morning."

Shmuel toyed with his food, not able to eat. He pushed the plate away and looked at the people gathered around the table. Finally he singled out Kosky. "What happens after this? How many more fights?"

Kosky ticked them off on his fingers. "Semis and then the

final. After that you go against the boys from the northeast, the northwest, Scotland, and Wales. And then you're heading the line for a crack at the heavyweight title."

"I don't like what I did to that man tonight," Shmuel said quietly. "I'm . . . ashamed."

"*Why*, for God's sake? You were fighting. Boxers know the chance they're taking every time they step into a ring—"

"Shut up, you damn fool," Lazar told him.

Kosky looked at Lottie and bit his lip. "Sorry," he muttered.

"Everything's changed," Shmuel said. "When I fought in the baths − against O'Brien, against the others − I could have killed because we needed the money so badly. We don't need it that way anymore."

"What are you trying to say?" Josephson asked. The trainer wasn't very good at subtleties . . . he only understood words that were like punches, straight from the shoulder.

"I want one crack at the championship. If I win it, I'll retire."

"And if you don't win it?" Kosky asked. "Supposing you come unstuck in one of the regionals?"

"Then I'll retire earlier."

"You're nuts," Josephson said. "If you've got a chance for the title you've got to keep on trying. And once you get it you hang onto it for as long as you bloody well can."

Shmuel shook his head. "I don't want the money, I just want one chance to prove I'm good enough. After that I'm through." He looked around the table, at Lazar, Sherman, Josephson and Kosky. And Lottie . . . she smiled back at him. At last Shmuel had set a limit to his boxing. She felt for the man who'd been injured . . . she couldn't even remember his name or the round he'd been knocked out in . . . And yet at the same time, in a way, she was glad he'd been hurt . . . because it had forced Shmuel to seriously question his fighting career. There was nothing Lottie wanted more than to see Shmuel quit the ring before what happened to Fredericks happened to him . . .

Long after Shmuel and Lottie had taken a taxi back to

Stamford Hill, Lazar stayed in a pub with Sherman, Josephson and Kosky, drinking leisurely. The main topic of conversation was not the fight but Shmuel's decision to quit once he'd either won the championship or lost one bout.

Kosky was strong against it. "Of all the boxers I handle right now, Shmuel's got the most ability. Now he wants to throw it away because he hurt a man."

"Don't look at me," Lazar said quickly, feeling Kosky's eyes on him. "If he wants to stop, that's his business."

"Some brother you are," Kosky said. "You'd let him throw away a chance like this?" He'd gotten up from his chair as he spoke. Sherman moved forward quickly. Lazar held out a hand to the bald man.

Kosky sat down again, keeping an eye on Sherman. He hadn't known Sherman was Lazar's bodyguard. "My bloody luck," he moaned. "I finally get someone who could go all the way and he goes soft on me."

"Maybe he'll change his mind," Sherman said, glad to see Kosky back in the chair again. He outweighed the ex-middleweight by a good forty pounds, but the man had once held three titles.

Kosky pulled a cigar from his top pocket, lit it and blew the smoke in a steady column toward the beamed ceiling. "I hope someone puts some sense in his head . . . or his wife's. God . . . what I'd give to get rid of the women. They're the real killers." He didn't smile when he said it.

Lazar got home just after midnight. Katya was asleep but he woke her up to tell her what had happened. "How did Shmuel take it?" she asked.

"Bad."

"I'm glad he decided to quit."

"So's Lottie. Kosky hopes he or someone can make him change his mind, but I don't think he'll have much luck."

"I hope he doesn't . . ."

The next morning Lazar knew that nothing would make Shmuel change his mind. He'd fight for the championship and then quit, win or lose. During the night Tim Fredericks had died from a blood clot in the brain.

Morning traffic on the road from London to Southampton was light. Lazar made good time, enjoying the warm sun that streamed in through the open roof. Glancing at the dashboard clock he estimated he'd be there just about the time the ship bringing Leah and Manny back from New York docked. Accompanying him on the long drive was Harry Sherman. With passes from the steamship company, they'd eat lunch on board.

Sherman closed his eyes and drifted off to sleep, leaving Lazar alone with the driving and his thoughts. It was easiest to think about Shmuel, if for no other reason than it took his mind off meeting Manny. He'd gone with Shmuel to Tim Fredericks' funeral in South London. It had been a dismal, overcast afternoon, and he'd watched the gently falling rain mingle with the tears that rolled down his brother's face as the casket was placed in the earth. Afterward Shmuel had gone to Fredericks' widow and parents, tried to express his sorrow once again. They'd all held onto each other, a tight group sharing one grief in the mud and rain.

Ben Kosky had been there too. After the interment he had buttonholed Lazar to ask again for help in making Shmuel change his mind. "Look where you are, man," Lazar had snapped back. "Haven't you got any decency?" Kosky had looked around, at the minister, at the mourners, finally at Shmuel. Then he'd shaken his head. "Not where my fighters are concerned." . . .

Sherman woke up as the car bounded over the railway lines on the dockside. The first thing he saw was the towering white wall of the ship's side directly in front of him. Lazar guided the car into a parking space and they got out. High above them passengers crowded the rails, stared down trying to identify waiting friends. Lazar strained his eyes as he looked up. Neither Leah nor Manny was visible. Pulling the steamship company passes from his pocket, he approached the gangplank and walked on board with Sherman at his heels.

They found Leah and Manny in the first-class dining room,

eating lunch. As soon as he spotted Lazar and Sherman, Manny snapped his fingers for the steward to set two additional places.

"Good to see you again. What's been happening while I've been away?" Manny wanted to know. Lazar wondered if it was his imagination playing tricks, or had Manny picked up an American accent in only a few weeks?

"A couple of things. I'll tell you about them later, in the car." Lazar leaned back as the steward set a dish in front of him. "Did you have a good time?"

"Great. We saw it all, did it all."

"What about you?" Lazar asked his sister. Leah sat quietly at the table, knife and fork balanced delicately in her hands. He wondered how she could stand to wear a long-sleeved dress on such a hot day.

"It was tiring. I don't have the energy Manny does."

Manny grinned. "We spent a fortune over there, an absolute bloody fortune. Staying in nothing but the best hotels, ate nowhere but the finest restaurants. Am I right, Leah?"

Leah nodded.

"Are you feeling all right?" Lazar asked his sister. She seemed awfully withdrawn for someone who'd just returned from her honeymoon, a once-in-a-lifetime trip, twice across the Atlantic on a luxury liner and six weeks in New York.

"I told you, I'm a bit tired."

"Never mind her," Manny said. "She can sleep all she wants when we get back home. What's been happening while I've been away?"

Lazar looked to Sherman. He might as well tell Manny the bad news here, the dining room was full, maybe he wouldn't make a scene in front of so many people . . . "The three spielers are out of business."

"*What*?" The single word cracked like a rifle shot across the table. "What do you mean out of business?"

"Pearl's was raided by a razor gang." And Lazar described what had happened, how he'd been hit on the head and knocked unconscious. "The other two were burned out. Two people were burned to death."

151

"When did this *happen*?"

"A few weeks ago."

"Why in hell didn't you send me a telegram?"

"I didn't see the point—"

"Who the hell are you not to see the point?" Manny's voice had gone up two octaves. Other diners turned their heads. Manny took no notice of them. "Who was it?"

"I don't know."

"What do you mean you don't know? Were you blind that you couldn't recognize anyone?"

"I'd never seen them before," Lazar lied.

"What did you do then?" The trace of an American accent had disappeared completely. Manny's old Cockney tone was back. "Did you see Joey Taylor? Did you try to find out from him what's going on?"

"I saw him."

"What did he say?"

"He'd heard something about a new mob. Down from Scotland. Trying to muscle in on the London business." Lazar now began to sow the seeds of his plan.

"Gorbals," Manny muttered. "Razor gangs. That makes sense. What else did he say?"

"He told me to do as I saw fit. Our firm had been singled out by this mob. I didn't want to do anything until you came back, so I closed down Leman Street, let the women go."

"You did *what*?" Manny's eyes turned glassy, the tic started jumping below his left eye as he tried to come to terms with the catastrophe. He glared at Sherman. "Do you know anything about this?"

"Only what Whitey told me. I wasn't at Pearl's when it happened."

"*Why* did you close down Leman Street? We've got no real money coming in now—"

"I didn't want anyone else to get hurt," Lazar said evenly. "Two people were burned to death when the spielers were fire-bombed. Goris will never be able to speak right again—"

"Screw Goris. Who gives a damn about that moron?"

Lazar wondered what would have happened if Shmuel had

152

accepted the job as enforcer at Pearl's. Would he now have his face scarred for life, his tongue so badly damaged he couldn't form words right? And would Manny be saying "Screw Shmuel. Who gives a damn about that moron?" It all hugely served to ease Lazar's conscience . . . not only would he set Manny up, he'd laugh, damn it, when the little bastard took the drop he so richly deserved.

A steward approached the table, whispered that other passengers were complaining about the noise. Manny turned to swear at him too. Leah, who had been a silent observer to the argument, put a tentative hand on Manny's wrist. He brushed it off. "You stay out of this."

By then Lazar and Sherman were also telling Manny to control himself as other stewards headed toward the table. Manny saw them, pushed himself back from the table and stood up. "The food here stinks anyway," he muttered, throwing his napkin onto the plate. "Let's get off this tub." Without waiting for the others, he walked back to his stateroom . . .

It took three hours before the baggage was unloaded and cleared through customs. On the return trip to London Manny sat in front with Lazar while Leah shared the back seat with Sherman. Manny kept up an almost incessant commentary on what he would do when he found out who had knocked over his clubs. His anger was transferred from Lazar to the Scottish mob he believed was responsible. Lazar let him rant on, busy with his own thoughts. Of course there was no Scottish mob. But it wouldn't do any harm for Manny to think there was. It would keep him busy until Lazar was ready.

They reached Stoke Newington by seven in the evening. Katya appeared at the front door. Leah, showing her first animation of the day, ran toward her, hugged her tightly, commenting on her size.

"Katya made dinner for us," Lazar told Manny.

"I don't want dinner. I want the telephone." He marched through to the living room, calling over his shoulder to Lazar and Sherman not to make themselves comfortable; they'd be going out very damn soon.

"Right now he's mad enough to spit blood," Lazar said to

Sherman. "Can you imagine what he'd be like if he knew it was Vanetti who did him up?"

"Whitey . . ." Sherman pulled Lazar down to the end of the hall, close to the front door. "Forget about that, I've got to talk to you."

"What about?" Lazar tried to move back toward the living room, wanting to eavesdrop on the call he knew Manny must be making to Joey Taylor. Sherman wouldn't let him go.

"It's about your sister."

"What? What about Leah?"

"When I was sitting with her on the back seat . . . she didn't think I could see, but—"

"See *what*?"

"Her left sleeve came up a bit. Like this." He pulled back his own jacket sleeve to demonstrate. "Whitey . . . your sister's arm is black and blue."

Lazar forgot all about the conversation he wanted to listen to. His eyes searched Sherman's face. "Did you say anything to her?"

"What was I supposed to say?"

"All right." He concentrated again on the living room. Manny was still talking, his voice quiet but urgent. "I'll be right back," he said to Sherman, leaving the bald man standing alone in the hallway. He walked quickly to the kitchen, where he found Leah and Katya standing by the sink chatting about the impending birth. Again the strangeness of his sister choosing to wear a long-sleeved dress on such a warm day attracted his attention. Now he understood. Too well. He also grasped something else. During the entire ride home, in Manny's presence, she'd hardly uttered a word. Away from Manny, if only for a few minutes in the kitchen with Katya, Leah was warm and talkative. Lazar could well believe there were bruises on her arm. He could also believe they were all over her body.

"Katya, can I have a word with you?"

"What is it?"

"Alone . . . please." He smiled at Leah. "Domestic problem." He took Katya out into the hallway, past the living

154

room, where he could still hear Manny's voice, and into the front room, where the table was set for dinner.

"What is it—?"

"We're going to have to go out for an hour, maybe more. To see Joey Taylor. While we're out, see if you can get Leah to tell you what happened to her. Harry Sherman says her arm's black and blue."

"You mean from Manny . . . ?"

"That's what I want to find out. She might talk to you if you handle it right."

"Whitey!" Manny's voice came from the hallway, the telephone conversation with Joey Taylor finished. "We're going to Bishop's Avenue."

Lazar kissed Katya quickly on the cheek. "Get her to tell you what happened."

"I'll try." She walked into the hallway, stood by the front door as Lazar drove away with Manny and Sherman. Then she turned back inside the house. Leah was still in the kitchen; she hadn't even come out to see her husband leave.

"You've heard enough about what it feels like to be an expectant mother," Katya said. "Let's hear about you. How was your honeymoon?"

"All right."

"That's it? Just all right? You went on a trip everyone else dreams about and you can't say anything more than that?" Katya wiped the back of her hand across her forehead. "Phew, it's hot in here . . . all the cooking I did . . . my God, how on earth can you wear that dress? You must feel like you're sitting inside an oven. Here . . ." She reached out quickly and grabbed hold of Leah's arm before she had the opportunity to move away. "Roll your sleeves up before you melt away—"

"*No.*" She was too late. Katya already had the sleeve up to the elbow and was staring in horrified fascination at the massive bruise on Leah's lower arm that Sherman had seen in the car. "How on earth did you get that?"

"I fell," Leah said weakly. "A couple of days ago, the ship was rolling badly in a storm . . . I fell and caught my arm on

155

the corner of a table."

"Really." Katya snatched at Leah's other arm, pulled back the sleeve. "Did you catch this arm too?" she asked, pointing to another, smaller bruise. "Or did you get this on a different table, in a different storm?"

Leah said nothing, offered no resistance as Katya unbuttoned her dress and peeled it down from her shoulders. The creamy white of her skin was desecrated by more bruises, some old and almost faded, others vividly fresh.

"My God . . . Manny?"

Leah nodded.

"When did it start?"

"The night we were married. In the hotel before we went to Southampton to catch the boat."

"Why?"

Leah pulled up her dress, fastened the buttons. "He never wanted to marry me. That's what he told me on our wedding night. He said he was forced into it, it was a marriage of convenience—"

"Convenience? You weren't pregnant, were you?"

"Of course not. I did enough stupid things but I at least managed to avoid that. No, it was convenient for Manny to marry me because it would keep Lazar in his place. Lazar would do as he was told, Manny said, because he had me to bargain with. And then he started to knock me around because I cramped his style and he hated me for it—"

"You were in love with him when you married him, weren't you? You acted like you were."

"Yes . . . or at least I thought I was. I thought I was a very smart lucky girl—"

"And now?"

Leah shook her head. "I'm just scared to death of him now. I'm even scared to say this to you. Scared for you to know it . . ."

Katya remembered Harry Sherman at the wedding. Drunk as he'd been he'd been right. Should she tell Leah she wouldn't have to put up with Manny for much longer? That Lazar and Joey Taylor were working to rid London of two dangerous lunatics . . . and Manny was one of them? No . . .

156

the less Leah knew at the moment the better it would be for all of them . . . somehow Leah would have to put up with Manny for another month. God help her . . .

"I made dinner for five people," Katya said. "Can you believe that? Looks like we're going to face a full table all by ourselves."

"Why should you worry . . . you're eating for two." Leah could actually smile. "That should help."

Katya put an arm around her sister-in-law's shoulders and guided her into the dining room. As much as she ached to tell Leah that there was a limit to her suffering, she knew she couldn't afford to. Something might slip out in an unguarded moment and Manny would be forewarned. And then all their futures would be as black as those awful bruises on Leah's body.

Seated behind the desk, Joey Taylor lit a cigar and studied his three visitors. Sherman and Lazar had been silent. Only Manny had spoken, and he had said enough to make up for the others. From the moment he'd been shown into the study Manny had demanded to know what was going on. Who was this new firm? Why had they picked out his clubs?

"I told you . . . I don't know a thing. No one does yet," Taylor said, eyeing the glowing tip of his cigar. "When I know, I'll tell you. And then we'll decide what action to take. Until that time you will do absolutely nothing."

"The hell I'll do nothing. I'm putting together an army. And then I'm going out there to chop the head off any bastard with a damn brogue."

Taylor glanced at Lazar and Sherman. Were they thinking, as he was, that Manny was his own judge, jury and executioner? What better evidence did any court need that Manny was unfit to control a firm than this tantrum? "You will do no such thing," Taylor said quietly, switching his gaze back to Manny. "You will just sit tight at home and wait until I have instructions for you. There's enough bloodshed at the moment to raise questions not only among the public but in the House of Commons itself. The burning of your two clubs, the attack on the other, have brought embarrassing pressure. There is talk of a Parliamentary commission being formed to investigate crime in London." It was a lie. Taylor knew; so did Lazar and Sherman. But it might scare Manny into cooling his heels for a while. "Anyone who steps out of line now, until we locate and take care of this Scottish mob, will be dealt with severely. Do you understand me?"

Manny's bluster cooled some. "All right, but once this thing is over do I get back my spielers? My territory?"

"Of course. Everything will be as it was. You have my word."

Manny understood he had to be satisfied with that promise. He wasn't big enough to go against Taylor and the force he represented. No firm was. Taylor had the real power on his side . . . top people . . . the governors who wore navy blue uniforms and worked out of Scotland Yard.

"You'll keep me informed, Mr. Taylor?"

"I'll keep you informed." Taylor stood up and rang for the butler to show the visitors out. The meeting was over.

Lazar was the last to leave the house. As the butler held open the door, he whispered that Mr. Taylor would expect a telephone call from him later that night. Lazar nodded and hurried to catch up with Sherman and Manny.

After dropping off Sherman, Lazar picked up Leah from the house and drove her and Manny back to the East End. When he finally arrived home he asked Katya what she had found out from Leah. She told him, and it was all he could do to stop himself from getting in the car and driving back to the East End. He could feel Manny's neck between his hands, hear the crack as it snapped, see Manny's face turn blue, his eyes roll up . . .

As hard to bear as his own fury was, Lazar tried to put himself in his brother's shoes. If Shmuel knew what Leah had been through he wouldn't hesitate . . . he'd go there and club Manny to death with his fists. He'd already been responsible for the death of a man to whom he'd felt no hatred. If Manny was in front of him, what Shmuel showed in the ring would be doubled, quadrupled, as he battered Manny's face to a pulp . . .

Lazar managed to console himself by visualizing the plan he'd worked out. Manny's eventual end would be more fitting. It would serve more purpose than merely appeasing his own private rage. Thinking about it, he called Taylor, as requested.

"He's back," Taylor said. "How long do you intend to wait?"

"I'm giving it another few weeks, until after Katya's had the baby."

"Very well. But don't leave it too long. Goodman's a hothead. If he stays out of business for too long without this alleged Scottish mob appearing, there's no telling what he might do."

"I understand." Lazar replaced the receiver and sat back.

When Katya came home from the hospital with the baby he'd have a small, intimate gathering at the house. He'd invite Leah and Manny. And Sherman. Shmuel wouldn't come . . . not with Manny there. Just as well. He didn't want to drag Shmuel into this. The less he knew about Leah's situation the better. Shmuel's presence might work against Lazar's carefully laid-out plan. Katya and Sherman would lie for him. Leah, too, if necessary, he felt. After what she'd been through with Manny . . . Shmuel wouldn't, and Lazar would not want him to.

And while that small, intimate party was going on, while everyone was ogling the baby, Lazar would find a reason to slip out for a while . . .

CHAPTER TEN

In the greengrocer's shop on Booth Street Lazar had to contend with Manny's carps about Joey Taylor's inaction and his inability to locate the mob that had attacked the spielers. Lazar also had Katya to worry about. In bed early that morning she'd suddenly grabbed his shoulder and said she thought she was starting to go into labor. Lazar had thrown her ready-packed suitcase into the car and driven her to the hospital. He'd waited two hours until a nursing sister had told him to go home. A false alarm but they were keeping her in. When anything happened they'd contact him. Knowing he wouldn't be able to stay at home by himself he'd given the hospital two other telephone numbers – Shmuel's furniture shop on Stamford Hill and Manny's flat on Booth Street.

Manny shouted across the shop to pay attention to a customer. With money no longer coming in from the spielers or the house in Leman Street the greengrocer's shop had become a real source of much-needed income. Even with the money generated by the rented houses Manny was hurting. So, of course, was Lazar. Except Lazar could comfort himself with the knowledge that there was a light at the end of the tunnel.

Manny walked away from the counter, leaving behind him women who had been shocked to learn that after years of cheap produce they were expected to pay the *market* price . . . Manny's little charity had been shelved. He went through the back of the shop to the alleyway and yelled up to the flat. "Leah, your brother and I say it's time for a tea break. Hurry it up."

Lazar pretended not to hear Manny give out his orders.

"Did you give the hospital the number upstairs?" Manny

asked as he poured five pounds of potatoes into a waiting woman's shopping bag.

Lazar nodded.

"Who's going to be the godfather?"

Lazar looked up from the display of fruit he was arranging. "We hadn't thought about it yet," he lied.

"You should, and I reckon you should give the honor to the bloke who's done the most for you. The same bloke you shunned when it came to choosing a best man for your wedding." He turned to the woman holding the potatoes. "Tenpence, darling," he said, taking the two sixpences she held out. "Twopence change . . . there you are, love."

"Let's wait for the baby to be born first," Lazar said.

Leah came down from the flat carrying a tray of cups and a plate of sandwiches. Lazar noticed she was wearing a longsleeved dress again, the collar high up around her neck.

"Go back upstairs and listen for the phone," he said.

Lazar watched her go. Pretty soon they'd be rid of Manny Goodman. And Katya would have the baby and be home . . .

"What are you going to call this kid?" Manny asked.

"If it's a boy, Aron. Sophie if it's a girl. After my parents."

"You name your kid after your parents . . . I name a spieler in honor of mine." The thought of Pearl's threw a shadow over Manny's mind, he became less talkative. He stood behind the counter, serving customers, brooding. Christ . . . if that Joey Taylor and all his friends at Scotland Yard didn't come up with something soon he'd explode. He hadn't been kidding when he'd told Taylor that he'd turn over every Scot he could lay his hands on. He'd leave such a trail of dead Jocks that the police would think war had broken out. And to hell with whatever those idiots in Parliament thought about it.

Half an hour later Leah came down again, running through the shop toward Lazar. "They just called! Katya's having the baby! Go!"

Lazar left the display of fruit he was arranging, threw his apron on the counter and ran from the store. His hands were dirty. His clothes were covered in dust. This was no way to visit a hospital where his wife was giving birth, but he didn't

161

care. He, by God, was going to be a *father*.

Reaching the hospital he jumped from the car and ran inside, racing up the two flights of stairs to the maternity ward. "Boruchowicz! Katya!" he gasped to the sister at the desk. "Has she had it yet?"

"Had *it*?" the sister asked humorously. She consulted a chart on the desk. "Your wife's just been delivered of a nine-pound boy."

"Nine pounds!" Lazar repeated numbly. A giant. He'd fathered another Shmuel. "How is she . . . he . . . them . . . ?"

"They're all fine. Why don't you sit down and relax for a couple of minutes?"

"Relax? Who can relax?" He looked at the waiting room, saw the other nervous men, the pacing, the spirals of gray smoke from countless cigarettes, and decided he didn't want to be one of them. He ran from the hospital, got back in the car and began to drive. Where was he heading? He had no idea. He took a hold of himself. He'd drive to Shmuel's shop. The hospital had probably tried there before they rang Booth Street. Shmuel would want to know the news . . .

"Well?" Shmuel asked when Lazar entered the shop. "Boy? Girl? Or twins?"

"Boy. Nine pounds."

"Big." Shmuel looked duly impressed.

"Did they call here first?"

Shmuel nodded. "Do you want anything? Cup of tea? Something stronger?"

Lazar waved away the offers. He was too tense to even think about drinking. He wasn't even sure he would be able to keep anything down. The excitement was all over him. His legs felt weak. His stomach was jumping. And his heart was beating ten times faster than it was possible for any heart to beat.

"Why don't you sit down before you fall down."

Lazar let Shmuel guide him to one of the chairs on display.

"Stay here. I'll run upstairs and tell Lottie."

"No school today?"

"It's five thirty," Shmuel said.

Lazar watched his brother leave. Moments later he returned with Lottie.

"Congratulations." She kissed him warmly on the cheek. "How does it feel to be a daddy?"

"How does it feel to be an auntie?"

"Katya's all right?"

"So they keep telling me." Lazar stood up and began to walk around the shop. He felt more in control of himself. He'd return to the hospital and join the other fathers in the waiting room until it was time for him to see Katya and his child.

"Will you be able to come to Holborn this Saturday evening?" Shmuel asked.

"Holborn?" Lazar had to repeat before he remembered. The Southern Area semi-finals, another step for Shmuel. "If Katya's still in the hospital, I'll be there. If she's home already, I wouldn't leave her."

"I understand."

"How do you feel about the fight?" Lazar asked, realizing that his own anxiety about Katya, about Manny, was no worse than what Shmuel must be experiencing.

"I'm worried about . . . hurting someone again."

"Tell Lazar what you're going to do with your purses," Lottie cut in.

Shmuel seemed embarrassed. "It's nothing, I've only got a few more fights before I quit. Whatever I make from those fights — whether I lose in the regionals or go on to win a Lonsdale Belt — I'm sending it to Tim Fredericks' wife." He couldn't bring himself to use the word *widow*. "He had two young children, did you know that?"

Lazar felt something burning in his eyes, then "Does Kosky know?"

Shmuel shrugged his massive shoulders. "He knows. He just thinks I'm even more *meshuggah* than he originally thought I was."

"Is he still nagging you about your decision to retire?"

"He's given up. He knows my mind is set and that nothing can change it."

"Good. You keep it that way."

Kosky must be feeling sick to his stomach, Lazar thought.

163

Shmuel had been his ticket to easy street. Lazar wondered if Kosky had gone into a hole, had spent a fortune before it was in his hands. And if he had, how did he plan to make up for it? Who would pay. Shmuel . . . ?

On Saturday Katya was still in the hospital, so Lazar stayed with her for the hour of visiting time, then drove at breakneck speed to Holborn Stadium for Shmuel's semi-final bout.

He missed the first two rounds. Harry Sherman, sitting at ringside with Lottie, brought him up to date. The Brick Lane Lion had adopted a new approach. Instead of swinging those awesome fists with punishing power he had come out of his corner boxing well enough to win both rounds on points. Lazar knew why . . . after all, he'd killed a man in his last fight.

The crowd understood too. At the end of the last round, when the referee announced the unanimous decision that put Shmuel into the Southern Area heavyweight final, everyone in the hall stood up to give the victor a standing ovation. Even Lottie applauded. She could appreciate that Shmuel had boxed, not fought. And boxed well enough to win, though he'd never taken an opportunity to finish off the other man.

"When's Katya coming home?" Lottie asked as they waited in the lobby after the fight.

"Another four days."

"Everything ready in the nursery?"

"What's to get ready?"

"You mean you haven't done a thing? Your newborn son's going to move into a bare room?"

"You should see that bare room!" Harry Sherman said. "Whitey's had me up there every spare hour helping him. New carpet. New wallpaper. The biggest toys you ever saw in your life."

Shmuel came out dressed, face unmarked. With him was Ben Kosky and Steve Josephson. Since the time he'd last refused to help persuade Shmuel to go on fighting – after Tim Fredericks' funeral – a distinct coolness had set in between Lazar and Kosky. The manager knew that Lazar wouldn't help, so he had no further use for him.

"You looked pretty good in there," Sherman told Shmuel.

"Thanks. I hope I look that good in the final."

"When is it?"

Kosky answered. "Three months' time at the National Sporting Club."

"Against whom?"

"Depends on the fight going on in there now." Kosky gestured toward the arena. "Bomber Harris against Danny MacAlinden." As Kosky spoke a roar swept up from the arena, reverberating around until the stadium seemed to shake from the noise. Kosky pulled back the swing door and looked inside, trying to see over the heads of the spectators who had gotten to their feet. "Harris," he said. "Harris just knocked out MacAlinden. That's who Shmuel's fighting for the Southern Area heavyweight championship."

Lazar pushed his way past Kosky to see for himself. In the ring, through the haze and smoke, he could see the blond-haired figure of Harris prancing around in triumph. Lazar felt disappointed. If he'd had his choice, Shmuel would fight MacAlinden. Bomber Billy Harris was a powerhouse, a walking arsenal. Shmuel couldn't afford to box him, to try to go for the distance and win on points like he'd done tonight. Harris would just wear him down, take everything Shmuel had to offer, hit him where he could and wait for an opportunity to take him out. To win against Harris and take the regional championship Shmuel would have to overcome his reluctance to slug it out. He'd have to be prepared to stand toe-to-toe in the center of the ring and prove he was the strongest.

"Would you like to come back to the flat for a bite?" Lottie asked Lazar and Sherman.

"I sure would," Lazar said. "Anything's better than trying to cook for myself." Leaving Kosky and Josephson, they walked quickly from the stadium.

Lottie made omelettes and toast, served tea in delicate china cups. Shmuel asked Lazar how Leah was, Lazar told him she was fine. If he told the truth Shmuel would find all the fury he'd need to beat Bomber Billy Harris . . . only he'd

165

channel it in the wrong direction. Manny would be taken care of, all right. But according to plan. His, Lazar's plan. After all, he was still the big . . . well, at least the older . . . brother . . .

Sherman and Lazar left the flat just after eleven. Knowing exactly when Katya would be coming home cleared Lazar's mind. He'd arranged the welcoming party for the following Saturday. Hours had been spent in planning. Now was the time to take that first step. The most dangerous step, because it meant winning the confidence of Davey Vanetti.

Lazar drove, heading for Gerrard Street, a narrow thoroughfare running north of Leicester Square. On the second floor of a building close to where Gerrard Street joined Wardour Street was an after-hours drinking club that Vanetti frequented. The club was minded by the West End's top governor. It was known as neutral ground. No one would dare to start trouble there.

The man on the door recognized Lazar and Sherman as they entered, murmured a few polite words. They made their way to the bar, looking over the crowded premises, recognizing sporting personalities and thieves, entertainers and bookies. There was no sign of Vanetti or any of his henchmen. Lazar and Sherman would have to be patient.

They nursed drinks until almost one o'clock in the morning, when Vanetti entered, accompanied by another man whom Lazar recognized as the razor wielder who'd carved up Goris. Vanetti's dark eyes swept over the club, past Lazar and Sherman. Then back. As Vanetti slipped his right hand into his jacket pocket, Lazar raised his own hand in a gesture of peace.

Followed closely by his lieutenant, Vanetti slowly approached the table where Lazar and Sherman were sitting. "What are you doing here?"

"Having a drink." Lazar guessed that the hand Vanetti continued to hold in his jacket pocket was caressing a razor. The Malt wouldn't dare to bring it out here. He might get it clear of his pocket, but before he had time to use it at least four men would be on him and his lieutenant. Not wanting to disturb the club's other patrons, they'd wait until they got both men outside before breaking their arms.

166

"Where are your women this time?" Vanetti said. "Aren't you hiding behind skirts anymore? Or are you the bait yourselves?"

"That's over."

"What? You've quit Goodman?" Vanetti looked skeptical.

"We'd like to," Lazar said, and Sherman nodded his bald head.

"Why?"

"Because you've put him out of business," Sherman said. "And he's a nut. He was told to lay off you and he didn't. Instead of keeping the peace so we can all make a living he runs around asking for trouble . . . like you gave him at the spielers."

"So?" There was nothing Vanetti wanted more than to attend Manny's funeral. But first, before he agreed to go in with these two men, he wanted them to beg. He wanted to see them down on their knees. They were the ones who'd helped to hold him down that night . . .

Lazar's next words told Vanetti he was wrong in assuming they wanted his help to take care of Manny. "If we fix him, can we expect no more trouble from your firm?"

"You fix him? By yourselves? How?"

"He trusts us," Lazar said, looking at Vanetti's lieutenant. He wanted to remember that face when the time of reckoning came. The man stared back with cold blue eyes, recognizing Lazar from Pearl's. "We'll be able to get Manny."

"I tell you what I'll do," Vanetti said. "If you bring me both ears of Manny Goodman I'll forget everything that's gone between us. You and me will start fresh."

Lazar looked at Sherman . . . getting rid of this bastard would be a true pleasure. "Be home next Saturday evening around nine o'clock," he told Vanetti. "The postman will be making a very special delivery."

Katya came home to find the entire house decked with flowers. Carrying the baby with exaggerated care, Lazar led the way upstairs to the nursery. Katya clapped a hand to her mouth, felt tears starting from her eyes as she surveyed the work that

167

had been done. The wallpaper was a pastel blue — purchased the very day Lazar learned he had a son. Pale blue carpet covered the floor. White drapes hung from the windows. There was a chest of drawers decorated with pictures of animals. A closet was filled with tiny clothes hanging neatly from the rail. And in an armchair by the window was the biggest stuffed dog Katya had ever set eyes on.

"This is fantastic . . . you and Harry did all this?"

"Mostly Harry," Lazar said. "I supervised." He turned the sleeping baby from one wall to another. "What do you think of your new home, young man?"

"It's a lot more comfortable than his old one," Katya said. "At least, as far as I'm concerned."

Lazar gently handed the child back to Katya, became serious . . . "We're having a party this Saturday evening. Manny's farewell . . ."

"Oh?" Katya asked. Lazar had told her what she had to know. "What do I do?"

"Settle Leah down. Make sure she tells the same story as the rest of us." If anyone could do it, Lazar knew Katya could. She was probably closer to Leah than any of them.

Katya moved aside the stuffed dog and sat down in the armchair, cradling the baby in her arms. He woke up, began to cry. Katya crooned softly to him. She was glad that the baby would take up so much of her time, and her thoughts. She didn't want to think about what had to be done, even though, God knew, Manny Goodman deserved it . . . what he'd done to Leah, to so many others . . .

Leah's reaction to the nursery was much like Katya's. She clapped her hands delightedly as she looked around, taking in every detail, almost unable to believe that her brother and Harry Sherman had been responsible.

"It's marvelous . . . gorgeous. Aron's going to be the most spoiled child in all of London."

"I only hope you can know — " Katya stopped abruptly. "I'm sorry, is he—?"

"He's worse than ever," Leah answered softly. "Every

night I pray that something happens, that they find this . . .
this Scottish mob that burned out his clubs, that he can at
least get back into business and leave me alone."

"Leah." Katya went to the door and listened. From downstairs she could hear men's voices. Lazar, Sherman and
Manny, drinking and talking before she served dinner. She
pushed the door closed.

"How much do you really want to be . . . rid of Manny?"

"Rid of him? More than anything. But how? He'd kill me
if I left him."

"Don't ask questions. Just listen to me. I need the key to
your flat."

"What?"

"Never mind the what and why for now. The key, Leah. . ."

"It's downstairs, in my bag—"

"Get it. Give it to Lazar."

"What's going to happen?"

Katya went to the door and listened again. The voices were
still coming from downstairs. "I'm going to tell you something.
Listen very carefully."

Leah listened. When Katya had finished, Leah, shaken,
nonetheless went downstairs and searched in her bag for the
key to the flat. She passed close to Lazar and dropped the key
into his hand. Then she sat down . . . Yes, once she had been
in love with Manny, not able to see anything but him.
Marriage to him . . . a hellish time . . . had changed all that.
Now, to be free of him . . . be patient. She had no choice . . .
and she could use the time to think on what had driven her to
be attracted to the likes of Manny in the first place. Be
honest, she told herself, you wanted it, him, and even fought
for him . . . but did she have to pay with her life for that
mistake? Hadn't she paid enough? And, in fact, hadn't
Manny gotten progressively worse, so that the redeeming
charm and intimacy had long since been abandoned . . . with
a vengeance since their marriage . . .

Shortly before eight o'clock, as they were sitting around the
dinner table, the telephone rang. At the first ring Lazar
stiffened, abruptly nervous. The wheels were in motion,

169

rolling faster with every second. Even if he wanted to stop them now, he couldn't . . .

"Lazar . . ." Katya said, glancing anxiously at him. "The phone."

He got up from the table and lifted the receiver, pressed it tightly to his ear. "Hello?"

The voice at the other end was Joey Taylor's. "Your call . . . as requested."

Lazar could swear he detected a hint of amusement in Taylor's voice, as though he were enjoying his protected role in the evening's intrigue.

"Hold on a minute." He swung back to the table. "Harry! It's the police! Your shop's been broken into."

"What?" Sherman moved quickly, snatched the receiver from Lazar, held it to his ear. When the short conversation was ended, his face was white with anger. "Can you believe that? Some sod's had the nerve to break into my shop."

"I'll go with you," Lazar said.

"How did they know where to find you?" Manny asked.

Sherman thought fast. "My missus must have told the police I was here." Without waiting for another question he hurriedly left the room. Lazar was close on his heels. Before Manny had the opportunity to say that he too would accompany them, they were in Lazar's car. Heading not toward Sherman's shop, but to Booth Street in the East End.

"You figure he went for it?" Sherman asked.

"I hope so."

"What if he checks? Calls my home or goes to the shop?"

"Why should he? He's laughing himself sick that you've been robbed. You're in the same boat as him . . . out of business."

Sherman nodded uneasily.

In Booth Street, they entered the shop first. A piece of cloth wrapped around his hand, Lazar reached under the counter and grasped the lead-weighted chair leg. They went upstairs. Lazar forced himself to search through Manny's wardrobe. He found a pair of gold cuff links engraved with the initials E.G. – Emanuel Goodman. He took one.

At eight fifty-five they were parking the car in front of

Vanetti's block of flats off Tottenham Court Road. Hurry. If they were away too long Manny would get suspicious.

As they got out of the car a man approached. A woman walking by peered quickly at the man's disfigured face — the puckered scar that stretched his mouth into his cheeks — and hurried away. Goris didn't even notice her reaction. He'd gotten accustomed to the curious, often horrified stares. Besides, this night left no room for self-pity. Pity of any kind.

"Did you see anyone go in?" Lazar asked.

Goris' speech was difficult to understand; the missing tip of his tongue tended to confuse his consonants, turn his T's into D's. "Just one. The one who did this to me." He pointed to his mouth.

Lazar held the chair leg inside his jacket, keeping the piece of cloth between it and his fingers. The plan had been that Vanetti would die to set up Manny. Now Goris could also dispatch the man who'd marked him.

Lazar pulled up his sleeve to check the time. "Two minutes to nine," Sherman announced. "On the nose." Lazar led the way into the building, taking the stairs two at a time to the second floor. Vanetti's flat was at the far end of the corridor, the door flanked on either side by a wide expanse of wall. Lazar motioned for Goris and Sherman to stand on either side of the door, backs pressed against the wall, invisible from inside the flat. He rang the bell, heart pounding. He forced himself to see Manny beating his sister, summoned up the image of the Brownshirt—

The door swung back. Vanetti stood there. Behind him, Lazar could see the man who had been at Pearl's.

"Is this the special delivery you promised me?" Vanetti said. "I don't see any ears."

"In my pocket. Shall I come in, or do you want me to hand them over in the corridor?"

Vanetti smiled. Manny Goodman was dead. The man who had killed him was standing in front of him, Goodman's ears in his pocket. Who would he send these ears to? he wondered. And what would he do with the body of the late Manny Goodman's white-haired lieutenant? Fool . . . to believe that

171

he, Vanetti, would want anything to do with him, would risk letting him live. "Come inside."

Lazar moved through the doorway, looking straight ahead. The pressure of the chair leg against his chest was a counterpoint to the rapid beating of his heart. Vanetti started to close the door. It exploded in his hand, crashing back to knock him off his feet as Sherman and Goris charged through it.

Goris was first through. He took one look at the body of Vanetti sprawled on the floor and didn't stop. Hands outstretched, he moved at the man who had disfigured him. The man tried to reach into his pocket. Goris' hands reached him first. Fingers pressed into his throat, crushed his windpipe. His face turned blue. Goris continued to apply pressure, the man's flailing arms fell to his side. His legs buckled. His head lolled back. Goris opened his hands, the man fell to the floor.

Goris turned around to see Lazar and Sherman dragging Vanetti to his feet. He stepped forward to help but Lazar waved him back.

"Watch the corridor," Lazar told him.

Goris opened the door a fraction, looked out. The corridor was empty. From behind he heard a sound, turned to see Sherman hold Vanetti upright. Lazar's arm, raised with the lead-filled chair leg grasped in his hand, came down . . . Sherman let the body drop to the floor. Lazar placed the chair leg alongside it, still using the cloth to avoid fingerprints.

For the second time in his life Lazar had killed a man. A Nazi and a sadistic maniac. Still . . . stop thinking, get *on* with it . . . He took the engraved cuff link from his pocket and tossed it into the centre of the room. It rolled to a halt under the body of the man Goris had strangled.

The three of them walked quickly down the stairs to the street, got into the car and sped off. A mile away Lazar stopped to let out Goris. Seeing a telephone booth, he called Joey Taylor. The message was – mission completed. The rest was up to Taylor and his friends.

By nine forty-five they were back at the house in Stoke Newington. While Sherman told Manny and Katya that his shop had not only been robbed but vandalized, Lazar returned the key to Leah. She didn't want to let his hand go.

Superintendent Alan Withers looked at his reflection in the mirror, applied the comb to both his hair and his moustache and decided he was ready. A police officer's appearance mattered. Especially when he was investigating a major crime, the murder of a leading racket figure. One never knew if a photographer would turn up, a picture would be in the paper.

Joey Taylor had telephoned Withers at home the moment Lazar had called in to say that Vanetti was dead. Withers had decided to wait several hours before investigating what he would say was an anonymous tip. Five o'clock in the morning would be a good time to see Vanetti's body for himself, to make the Malt's death an official statistic on police files.

Precisely at five o'clock Withers stepped from a police car in front of Vanetti's building. The drizzle that had been falling since midnight started to increase in intensity and he pulled up the collar of his raincoat. Leaving a uniformed constable sitting in the driver's seat, the superintendent led two plainclothes officers up to the second floor. He rang the bell twice. When there was no answer he stepped aside and let one of the detectives — a solid, heavy man who played rugby for the Metropolitan Police team — charge at the door with his shoulder. The lock was strong enough to withstand the first two assaults. On the third it gave. The door slammed back against the wall, tearing paper, chipping plaster. It rebounded and was shoved aside by the detective. Along the corridor another door opened, a tenant curious about the noise. "Police," Withers called out. "Sorry to disturb you."

Vanetti's body was closest to the door. Withers knelt beside it, not bothering to check for a pulse. He wrapped a handkerchief around the chair leg, lifted it, saw the dried blood, hair and skin attached to it. Surprised at the weight of the chair leg, he inspected it more closely. It was hollowed out, filled with lead.

"Looks like your tip was right, sir," said the detective who had charged down the door.

"Yes, it does rather, doesn't it?" Withers stood up. "One

less of them to worry about. Is he dead too?" He gestured with the chair leg at the other man.

"As a doornail, sir."

"Do you know him?"

"Jack Gardner," the detective said. "Vanetti's persuader. Kept his women in line."

"Won't be keeping anyone else in line, will he? Let's look around." Withers knew the gold cuff link was underneath Gardner's body. He wanted one of the other men to find it.

It didn't take long. While Withers was checking through a bureau an excited shout came from behind him. Gardner's body had been rolled over. Strangulation was the obvious cause of death. Bruises covered the dead man's throat. One of the detectives was holding the gold cuff link by its edges. "Look at this, sir."

"What is it?"

"Gold cuff link, sir. Not Gardner's. He's still wearing two and they're silver. It's initialed."

"What initials?" he asked, stepping closer.

"E.G."

"E.G.? Who do we know with the initials E.G.? Who carries something like this around?" He held up the chair leg.

Both detectives answered simultaneously. "Manny Goodman . . . Emanuel Goodman."

"That's what it looks like to me too. Well, well . . . Vanetti and Goodman were at each other . . . Goodman must have come into the flat, clobbered Vanetti with the chair leg, then gone for Gardner. Strangled him. Once he was dead, he went back to Vanetti . . ."

"When do you think it happened, sir?"

"Hard to say without a medical examiner's opinion. Bang on a few doors along the corridor. Wake up the neighbors, find out if they heard anything." As the two detectives went out Withers called the Yard to send a medical examiner immediately.

Only the tenant in the adjoining flat could offer any help. Groggy from being awakened, he told Withers that he'd heard a burst of noise around nine o'clock the previous evening. He hadn't taken any undue notice because Vanetti was a noisy neighbor, parties that lasted all night . . . Withers thought that pinpointed things nicely. He told the two detectives to wait in the flat for the medical examiner. He left. It was time to pay Manny Goodman a visit.

Withers told his driver to head for Commercial Street police station in the East End. Manny's home was in their jurisdiction. It would be common courtesy to involve them. Withers was pleased when he learned that Ivor Davies was duty officer. To include Davies in Goodman's arrest would put the Welshman on his side. Lazar had said that Davies was causing problems . . . this was an ideal opportunity to stop those problems before they got out of hand.

"Superintendent Withers." Davies stood at attention as he greeted the Yard man. "What can we do for you?"

"I want you and a couple of your men. For a little job I think you're going to enjoy."

"What would that be, sir?" Nothing enjoyable, in Davies' experience, happened so early on a rainy Sunday morning.

"I want to pick up Manny Goodman for questioning. On suspicion of murder."

Davies looked at Withers with undisguised interest. "The murder of whom, sir?"

"Davey Vanetti and Jack Gardner."

"Vanetti?" He didn't know who Gardner was . . . and didn't care. Vanetti was the important name. Davies had heard that the feud between Goodman and Vanetti had been cooled, that Goodman had been ordered to toe the line. He hadn't. He'd done exactly what anyone who knew him would have expected him to do. He'd come back from America and his honeymoon to learn that his clubs had been closed and he'd gone berserk. "When did this happen, sir?"

"Last night. I received an anonymous tip." He related what they had found in Vanetti's apartment — the two bodies, the chair leg and cuff link. Davies nodded . . . the chair leg was Manny's signature. He kept it under the counter of his shop. They had him. At last, they could take care of that little bastard . . .

175

Something nagged at Davies, though. "I can understand him losing the cuff link, sir. The struggle with the other man. But to leave the chair leg behind . . . wasn't that more than asking for trouble."

Withers noted the question. Maybe he'd underestimated Davies. Must be slipping . . . "He might have been disturbed. Panicked. This is a man who has just committed a double murder. I'm grateful he left it there. Whatever the explanation. Now . . ." Withers became businesslike, he didn't want to give Davies time to think too much . . . "I want you to come with me to Goodman's home. Have two of your men follow us. We'll bring Goodman back here for questioning."

"Right away, sir."

The car carrying Davies and Withers traveled slowly to Booth Street, allowing the two constables from Commercial Street station to keep pace on their bicycles. The rain was falling more heavily now, dripping off the constables' rubberized capes onto the road as they pedaled furiously to keep up with the car.

"That's Goodman's shop, sir." Davies pointed out the greengrocer's shop to Withers. "He's probably still in bed." Which made him think about Leah . . . she'd be with him . . .

Davies led the way into the building and stopped in front of Manny's door. He moved aside for the superintendent. Withers hammered on the door. A muffled yell from inside demanded to know who it was. Withers knocked again, and kept on knocking until the door swung back to reveal Manny in red-and-white striped pyjamas.

"Christ Almighty! Davies and a whole bunch of bogies!" Manny stared into Withers' face, trying to place him. The moustache and red face were naggingly familiar. He wasn't a local copper, he looked too important for that. "What do you lot want?"

"We want you to come down to the station," Withers said. "To assist us in our enquiries regarding the murder of Davey Vanetti and Jack Gardner."

"What! You're bloody mad—"

"We'll see," Withers said quietly. He pushed past Manny

176

into the hallway of the flat. Manny turned around to follow. Withers went straight to the bedroom. Without knocking he walked in to find Leah getting out of bed, slipping into a robe. He noticed bruises on her arms and shoulders but said nothing. She covered them up before Davies came in.

Manny yelled at Withers, "I didn't even know Vanetti was dead—"

"Sure you didn't," Davies said from behind him. "And that lead-filled chair leg of yours is still downstairs in the shop, under the counter where it always is."

Manny swung around to face the inspector.

"The one you used to beat Vanetti to death with last night. And left in his flat."

"You're crazy, what time last night?"

"Around nine o'clock."

"Nine o'clock, eh?" Manny relaxed a little. "I've got half a dozen witnesses who'll tell you where I was at nine o'clock last night."

"What kind of witnesses? Paid ones?"

"I don't have to pay witnesses like you do. I've got real ones. Like Leah. Her brother and his wife. We were over there last night. Till eleven o'clock. Celebrating the birth of his kid. Harry Sherman was there too."

"Leah?" Davies gazed at her as she sat on the edge of the bed, holding the robe tight around herself. "Were you and Manny at your brother's home last night?"

Leah avoided answering as she watched Withers go through Manny's wardrobe. He found a tray of jewelry, spilled it on the bed, separated the cuff links from the tiepins and collar studs. He selected out a solitary initialed gold link.

"Nice cuff link," he said to Manny. "Where's its partner?"

"With it, I suppose. Use your bloody eyes." Manny went over to the pile of cuff links, sorted through them. He checked the other jewelry, turned angrily to Leah. "What did you do with it? You always put my things away—"

"Would this be it?" Withers asked softly. The chief superintendent pulled a sealed envelope from his raincoat pocket, ripped it open and held it upside down. Into the palm of his hand tumbled the matching cuff link.

"Where did you get that?"

"In the same flat as we found your chair leg," Withers said. "It was underneath Jack Gardner's body."

"Who's Jack Gardner?"

"Vanetti's lieutenant. The second man you killed. The cuff link must have fallen from your shirt when you struggled with him."

The tic started below Manny's left eye. He began to shake . . . for once not from anger but a dawning fear. "Someone's had me," he whispered in disbelief. "Someone's gone and bloody had me."

"Leah . . ." Davies tried again. "Can you vouch for your husband's whereabouts last night?"

Leah seemed dazed. She clutched her robe tighter. "He . . . he . . ."

"*Tell him* . . ." Manny slapped her across the face with his right hand, sending her falling off the edge of the bed. Before he could draw back his hand again Davies was on him, applying a half-nelson, bending him double with the pressure.

"You lay your hands on her one more time and I'll break your bloody arm," Davies promised.

"Call anyone, call Whitey, his wife . . . Call Sherman. Yeah, that's it. Sherman. While we were at the house last night Sherman got a call from the coppers. His shop had been broken into. He and Whitey went out to look, to check on it. They were out . . . for . . . a . . . couple . . . of . . ." Manny's voice faltered as he realized what he was saying. At the same time he remembered where he had seen Withers before. In The Bishop's Avenue. The superintendent had been leaving as he'd arrived one night at Joey Taylor's house. They'd crossed in the doorway.

They were all in on it. From Taylor . . . right down to that little white-haired bastard *and* his sister. They'd set him up for the drop. Vanetti was out of the way and now he'd been taken care of. It must have been a deal. Taylor must have offered it to Lazar. They were rushing him straight to a date with the hangman's noose.

178

Withers and Davies took Manny to Commercial Street police station in the car. There, in the same bare, green-painted room where Davies had once tried to reassure Leah about the fate of her brothers, Superintendent Alan Withers made it official: "Emanuel Goodman, I am arresting you for the murders of Davey Vanetti and Jack Gardner. I must warn you that anything you say will be taken down and may be used in evidence against you."

Manny calmed down enough to know he needed legal representation. He also understood the situation. Lazar and Sherman had somehow killed Vanetti and Gardner . . . he didn't know exactly how but he was sure they were responsible . . . they must have gotten the key to the flat from Leah, goddamn her . . . Anyway, Lazar had the key to the shop. They'd taken the chair leg and a cuff link. And the whole deal had been approved by Taylor. Which was why Withers was in it . . . he was Taylor's man, his control, at the Yard . . .

The solicitor questioned Manny about his alibi. Manny went over the previous evening in detail. The solicitor checked. Sherman's shop had not been broken into. The police had never called Lazar's home. Sherman had spent the evening with Lazar and Katya. Leah had stayed at home with Manny. He'd gone out around eight thirty without telling her where. (As vicious as he'd been to her, she still was barely able to say it.) She waited until nine thirty and had then gone to bed, falling asleep before he returned. The solicitor's one consolation as he undertook Manny's defense was that a wife could not be forced to testify against her husband. But Manny had no defense except his own testimony. The chair leg and cuff link — along with the feud that had existed between him and Vanetti — were damning evidence. Even the solicitor didn't believe in his client's innocence.

Davies went off duty at midday. Withers had already returned to Scotland Yard, and Manny was in a cell, waiting for a hearing in the magistrates court the following morning. The rain had stopped and Davies walked slowly along Wentworth Street, looking at the stalls, chatting to vendors he knew. Manny's arrest was already public knowledge. All the street traders were talking about it, asking him questions. Yes, he nodded. It was true. We've got him . . . the evidence is overwhelming.

But was it? he asked himself. Didn't it all seem a bit too neat? Leaving the chair leg and cuff link like that? The prospect of Manny getting it didn't faze Davies at all. Even if it was for something he hadn't done. He'd committed enough horrors and never been brought to book. If he hadn't killed Vanetti and Gardner, though, whoever had done it was still out on the loose . . . out of control . . . ? That at once bothered and interested him . . .

Davies walked to Booth Street, studied the closed greengrocer's shop and wondered when it would open again. Who'd run it with Manny gone? Lazar? Strange how all of Manny's people had given stories that contradicted their governor's version. They'd all denied Manny's story. And wasn't it convenient the way Harry Sherman had spent the evening with Katya and Lazar . . .

Before he realized what he was doing Davies found himself climbing the stairs to Manny's flat for the second time that day. He was curious about Leah. When her two brothers had been arrested she'd followed them to Commercial Street police station, crying hysterically. Now her husband had been arrested, charged with the most serious offense possible, and she'd scarcely shown interest. Davies knocked on the door, waited.

Leah was dressed in a long-sleeved blouse and skirt when she answered. When she saw who it was, she stepped back in shock.

"May I come in?"

"Oh . . . well, what do you want . . . ?"

"I just got off duty and was walking around. My feet . . . they just kind of brought me up here."

"You'd better come inside." She led him through to the flat's living room. "What happened with Manny?"

"I was wondering if you'd ask."

She said nothing.

He watched her closely as he said, "Your husband's been charged with murder and locked up. Committal proceedings

180

are tomorrow. Old Bailey within two months."

Leah digested the information, tried not to show her feelings, which, God help her, were still mixed. "Would you like a cup of tea, Inspector Davies?"

"Inspector Davies? I thought we were on a first-name basis."

"That was a long time ago—"

"It was also a long time ago when you last made me a cup of tea. As I recall, I never got the chance to drink it." He smiled at her and thought he saw the faintest hint of a reciprocal smile on Leah's face.

"One sugar, wasn't it?"

"One sugar." He sat down, made himself comfortable while he listened to the sound of Leah moving around the kitchen. If he closed his eyes he could believe he was back in the room in Brick Lane, next to Shaffzics steam baths. Those few times he had been out with Leah, Davies had grown fond of her, he had been attracted to her, had wanted to see even more of her. He'd been careful not to push, though, figuring she'd been through so much, the last thing she could handle at that time was a man like him in her life. Now he wished he had pushed, had involved himself. Well, it might not be too late . . .

Leah brought in two cups of tea and a plate of biscuits. Davies asked after her family. She told him that Lazar had just become a father and that Shmuel was married and owned a furniture shop on Stamford Hill.

"Too bad about that boxer who got killed," Davies said. "That must have shaken up Shmuel."

"I haven't seen Shmuel for a long time," Leah said quietly. "Lazar told me he was very upset, though. In spite of his size, and his reputation in the ring, Shmuel's a very gentle man, let me tell you . . ."

Trying to lighten the atmosphere, Davies added, "So you're an aunt now."

"That's right." Leah raised the cup of hot tea to her lips. She was glad that Davies had come back to the flat. He'd stuck up for her that morning when Manny had nearly hit her again. He was a decent man, at least he cared . . .

"When you were over at Lazar's last night, was that the

first time you'd seen your nephew?"

"Yes," Leah said without thinking.

The moment the words were out of her mouth the blood drained from her face, her hands shook and the cup of tea dropped to the floor, splashing over Davies' trousers.

Davies watched her, certain now of his earlier speculations . . . For the first time in his miserable life Manny Goodman was telling the truth . . . and no one was going to believe him.

Leah knelt down, started to pick up the broken china. Davies got down on his knees to help her, and as her sleeves hiked up he got a good look at the beginning of the ugly bruises inflicted by the "innocent" Manny Goodman . . . he was neither innocent nor naive.

Davies understood how London worked – the relationship between forces on opposite sides of the law – and accepted it as long as other people didn't get hurt. Now an innocent man was going to be hanged, literal justice was being twisted and Davies knew that he'd do nothing about it. Manny Goodman deserved to swing, if only for the hell he'd put Leah through. It wasn't legal, but it was right.

"I'm not a very good liar, am I?" Leah said quietly, breaking into his thoughts.

"Not many people are." Davies said it as a compliment.

"Are you going to . . . do anything—?"

"Yes. I'm going to finish this cup of tea. It was worth waiting for."

CHAPTER ELEVEN

Four weeks after Manny's arrest Joey Taylor called Lazar to invite him to the house in The Bishop's Avenue. Lazar made the now familiar journey immediately, trying hard to keep down his excitement.

There was a new respect in the butler's manner when he showed Lazar through to Taylor's study, as if even he understood that a change of command had taken or was taking place. The white-haired man who'd been Manny's lackey — deserving nothing more than a courteous inclination of the head — was now "the governor of the firm."

"Congratulations, well done, Whitey," Taylor greeted him. "And my associate in the C.I.D. is well satisfied. London is rid of two despicable characters. Vanetti's under the earth, where he belongs. Goodman's on his way to join him . . . But enough of the past. Let's hear your plans for the future."

"I'm going to reopen Pearl's," Lazar replied after a pause. "The other two spielers — the ones that were burned out — I'll forget about. I think I'm better off out of the East End. Let someone else have it."

"Will you be able to survive on just one spieler? What about the women? The houses? Goodman's receiving business?"

"I threw out the women the day after the spielers were attacked and I don't want them back . . . I don't want any part of that. The same goes for receiving." He saw Taylor nod his approval. "As for the houses themselves, they belong to my sister."

"I understand. And she ought to be a grateful widow, from what I hear. A brotherly gesture."

Lazar almost smiled at the irony of the comment. He could have used the money those houses would have realized on the market. After Manny's arrest Lazar had gone over his estate, had had a solicitor work on preparing the transfer of the house titles from Manny to Leah, sure that she would sell them and turn over the proceeds to him. He'd been shocked when she'd refused. And even more so when he found out who had advised her not to sell. True-blue Ivor Davies. The news that his sister had taken up with Davies again hardly pleased Lazar. He'd assumed that with Manny gone Leah would return to the family, find a man who was worthy of her, marry and settle down properly. Still, thinking further on it, it might just work out . . . Leah's welfare was more important to him than the houses, the money they might bring. Davies *had* been good to her during their early days in London. Maybe he could provide the support she so badly needed now . . . even if he were part of the opposition. Well, that too could be a plus . . . at least Leah would have total respectability . . . a complete change from Manny . . .

As though reading Lazar's thoughts, Taylor asked, "Did my friend's decision to involve Inspector Davies from Commercial Street cure the problem you mentioned?"

Lazar looked up sharply, shrugged noncommittally.

"There's only one thing better than having old Bill as a friend . . . and that's to have him as a relative."

His solicitor visited Manny in Pentonville Prison twice a week to keep his client briefed on the latest developments in the case. He'd been to see everyone Manny claimed could give him an alibi. They'd all stuck to the stories they'd told the police. Even Leah. The slip she'd made with Ivor Davies was not repeated. If the solicitor had been as understanding and sympathetic as Davies had been, perhaps Leah would have made a mistake. He was not. He was overbearing. He tried to browbeat her into changing her story about that Saturday evening, and so he failed.

Manny told his solicitor, "I'll tell you one thing . . . they aren't going to hang me. I'm going to come back, I'm going

184

to get Lazar, and Sherman, and Leah . . . everyone who framed me . . ."

The solicitor listened, nodded. His client was obviously cracking. What harm to indulge him . . . ?

A family dinner party at Lazar's and Katya's. Shmuel and Lottie, Leah and Davies were there too. No ulterior motives. This time.

Around eleven, when the evening finished, Davies pulled Lazar aside. "Whitey . . . is that the name you prefer now?"

"You can call me Lazar."

"I think it's about time you and I had a talk." Davies had been thinking about it the whole evening. And before. And it erupted in an unstoppable torrent.

"I want you to know that I know the real story about Manny. Nobody said anything, didn't have to. Manny may have been a lot of things, all of them bad, but he was never stupid enough to leave all those clues lying around. It's working out as planned. My very educated guess is that you came to an agreement with Joey Taylor, you took care of Vanetti and set Manny up for it. Your payoff is Manny's firm. Don't bother to deny anything, just listen. You're smarter than Manny, you've proved that. I don't care about spielers. I don't care about drinking clubs. Just remember our little chat a while ago . . . You want to get to the top, fine. Get there by being clever, by keeping people sweet, not by causing trouble."

"Is that official advice?"

Davies shook his head. "The only official advice I'm giving you is to stay out of the East End . . . For Leah's sake . . . and your own . . ."

"I'm not in the East End anymore. I've let those two spielers go. Pearl's is reopening soon, and that's all I have planned. When I do move, it'll be to the West End, not the East End."

"Glad to hear it." And he was, for more than the reasons he'd given Lazar.

"Just make sure you don't get a transfer to the West End,"

Lazar joked and held out his right hand. Davies took it, and his grip made Lazar wince.

Lazar took his mind off Manny's trial by preparing to reopen Pearl's in Dalston Junction. The builders had finished redecorating. Plush paper had replaced the cheaply painted walls. The floor had been stripped and varnished to a high gloss. New card tables were in evidence. Lazar was taking over and he wanted everyone to know it. Spielers had never been known for their decor. He wanted the new Pearl's to be the first. It would be good practice, valuable experience for when he was strong enough to move those few important miles into the West End of London.

Before Manny's trial at the Old Bailey, Lazar's only previous appearance in a court had been at Old Street when he and Shmuel had been accused of assaulting a police officer. The difference between the lowly magistrates court and the bustling but solemn splendor of the Old Bailey was staggering. Lazar found it hard to believe that both courts could be a part of the same judicial system. Bewigged barristers thronged the corridors, robes flying behind them as they moved imperiously from one appointment to another. Police officers were everywhere.

The prospect of Manny Goodman being sentenced had drawn crowds. The judge was a slight man in his late sixties, dwarfed by his red robe and long white wig. Above pale blue eyes bushy brows stood out.

It was not the judge who spoke now, though. It was the clerk of the court. "Prisoner at the bar, have you anything to say before sentence is passed?"

Manny said no. Courage? Fear? Lazar wasn't sure.

The judge reached for something in front of him. A gasp erupted from the spectators in the public gallery as the judge ceremoniously placed the black cap, signifying the death sentence, on the back of his head.

"It is the sentence of this court . . . a place of execution . . . and may the Lord have mercy on your soul."

Manny Goodman, though white-faced, was still, all agreed,

186

remarkably composed. He said nothing, kept his eyes firmly ahead. Could it be that the "miserable little spiv's" quality had been so underrated? Or was he merely numb, drained of all feeling and emotion . . . ?

At the moment it seemed almost idle, irrelevant, speculation. It would prove to be something of considerably more significance – especially for those who had arranged this final moment.

CHAPTER TWELVE

Lazar could not sleep that night. Katya was in the nursery. The baby was still crying, lying on his back, arms and legs waving. She picked him up, cradled him in her arms, spoke softly until he was quiet, then went back to the bedroom.

Lazar was sitting on the edge of the bed, bending down to tie his shoelaces. "Where are you going?"

"For a walk."

"It's two o'clock in the morning, for God's sake."

"I need some fresh air." He looked out of the window. Light rain flickered past the gas lamp down the street.

"Take a coat," she whispered.

"I will." He kissed her, went downstairs and let himself out of the house.

The light rain, the coolness of the night air calmed him only a little. He was still impressed – chilled – by Manny's apparent calm after sentence had been passed . . . He was surprised to find himself at Dalston Junction. Checking his watch under a streetlight, he saw it was just after two forty. Pearl's would still be open. He'd go there for a cup of tea, a talk with Goris before he closed up for the night. Afterward he'd get a taxi home from the cab rank opposite the railway station.

He picked his way between the puddles in the narrow alleyway that led to the spieler. Two men came out of the club, recognized him and nodded a greeting. "Have a good evening?" he asked. They said they'd lost a hundred pounds between them. They'd be back, though, because Pearl's was the classiest spieler in London.

Lazar felt a little better as he entered the club. It was almost deserted. The woman who ran the tea bar was sweeping the floor. Goris, in suit and tie as always, was standing by the only rummy game that was still in progress. When he saw Lazar he walked over.

"You're soaking, hold on, I'll get you a towel."

"Never mind . . . Been busy tonight?"

"Early on. I must have passed out three-or-four-dozen packs of cards." Goris pulled another half-dozen packs from the pockets of his jacket, threw them on the counter. The bottom of his jacket was baggy, shapeless.

"Who was in?"

"Harry Sherman came by for an hour or so around midnight. Lost quite a bit of money."

Sherman? Lazar was surprised. Harry Sherman couldn't sleep either.

Lazar picked up one of the decks of cards, broke the seal and took a cup of tea to an empty table. From the counter, Goris watched as Lazar started to play solitaire, setting out the cards, laying black on red, red on black, building up his suits. He played six games before Goris announced that the last players had left and he might as well close up for the night. He handed Lazar a pile of money, large white five-pound notes bundled together unceremoniously with green one-pound notes and orange ten-shilling ones. Lazar took it, peeled off a fiver and passed it to Goris. "Buy yourself another suit."

Goris smiled. How different from Manny . . .

"I'll lock up."

"Okay." Goris went behind the bar, found his raincoat and was about to leave when two men entered the club. When Lazar recognized them, he relaxed.

"Just looking around," Joey Taylor told him. He wore a hand-tailored overcoat and a bowler hat. A rolled umbrella dangled from the crook of his arm. Behind him was the heavier figure of Superintendent Alan Withers, protected more sensibly from the bad weather by a trilby hat and a tan belted raincoat.

"Would you gents like a fresh pot of tea?" Goris asked.

Taylor shook his head. "You can go on home, Goris. We've

got business with your guv'nor.''

Taylor and Withers pulled up chairs to the table where Lazar was playing solitaire. Withers studied the cards. "Red ten goes on the black jack. Then you can move the black-nine column over. Gives you space for the king.''

"I already saw, thanks." Lazar pulled out the money Goris had given him. Taylor waved at it.

"Since when do I have to visit spielers to collect? Still . . . it's nice to see you're doing so well.''

Lazar replaced the money in his pocket. "You were just in the neighborhood, is that it?"

Taylor bestowed a warm smile. "You could put it that way.''

Lazar noticed that Withers was searching for something in his jacket pocket. To his surprise the superintendent pulled out a photograph, dropped it casually onto the table to cover some of the cards. It was a postcard-sized picture. A group shot, men and women, children in swimming trunks, all posing for a summer snapshot on a beach somewhere. Withers was at the left of the group, trousers rolled up above his bare feet as though he'd been wading in the sea.

"Recognize anyone?" Taylor asked.

"Only the superintendent.''

"It was lowly chief inspector in those days," Withers said. "That picture was taken ten years ago. What about him?" He pointed a stubby finger to the other side of the group, indicating a powerful youngster in swimming trunks. His curly blond hair was awry, a posed grin for the camera was fixed on his face.

"Should I?"

"That's my nephew," Withers said proudly. "My sister's only boy." He pointed to his sister who stood behind the blond-haired youngster. "She thinks the world of him . . . so do I.''

Lazar looked from Withers to Taylor. What was this all about? What concern of his was Withers' family?

"Remember me telling you favors sometimes have to be paid back?" Taylor asked quietly. Lazar nodded. "We've done you quite a few. Your own firm. Got your sister out

190

from under a little sadist . . . I think the time's come to call in some of those favors."

"I'll pay you back, you know that . . . but what's it got to do with the superintendent's nephew."

"I didn't tell you his name," Withers said. "My nephew's name is Billy."

"Billy?"

"You know him better as Billy Harris. Bomber Billy Harris."

And now it all became too clear. "The one who's fighting . . . against my brother next week?"

"Not quite," Withers said with an ice-cold smile. "He's the one who's going to beat your brother next week. My nephew Billy's going to win the Southern Area heavyweight championship. Because if he doesn't, you're not going to be in business for very much longer. You're not even going to be breathing. And add in your precious sister *and* big brother."

Lazar got home at about six o'clock. He made tea, took a cup to Katya in bed and told her what had happened . . . How could he possibly persuade Shmuel to throw a fight? Shmuel's honesty, his pride would never allow him to do such a thing. And Lazar knew he would be damned in his brother's eyes for even suggesting it. Yet he had to, for *all* their sakes. Withers had made it clear that it wasn't only his neck that would be on the chopping block.

"You'll just have to tell Shmuel what the situation is—"

"And tell him what I've done?"

"Give him some other reason then. You'll think of something." She hoped.

Lazar was trying. What *could* he tell Shmuel? That he'd been threatened? That if Shmuel won, Lazar's life would be in danger? A top governor stood to make a lot of money on Harris winning the fight and wanted to make sure that nothing went wrong? The best he could do was tell Shmuel a limited version of the truth . . . he was repaying a huge debt. When Shmuel saw how much it meant to him . . .

He went to the door and Katya called after him, wanting to know where he was going. "To Stamford Hill. Shmuel runs this time of the morning. I'll catch him there." . . .

At Stamford Hill lights showed in the flat above the furniture shop, and Lazar guessed Shmuel was already running. He began to drive slowly toward Tottenham, looking for the heavy figure of his brother, boots pounding the concrete as he put in his morning quota of exercise. He passed Seven Sisters Road and still no sign. To Bruce Grove. And there, in the misty distance that hemmed in Tottenham High Road, he saw Shmuel, arms and legs pumping like pistons as he covered the ground in swift, sure strides.

Lazar knew where his brother turned around to begin the return run to Stamford Hill. He pushed down on the accelerator, passed Shmuel who was too involved in running to notice the car, and swung around in a wide U-turn to stop by a public house on the corner of a narrow lane. He switched off the engine and waited for the distant figure of Shmuel to come closer.

He looked through the side window at the narrow lane, and at the huge, blue-painted structure that towered majestically behind it. Football, he thought. The only similarity between the country he'd left and England – they had the same national sport. The West Stand of Tottenham Hotspur's ground rose like an ocean-going liner to dwarf the rows of terraced houses and shops that were adjacent to it. Lazar had been there a few times to see the games. With Manny, who had been a regular supporter.

The figure of Shmuel came closer. Lazar flicked his headlights on and off to signal. Shmuel reached the car, leaned down by the open window.

"What are you doing here?" Rain poured off his face, dripped from his chin.

"You want a ride back?"

"I'm in training, I can't ride."

"Ride for once, I want to talk to you."

Shmuel sensed the urgency in his brother's voice and climbed in. Lazar took his time starting the engine. "You figure you'll beat Billy Harris?"

Shmuel nodded, gulping to catch his breath. "I think so.

192

Kosky thinks so. And the newspapers think so. Is that why you got up so early, to ask me that?''

Lazar pulled away from the curb, turned on the windshield wipers. "Shmuel . . . I need a favor."

"What . . . ?''

Lazar took a deep breath and stared straight ahead. All right, say it . . . "Would you lose that fight for me?''

"What did you say?"

"I've got a debt to repay. The only way I can do it is by you losing to Bomber Billy Harris—"

"You're crazy . . ." Shmuel turned in the seat and, for a moment, Lazar thought his brother was going to hit him. "You're crazy even to think such a thing—"

"Shmuel . . . you'll get another chance. This one fight, that's all I'm asking—"

"I *won't* get another chance. You know what I promised. If I lose that's the end of it. I promised Lottie . . . nothing would make me go back on my word. Damn it – stop the car, I'm getting *out*."

Lazar saw Shmuel clutch the door handle and pressed down harder on the accelerator. "You're not getting out, you're staying in this car at least until I've finished my say—"

"As far as I'm concerned you have finished. My God, what sort of mess have you got yourself into this time? I thought you were . . . free of everything now. Free of Manny—"

"There are other people besides Manny."

"Like the man with the house big enough for—"

"That's exactly who I mean."

"What favor did he do you this time? Did he tell you that whatever Manny owned, whatever little racket he ran, was yours? Did he have to give his permission for you to move in, to take over the spieler in Dalston?"

"He gave me his . . . protection—"

"Protection from what . . . from whom? From himself?"

"That's it, I'm afraid." Lazar began to slow down as the car approached the crest of Stamford Hill.

"Lazar . . ." Shmuel waited until the car had come to a complete stop before continuing. "I've paid you back for

193

waiting in Maastricht. I've paid you back more than once. I'm all *square* with you."

"All right, you've paid me back . . . Now I'm asking you to do me a *favor*. Not out of gratitude but because you're my brother—"

"I can't, and you know it. I suggest you pray Billy Harris beats me fair and square. Because that's the only way he's going to win the Southern Area championship." He slammed the car door and ran across the road to the flat.

Sherman listened to Lazar's report of the late-night meeting with Taylor and Withers. He felt what Lazar felt . . . if they came down on Lazar, they'd come down on him too. Another firm trying to take you over could be fought off . . . muscle against muscle. But Joey Taylor and his control from the C.I.D. could not be fought off. They were, after all, the law of the land.

Shmuel *had* to lose that fight, no matter what . . . "Kosky," Sherman said. "Go see him, he's running Shmuel. And he knows he isn't going to make much more out of him. Maybe he'll be interested in a few bob."

Sherman was right. Hurting financially by the loss of income he'd anticipated from managing Shmuel to a long and successful career, Kosky was willing to listen. He could make certain Shmuel lost, but he wanted a thousand pounds. *Before* the fight.

Lazar gasped. "That's robbery—"

"Stealing a championship isn't?"

CHAPTER THIRTEEN

Shmuel could hear his own heart pounding inside his chest as the minutes ticked away with agonizing slowness toward the regional championship fight with Bomber Billy Harris.

Was Harris nervous too as he sat in his dressing room, having his hands taped, his gloves tied? Or would he be at ease with the knowledge that he was going to win? That a business arrangement had been worked out? . . .

"How do the hands feel?" Steve Josephson asked.

Shmuel flexed his hands, banged the gloves together. They felt fine.

"Okay, you know exactly what you've got to do." Kosky appeared in front of him, joining Josephson. "Bomber's big gun is that right hook. Stay away from it. He's going to try to sucker you inside by showing his belly. Don't go for it. You couldn't hurt his stomach with a pickax. Just box him and wait for your chance."

"Don't worry about me," Shmuel told Kosky. He had his own fight plan all worked out. If Harris was certain that victory had been bought, the last thing he'd expect would be an all-out assault in the opening minute. Shmuel was going after him from the bell . . . and he hoped to God he was doing the right thing. This was the National Sporting Club, the Southern Area heavyweight championship. It wasn't the baths. Here you didn't get a second chance. Most important, Lottie was out there. With her own . . . *their* own secret. Only two days earlier she'd learned she was pregnant. Shmuel was glad he'd decided not to tell her about Lazar's proposition. God knew how that would have affected her. Just as losing tonight would affect her. He *had* to win . . . and afterward, when he held the Southern Area heavyweight title, they'd tell Lottie's news too . . .

A knocking sounded on the dressing-room door. Ivor Davies poked his head around and asked if he could come in. "Come in, come in," Shmuel bellowed, glad to see the inspector. "Come in and arrest all these butterflies trespassing in my stomach."

Davies grinned. "What round are you going to knock Harris out, champ?"

"Champ? What are you . . . a fortune-teller?"

"All *good* cops can tell a fortune." Especially ones like himself . . . with their eye on the future's main chance . . .

"How's Lottie?"

"Worrying about you, of course. So is Leah."

"And Lazar?"

"He's sitting with us. With his pal Sherman."

"Are they worried too?"

Davies was intrigued by the question. "I guess so. Why?"

"Nothing," Shmuel said. He looked at Josephson. "How much longer?"

"Next bout."

"I'd better get back," Davies said. "I'd hate to miss a first-minute knockout because I wasn't in my seat." He left the dressing room and waited for the round to end before making his way back to his seat. He passed a man who looked familiar. It wasn't until he sat down that he realized it was Superintendent Withers.

"How's Shmuel?" Lottie whispered.

"Raring to go."

She closed her eyes and started to pray softly. If there was truly a God He'd hear her prayers. Shmuel would win. There would be one less fight for him on the road to the championship. One less chance of him being hurt.

Along the row, in a seat on the aisle, Lazar stood up. He muttered something to Sherman in the next seat and then walked toward the dressing room.

At the dressing room door Lazar knocked and entered. When Shmuel saw who the visitor was, he waved Kosky and

Josephson away. He knew why Lazar was there. A final effort to make him change his mind. Shmuel did not want Josephson or Kosky to hear, he wanted no one to know about his brother's shameful request.

"I'm asking you for a final time," Lazar said quietly. "For me. For *everyone*."

"Lazar, I'm going to put Bomber Billy Harris away. For my sake and my wife's sake and—" He cut himself off before mentioning their yet-to-be-born child. That news would come later.

Lazar gave him a last look, then as he turned around to leave he caught Kosky's eye. Lazar waited outside the dressing room. Moments later, Kosky came out.

"I'm leaving it for one round," Kosky said. "And hoping he walks straight into one of Harris' right hooks. If he's still on his feet after one, I'll slip him the bottle."

"What if he knocks out Harris in the first round?"

"He won't. He'll box him for the first round. That's what I told him to do. I've got that thousand quid you gave me riding on Harris. I can't afford mistakes either."

As Lazar walked away he too spotted Withers. The superintendent didn't acknowledge his presence.

"What happened?" Sherman asked when Lazar returned to his seat.

Lazar concentrated on the figures in the ring, ignoring Sherman. But before Lazar realized what was happening the master of ceremonies was announcing the main event of the evening . . . the Southern Area heavyweight championship contest between Bomber Billy Harris and Sammy Brooks. Lazar looked up through the ropes, tried to get his brother's attention, see into his mind. Shmuel, looking fitter than Lazar had ever seen him, looked down just once. His eyes focused on Lottie, and he smiled. When he saw his brother gazing up, he looked away.

From the opening bell Shmuel charged after the shorter Harris, peppered his face with stinging jabs. Harris tried to entice Shmuel in close. Shmuel feinted to do so, then as Harris waited to unleash the right hook Shmuel danced aside, let loose a combination of punches that had Withers' nephew

197

rocking back into the ropes. One savage right to the body blasted the wind right out of him; his mouthpiece flew across the ring. Harris reeled around, saving himself from further punishment only by grabbing hold of Shmuel's arms and hanging on.

Lazar felt ripped apart. He knew how much this fight meant to Shmuel. And to him *and* his family. But for a moment at least Shmuel's happiness was more important than any threat to any of them.

By the end of the first round Harris' holding tactics had run out of steam. Bleeding from the mouth and nose, and badly cut above one eye, he'd been warned by the referee for holding. His sole aim now was survival. He couldn't understand what had happened. The big ox beating the hell out of him was supposed to have been paid off. What kind of stupid game was he playing? Making it look good? So good that he'd even win it in the second round if he didn't lay off?

Lottie, who'd watched only in spasms, didn't feel well and wished she hadn't come to the fight. She'd agreed to come only because she understood how much Shmuel needed her. But she hurt. Twinges of pain squeezed her lower abdomen. Sympathy pains, she thought, trying to ignore them, in sympathy with Shmuel the couple of times he'd been hit . . .

"Someone isn't going to be enjoying this," Sherman whispered to Lazar just before something was thrust into his hand by a man walking quickly along the aisle. It was a small square of paper. No words were printed on it. No words were necessary to explain the roughly scrawled drawing of a hangman's noose. He looked across the ring to where Withers sat. He couldn't see him. He turned his attention to Shmuel's corner. Kosky saw him, closed one eye in a quick wink. Josephson passed Shmuel the bottle of water. Shmuel took it, drank deeply, spat some out, swallowed the rest. Lazar closed his eyes, not able to watch.

The bell sounded. Shmuel quickly got up and advanced to the center of the ring. Harris was slower leaving his corner. He came out cautiously, touching a glove to his nose, his mouth, his eye. The glove came away dry. His seconds had done a good job and he felt more confident.

Shmuel seemed surprised when the vicious jab that had caused Harris so much trouble in the first round failed to connect. Harris ducked the blow easily and came up underneath it. Two sharp jabs made Shmuel blink and lift his guard. A right slammed into his solar plexus. Another right crashed through his guard and exploded against the side of his head. He reeled under the impact. His head felt light. His stomach churned. His legs were turning to rubber. How hard had Harris hit him? Not that hard, surely. There couldn't have been enough power in those punches to numb his senses like that.

As Shmuel thought about it Harris closed in, launched a wicked series of punches. Lefts and rights to Shmuel's face and body, while Harris always seemed half a second ahead of Shmuel's now clumsy efforts to counter. Another right detonated on the side of Shmuel's jaw. He dropped down onto one knee.

"One . . . two . . . three . . ."

Through a fog of noise and pain, Shmuel could barely hear the count. He looked through the ropes, saw Lottie with her eyes shut tight. Davies was yelling at him to get up and box. Leah, hands clenched, seemed to be praying. Lazar was on his feet, shouting.

Shmuel concentrated. "Stay down," his brother seemed to be screaming. Lazar wanted him to stay down. To give in. The hell with him. Sammy Brooks, the Brick Lane Lion, didn't stay down for anyone . . .

He got up unsteadily and walked straight into another right that sent him rolling back into the ropes. His legs threatened to buckle. Only his huge heart kept him going. He blinked, found the strength to lift his gloves — why did they feel like they were full of lead? — and advanced on Harris. He didn't notice the blows that rocked him. All Shmuel could see was his opponent's face, the thatch of blond hair. Moving . . . moving . . . always moving out of range of his own flailing fists. Even Harris seemed to be telling him to go down. He could see the man's mouth forming the words, could feel the savage punches that punctuated them.

From her ringside seat Lottie could take no more. She buried her face in her hands, sobbing hysterically as she heard the sounds of punches landing. It was a slaughter. Shmuel had lost and he refused to accept it. He'd force Harris to beat him to a pulp before he'd give in. God Almighty, why didn't the referee *stop* it?

The pain in her stomach intensified. And it wasn't a sympathy pain. Her sobbing became an anguished scream as she realized what it was. *She . . . was losing the baby . . .*

Shmuel felt the ropes at his back. If they weren't there he knew he would fall down. His legs had now gone completely. There was no longer the strength even to lift his arms in defense. His head rattled from side to side. His eyes were closing. His brain felt like it had been knocked loose inside his skull.

Another figure intervened, dived between the two boxers. Shmuel felt arms wrapped around him, a stool shoved roughly under his collapsing body. He was only vaguely aware of the referee calling out Harris' name as the winner, raising his arm in victory. Then Shmuel's head dropped onto his chest. He slid off the stool and passed out on the canvas.

Lazar ran to Shmuel's corner, hardly noticing that something was terribly wrong with Lottie. Leah was helping her. So were Davies and Sherman. Helping her out of the auditorium, calling for a doctor. With Josephson and Kosky, Lazar carried Shmuel from the ring through the noisy crowd to the dressing room. When he looked closely at Shmuel's face, he was sick. Both eyes were battered shut. The nose and lips were smashed. He was having trouble breathing.

"Shmuel, Shmuel, why didn't you stay down . . . ?"

No answer.

A doctor appeared. He gave Shmuel a cursory inspection and ordered him to the hospital. Lazar went outside with Kosky and Josephson, watching the stretcher being carried away.

"Why didn't he stay down?" Lazar kept repeating.

"Don't ask me," Kosky said. "He drank enough to knock out a bloody horse." He started to walk away and Lazar grabbed him by the arm, demanding to know where he was going. "To see my bookie."

"How much did you win?"

"Fifteen hundred quid. Harris was the six-to-four under-dog—"

"It goes to Shmuel."

"It what?"

"You heard me. All of it. Or I put out the story you drugged your boxer and bet against him."

Kosky shook his head slowly, partly in amazement, partly in admiration. "Jesus . . . you're something, aren't you?"

By the time he reached home after four o'clock the following morning, Lazar knew that fifteen hundred pounds wouldn't even begin to compensate Shmuel.

Lazar had stayed at the hospital until the doctors had ordered him to go home. There was nothing he could do. Nothing any of them could do to save the sight in Shmuel's left eye. It had been reduced to jelly by the repeated right hook of Bomber Billy Harris. There was no alternative but to remove it.

Katya was up when Lazar arrived home. Harry Sherman had been to the house earlier, had told her the result of the fight, the beating Shmuel had taken. She had waited up, knowing how Lazar would be feeling.

He told her that Shmuel and Lottie were in the same hospital. "Shmuel loses his eye, his wife loses her baby. At least I make sure it happens where they can both go to the same hospital—"

"Don't talk such rubbish. You couldn't know what would happen—"

"Of course I did. I know Shmuel. A knockout drop like Kosky gave him wouldn't put him out. He wanted that title so badly — wanted what it would mean to him and his family — he kept on going even when even he knew he should stop." He went into the living room, sat down heavily, stared at the fireplace.

Katya decided she would leave him alone. Nothing she

201

could say would relieve this moment for Lazar. He'd have to face it — and learn to live with it — by himself.

Five days passed before Lazar could get up the nerve to visit Shmuel, who had been transferred to Moorfields Eye Hospital for his operation.

Shmuel was in a private ward, paid for by the insurance he carried as a professional boxer. A white patch covered the empty eye socket, held in place by strips of plaster to his cheek and forehead. The swelling on his face had subsided. His right eye was almost fully open. Expecting an outburst, Lazar closed the door.

"You think I don't know what happened?" Shmuel said. "What was in that bottle Kosky gave me between rounds? How much did you pay him? I tried to stay up, Lazar, even when I knew I'd been drugged. One lucky punch, that was all I wanted. One punch . . . not to put Harris away. To put *you* away—"

"Shmuel . . . I didn't want this to happen, you at least can believe that."

"It happened though, didn't it? You could start it, but you weren't strong enough to stop it."

Lazar turned away, unable to face that one good eye.

"Oh, don't you worry, brother . . . my lips are sealed. You think I want people to know I've got a brother who would do this to me? I wouldn't even tell Lottie."

"How is she?" Lazar was grateful for an opening to change the subject.

"Why don't you go and ask her for yourself? She's staying with her parents in Palmers Green, you know the address. Try explaining to her that she lost our baby because things didn't quite work out the way you planned—"

"I didn't even know she was pregnant until—"

"We only found out two days before the fight. We were saving the news for a surprise. We were going to tell people after I'd won . . ."

Get it over with, Lazar told himself, and pulled out an envelope containing the fifteen hundred pounds he'd taken from Kosky. "This is for you . . . we had a collection—"

"We?"

"Harry Sherman, Kosky, all of us . . ."

Shmuel reached out to take the envelope. He gazed inside at the thick wad of notes. Then he drew back his arm and threw the bulky envelope at Lazar's face. Lazar made no attempt to duck as it hit him and fell to the floor.

"Keep it for yourself. You earned it . . . You know, I left you once because I thought I had to get away, from Manny and his influence. I was wrong . . . it was you I had to get away from." He turned over on his side and faced the wall.

Lazar sighed, left the private ward, closing the door quietly behind him.

He drove from Moorfields Eye Hospital to Booth Street. The greengrocer's shop was open, and he went upstairs to the flat. Leah let him in, sat with him in the living room while she waited for him to speak.

"I've just been to see Shmuel," he said finally.

"How is he?"

"You know . . . Leah, do you . . . do you believe that I never intended it to happen?"

"Intended what to happen?" She moved close to him, mystified by what he was trying to say.

"You don't know, do you?" He looked at her, marveling how little she had really changed since they had fled from Germany. Once she had told him that she was grown up, she could look after herself. Manny had put her through hell. And still she was his little sister, those large brown eyes defining her innocence. God . . . it didn't seem possible that she was married to a man who would soon hang . . . "I had Shmuel drugged, Leah . . . I couldn't let him win—"

"*Lazar.*" The brown eyes widened. "My God . . . *why?*"

He told her then, all about Joey Taylor, about Withers, about how they'd threatened not only him but the whole family . . .

"All because of what we did to Manny?" Leah whispered when he had finished. "These people, they've got you under their thumbs, haven't they? Whatever they want, you have to do or—"

"Until I'm strong enough to fight back, beat them at

their own game—"

"Lazar . . . Lazar. Manny thought that way. And these men . . . this Taylor and Withers . . . they didn't even have to soil their hands. They had you to do it for them—"

"That's the way it *works*, Leah . . ."

"Does Ivor know about these men?"

"I'll telephone him right now, he's at the station . . ."

Lazar watched Leah dial and wondered what involving Davies would solve. Shmuel had refused to tell anyone what his brother had done, he'd been too ashamed for him . . . Now Lazar was doing the job himself.

Davies arrived fifteen minutes later. He spoke to Leah and she left the flat, giving the two men privacy.

"You really had Shmuel drugged?" Davies asked.

"There was no other way."

"I suspected as much," Davies said. Lazar wondered why he was taking off his uniform jacket, laying it neatly across the back of the chair. "When he came out for that second round he was a totally different boxer. In the first round he was a holy terror. In the second" − Davies walked to where Lazar was sitting, lifted him up by the lapels of his jacket − "he was staggering around like a drunk."

Lazar saw the punch coming but did not try to duck it. Pain was welcome, a cheap expiation. Davies' fist hit him square in the mouth. Arms flailing for balance, he fell back onto the couch.

"You're quite an operator aren't you?" Davies said as he stood over Lazar. "I've some news for you . . . I'm going to marry your sister. After Manny gets what's coming to him Leah and I are going to wait a bit and then we're getting married."

"*Mazel tov.*"

"Just shut your mouth and listen," Davies told him. "Marrying the widow of an executed murderer might be rough on my career, but I can live with it. What I don't need is a brother-in-law with a bad reputation. For God's sake, be smart. Work with the law, not against it." He put his jacket on, buttoned it up and held out a hand to help Lazar to his feet.

"Clean your face up. Leah doesn't need to see it like that

when she comes back." He waited while Lazar went to the bathroom and held a damp cloth to his mouth. When the bleeding stopped he returned to the living room.

"Do you know how Joey Taylor got where he is today? Why he's respected? Because he used his brains. He kept everyone sweet. If you want to get out from under him, you'll do the same thing. You'll be smart. You won't chop off heads unless you absolutely have to. And when you do have to . . . you'll make sure you've got approval."

"Approval . . . from whom?"

For the first time since he had entered the flat, Davies smiled. "Who do you think, future brother-in-law?"

The next time Lazar spoke to Ivor Davies was midway through the following week. That very afternoon Manny's appeal had been turned down, the date of execution had been set.

In Pearl's that evening, the telephone rang. The woman behind the bar answered it and called Lazar over. He took the receiver, listened.

"You'd better find a comfortable chair to sit on," Davies said.

"Why?"

"Manny just escaped from Pentonville." Before Lazar could interrupt, Davies rattled off the facts . . . the escape had taken place an hour earlier, doors had been left unlocked, backs had been turned, a car had been waiting outside, two guards were being held for questioning.

"Who arranged it?" Lazar asked him.

"You'd better ask your pal Taylor. After you get Katya and your son out of the house."

"What about Leah?"

"I've already sent a man over there. She's on her way to a hotel."

Lazar slammed down the phone and rushed from the club, then went back and told Goris to come with him. When Goris heard that Manny had escaped, he turned pale.

"We're moving my wife and son," Lazar said.

"What about Harry Sherman?"

"I'll call him from the house." Lazar drove the short distance at frightening speed. While Goris stayed in the car as lookout, Lazar ran inside. Katya bundled the baby in a blanket, Lazar telephoned Sherman to warn him. And then he called Taylor. Taylor, remarkably calm, said he knew about the escape. His next words stunned Lazar.

"I wouldn't lose sleep over it if I were you."

"Lose sleep? I set the man up, now he's free. My house will be the first place he comes—"

"The first place he's going — and by my watch he should have been there half an hour ago — is a private airfield in Elstree, just north of here. By now he's probably on his way to France . . . perhaps it would be best if you came over here. Drop by in half an hour or so. I'll explain everything then."

Lazar replaced the receiver, baffled. Katya was equally mystified when he told her to stay in the house. She'd be safe, he said. He got in the car with Goris and drove to Hampstead Garden Suburb. The butler opened the front door as Lazar drew up.

"Mr Taylor is expecting you, sir."

"Thank you." Again Lazar left Goris in the car while he went into the study, where Taylor was waiting.

"It seems Manny Goodman had more brains than I gave him credit for," Taylor said. He motioned for Lazar to sit down. "Apparently he kept a dossier on every one of our transactions. It's in the hands of a lawyer — Lord, how I wish I knew which one — with the instruction that it be turned over to the press exactly one minute after he was hanged."

"Which transactions?"

"Every penny he ever paid me, every deal I ever worked on with him. Territories. That unpleasant business with Vanetti."

"Couldn't you have denied it? Your connections . . ."

Taylor shrugged. "Whether I denied it or not, I could never afford the scandal of the allegations. And neither could Mr. Withers."

Lazar nodded. "Where's Manny going?"

"Eventually to America. He'll wait in France until I furnish him with a new passport. Then with a new identity, money, whatever else he needs, he'll sail for America."

"What about when he decides to come back?"

"I said Manny was smart . . . he's been clever, he's evened it up with us this once. He knows enough not to push us further. If we can't stand scandal this time, we surely couldn't afford to give in to a second challenge. That would be worse than scandal . . . that would destroy our credibility – which is to say it would put us out of business. Obviously we'd have no option but to kill Manny if he ever comes back. He understands that."

Lazar shook his head, still in shock. "So you got him out of prison . . ."

"I paid for it," Taylor corrected him. "Paid heavily. There are two guards who will lose their jobs, will face prosecution. Compensation for that kind of sacrifice is expensive."

Lazar began to feel easier. He'd learned something too, he realized, as he stood up and prepared to leave. Manny had covered himself, taken out insurance . . . he would do the same thing.

At the door Lazar stopped and looked back at Taylor. He couldn't resist saying, "By the way, Mr. Taylor, my brother's recovering real nicely—"

"Your brother?"

"You remember . . . Sammy Brooks. He lost an eye in the fight with Superintendent Withers' nephew. He doesn't miss the eye at all." He swung the door closed and walked quickly to the car.

After he had dropped off Goris at Pearl's, Lazar sat in the car a while. So Manny was on his way to America. Saved from the hangman's noose because he'd had more sense than anyone had given him credit for. Sense enough, too, not to come back and stupidly push his luck, as Taylor had said.

Taylor . . . the big house on The Bishop's Avenue. Lazar no longer wanted just any big house. He wanted Joey Taylor's big house. He wanted Joey Taylor. And Withers. Lazar wanted him too.

Putting the car in gear, he drove slowly home. He'd do what Ivor Davies had told him. He'd take it easy. He'd keep people sweet. He'd wait . . . wait until he'd gotten enough

207

strength, become big enough to be able to take them on.

Until that time, he'd use them. He'd let them help him to become stronger than they were. And then, when the time was right, he'd chop their heads clean off.

1946

CHAPTER FOURTEEN

The moment he finished writing the check Lazar noticed the mistake. Every year it was the same. At least two weeks in January had to pass before he could remember to write in the proper year.

Crossing out "1945" he wrote in "1946" and initialed the correction, then slipped the check for one hundred pounds into an envelope that bore the name and address of his solicitor. He wondered what Shmuel would think when he eventually received the hundred pounds. It was by far the largest amount of money Lazar had ever sent to support Clapton Boys' Club, the youth organization his brother had formed during the war. Shmuel would simply believe that somewhere a philanthropist sufficiently appreciated his work with youngsters to go on funding the club.

The thought saddened Lazar. He had already donated four hundred pounds to the club, and still Shmuel did not have any idea where the money came from. The solicitor was too clever for that . . . he banked Lazar's check, waited for it to clear and then forwarded one of his own to Shmuel. Each time, Shmuel called the solicitor to thank him, and to ask the name of his benefactor. And each time, on Lazar's strict instructions, the solicitor refused to tell him. Lazar had little doubt that if his brother knew the source of the money he would refuse it.

Shmuel had opened the club as part of his own war effort. Rejected by the army to fight against the country of his birth – because he had only one eye – Shmuel had looked for other ways to serve. He had seen boys who had not been evacuated, whose fathers and older brothers were away in the army and had decided to adopt as many as he could. After persuading a local school to allow him to use the gymnasium in the evenings he had searched for volunteers and money. The volunteers — men who would supervise the youngsters, coach them in sports — had been easy. Money had been the difficult thing. At first Shmuel had used whatever he could spare from his own pocket to buy secondhand equipment he stored in the back of the shop. It was never enough, and he had turned to organizing charity drives. News of them had appeared in a local newspaper, alerting Lazar to what his brother was doing. Immediately, he had sent twenty-five pounds through the solicitor, following it at regular intervals with other sums.

Was it guilt money . . . blood money? Lazar stared at the envelope that bore the solicitor's name and address. Was it his way . . . and a very small way at that . . . of paying back Shmuel for the tragedy Lazar knew was his responsibility? Lazar well understood another reason why Shmuel was so involved with the youngsters . . . he and Lottie could not have children of their own. After her miscarriage during the Southern Area championships Lottie had been warned never to try again for children.

Lazar pushed the envelope away. Blood money or not, at least he'd been able to help his brother. During the war he'd opened another spieler . . . the least he could do was help Shmuel . . . even if he could never know the pleasure of Shmuel thanking him, or even speaking to him, acknowledging his existence. The last time he'd seen Shmuel had been at Leah's wedding to Ivor Davies, the week before war started. Shmuel had stood apart from his older brother, never even looking at him. And Lazar had been almost unable to take his gaze away from the patch that covered Shmuel's injury, made him look like a screen buccaneer . . .

Katya came into the living room. She saw the envelope and silently observed Lazar's way of trying to make it up to his brother. Not that it would ever work. Like Lazar, she felt that if Shmuel ever learned the source of the money he would have to reject it. But if giving helped salve Lazar's genuinely agonized conscience, it was worthwhile. She would watch him scour the newspaper for some mention of Shmuel's club, and she understood how he could take at least some small consolation in the knowledge that it was his interest, his money that helped to make possible the club's continuing existence . . .

"Lazar . . ." Katya said softly, reluctant to break into his reverie. ". . . the boys won't go to sleep until you say goodnight." She stood by his chair, held his hand as he put his arm around her waist, toyed with his fingers.

"I'll go up." He slipped the envelope into his jacket pocket, stood and walked toward the door. Halfway through, he turned around. "Do you think I'm doing the right thing?" He tapped the pocket which held the envelope.

"If you do . . ."

He nodded, then took the stairs two at a time. His two sons – Aron, now nine, and David, who had been born just before the war started – shared a room on the second floor. The third floor, where Leah and Shmuel had once lived, was empty. The boys were sitting up in bed, expectant expressions on their faces as they waited for their father. Aron looked like Shmuel as a boy, a heavy child with thick black hair and solemn brown eyes, while David had Katya's fair skin and auburn hair. Lazar knew that other parents, other fathers, might have favorites among their children. He had none. He loved each son as dearly as the other, taking real pleasure in them both.

"Are you going to work now?" Aron asked his father.

"Soon." Lazar sat on the edge of his older son's bed and wondered how he would have felt if all that was left to him was running a boys' club because he'd been denied the opportunity to have children of his own . . .

"Why do you work at night?" Aron pressed. "Why don't you work during the day like everyone else?"

How could he ever explain to his children what he did for a living? And once they were old enough to realize how he made his money, would they understand? "Not everyone works during the day."

"Only burglars work at night," Aron remarked with a child's solemn wisdom.

213

"Oh . . . where did you learn that?"

"At school."

"I see." Lazar looked from one boy to the other. "Your Uncle Ivor often works at night . . . and he's a policeman. Just because I work at night, do you think I'm a burglar?"

Aron shook his head in a decisive rebuttal, and Lazar glanced at his younger son. "What about you?"

"What's a bur- . . . burglar?"

While Aron tried to explain to his younger brother the meaning of the word, Lazar listened, and prayed a little that these two would not break away from each other when they grew up, as he and Shmuel had done. Brothers ought to remain close . . . a damn sight closer than anonymous donations to a boys' club. The only uncle Aron and David had was Ivor Davies. Even if he were now a detective-chief inspector, Davies could never compete with an uncle who had once been a contender for the heavyweight title . . . who might have gone on to win if his brother hadn't helped sabotage his chances so as to save his own neck. Jesus . . .

"Does Uncle Ivor ever catch any burglars?" David asked, once he thought he understood the word.

Lazar never got the opportunity to answer because his older son moved in with, "Of course not, stupid. Uncle Ivor's too important. He catches spies, not just burglars. And after he catches them he *hangs* them."

Lazar could barely control the shudder he felt at the word. He could still close his eyes and bring to mind the picture of the judge's face, the black cap at the back of the head; hear those awesome words . . . "There aren't any spies left for Uncle Ivor to catch," he pointed out, grateful that neither of his sons had noticed him flinch. "The war's over . . . so he's gone back to catching burglars."

The war had been good to Ivor Davies as well . . . Early on, Davies had transferred to Special Branch to work against Irish nationals who might be sympathetic to the Germans. In 1941 he'd been responsible for the arrest of an Irishman living in London who had acted as a conduit for Nazi spies; the man had been executed for treason. After D-Day, certain that

214

the war would end soon, Davies had forecast a tremendous rise in crime once the armies came home. Disregarding warnings from fellow Special Branch officers that he was leaving an elite force and hurting his career prospects, he'd transferred again . . . this time to the Criminal Investigation Department. Back in his bailiwick.

Lazar kissed each son in turn, tucked them in and quietly left the room. He stopped off in his own bedroom for a heavy winter coat and returned downstairs to where Katya waited. She gave him a lingering kiss, knowing he wouldn't be home until the early morning. It was the second Saturday of the month . . . the night he traditionally met with Joey Taylor, paid him for his protection.

From the house Lazar drove the short distance to Ruby's, the second spieler he had opened in 1943. When Katya and the two children had been evacuated to Reading, west of London, Lazar had stayed on in the city. He'd opened Ruby's when Allied troops had started to flood into London. The rummy games which had been the backbone of the peacetime spielers were replaced by faro, blackjack, dice games. Fortunes had been won and lost on the turn of a single card, the roll of dice. No one had cared about money . . . at any moment a bomb might drop on the building.

Two hours passed while he stayed at Ruby's, watching the action begin to build as the evening wore on. Nothing like it had been during the war. Those had been exciting times. The club membership swollen by men in American and Canadian uniforms, a lively action that lasted until dawn when the remaining gamblers would force themselves to leave. Peacetime meant belt-tightening. The days of easy money were gone.

By ten thirty he was at Pearl's in Dalston Junction, standing at the tea counter with Goris. While he listened to the club manager describe the evening's business in his garbled speech, Lazar marveled at how it seemed like just a couple of weeks ago that three men had walked in and Goris had rushed across to tell them that the club was for members only . . . and had been punched in the mouth with a razor.

215

That wouldn't happen again . . . Goris no longer worked alone. Each of the clubs had half a dozen men. Not that Lazar needed so many when he had Taylor's protection, but since the end of the war he had taken on men who had returned from the army and were looking for work. The strength of his operation had grown . . . and with it his confidence and ambition.

Harry Sherman came by just after eleven accompanied by two men in their late twenties whom Lazar had never seen before. For Sherman the war had been a heartbreaking tragedy. If the bald man had not been in Pearl's with Lazar that Wednesday night two years earlier, he too would have been killed in the V-2 explosion that had destroyed his house and killed his wife and children. Sherman had gone home from Pearl's that night to find his street blocked by ambulances and fire engines. When he'd fought his way through the crowd, all he could see was rubble. His own home and four adjoining houses had been demolished. A civil defense warden had tried to comfort him, saying the people inside could never have known what happened. Sherman had poked among the bricks, looking for . . . anything. He'd scraped the skin off his fingers as he dug feverishly in the rubble until at last he'd uncovered a hand. It was his wife's, wearing the diamond ring he'd given her on their engagement. Sherman had sat down on the bricks, crying unashamedly until the ambulance had taken him away as well.

No mother, no nurse could have taken better care of Sherman than Lazar did. With Katya and the two boys away in Reading, Lazar had moved Sherman into the house. He never let the bald man out of his sight. Even when he traveled to Reading to see his family he took Sherman along. The two men had lived together for almost a year, until Sherman felt well enough to find a flat of his own, to pick up the pieces of his life again. Often he embarrassed Lazar by saying he owed him his life . . . not once, but twice. Because had he not been in Pearl's, he would have been at home when the rocket hit; and without Lazar's friendship he surely would have committed suicide during those first months without his family.

Sherman now greeted Lazar, clasping him around the shoulders, hugging him, then introduced the two young men he had brought to the club. "Whitey . . . I'd like you to meet Johnny and Jimmy Peters, the two boys I told you about."

Lazar noticed for the first time that both men were identical. Each stood a little over six feet, broad-shouldered, muscular. They had curly brown hair, parted on the right side at exactly the same spot. Their light blue eyes and square, solid chins looked interchangeable. Even their choice of clothing was identical . . . dark blue suits with white shirts and wine-colored ties. The only difference Lazar could discern was a narrow white scar above Johnny Peters' left eye.

"Twins?" Lazar asked unnecessarily.

"I'm older by ten minutes," Johnny replied, grinning cockily. His voice held the faintest trace of a Belfast accent.

"How did you get the scar?"

"The war. Grenade."

"What about you?" Lazar asked Jimmy Peters. "Weren't you in it?"

Jimmy rolled up his right trouser leg. The calf was mutilated by a jagged, diagonal scar. "Same grenade. We were together at Normandy. Commandos."

Lazar's earlier thoughts about brothers remaining close came back to him. But this close was too much. "All I can offer you right now is work in the spielers . . . keeping an eye on things."

"Sounds fine," Johnny Peters said. He touched his hand respectfully to his forehead, then the twins walked away to stand by one of the tables, watching a game.

"Let's go see Joey Taylor," Lazar said to Sherman. "We don't want to keep an old man waiting up all night long."

Sherman nodded. Visiting Taylor had once been an almost awesome experience, being allowed into the presence of the man who controlled London's underworld with a rod of iron. Now it was a drudgery, almost like paying a call on a sick relative. Joey Taylor had aged greatly, never able to recover from the shock of having his only grandson – a nineteen-year-old boy – killed at Arnhem. Sometimes you were better off being at the bottom of the ladder, Sherman thought as he

217

sat with Lazar in the car on the way to Hampstead Garden Suburb. Then you had friends to help you through. Who did Taylor have? His colleagues at Scotland Yard? The men on the other side of the law that he controlled? He had no one . . .

"You like those two?" Sherman asked Lazar.

"The Peters twins? Where did you find them?" Sherman had told him when he'd asked if he could bring them to the club. But Lazar couldn't remember.

"I've known them for years. Moved over from Belfast in thirty-seven. Always up to things. Now they're back from the war and, you know . . . they looked me up, said they wanted work."

"Just two of them?"

"They've got another brother . . . much younger. He lives at home with his mother. Jimmy and Johnny are tough boys, though. They've got medals and decorations for a regiment."

Lazar became silent. Thinking about the Peters twins . . . numbers . . . turned him to arithmetic of another sort . . . and economics. He had twenty men on his payroll now. There was no way the two spielers and the black market could feed that kind of an army. He needed more revenue . . . room to expand. It was time for serious talk with Taylor.

The scar on Taylor's right cheek had virtually disappeared in the maze of wrinkled flesh that covered his face. He was still a dapper dresser — with a red velvet smoking jacket to cover his shirt — but his body was bent, his face sunken.

After offering his visitors a drink Taylor sat down behind his desk in the study and waited for Lazar to speak. From a briefcase he'd brought in from the car Lazar took out the accounts, then reached into his pocket for a sheaf of banknotes. With them came the letter to the lawyer. He tried to stuff it back, out of sight, but it fell to the floor.

"What's that?" Taylor asked as he took the money from Lazar and began to count.

"A personal letter."

"Let me see."

Lazar bent down to pick up the envelope from the floor, offered it to Taylor. "A lawyer?" Taylor remarked drily.

"You wouldn't be doing a Manny Goodman on me . . . ?"

"It's a check," Lazar said. "See for yourself." He unsealed the envelope, showed Taylor the check he had rewritten for two hundred pounds; this time he'd got the year right on the first try. "It goes to my brother's boys' club. Anonymously."

"Very noble . . . very noble indeed." Taylor studied the check for several seconds before he returned it to Lazar. "It's just that I wouldn't like to be blackmailed twice. One Manny Goodman was enough, thank you." He finished counting the money and a look of disappointment formed on his lined face. "It goes down every week, Whitey. Maybe you're paying too much to your brother and not enough to me."

"I'm giving you the percentage we agreed on. There are the books . . . see for yourself. Business is bad." Lazar wondered if Taylor had any idea of Manny's whereabouts. Friends Lazar had made among the Americans during the war had promised they would try to locate him, but it would be a virtually impossible task. The only photographs Lazar had to show were those from Leah's wedding. And what would he do if . . . by some miracle . . . Manny was found? Put out a contract on his former boss . . . his former brother-in-law? Or just forget about it . . . let bygones be bygones and hope that Manny was as realistic, and forgiving.

"You'd better see about improving your business," Taylor said. "Otherwise I might have to give my protection to someone who can better afford to pay for it.

"I need more territory," Lazar said bluntly. "If I make more, then you make more."

"Oh? What do you have in mind?"

"The West End."

"Where the real money is," Sherman cut in when he saw Lazar pause to reseal the envelope that contained Shmuel's check. "Right now we're earning pennies. We can't live on pennies . . . and neither can you."

Lazar put the envelope back in his pocket. "Mr. Taylor . . . the war's over and all the outfits are starting to reorganize. Everything's up for grabs, you know that. Is it better to have half a dozen fighting it out . . . or just one strong organization taking control? A strong one that is directly answerable to *you*?"

"Why should that one be yours? Why not one of the others?"

"Because they're all −" Lazar was going to say something about the others still being in a transition state, changed his mind, deciding to be more direct − "because I'm ready to move right now."

Taylor got up from behind the desk and started to walk around the study. He pulled back drapes, looked out onto the floodlit grounds. "I need time to think about this. Discuss it with Mr. Withers."

Withers. The name dug into Lazar's gut. Withers shared the blame for Shmuel's disfigurement. Withers and his nephew, Bomber Billy Harris. Lazar remembered with pleasure Harris' next fight, a bout against a heavyweight from Newcastle . . . one that Withers had not been able to fix. Harris had been knocked senseless in the third round, and Lazar had bought every newspaper he could put his hands on to observe the different versions of Harris' humiliation. Shmuel, he hoped, bought them too. Probably not, though . . . Harris wouldn't be the one he would blame . . . it hadn't been Harris who'd robbed him of the championship, and his eye. It had been his brother . . .

"This needs careful consideration," Taylor said.

"All right, Mr. Taylor. I'll wait to hear from you." Lazar motioned to Sherman that he was ready to leave."

"God, that man's gone bloody senile," Sherman grumbled as they drove away from the house. "He's so soft . . . indecisive."

Lazar nodded. Taylor should retire already. He no longer had any business controlling anything. Surely Lazar couldn't be the only one to see it? Or maybe he was . . . the others were still getting straight after the war. Lazar had been ready for a long time . . . he could see better what was going on . . . "How old is he?"

"Must be close to hitting seventy."

"What does it say in the Bible?" Lazar mused. "That part about a man's life span being three-score years and ten."

"Taylor's time is almost up."

"I know." Lazar made up his mind that he would be as decisive as Taylor had once been — as strong as the controller was now weak. He'd go out on his own, create a whole operation for himself. He didn't need men like Taylor anymore. He had an army of his own. And with it he didn't have to ask permission from anyone. Taylor could make his own choice whether he wanted to retire gracefully . . . or be pushed out. What the hell — he'd had his. Time to move over and retire in peace . . .

"Where are you going?" Sherman asked as Lazar braked to a sudden stop. The bald man pushed forward against the dashboard to prevent himself sliding out of the seat.

"I want to mail this letter." Lazar got out, checked the collection time on the mailbox and dropped in the envelope containing Shmuel's check. Thinking about the check made Lazar smile grimly. Taylor had been worried about him keeping records . . . storing insurance with a lawyer. The man had every right to be worried. But not because of blackmail.

He had a revolution on his hands.

Shmuel received a check from Lazar's lawyer five days later. The money from his mysterious benefactor could not have come at a better time. Because of the club's popularity the school facilities were hopelessly inadequate. He refused to turn potential members away, couldn't stand to disappoint them, so he had to find new premises for the hundred young-sters who belonged to the club. The money he had raised through charity drives was much less than what he needed.

Shmuel knew he could never drop the club. He found great pleasure in helping the youngsters, got as much out of it as they did. While they played soccer and cricket, boxed in leagues Shmuel had entered them in, he shared in their fulfillment. Lottie and the club were his reasons for living, and thank God she shared his pleasure. She was like a second mother to many of the boys . . . at least twice a week she would have a load of laundry cluttering up the flat above the furniture shop, washing and ironing to have their uniforms ready for the next game.

When Lottie returned from school that afternoon and

221

popped her head into the shop, Shmuel showed her the check for two hundred pounds. "Who said there were no angels?"

"Be grateful this one reads the newspaper," she said. "Have you called the solicitor yet to thank him?"

"As soon as I opened the letter. He told me I was welcome. And no . . . he wouldn't say who'd sent the money. But he did ask me to forward all details of the club to him, his client would like to know."

She took the check from Shmuel and told him she'd deposit it the next morning in the special account that had been opened for the club. "I'd better go upstairs and finish off ironing the football kit for this Saturday's game. Chris will be coming around soon to collect it."

'All right. Tell him to drop in here before he goes. I want to see him."

Chris Peters was one of Shmuel's special cases, an eighteen-year-old boy who lived with his widowed mother in Clapton. His father had died six years earlier from lung cancer and Chris had come under the influence of his two older brothers. At thirteen, Chris had spent six months in reform school for acting as a lookout while his brothers robbed a jewelry store. They had also been caught, but not yet having received their conscription papers they had traded prosecution and certain jail for volunteering for the army. Shmuel had met Chris when he'd come out of the reformatory. He'd worked with him at the club, had persuaded him to finish school and had then helped to find an apprenticeship for him at a local weekly newspaper. The training period was almost over, and Chris had shown enough determination and ability to indicate a promising career as a reporter.

Chris came by a half-hour later, went upstairs to collect the laundry Lottie had finished, then came into the shop. Shmuel was taking an order from a customer and the youngster waited off to the side; two shopping bags containing the clean clothes were at his feet. As well as playing on the team, Chris helped manage the club. He could type, which was a considerable bonus for Shmuel, who, having mastered spoken English, still found trouble with the written word. And he had made certain that the club received adequate editorial space in the newspaper. Shmuel had taken a particular pleasure in watching Chris blossom from an awkward, surly teenager with a chip on his shoulder to a responsible young adult.

The order taken and the customer departed, Shmuel walked over to Chris. "How did you get on today?"

"Magistrates court this morning. Two drunk and disorderlies and a traffic offense. We live in crime-ridden times." Chris' blue eyes sparkled as he spoke, echoing his irony. Shmuel laughed and said he should be glad, and Chris complained that he'd never be famous reporting a magistrate's lecture to a hungover drunk.

"How's your mother?"

Chris made a face, the blue eyes lost their laughter. "Not too good . . . my brothers got out of the army . . ."

"They're not living back at home, are they?"

"*No*. They've got a flat of their own, in Hackney."

"Are they working?"

"So they said." Chris couldn't look Shmuel in the face. He stared down at the bags of clean laundry at his feet. "They're working for your brother. At Pearl's."

"How did you find that out?"

"They were round the house last night. Johnny gave me this" − Chris fished in his trouser pocket − "said it was a souvenir from the war." He showed Shmuel a silver ring with a death's-head insignia. "Took it off a dead SS officer, Johnny said."

Shmuel could not help grimacing as he looked at the "memento." What a thing to give a younger brother. Suddenly he felt even closer to Chris Peters. He and the youngster had something in common . . . older brothers who'd chosen to go against the law . . . He hoped Chris never got taken in by his brothers the way he'd been by Lazar. "What did they say they were doing at Pearl's?"

"Nothing much. But they hinted they'd be in the money, real money. I think they were just exaggerating, so they could tap my mother for a few bob."

"Did she give them anything?"

"Are you kidding? She told them to leave and not to come back."

Shmuel could believe it. Chris' mother was a strong-willed woman, determined that her youngest son would not grow up to be a carbon copy of his brothers. She'd done a good job so far . . . with Shmuel's help. On reaching seventeen Chris' juvenile record had been expunged and he'd been given a fresh start. Shmuel was sure the kid was going to make it.

"Take your things home, then come on back this evening for a cup of tea with Lottie and me," Shmuel said. "We've got some things to decide."

"What about?"

"Our guardian angel dropped us some more money this morning. Two hundred pounds. We can start thinking about a proper clubhouse."

"That's great!" Chris' eyes brightened, then dulled as he showed the ring again to Shmuel. "What should I do with this?"

"Drop it in the collection plate. Maybe they can melt it down for scrap . . ." If Chris' brother Johnny was to be believed about taking the trophy from a dead SS officer, the silver in the ring had probably been stolen anyway, melted down from looted valuables and recast. Had it belonged to anyone he might have known? Shmuel couldn't help thinking. Been part of goblets like those he and Leah and Lazar had brought over from Germany . . . ?

He shook his head, wanting to clear away such thoughts. Cologne and the house in Koenigstrasse seemed so distant, so far removed from a furniture shop on Stamford Hill and a boys' club in Clapton . . . it almost seemed it might never have happened at all.

Ivor Davies and Leah lived in Ilford, on London's eastern edge, halfway to Southend and the sea. Every Sunday during the summer the main arterial road would be chock-full of traffic, buses and cars making the pilgrimage to the coast. In winter, though, the road was almost deserted, and Lazar enjoyed pushing the car up to fifty miles an hour, only slowing when Katya's anxious glances at the speedometer were emphasized with reminders that the two boys were in the back.

Lazar had not been to Ilford for a month, not since Leah and Davies had hosted a combined Christmas-Chanukah party. Despite his own ambivalent attitude toward religion, Lazar had not been able to keep down his curiosity at the blend. Leah had said that she and Davies saw no conflict in following their own beliefs. They complemented each other. And their four-year-old daughter, Adele, would learn about both religions and make her own choice when she was old enough to understand.

Outside a modest three-bedroom, semi-detached house Lazar brought the car to a gentle halt. The two boys spilled out of the back, ran eagerly toward the house. Katya followed while Lazar went to the trunk and removed a large cardboard box, struggling with its size. Ivor Davies appeared at the front door, wearing a bulky white Shetland sweater and gray flannel trousers. He patted the boys on the head, kissed Katya and came to Lazar's aid.

"What have you got in there?" Davies took the box from Lazar. All the years in London had failed to blunt Davies' musical Welsh accent.

"Sugar and spice and all things nice," Lazar said with a smile.

"Black-market sugar and spice? There's a law against that, you know."

"Do me a favor," Lazar said. "I don't stoop to stealing ration books. You should know me better than that."

"Oh . . . trading with your American friends again?"

"Nothing wrong with that, is there?"

"Only as long as your friends don't wind up in front of a court-martial, there isn't."

"I pay them enough for their risk."

"I bet you do." Since the end of the war, Davies had split his time between combating the ever-growing black market and trying to control the rise in crime that he had prophesied would come with the return of so many men from the armed forces. Most of the black marketeers dealt in stolen or forged ration books, coupons that could be used to obtain foods and articles in short supply. Lazar had proved himself to be much more imaginative, winning contracts among the massive American supply machinery.

Davies carried the carton easily into the house; Lazar slammed the trunk and followed. His eyes caught the *mezzuzah* on the door-frame and he smiled to himself, knowing that somewhere inside the house he'd also find a crucifix.

Katya was in the kitchen with the children, talking to Leah who was preparing dinner. Lazar called out a greeting and went into the living room, where Davies had placed the carton on the floor. He opened it and whistled at the two bottles of Scotch and the dozen cans of beef.

"American servicemen live better than British royalty," Lazar said, enjoying the expression on Davies' face.

"They sure do. I wonder if this constitutes trying to bribe a police officer."

"No bribe. I'm just following your advice . . . keeping people sweet. By the way . . ." Lazar added, ". . . you remember that raid at the docks a few weeks ago? The cognac?"

Davies nodded. A bonded warehouse had been broken into, hundreds of cases of imported cognac had been stolen . . . and most importantly, the night watchman had been beaten so brutally he was paralyzed. "What about it?"

"I heard someone's offering the stuff." He handed Davies a scrap of paper. "The information's there."

Davies looked at it quickly, stuffed the paper into his pants pocket. "Thanks . . . we'd like to get that one off the books."

"Now you can do me a favor."

"You in trouble?" Lazar had passed on plenty of tips, like the one about the bonded warehouse job. But he'd never come to him for help. There'd been no need. He was protected by Joey Taylor. And as far as Davies was concerned, he was carrying on an almost legitimate business with the spielers and his dealings with the Americans.

"I might be."

"How?"

"I've got too big for my britches. Or rather, my wallet."

"We'll talk about it in a minute," Davies said when he saw Leah enter the room with Katya. The sound of footsteps pounding up the stairs marked the children's passage to the spare room.

"Have you seen Shmuel and Lottie lately?" Lazar asked his sister.

"We were there the other night for dinner."

"How were they?"

"Fine. Shmuel was in heaven over the money. He'd only got the check a day earlier."

"I thought he'd be pleased." As he pictured his brother's pleasure at receiving the two hundred pounds, Lazar experienced the same good feeling he'd had watching Davies open the carton . . . "You didn't say anything, I hope."

Leah shook her head. "I wanted to . . . but I didn't."

"What does he plan to do with the money? Did he say?"

"He wants to rent a hall they can use for a permanent clubhouse. They're so popular, they've got too big for the school."

"And when you get too big, you've got to look for ways to expand," Davies said, returning from the kitchen to catch Leah's last sentence. He motioned for Lazar to follow him into the front room. "What's your problem?"

"I've got to buck Joey Taylor. I can't afford to operate the way he wants me to operate . . . not with the payroll I've got now—"

"Payroll? Who told you to take on every guy who came out of the army looking for a job? What do you think you are . . . the employment exchange?"

"I was planning for the future, building myself up."

Davies pulled out a chair and sat down at the table. "Keep talking. I'm listening."

"You must know what the situation is now, Ivor. If I don't grow big myself I'll just get swallowed up. Taylor's getting old. He's not the man he used to be. He's unsure . . . he's losing his clout. I can't look to him for protection much longer."

"What do you intend to do?"

"I want to move into the clubs – the best ones – that Taylor protects. Persuade him that it's time he called it a day."

"Taylor might be old. He might be wiped out by the death of his grandson. But he's still working hand-in-hand with

227

Withers. And *that's* where his strength is. While Withers stays at the Yard, Taylor can't be touched."

A knock on the door. Leah's voice called out that she wanted to set the table for dinner. Davies told her that they'd be ready in five minutes.

"Do you . . . see much of Withers?" Lazar asked.

"We're doing a bit of work together at the moment. Been a few bank jobs lately . . . you might have read about them." Lazar said that he had. "Withers seems to think it's the Irish trying to fund themselves for a big operation." It seemed strange working with Withers, Davies thought. The first time was that rainy Sunday morning when Withers had asked him to help in arresting Manny Goodman. Davies wondered if Withers knew that *he* knew the truth of that case.

He thought again about what Lazar was proposing. It would be fine if there were no crime and he could be true-blue and spend his life giving directions to sweet old ladies. Such was not the way of the world. A setup where the police selected the crime governors themselves so they could control what was going on was the best practical arrangement . . . Withers had it with Taylor. And Davies had it − to a much lesser degree − with Lazar, whose dealings on the fringe of the underworld helped him and helped the police. Davies figured that eventually his arrangement with Lazar might rival Taylor and Withers, given time as they both moved up to need and justify each other. It would be a feather in his cap, no question. When he cracked the whip, Lazar would jump. And everyone under Lazar would too.

The only problem, as far as Davies was concerned, was that neither he nor Lazar was really ready yet . . . "I wouldn't be too quick to try to persuade Taylor to retire," he said quietly.

Lazar seemed surprised. "Why not?"

"Remember Manny. He's got a Mexican standoff with Taylor. Taylor would have him wiped out if he ever set foot over here again . . . but he can't touch him now, wherever he is, because of Manny's little insurance policy. If you push Taylor out of the way, what's going to stand between you and Manny? And it's not just you," he added pointedly. "There's

Katya to consider. And Leah."

Again, Leah's voice called from the hall. Davies stood up and opened the door. Leah was outside, hands laden with plates. "Remember what I said," Davies said. He took the plates from Leah and set them on the table. Katya came in, carrying napkins, cutlery. Lazar turned around and looked at the small fire burning in the grate, poked it into life. He wasn't afraid of Manny coming back. For all he knew, Manny might be dead . . . no one had ever been able to trace him. And if he were still alive . . . and even if he decided to return once Taylor was out of the way . . . well, he would be strong enough to put the little maniac away forever.

He smiled as his two sons entered the dining room and sat at the table on raised chairs. Adele took the place between them, still young but already wise enough to play one boy against the other.

Lazar's two sons were so different in appearance that many people found it difficult to believe they were brothers . . . There was no possibility of committing the same error when it came to Johnny and Jimmy Peters, Lazar thought. Even their voices were alike . . . with that faint trace of Belfast that sometimes sneaked through.

Lazar decided he might have a job for them.

CHAPTER FIFTEEN

The Germans had made sure that Harry Sherman would never have grandchildren of his own when they'd launched the V-2 rocket that had blasted his home and destroyed his family. The only family he had now was Lazar's. The two boys – Aron and David – were as close to grandchildren as Sherman would ever come, and he spoiled them whenever he got the opportunity.

Every Friday night Sherman had dinner with the family. It was an occasion he eagerly anticipated all week . . . the one night he could enjoy home cooking instead of the restaurant food he ate the rest of the week. And every Friday night he would bring toys, or comics . . . anything he thought would please the boys. Even if Katya did regularly accuse him of making her life miserable by overindulging the children. Sherman just laughed, and Lazar encouraged him.

This Friday night, though, he turned up at the house with two cowboy outfits, complete with stetsons and authentic-looking, cap-firing six-guns. Katya's disapproval was obvious the moment Sherman opened the packages and handed out the presents.

"I don't want my sons playing with guns . . . even toy guns," she said. "Please take them away."

The boys looked disconsolate as Sherman regretfully removed the six-guns from their hands and stuffed them into his jacket pocket.

"Every boy plays cowboys and Indians," Lazar said, feeling sorry for his sons *and* Sherman. He didn't know who was more unhappy about Katya's decision. "What's wrong with it?"

"They can play perfectly well without guns," Katya said firmly. She'd witnessed enough violence, God knew, and was determined that her sons would not be exposed to it . . . even through toys.

Lazar knew Katya was right. He'd never seen a gun fired, but Leah and Shmuel had. At the railway station in Aachen . . . when their parents had been killed. Suddenly, Lazar didn't want toy guns in his children's hands either . . .

After dinner, Lazar went to the bureau in the living room where he filed his papers, and pulled out a newspaper clipping. "This came a couple of days ago," he said, passing the clipping to Sherman. "My brother's coming up in the world."

Sherman read slowly, his mouth moving to form the words. The story concerned a small, disused warehouse which Shmuel had leased as premises for Clapton Boys' Club. A picture showed him and Lottie standing with the mayor at the ribbon-cutting ceremony. In the background was a group of boys, members of the club.

"Very nice," Sherman remarked.

"I'd love to see that place when he's finished with it," Lazar said wistfully.

Sherman looked at the article again. "It says here they're planning a big boxing tournament. Why don't we go along?"

"He might feel uncomfortable if I turned up."

"Lazar's right," Katya cut in. "Perhaps one day the time'll be right for Lazar and Shmuel to be friends again. But now . . ." She left the sentence unfinished as she stood up and began to clear the plates from the table. Lazar helped, followed her into the kitchen.

"Harry and I have to go out," he said.

"Tonight?" She turned around, disappointed. "You never go out on Friday nights. It's the one night you always stay in."

"I'm sorry," Lazar said, and meant it. He didn't see much of his family in the evenings — leaving for the spielers by eight o'clock as a rule — so he always looked forward to spending Friday night with them. Tonight, though, he had no other choice. "It's important, believe me."

"It's always important, isn't it?" Katya put her arms around

231

Lazar's neck and kissed him.

Lazar, though, was preoccupied . . . He knew he was fast becoming financially strapped. He had to make his move soon or he would be forced to let his men go. And if he did that he'd show the world he was weak. Word would get around. And his spielers would become the first target for any expanding firm.

They took Sherman's car. Lazar sat in the front passenger seat while his bald-headed lieutenant drove slowly toward Dalston Junction and Pearl's. "How reliable are the Peters twins?" Lazar asked Sherman after a while.

"You've seen them."

"Only in the spieler. They stand around at attention like a couple of guardsmen and look polite and tough at the same time. I don't want a pair of tailor's dummies. I need people for a big job . . . a whole series of big jobs."

"What have you got in mind?"

"Bank robberies," Lazar said quietly. He reached out a steadying hand when he saw the steering wheel twitch under Sherman's suddenly nervous touch.

"Banks, Whitey? That's not our kind of business. We're in the clubs, the market. Why for God's sake would you want to change to something dangerous like that?"

"Two reasons. First . . . we're desperately short of funds. We've got too many bodies on the payroll and we can't afford to keep them unless we get a new racket going. Banks offer easy money. And secondly . . ." He paused for a few seconds to allow Sherman's curiosity to build. ". . . I want to set Withers up."

"Set him up?" Sherman was scared now. "What do you mean . . . set him up? Do away with him?"

Lazar laughed. "No . . . as much as I'd like to." Lazar then slowly explained that he would not dare move against Taylor as long as Withers was protecting him. Withers had to be distracted. And Ivor Davies had inadvertently suggested a way. "I want to make him so busy chasing bank robbers – IRA thugs he thinks are funding God alone knows what revolution – that he won't have the time to look after Taylor.

232

He'll be too damned busy doing, for a change, what he's paid to do by the police."

The more Sherman thought about it, the more the idea appealed to him . . . He didn't like Withers any more than Lazar himself did . . . not after what had happened to Shmuel. Here was a way to kill two birds with one stone. And the Peters twins would be perfect for the part. With their Irish background they could slip back into the accent with no trouble at all . . .

"Like it?" Lazar asked Sherman as he stopped the car near Dalston Junction Station.

"Yes . . . I do. You can hit banks all over the city. Even outside. Run Withers ragged."

"That's just what I plan to do." Leaving Sherman in the car, Lazar walked down the alleyway and entered Pearl's. The club was fairly quiet with only half the tables in use . . . a reminder to Lazar of how necessary it was for him to move quickly. Next to the door stood the Peters twins, dressed in identical royal blue suits with padded shoulders and sharply creased trousers. Guardsmen, he thought again. They looked pretty but could they really fight? Lazar told the twins that he wanted to see them outside and led the way to the car. Sherman drove toward Stoke Newington and Stamford Hill. Lazar turned around to talk to the twins in the back.

"How would you like the chance to earn some proper money, not the loose change I pay you for looking after the spieler?"

"Sure." Johnny's face lit up at the prospect. "How?"

"Rob a few banks for me."

Both twins laughed out loud. Then: "Are you serious?" Jimmy asked.

"If I wasn't, I wouldn't have asked you."

Their amusement died quickly. "Go ahead," Jimmy said.

"You'll be doing it for the firm, but you'll get to keep a quarter of whatever you take."

"Which banks?" Jimmy asked.

"I'll let you know that later. But rest assured they'll be easy to take."

The twins mulled over the offer . . . They'd been chosen by

233

Lazar from everyone else, given this opportunity to make some real money. "Banks won't hand over the money just because we say please," Jimmy finally said. "We'll need a little . . . persuasion."

"I can get you all the persuasion you'll need," Lazar promised.

"Like this?" Sherman dug into his pocket and pulled out one of the toy guns which Katya had made him take back from the children.

Although it was a child's plaything it looked menacing enough, especially in the darkness of the car. The twins could possibly use this and get away with it, he thought, then shook his head. He needed a real pistol, knew where to get one.

"No one is to get hurt, do you understand that?" he said to the twins. "No one gets hurt at all. You fire . . . yes . . . but just one shot into the ceiling when you enter the bank. To get their attention and show you mean business. And while you're in the banks I don't want you looking like professionals."

"Why?" Jimmy asked.

The questions all came from Jimmy, Lazar noticed. Johnny might be proud of the fact that he was older by ten minutes, but Jimmy was by far the smarter of the two . . . Johnny would do anything you told him . . . but Jimmy would want to know why.

"We need a bankroll to expand our operation," Lazar explained. "What we don't need is the coppers looking for professional thieves and coming back to us. You two have the know-how already, what with that jewelry store robbery. So if the coppers are looking for a pair of clumsy amateurs they're going to start looking somewhere else."

"Where?"

"At your countrymen, the Irish. There's been a whole bunch of bank robberies lately. The coppers think it's the IRA, raising money to buy weapons or explosives. You and your brother are going to make it look like they're getting even busier."

"For the love of Christ!" Johnny exclaimed. "Who ever thought it'd pay to be Irish? We'll be the only Orangemen in the IRA."

"That's right. Just don't get greedy. Be satisfied with whatever you can grab within a minute, and then get out."

"We'll make you rich," Johnny promised.

"Just don't make me famous," Lazar warned. He turned around and gazed through the windshield, momentarily lost. "Where are we?"

"Coming up to Stamford Hill," Sherman answered.

"Turn right," Lazar said suddenly. "Drive toward Clapton."

At the crest of the hill Sherman swung the car to the right. They drove past a line of shops, houses. On Clapton Common was a partially constructed estate of low-rent council flats, anonymous red-brick buildings that had been started at the end of the war. At the end of the common Sherman stopped the car and turned out the lights. "There it is," he said, understanding now why Lazar had told him to drive through Clapton.

Lazar rolled down the window and looked out at the single-story wooden building. The new headquarters of Clapton Boys' Club lay back from the main road. Lights were on inside, shining through the windows to illuminate the gravel-covered forecourt which had once been the warehouse's loading area. An ancient van was now parked in the forecourt. Painted in gold on the side was the name S. BROOKS.

"What's this then?" Jimmy Peters' voice came from the back of the car. "This one of your sidelines, Whitey?"

Lazar didn't bother to reply. He sat and looked at the building. Shmuel was probably inside, doing whatever it was that people who ran boys' clubs did. Was Lottie in there with him?

"What are you thinking about?" Sherman asked quietly.

Lazar took his time answering. His thoughts were so jumbled that he was not even certain he could explain them to himself. "Just that we've all come a long way from Cologne, I guess. And I'm wondering which one of us made the better choice."

"Don't upset yourself," Sherman counseled. "You had to go your way . . . and Shmuel had to go his." Sherman kept his voice to a whisper, not wanting the men in the back to hear. He tried to read what was going through Lazar's mind

. . . Probably a bit of pride as he looked at what his money had helped to purchase . . . and a whole lot of sorrow that he couldn't share in Shmuel's pleasure. Inside that building was the brother who hadn't spoken to Lazar since long *before* the war. What would it take for Lazar to get out of the car and go inside?

The door to the warehouse opened and two figures came out. They went to the back of the furniture van, opened the tailgate. Lazar could recognize the heavy figure of Shmuel. The kid with him was a stranger; most probably one of the club members, he decided. He watched while they carried folding tables from the van toward the building.

Suddenly the back door was flung open and Johnny Peters yelled out, "Chris! Hey . . . Chris! Over here!"

The boy turned around, looked at the dark shape of the car fifty yards away. Lazar also turned, his face contorted with anger. "Why don't you keep your bloody mouth shut?"

"That's my kid brother!" Johnny said. Chris had put down the folding tables and was slowly approaching the car. Shmuel stayed where he was, eyeing the car cautiously.

The boy's walk quickened as he recognized his brother getting out of the car. "What are you doing here?" Johnny asked. "I thought you were working on some newspaper or other . . . not in a warehouse."

"This is a club I belong to." Chris looked inside the car, nodded to Jimmy, then moved his eyes to the front. Sherman he'd never seen before, but he could guess who Lazar was from the white hair.

"Who's that big bloke with you?" Jimmy asked.

"That's Sammy Brooks," Chris said, unable to believe that his brother could not recognize the man who had once been a heavyweight contender. "You must remember him. It's his . . ." Chris pointed a finger at Lazar. ". . . It's his brother."

"Let's get out of here," Lazar said to Sherman. He wished now that he had not stopped. All he'd wanted was a look at the clubhouse he had helped to finance. How was he to have known that Chris Peters – the twins' younger brother – would be working with Shmuel on his damned club?

236

Sherman pressed down on the clutch and turned the ignition key. He would have driven away with the rear door hanging open and Johnny Peters out in the road had he not noticed Shmuel walking toward the car.

"He's coming over," Sherman said.

"I didn't know you had a brother," Jimmy spoke up from the back. "Especially him."

"You didn't have to know."

Jimmy ignored the rebuff. "I've heard about him. He was a tough fighter, he was."

Shmuel reached the car, still not sure who was in it. He could only see Johnny, could guess who he was. Without waiting for any introductions from Chris, he stooped and looked through the window, saw Sherman and Lazar.

"We've got some other stuff to unload, Chris. We'd better get on with it, otherwise we'll be here all night long."

Lazar knew he had to speak, had to say something that might explain his presence at the clubhouse. "Congratulations," he finally said through the open window. "I wish you luck with it."

"Why are you here?" Shmuel asked. They were the first words he had spoken to Lazar in years.

"I saw the story and picture in the newspaper. I wanted to look at the club for myself."

"Good . . . now you've seen it."

Lazar felt his throat tighten. "Get back in the car, Johnny. We're leaving."

"I want to talk to my brother," Johnny protested.

"He doesn't want to talk to you," Shmuel said. "He's too busy right now." He tapped Chris gently on the shoulder and reminded him again that they had more unloading to do. Chris turned around and began to walk back to the van.

"Hey! Wait a minute!" Johnny roared. He walked furiously away from the car, and Jimmy jumped out to follow him. "You don't tell my little brother who he can talk to, you fucking one-eyed moron!"

Sherman jerked open the door, knowing he was needed to calm things down. Lazar jumped out the other side. But before anyone could reach Johnny he had his hand on Shmuel's shoulder and was roughly swinging him around.

Shmuel had put on weight since his fighting days; the years had softened his muscles with fat. But though he might have lost his timing and devastating power, in a fair fight he was still more than a match for Johnny Peters. He lifted his hands, clenched them into hammers of fists. Johnny tensed up. Expecting the blow to be aimed at his face, he raised his own hands. Shmuel feinted with his left, made to jab. Then he slammed his right into Johnny's stomach. Johnny doubled up, sprawling on the gravel as he clutched his stomach and screamed in pain. When Jimmy sprang forward to his aid, Lazar dived at him.

"Get back in the car! Don't say a word . . . don't do a thing except get back into that car!" Lazar half-dragged, half-wrestled Jimmy away from his fallen twin, pushed him savagely toward the car. He threw a look at Shmuel and Chris Peters. Shmuel stood his ground, both hands still clenched. The eyepatch made him look even more menacing. Chris stood next to him, hands also closed into fists. It was obvious to Lazar that Chris would have fought alongside Shmuel . . . even against his own brothers.

Sherman lifted Johnny to his feet, dragged him to the car. Lazar stared at Shmuel, tried desperately to find words, anything to bridge the terrible awkwardness he felt. How could he tell his brother that he had not intended this to happen . . . just like he had not intended for Shmuel to be half-blinded in his last fight? He had only driven by for a look . . . not to start trouble. Surely Shmuel could understand that. You didn't start trouble after paying out hundreds of pounds to help with a club.

But Shmuel was already moving back toward the van as if the incident had never taken place . . . as if his brother were not even there. Trembling, Lazar turned around and got into the car, and the moment he closed the door Sherman drove away. He, too, was sweating profusely . . .

At first, no one in the car spoke, then Johnny broke the silence, his words hoarse as he rubbed his aching stomach, fought to regain his breath. "I'm going to get him," he

238

swore. "So help me, I'm going to get that one-eyed bastard."

Lazar never bothered to turn around. "You ever go near him again . . . and I'll chop your head off." He heard Johnny suck in his breath, prepare to say something else. Then Jimmy whispered something he couldn't hear in an urgent, threatening hiss. Johnny shut up. Lazar stared through the windshield as Sherman continued toward Dalston and Pearl's. It had been a mistake to look at the club. He'd come face-to-face with Shmuel . . . and instead of bridging the gap, he'd made it wider . . .

Johnny Peters was a hothead, a punk who acted first and only considered the consequences afterward . . . if he considered them at all. Lazar knew he should get rid of them both . . . Johnny and Jimmy . . . throw them out on their necks. How could he do that now, though . . . when he'd already involved them so heavily, made them privy to his plans because he'd looked on them as trusted henchmen? He'd work on the more reliable one to control the other. For better or worse, he had to stay with them. Just try to watch them even more. Or kill them. If necessary . . .

Shmuel's friendship with their brother complicated matters. Without Chris there would be no link between the twins and Shmuel. No reason for Lazar to worry . . . Shmuel would never come into contact with the twins. Chris was the link. While he was around Shmuel there would always be danger.

So help me God . . . Lazar swore to himself. If either one of the twins ever goes after Shmuel . . . even looks the wrong way at him . . . mentions his name . . . I'll slit their throats.

CHAPTER SIXTEEN

Lazar could have gone to a small hardware shop in Cable Street, at the very heart of the East End, to place his order for a gun. He chose not to . . . he didn't want anyone in the underworld to know that he was in the market for a weapon. The use of guns in London was so infrequent that his order would stand out, be remembered, even talked about.

Instead, he went to one of his American contacts. An Air Force supply sergeant being rotated back to the States in three weeks' time acquired a government-issue Colt automatic and two dozen rounds of forty-five-caliber ammunition. Lazar arranged to meet the man at a public house in the West End. Money changed hands. Lazar slipped the anonymous brown-paper package into his coat pocket and bought the supply sergeant a drink.

Lazar had never realized a pistol could be so heavy. It had cost him fifty pounds, equivalent to the two hundred and fifty dollars which the supply sergeant had wanted as a fee for stealing the weapon and falsifying records. It was a sum Lazar could barely afford.

Katya was fast asleep when he arrived home. He went straight up to the third floor, removed a floorboard he had loosened earlier and placed the gun and ammunition beneath. God alone knew what Katya would do if she learned he'd brought home a gun – a real one . . . not a toy this time.

Over the next few days he researched banks with easy escape routes. Listening to Harry Sherman's advice, he chose them in different parts of the city. He picked a bank in Kilburn, a north-west suburb with a heavy Irish population; one in South London; one in West London; and one out of the capital altogether, in a sleepy market town in Bedfordshire, forty miles north of London where the local police force comprised two bobbies on bicycles.

When he was ready he met with the Peters twins in Sherman's three-room flat in Highbury, north of where Lazar lived. Lazar was the last to arrive, carrying with him maps of the areas in which the targeted banks were located . . . and the gun. The twins had already seen the banks for themselves, but Lazar wanted to go over the areas again and again until he was satisfied there would be no mistakes.

An hour passed before Lazar was certain that Jimmy and Johnny knew every street within half a mile of each bank. Then Lazar moved on to the actual operation.

"When do you steal a car?"

"The night before," Jimmy answered immediately. "Very late. And switch plates so we can leave it overnight without the coppers finding it."

"Who drives the getaway car?"

"I do," Johnny replied. "Jimmy goes into the bank with the gun."

"How long do you stay in the bank?" Lazar asked Jimmy.

"One minute . . . not a second more."

"Where do you go when you're finished?"

"Back home. Then to Pearl's in the evening to meet with you," Johnny said. He looked at Lazar only briefly while he spoke, then dropped his eyes to the table, obviously fascinated by the gun . . .

"What if we run into any trouble?" Jimmy asked. "Suppose something unexpected happens . . . do we use that?" He motioned toward the gun.

"You won't run into any problems. I told you before . . . I don't want anyone hurt. Avoid trouble at all costs, even if it means abandoning the job."

"Seems a pity to have this and not be able to use it," Johnny broke in. Unable to control himself any longer he reached forward to pick up the gun, worked the slide and chambered a round. "I bet this could knock a copper off his bike."

Sherman glanced nervously at Lazar, who reached across

the table and took the pistol from Johnny's grasp. "You hang onto this," he told Jimmy. "I don't want any accidents."

Jimmy dropped out the magazine and ejected the chambered round. "No problem," he assured Lazar. "Just one shot into the ceiling to show that we mean business. Then we take the money and run."

"What did they use in other raids the cops are blaming on the IRA?" Sherman asked. "What kind of gun?"

Lazar thought back to the newspaper stories. "Sawed-off shotgun in a couple, I think. Pistols other times. One of the reports said the bank manager recognized a Webley forty-five."

"Webley forty-five, Colt forty-five . . . what does it matter?" Jimmy asked. He slipped the gun into his belt, dropped the ammunition and clip into his jacket pocket. "We'll do Kilburn tomorrow afternoon. The others at two-day periods, starting Monday."

Lazar nodded. They'd hit the town in Bedfordshire the following Friday . . . market day, when the bank would be at its busiest as the local farmers brought in their produce and livestock. The sooner they got this over with, the happier he would be. So low were his funds now that he had been taking money from Harry Sherman to pay salaries. That couldn't go on for much longer; Sherman couldn't afford to continue dipping into his savings to keep the outfit solvent. He folded the maps and tossed them to Jimmy. "After Pearl's closes tonight, see about a car. Nothing flashy."

The twins left the flat. Lazar stayed at the table while Sherman busied himself in the small kitchen, making tea. He came back with two cups and some biscuits on a tray. Lazar sipped the tea thoughtfully, grateful that the gun was out of his house . . . But he did have some nagging doubts about how smart it was to have given it to the twins. Jimmy he was fairly certain about . . . it was Johnny who worried Lazar. The confrontation with Shmuel two weeks earlier still haunted him. Could Jimmy control his twin brother? He'd done it in the car that night, hissed at him to shut up. But would he be able to do so when the pressure was on? Thank God it was Jimmy who had the gun . . . and not Johnny. There was no telling what the older twin would do if something went wrong . . .

"Don't worry about them," Sherman said softly. The two men had become so close following the death of Sherman's family that a tight bond had formed, and Sherman had somehow come to be able to read Lazar's mind, to understand what was tormenting him. "Jimmy can take care of his brother. Johnny's driving the car . . . that's all."

"I hope to God you're right. Anyway, it's too late now to worry about it. We're committed."

Sherman grinned at Lazar. "What wouldn't I give to be able to see that bastard Withers start running around in circles after this phantom Irish gang."

"Irish phantoms . . ." Lazar liked that. "It'll be a bit like the Scottish mob we once used, won't it?"

Pearl's closed shortly after two thirty the following morning. Jimmy and Johnny Peters watched the last players leave, said goodnight to Goris and walked out into the chilly night.

For a half-hour they drove around in Johnny's car before Jimmy pointed to a Riley parked in front of a row of shops in Finsbury Park. Johnny pulled in behind, waited with the engine running while his brother worked on the Riley's doors. The driver's door swung open. In the darkness Jimmy gave a triumphant grin. Half a minute later, the Riley's engine was purring. Its sidelights were on. Jimmy pulled away, followed by Johnny.

They drove to Kilburn, parked in a quiet residential street half a mile from the bank they planned to rob the following afternoon. While Johnny kept watch, Jimmy speedily changed the plates, dropped the original ones into a nearby sewer. Then they drove home, leaving the stolen car waiting to play its part.

When Lazar woke up the following morning the children had already left for school. Katya was in the kitchen, washing up the breakfast plates. She didn't hear Lazar come in, only felt his arms around her waist, his lips on the back of her neck.

243

"Good morning," he greeted her. "Any tea left in the pot?"

"It's probably cold by now. I'll make you some fresh." She dried her hands and put the kettle on the gas. Lazar leaned back against the sink, content to watch Katya move about the kitchen. "What do you want for breakfast?" she asked. "A couple of boiled eggs?"

How many other husbands got asked that question? Lazar wondered. Eggs were like gold, strictly rationed unless you had contacts like he had. Did Shmuel and Lottie have eggs for breakfast whenever they wanted? Leah and Ivor Davies did, because Lazar supplied them. Davies was a realist . . . Lazar liked that about him. He was bright enough to recognize those things that were useless to fight, better to go along with, take advantage of. As long as they were discreet . . . and not entirely illegal . . .

"Just toast will do," he answered. "I'm not all the way awake yet." He sat down at the table in the dining room, scanned the pages of the *Daily Mirror* while he waited for Katya to bring in tea and toast. A story about the trials in Nuremberg attracted his attention . . . He so often these days forgot that he was a Jew . . . and a German Jew at that. Those same bastards who had killed his parents were now standing in front of a war-crimes tribunal, protesting their innocence. Would the judge who sentenced them to hang . . . as Lazar prayed he would . . . wear a robe and wig, with a black square of silk balanced delicately on the rear of his head? . . .

"Here's your tea," Katya said.

Startled, Lazar dropped the newspaper onto the table.

"Are you all right?"

"You scared me," he admitted. "I was reading this." He picked up the paper and pointed to the story.

"They should all rot in hell," Katya said quietly.

"Amen to that."

She sat down on the opposite side of the table, watching while Lazar ate. Then she said, "I'm glad you got rid of that gun."

"What?" Lazar looked up. "What gun?"

"What gun do you think I mean? The toys that Harry gave to the children? I mean the one you hid under the floor upstairs."

244

Lazar saw no advantage in trying to lie. "How did you know?"

"How was I supposed to sleep when you were pulling up floorboards over my head? You never go up to the top floor . . . especially not late at night. I looked for myself the following day. And I looked every day, until this morning I saw that it was gone, thank God." She reached across the table and placed her hand on his. "Lazar, what are you doing with a gun?"

He glanced down at her hand, at the engagement and wedding rings that she took off only to rinse in soapy water when their sparkle was dimmed. "Someone paid me off with it. A gambling debt. They didn't have the cash so I took that in lieu."

"Don't lie to me, Lazar. I'm no fool. This is Katya. I know when you're lying. Why did you have a gun?"

What was he going to tell her? Katya expected the truth – and she deserved it. But this was one of those times when it would be kinder to lie . . . and keep on lying. Better that than to see her worried out of her mind. "We heard something about some other firm trying to muscle in on the two spielers. Joey Taylor put me wise to it." He looked deep into her green eyes, trying to see whether his words were ringing true.

"You never had a gun before. Why now?"

"Things are getting tougher. There are thousands of demobbed servicemen wandering around, all looking for some way to make quick money."

"Why did you keep the gun here then . . . and not at one of the clubs?"

"Because I don't care about the spielers. I care about you, and the boys. If the clubs were attacked, I've got men there to take care of it. I wanted it here because you and the children were here. Anyway . . ." he added brightly, relieved that she believed him but still wanting to quiet her fears, ". . . it's gone back to Joey Taylor. It was a false alarm."

Slowly, she withdrew her hand from his. Her eyes were filled with tears. "Lazar . . . make me a promise."

"Anything."

"Promise me that if it gets too dangerous, you'll . . . you'll pull out. Let someone else have the clubs. Invest the money you've made in something else . . . whatever it pays. But at

245

least I'll be able to sleep at night knowing that my husband and children are safe."

What money? . . . Lazar thought grimly . . . She should only know how much we've really got. "I promise you that," he said solemnly.

Katya wanted him to quit if things became dangerous. What was going into a head-on clash with Joey Taylor if not dangerous? Lazar had been married to Katya all this time, but since the Vanetti affair he had managed to avoid exposing her to any real danger. That made him feel good, proud.

"Thank you," Katya said.

Lazar didn't let the subject drop. "What kind of business do you think I should invest in?"

"You could buy a shop," Katya said.

"I don't know anything about shops."

"You could become an accountant then. Here . . . in this country. You could go to school, take the examinations to get your British qualifications."

Lazar could never become an accountant again, making figures talk for someone else's benefit. Those days were over. The spielers were in his blood . . . the excitement, the intrigue that went with them. "Katya, I'll make you a promise. When I've got enough money I'll at least put everything into opening a respectable club. A nightclub in the West End, with dinner and dancing, a cabaret, the works."

She thought about asking how long it would take, but didn't want to spoil the moment. She guessed he was indulging her, but . . . there always existed that possibility that he would walk away from the spielers and the rackets and go legitimate. If he did, she wondered, what use would he find for Harry Sherman? And all the others who worked for him? . . .

"Lazar . . . I don't want anything to happen to you," she heard herself saying. "Please be careful."

"I will." He got up from the table and went upstairs to dress. For a while he sat on the edge of the bed thinking about what Katya had said. An accountant she suddenly wanted him to be . . . that was from a different life . . . a life that was almost snuffed out by order of those Nazi thugs who

246

were even now standing trial in Nuremberg . . . He couldn't go back, not to Germany nor to being an accountant. Maybe the idea of a respectable nightclub wasn't such a bad scheme after all. He'd make his money in the rackets and get out . . . leave the trouble and grief for someone else.

When he returned downstairs, fully dressed, Katya was busy ironing, and did not bring up the earlier conversation. He told her that he was going out for a ride, asked her if she wanted anything. She shook her head and laughed. It was a standing joke between them, his complete inability to shop for basic household goods.

"I'll see you later then." He kissed her and left the house, sitting in the car for a couple of minutes while the engine warmed up. He wondered where the Peters twins were. Had they managed to steal a car the previous night and park it near the bank in Kilburn? God . . . he hoped so. That would be the bitterest blow of all . . . for Katya to learn how broke he really was. All the risks he'd taken . . . the enemies he was prepared to make. And for what?

He drove to Clapton, rolled slowly past the Common, his eyes peeled for Shmuel's clubhouse. To Lazar's surprise, the furniture van was parked in the loading area; he wondered why Shmuel wasn't working in the shop. The building's main door was open and Lazar could see inside. A boxing ring had been set up in the center of the club; Lazar recalled the tournament that had been mentioned in the newspaper article. Shmuel really had his heart in the place. Good luck to him . . . Lazar hoped it all worked out.

But he found himself hoping that Shmuel was not letting the furniture shop go downhill as he worked on the club. Until Lazar made his move against Joey Taylor he could not afford to send any more anonymous donations through the lawyer. For the time being Shmuel was on his own.

At two thirty in the afternoon, half an hour before the bank's business day ended, Jimmy Peters drove up behind the stolen Riley. He stayed in the car while Johnny started the Riley's engine. When it was running, Jimmy joined him.

While they drove toward the bank Jimmy busied himself by checking the pistol. He worked the slide back and forth, made certain he had the safety off. By the time he had slipped in the magazine and chambered the top round, Johnny was driving the Riley along the main road, approaching the bank.

"Pull in there." Jimmy indicated a space outside the bank.

Johnny stopped the Riley outside the bank's door. Jimmy thrust the pistol into his coat pocket, grabbed a large shopping bag from the floor, opened the door and got out. Johnny pressed down on the clutch, moved the stick into first, ready to take off the instant his twin brother reappeared. He felt jealous of Jimmy, wishing it were himself going into the bank, gun in one hand, bag in the other. What bloody fun was there in sitting outside while all the action was taking place inside?

Jimmy looked back just once, as he pushed open the door to the bank. Suddenly his stomach started to tremble, a feeling he hadn't experienced since he and his brother had gone onto the beach at Normandy in that first assault, wading through the cold water as machine-gun bullets and mortar bombs peppered the sea around them. Hell . . . he pushed the anxiety from his mind. This should be easy. It was an unguarded bank, not a heavily fortified beach. He pulled up his coat collar, tipped his hat low over his face and covered his chin with a scarf.

Once inside the bank he looked around quickly. Four tellers were on duty behind the counter – three men and one woman. At each position there was a short line of customers. The glass-paned door to the manager's office was open. Jimmy could see a middle-aged man inside, sitting behind a desk, a cup of tea placed conspicuously in front of him. Tea break, Jimmy thought. Tough luck, mister . . . this is one cup you're not going to enjoy in peace and quiet.

Taking the pistol out of his coat pocket he walked into the bank, raised his hand, cocked the hammer and squeezed the trigger. The shot blasted through the normally quiet bank. The bullet smacked into the ceiling, shattering plaster. Somewhere a woman screamed.

"Good afternoon, ladies and gentlemen. Please lie on the floor and no one will get hurt. This won't take long." The words were partly muffled by the scarf that covered his mouth, but the Irish accent was unmistakable. His earlier moment of tension was gone . . . Jimmy was enjoying himself. He walked toward the nearest teller's window. "Drop it in there, my boy," he told the man behind the window. He held up the shopping bag, eyes flickering from the money to the customers and other tellers. Movement from the manager's office startled him, and he jerked up the gun.

"What's going on?" the manager demanded.

"What does it look like? Come and join the party." He beckoned with the pistol, kept it trained on the manager until he was lying face down on the floor, hands clasped behind his neck. Then Jimmy moved on to the next window, waited a few seconds. Then on to the next. By the time he reached the final window he estimated that his minute was up.

"Thank you all very much for your cooperation. You have our everlasting gratitude." He backed toward the exit. "Don't anyone move!" he called out. Then he spun around and ran from the bank. Johnny was holding open the passenger door. The instant Jimmy landed in the passenger seat the Riley sped off.

"How did it go?"

"Fantastic. Look at this take, will you?" Jimmy opened the shopping bag. It was brimming with money.

"How many shots did you fire?" Johnny glanced in the mirror as he threw the Riley around a corner. No one had come out of the bank yet. Home free.

"Just the one into the ceiling. And will you watch your speed? We don't want to get stopped for speeding, you idiot!"

Johnny slowed down. "No one gave you any trouble then?"

"Who would . . . with this?" Jimmy patted the gun in his pocket. He tried to guess how much was in the bag but gave up. It needed to be counted properly . . . there was so much.

Johnny took another couple of turns and, two minutes later, swung the Riley into a cul-de-sac. They got out of the

249

car and walked away slowly, not wanting to arouse suspicion. Their own car was parked less than a hundred yards away. They got in and drove casually away from Kilburn.

Four minutes had passed since Jimmy had walked out of the bank with the money.

Lazar was reading the account of the bank robbery in Kilburn for the third time when the Peters twins entered Pearl's shortly after eight o'clock that evening.

The robbery had made the front page of the *Evening News* final edition. The account, though short, was fairly complete. One armed man. Another waiting outside in a getaway car . . . a black Riley which had been found dumped half a mile away. A single shot had been fired into the ceiling. Thirteen hundred pounds had been stolen in the raid, which had lasted no more than a minute. There had been no injuries . . . indeed, the bank manager described the robber as "charming."

On the back page of the *News*, mixed in with the racing results, was an additional paragraph. Police were working on the theory that the raid was the work of the Irish Republican Army . . .

Lazar led the twins to the back of the spieler into a small room that was used for storage, closed the door and locked it. "How did it go?"

"Like a piece of cake," Jimmy answered. "In and out like lightning." He handed over the briefcase. Lazar opened it, saw the neatly stacked bills and whistled in appreciation. "Have you counted?"

"Thirteen hundred and eighty quid."

"That's eighty pounds more than they reported in the paper." Lazar was glad the twins hadn't kept anything back for themselves. He counted out three hundred and forty-five pounds for the twins' cut; the remaining one thousand and thirty-five pounds he crammed into his pockets. The money felt good – very good. He now had the makings of a bankroll. Three more raids like this and he'd be able to afford the men who worked for him. "Your Irish accent seems to have come back all right," he complimented Jimmy. "The coppers are looking all over for Paddies."

Jimmy laughed. "After next week's over they'll be looking even harder." He became serious. "Look, Whitey . . . the way I see it we're helping you out pretty good right now."

Lazar saw what was coming and tried to avoid it. "You two just picked up a pretty good bundle of cash for a minute's work."

"We could have picked up even more if we'd done the job for ourselves," Johnny pointed out.

"I planned it for you . . . remember that."

"Sure you did, Whitey," Jimmy broke in quickly. "But we're the ones taking all the risks."

"Yeah, it's our necks if we get caught with a gun," Johnny said.

"What do you want?"

"Well . . ." Jimmy became coy, like a small child who has been offered anything he desires and becomes too embarrassed to ask. "We were thinking that maybe you'd do the right thing by us when all this is over."

"You're not trying to blackmail me, are you?"

"Blackmail?" Jimmy seemed shocked. "Christ, no!"

"Good." Lazar thought about Joey Taylor, and the old man's horror of being blackmailed. Every move you made left you open to it. "Then what do you want?"

"When you get big you won't be able to control it all by yourself," Jimmy said. "You're going to need a chain of command, responsible lieutenants."

"And you want to be high on that chain, is that it?"

"I think we deserve it."

"Ambitious, aren't you?"

"What's wrong with being ambitious?" Johnny wanted to know.

Lazar ignored the question. "Why don't we wait and see what happens? Once things start looking good, we'll talk about chains of command."

"Sounds okay to me," Jimmy agreed.

"What about you?" Lazar asked Johnny. He still wasn't sure about the older twin, didn't know whether he held a grudge over the beating he'd taken from Shmuel.

"Me, too."

"Good. In the meantime, don't go throwing any of that money around. Save it for a rainy day."

"Do you see any coming?" Jimmy asked.

Lazar laughed at the question . . . I'm having one right now, he thought. And I'm relying on the two of you to find the sun for me . . . He unlocked the door and returned to the front room of the spieler.

Of all the men he had taken on since the end of the war, the Peters twins were the only ones he could never afford to get rid of. They were tied in too tightly with him now . . . blackmailing him without even realizing it. He hoped that Harry Sherman's assessment of them was right. Because if it was not, Lazar knew he could be in big trouble.

But before that time the Peters twins would be gone. He'd make sure of that.

CHAPTER SEVENTEEN

When Katya invited Leah and Ivor Davies to Stoke Newington for dinner on Thursday night, Lazar was pleased, knowing it would enable him to gain a more "official" view of the three bank raids the Peters twins had so far pulled off.

As far as his coffers were concerned the raids were a magnificent success. In addition to the money from the robbery in Kilburn they had raked in more than five thousand pounds from the other two raids. The final job — in the Bedfordshire market town the following day — would, Lazar hoped, net at least another couple of thousand.

All the raids had gone like clockwork. Jimmy and Johnny Peters had obeyed Lazar's instructions to the letter . . . in and out before anyone had a chance to gather their wits. Lazar read in the newspapers that the government was gearing itself for an increase in Irish Republican Army activity . . .

Leah and Davies came by themselves, leaving their daughter, Adele, at home with a baby-sitter. After dinner Lazar brought his two sons upstairs to bed, kissed them goodnight, and stayed for a few extra minutes in their bedroom, talking, telling them stories, unable to tear himself away from the time of day he loved. When he eventually returned downstairs, he found Davies pouring an after-dinner drink.

"You sure get hold of the finest and the best," Davies complimented Lazar as he held up a bottle of cognac.

"It's a matter of knowing the right people." Lazar shook his head when Davies offered him the bottle. He never drank when he was working and, later, after his guests had left, he would be going to work. "I keep it especially for guests and visiting policemen."

"Do you get many?"

"Guests?"

"No." Davies finished pouring cognac into his snifter. "Visiting policemen?"

"God forbid!" Katya broke in, laughing at the question. "Lazar's too law-abiding for that."

Davies grinned as he sat down next to Leah on the couch, the drink cradled in his hands.

"The only time I ever see a uniform is at Pearl's," Lazar said. "When they come for a free cup of tea."

"That's the bloody trouble," Davies grumbled. "They're all too busy tapping you for free tea and sandwiches when they should be getting out there and catching bank robbers."

"I've been reading about that in the papers," Lazar said. "Things must be pretty hectic for you right now."

"Hectic!" Leah looked at her husband. "This is the first night Ivor's taken off in more than a week. I told him that if he didn't take off this evening to come over here I'd divorce him and sue the police force as corespondent."

Davies patted Leah's knee affectionately. "The lady doth protest too much, methinks . . . the only bloomin' trouble is, she's right."

"How many hours are you putting in each day?" Katya asked Davies.

He groaned. "How many hours are there in a day? We're all involved up to our necks. C.I.D. . . . . Special Branch . . . Flying Squad. We must have interrogated more Irishmen living in London than they've got in the whole of Ireland."

"Have you got anywhere?" Lazar asked.

"It's like banging your head against a solid brick wall. Every time we pull in an Irishman for questioning, we never know whether he's just plain dumb and telling the absolute truth . . . or bloody smart and lying his head off to us."

"How's Mr. Withers taking it all?" Lazar tossed in the question casually. Now that Davies was talking openly about the bank raids he could find out what he really wanted to know.

"Withers?" A trace of scorn crept into Davies' voice. "He's lost . . . like a Boy Scout whose compass has gone on

254

the blink. All of a sudden Withers is faced with doing solid police work and I think he's forgotten how to go about it. The contacts he's got don't stand up very well in this kind of work."

So Withers *was* running around in circles . . . Good. Pretty soon he'd be too busy to even think about protecting Joey Taylor. He'd be too occupied in protecting himself, his position . . . Then Lazar would make his move . . . "Have you spoken to Shmuel and Lottie lately?" Lazar asked. He had learned what he needed to know about Withers.

"We popped in there on the way over here," Leah said. "You both live so near each other that it seems silly not to. Especially when Ivor's so busy."

"I drove past his new clubhouse the other night," Lazar said. "Saw Shmuel and some youngster unloading tons of equipment."

Davies nodded. "He did mention that he'd seen you. That was Chris Peters with him, by the way . . . the younger brother of a couple of bad types you've got working at Pearl's."

"They're good for keeping an eye on the place." Lazar wondered if Shmuel had told Davies about the fight with Johnny Peters.

"Isn't Goris enough anymore?" Davies asked.

"They say there's safety in numbers."

"You mentioned that once before." Davies finished the cognac in the snifter, looked at the sideboard as if debating whether to take a refill. He decided against it and placed the empty glass on the table. "Why don't we go for a ride?"

Startled, Lazar looked toward Leah and Katya. "Would you mind?"

"Go ahead," Katya told him.

They took Davies' car and drove around aimlessly, up over Stamford Hill, past Shmuel's shop and toward Tottenham. "While you were upstairs before with the boys, Katya mentioned something about a nightclub. Is that true?" Davies asked.

Lazar shrugged. "She wants me out of the spielers. She's worried."

"What about?"

"About me getting hurt, I suppose." Damn! . . . he wished he knew what Katya had told Davies. Had she repeated the story Lazar had given to her? Had she said anything about the gun?

"Were you serious about the nightclub? Or were you . . . lying? Trying to keep Katya from knowing the truth?"

"What's the truth, Ivor?"

"Don't play games with me, Lazar. I'm a copper . . . remember? I can see right through you even if Katya can't." He looked into the rear-view mirror, made a wide sweeping U-turn and pulled into the curb. They were parked by the narrow lane that led down to the Spurs stadium. "You're going after Joey Taylor, aren't you?"

Lazar saw no point in denying the accusation. "Are you going to advise me against it?" He gazed at the public house on the corner of the narrow lane . . . remembered that dawn when he had parked in the same spot, waiting for Shmuel . . . to ask his brother to throw the fight with Bomber Billy Harris . . .

"I'm going to advise you to watch out for yourself."

"Thanks . . . I'll bear it in mind. Can we go home now?"

"Lazar . . ." Davies' next words came out slowly. "Do it sweet. Don't go in like an armored division storming a fortress. If any innocent person gets hurt . . . I'm going to come down on you like a ton."

"Who's innocent?"

"Katya is. So is Leah. If anything happens to you, they're both going to be hurt." Davies gripped the steering wheel. Sooner or later he knew he'd have to reach a painful decision about his brother-in-law . . . something he'd so far managed to avoid doing. He'd taken the gifts Lazar had showered on him . . . Used the information Lazar had given him to further his own career . . . And had advised him to do nothing.

But now Lazar had run out of patience. He was determined to move against Joey Taylor . . . ready to set himself up as Number One.

"Do it cleverly," Davies said between clenched teeth, "and I'll do whatever I can to protect you. Do it stupidly — and by that I mean leave a trail of bodies in your wake — and so help me I'll put you out of business."

Late that night Jimmy Peters stole a Morris family sedan and drove it forty miles north to the small Bedfordshire market town where the final bank was located. His brother followed in his own car. This time Jimmy didn't bother to change the plates of the stolen car; the police would still be looking in the area of the first three raids.

Market Street, the town's one main thoroughfare, stretched for a mile from the railway station to the broad cobblestoned expanse where the weekly market was held. They left the stolen Morris in the station parking lot and drove slowly through the town. The public house next to the station was the only building for half a mile, then the residential area began, half a dozen narrow roads running off Market Street. Beyond them were acres and acres of farmland.

The bank was situated at the end of the town's only row of shops . . . The town didn't even have its own police station, but came under the jurisdiction of the next town, four miles to the north. The two constables on permanent duty worked from their homes.

"It'll be like taking chocolate from a baby," Jimmy said confidently as they completed their swing through the town. He sat back in the passenger seat and closed his eyes as his brother began the return journey to London.

Just after midday they were back in the town, amazed that it was the same sleepy place they had visited early that morning. The parking lot at the railway station was now full of cars and trucks. The wide part of Market Street was bustling, lined with stalls selling every kind of produce. Horse-drawn carts mixed with automobiles. The smells — and sounds — of livestock were everywhere, and farmers in mud-encrusted boots unloaded vegetables at the stalls.

"Jesus . . . if it stays this busy we'll never be able to get away," Johnny said anxiously.

"Relax, will you?" Jimmy said. "The market is over at two. By two thirty they'll all have been to the bank to put their money away."

Opposite the bank was a stall selling refreshments. Jimmy bought two cups of tea, handed one to his brother. While they sipped the scalding hot tea, Jimmy looked around, taking in the activity. Then he spotted the uniform of a police constable. The man was cycling along Market Street toward them. The bicycle's front wheel wobbled back and forth as its rider guided it over the cobblestones right past them.

"Doesn't look like much, does he?" Johnny remarked, turning his head to keep the constable in sight.

"Leave it to Whitey . . . he knows how to pick a good one." Jimmy finished the tea. "Come on, we might as well get back to the station."

From Market Street they drove to the station parking lot and left their own car close to the exit. The stolen Morris was on the other side of the lot. After checking that the Morris' exit wasn't blocked they walked over to the public house. They still had an hour left to go before they could move.

Jimmy ordered a pint of beer. Johnny satisfied himself with tomato juice. When the bartender smiled at the order Johnny's glare wiped the grin off his face.

At two fifteen they left the pub. Through the window they had watched the parking lot empty as market day came to a close. Johnny started the engine of the stolen Morris and drove slowly along Market Street toward the center of town. Jimmy slipped the magazine into the Colt.

"This'll do fine." Jimmy indicated a space by the refreshment stand. The shutters were closed, the business day over. Johnny swung the car around to face it back toward the railway station. Jimmy pulled down his hat, hid the rest of his face with his scarf and picked up the shopping bag.

The pistol felt comforting in his hand as he entered the bank . . . Farmers and merchants were lined up at the two teller positions. He raised his arm into the air, pointed the gun at the ceiling and pulled the trigger. "Everyone on the floor!" he called out as the single shot still echoed. "Do as I say and no one will get hurt." He slipped easily into the heavy Irish accent, waved the gun to emphasize his words.

258

At the sound of the shot and the sight of the heavy automatic pistol the bank's customers sat down on the floor. Jimmy held out the shopping bag and marched toward the first teller. But before he could order the teller to fill up the bag a car horn sounded urgently. Jimmy stiffened, told himself it could not be his brother. Only an idiot would call attention to himself like that.

Outside the bank, Johnny pounded his gloved hand on the horn again. His eyes flicked from the bank door to the rear-view mirror, where he could see the uniformed figure on the bicycle wobbling unsteadily toward him. Damn that stupid small-town copper! Why had he chosen this one bloody moment to come cycling along Market Street?

Standing by the teller's window, Jimmy listened to the second blast of the horn. He knew now that it had to be his brother, giving him a warning . . . but what could have gone wrong? He took two steps toward the door, the gun wavering uncertainly. Then he changed his mind. He'd see himself in hell before he walked out empty-handed . . . not when all these farmers were banking big bundles of money. He swung back to the teller, held open the bag while the frightened man dumped in a handful of money. Then he ran to the second teller, repeating the performance.

"Don't anyone move for a minute," he yelled as he turned and ran for the door. He barged his way through it, saw the car . . . and saw what Johnny had his eyes riveted on. The constable was pedaling his bicycle furiously, his suspicions roused by Johnny's insistent honking. The bicycle bounced dangerously over the cobblestones as the constable raced toward where they were parked.

"Get in!" Johnny screamed, throwing open the passenger door.

Jimmy flung in the shopping bag. Before he knew what he was doing he raised his right arm and squeezed off a warning shot at the onrushing constable. The bullet flew high over the man's head. Jimmy dove into the car as Johnny let up the clutch and floored the accelerator pedal. At the last moment the constable plunged off his bicycle. His hands gripped the spare wheel cover on the trunk of the Morris. His helmet flew off, bouncing in the road as he hauled himself up onto the car.

"He's sitting on the bloody back!" Jimmy yelled out.

"Shoot him!"

Jimmy raised the pistol, looked along the barrel at the constable pressed against the rear window. And he couldn't pull the trigger . . . couldn't shoot the man at point-blank range . . . couldn't shoot to kill . . .

"Why the bloody hell don't you shoot?" Johnny screamed. He swung his head around, saw the constable with grim determination clinging to the back of the car.

Jimmy tried again. Johnny saw his hesitation and grabbed the gun away. With one hand controlling the speeding car, he pointed the gun toward the back and pulled the trigger three times. The roar of the explosions thundered through the inside of the car. Spent cartridges flew out. Jimmy saw glass shatter. The constable flew off the car and landed in a heap in the middle of the road.

"Why are you stopping?" Jimmy asked, confused.

"Why do you think?" Johnny threw the car into reverse. "To make sure he's fucking well dead. He got a good look at us."

Jimmy closed his eyes as the car lurched backward over the fallen police officer. When he opened them again Johnny had the Morris going forward over the crushed body before heading toward the railway station.

"You mad bastard," Jimmy breathed out. "You nut." He moved uncomfortably in the seat; his pants felt damp. He couldn't believe it. He'd been through Normandy, in with the first wave. And now he'd wet himself when faced by an unarmed copper. He'd been afraid to shoot, to kill a man. And finally pushed beyond his limits by the sight and feel of his twin brother rolling the car twice over the man's body.

"What did you want me to do?" Johnny snapped. "Leave him there so he could put us away?" He didn't notice Jimmy's pale face, the look of shame. He guided the car into the station parking lot. A man coming out of the public house

260

gave them no more than a cursory glance. Johnny thrust the gun into his pocket, slammed the door shut and walked quickly to the other car. Jimmy followed, walking awkwardly with his trousers sticking to his skin. He climbed in and Johnny drove off, heading south toward London.

"How much did we get?" Johnny asked.

"A few hundred, that's all." Jimmy looked nervously over his shoulder, half-expecting to see a posse following them. The road was empty and he began to feel better.

"A few hundred!" Johnny exploded.

"You started banging the horn the minute I stepped into the bank." He wriggled in the seat, tried to get more comfortable. "I had no time."

"A few hundred," Johnny repeated. "And for that we killed a copper!" He fell silent, replaying what had just happened in his mind . . . What else could he have done? Carried the copper all the way back to the railway station so that he could get an even better look at them? . . . He'd done the right thing. But, damn it, you didn't bump off the law . . . no matter how much you wanted to. That was one of the rules of the game. "You're in this with me," he said to Jimmy. "I'm not carrying the rap for this myself."

Jimmy said nothing. "What's the matter with you?" Johnny asked. Then he began to laugh. Jimmy's coat was open and Johnny could see the damp stain on his trousers.

"Shut up," Jimmy said with little conviction or force. His shame at losing control of himself was bad enough . . . what was worse was that he had lost control of his twin brother.

"Don't you tell me to shut up. I don't need that kind of advice from someone who pisses in his trousers. *You* shut up. And *you* listen to me. The only one who got a good look at us was that copper. He's dead . . . we've got nothing to worry about now. But Whitey'll know what happened. Even if we don't tell him he'll find out from the newspapers. He'd better stand by us . . . or by Christ we'll take him down with us." He started to laugh again.

"Jimmy, we're both on easy street. Don't you see? Whitey's got a whole lot more to lose than we do. He's got to stand by

261

us, be good to us . . . if he knows what's good for him."

Lazar hated the unexpected. The telephone call that evening
– shortly after six o'clock from Johnny Peters asking for an
immediate meeting – smacked of the unexpected.

"Where are you going?" Katya asked as she saw Lazar
fling on his coat and walk quickly toward the front door.
She'd been listening to the radio in the kitchen while she
prepared dinner and she heard the telephone ring. Only brief
snatches of Lazar's hurried words had been audible. Then
he'd made a call himself. Only when she heard him slam
down the receiver, saw him put on his coat, did she realize
that something might be wrong.

"I have to go out right away. I'm sorry . . . but something
important has come up."

"But you'll miss dinner. It'll be ready in half an hour."

"Wait for me. I'll try to be back in an hour and a half."

Lazar didn't know what else he could tell her. He didn't
even know himself what had happened . . . All Johnny had
said was that an emergency had come up and that he had to
see Lazar immediately. Lazar told Johnny to meet him in half
an hour at Harry Sherman's flat in Highbury. Then he'd
phoned Sherman, told him to expect company.

But why had Johnny made the call, not Jimmy? Jimmy was
the twin with brains. He should have made the damned call
. . . unless . . . unless he'd met with an accident.

"Lazar . . . what is it?" Katya pressed.

"I wish I knew . . ."

"At least tell me who called you."

"One of the Peters boys. Johnny. From Pearl's. Who
knows . . . maybe they've run out of cards and they don't
know where to buy any more," he joked feebly.

"That'll be the day when they run out of cards," Katya
said. "Goris manages that place too efficiently. Besides . . .
the Peters twins don't go on duty until eight o'clock. Lazar . . ."
She wiped her hands on the apron tied around her waist. ". . .
There was something on the six o'clock news just now. About
a policeman being killed up in Bedfordshire. He was run over

. . . after he was shot. Something to do with a bank robbery."

"What are you talking about?"

"Lazar. What . . . happened . . . to . . . that . . . gun?"

"Gun? What gun?" His mind was so confused by the phone call that he was having difficulty following Katya's words . . .

Bedfordshire? Lazar's face slowly turned a deathly white as he finally understood what she was saying. Bedfordshire was where the twins had been . . . the bank . . . "I've got to go," he said. "I'll see you later." Without another word he rushed blindly from the house and climbed into the car.

Harry Sherman was himself confused when Lazar arrived. The twins were not there yet; Sherman led Lazar to the living room. "What's this all about?"

"Did you hear anything on the news about a copper being shot?"

Sherman shook his head. "I haven't had the radio on. Did they . . . ?"

"I don't know *what* they did. Johnny just said it was urgent. And then Katya mentioned something about a copper being shot. In Bedfordshire."

"Christ . . ." Sherman ran a hand across his forehead. "Don't even think about it, Whitey."

The doorbell rang. Sherman moved to answer but Lazar beat him to it. He pulled open the door to see Jimmy and Johnny standing outside. Jimmy had changed his clothes; for once, the twins were not dressed identically.

"What went wrong?" Lazar pushed the door closed and stood between it and the twins. "Why in God's name did you kill that copper?" He put his hands on Jimmy's back and shoved him roughly toward the living room.

"We didn't have any choice," Johnny said as he followed his brother and Lazar.

"I wasn't asking you. I was asking *him*!" Lazar snapped back, his worst fears confirmed. He'd thought of them as obedient guardsmen . . . Crazy commandos was more like it. Give them a gun and they thought they were fighting the war all over again.

Jimmy bit his lip. "It's like Johnny said. The copper came

at us. Grabbed ahold of the car as we drove away from the bank. Wouldn't let go."

"Who fired? You? You had the gun."

"I fired!" Johnny shouted. "Because he was too bloody scared to pull the trigger. I grabbed the gun from him and fired three shots through the rear window where the copper was hanging on."

"Three shots?" Lazar gasped. "Wasn't one enough? Just to loosen his hold."

"He'd *seen* us. That's why I fired three times. And just to make bloody certain I ran the car over him a couple of times."

"You crazy bastard! Give me that gun!" Lazar advanced slowly toward Johnny. He couldn't understand what had happened between the two brothers . . . Johnny had suddenly taken the helm, become the dominating one. But Lazar really didn't care about the reason now. He just wanted to get the gun away from Johnny. Then he'd decide what to do.

Sherman also moved . . . quickly. He'd never before heard Lazar swear or seen him lose control like this. As Johnny's hand darted toward his pocket Sherman grabbed him from behind and wrapped a heavy, powerful arm around his throat.

"You stay where you are!" Lazar yelled at Jimmy. Jimmy stood still.

"Get off me!" Johnny yelled as Sherman tightened his grip even more. "You're choking me! I'm going to give him the gun like he wants."

"Do it then," Sherman hissed. "And very gently."

Johnny's hand came out of the pocket, holding the Colt by the barrel. Lazar snatched it away, nodded at Sherman. Johnny staggered away, gasping for breath, rubbing his neck where Sherman's grip had left a crimson mark.

Lazar was surprised to realize that he was pointing the gun at Johnny – the hammer was cocked. He ejected the ammunition, released the hammer. The last thing he wanted was more bloodshed. He needed to calm down, to think clearly.

"You!" He beckoned to Jimmy. "Come inside with me." He threw the pistol and clip of ammunition to Sherman, glad to be rid of it, and left the bald man to keep an eye on

Johnny. Lazar led Jimmy through to the flat's single bedroom. He closed the door and faced the younger twin.

"What happened out there today?"

"Everything went wrong," Jimmy replied quietly. "From start to finish."

"How?"

Jimmy explained how he had gone into the bank and how, before he'd had the opportunity to clean out the first teller's position, the warning signal had been given. "I tried to scare the copper when he was cycling toward us. I didn't want to hit him, Whitey . . . just frighten him. But he wouldn't back off. He threw himself at the car as Johnny drove away. And then . . . when he was hanging onto the back . . . I couldn't bring myself to fire at him."

As Lazar listened, he found it difficult to blame Jimmy. Deciding whether to fire point-blank at an unarmed man, he probably wouldn't have been able to squeeze the trigger either. He hoped not . . . "Then what happened?"

"Johnny grabbed the gun away from me. He fired three times through the rear window. The copper fell off. Then he backed the car over him to make sure he was dead."

"Any witnesses?"

"None. It was an empty stretch of road that led to the railway station. There wasn't a soul around."

"Damned fool," Lazar murmured. He knew he should be relieved that the single link which might have connected him to the crime had been severed. But all he could feel was a growing fury that his instructions to avoid trouble at all costs had been so flagrantly disobeyed. "You wait in here," he ordered Jimmy. "I'll let you know when I want you."

As he opened the door Lazar heard Jimmy call after him: "We didn't get very much either, Whitey. Only three hundred and forty quid."

"I don't give a damn what you got!" He walked into the living room. Sherman and Johnny stood a yard from each other. The bald man looked calm, sure of himself. Johnny fidgeted, glanced anxiously toward the hallway as he heard Lazar's footsteps.

"You bloody idiot!" Lazar lashed into him. "Who told you you've got the brains to improve on my instructions?"

"Whitey . . ." Johnny's earlier bluster, the confidence he'd displayed in the car, wilted in the face of Lazar's rage. "You've got to protect us."

"Protect you? I should kill you. Carve you up into little pieces and feed you to the dogs." With no warning at all, Lazar reached out and slapped Johnny across the face. Hard. Johnny stepped back a pace, touched his smarting face in confusion. Sherman stood still, ready to act should Johnny try to fight back. The Peters twins were Sherman's responsibility. He'd introduced them, recommended them. It was his duty to make sure they stayed in line.

Lazar drew back his hand to strike again. "We had no choice," Johnny said quickly. "We had to get him."

"Of course you had a choice!" Lazar lashed Johnny across the face again with his open hand. "It didn't matter a damn whether that copper saw you or not. I'd have given you both an alibi that no one would have been able to break." He dropped his hands to his sides, tried to control himself . . . He knew if he didn't he would be as bad as they were.

"Do you know how reliable the testimony of a man clinging for dear life to a speeding car is? It would have been thrown out of court. Any defense lawyer would have made mincemeat out of it. Especially when both of you would have had witnesses to swear that you were fifty miles away at the time. All you had to do was stop and throw the copper off. Maybe hit him a couple of times. You didn't think of that, did you? All you could see was shooting him . . . and crushing him with the car."

He turned away and slumped into a chair. Johnny remained cowering in the corner, waiting for the next attack. "Get Jimmy out here," Lazar told Sherman.

Sherman went to the bedroom. When he returned with Jimmy, Lazar was on his feet, hands clasped behind his back. "Where's the money you took today?"

"I've got it," Johnny said, pulling it from his jacket pocket, tossing it to Lazar.

"Three hundred and forty pounds, eh? That's how much a police constable's life is worth?" Lazar said. "How much do you think your life's worth?" he asked Johnny. "And yours?" he added to Jimmy. "More than three hundred and forty pounds? Less? The same?"

Both twins watched him nervously. Jimmy had heard the shouting, could see the marks on his brother's face. Right now Lazar was the last man on earth he wanted to tangle with.

"Turn on the radio," Lazar told Sherman. "We'll wait for the seven o'clock news."

Johnny rubbed his sore face and avoided looking at his brother. While Sherman turned on the radio and fiddled with the tuning Lazar sat down again, his mind racing. Like it or not he had to offer protection to these two. Either that . . . or make them both disappear so completely that no one would ever find them. No . . . that was impossible. Too many questions would be asked. Besides, Jimmy didn't deserve such a punishment. Lazar knew that he himself would have been unable to shoot the constable at point-blank range . . . But Johnny worried him. Three shots that couldn't miss . . . and then running over the man. It made Lazar sick to know that he had to stand by them . . . They had carried out the first three bank raids to the letter. The fourth raid had been one too many.

"Here's the news," Sherman said.

Lazar swung around as Sherman turned up the volume. The bank robbery was the lead item. He began to relax a bit when he heard that police were linking the killing with the string of IRA bank robberies that had recently been taking place. The car believed used in the raid had been found at the local railway station. Two men were being sought. The description given of Jimmy was useless . . . it could have fitted any one of a million men. Lazar was sure that even in a police lineup the bank staff would not be able to identify him with any certainty.

"See?" Johnny said from the corner, his confidence slowly returning. "We've got nothing to worry about."

"Shut up!" The command came from Sherman. Johnny

Peters had let him down. Badly. Lazar hadn't said anything, but Sherman knew that it was he himself who had recommended the men who had botched the job. Sherman vowed to himself that he would keep an extra close watch on Johnny Peters. If he screwed up again . . . Christ help him.

Lazar heard the newscaster describe the murdered police officer. Constable Henry Jeffries had been thirty-four years old . . . he'd left a widow and three young children aged between two and nine. Lazar closed his eyes. Three kids had been deprived of a father because one of his men had acted like an idiot. He couldn't forgive anyone for that.

He opened his eyes. "I'm sending a thousand pounds to that copper's widow," he told Johnny and Jimmy. "Half of it's coming from me. The other half is being taken out of your wages."

"What?" Johnny was stunned. "She'll get a pension from the state. She'll be all right."

His brother cut him off. "We'll give you the money tomorrow, Whitey. From what we made on the other jobs."

Lazar stood up and walked over to Johnny. "You step out of line just one more time, I won't use my hand on your face. I'll take a razor to it. You follow?"

Johnny looked into Lazar's eyes, at Sherman, at Jimmy. No sympathy anywhere. "I'll be careful."

Lazar swung around, opened the door, ready to leave. As an afterthought he called for Jimmy, spoke to him quietly in the hall.

"Jimmy . . . the other night you asked me about doing right by you."

Jimmy nodded, embarrassed now.

"Look . . . I'm not blaming you for what happened today. But I'm telling you this. You keep a leash on that brother of yours. You're responsible for him . . . you understand?"

"It won't happen again."

"It had better not."

Lazar's return journey to Stoke Newington was completed in a near-trance, turning left and right, braking and accelerating without thinking. When he arrived home, Katya

268

greeted him at the door. "What was the panic all about?" she asked. She had delayed dinner and was glad he had returned in time for it. The two boys, already washed and dressed for bed, were waiting in the dining room.

"It was nothing, after all." He forced himself to look cheerful, went into the kitchen and sniffed at the pots that were bubbling on the stove. "Smells good . . . worth rushing home for."

"Lazar . . ." Katya gripped his shoulders and turned him around so that they were face-to-face. "What's wrong with your eyes? They're red, puffy . . ."

"I've got a piece of dirt in my left eye, I was rubbing it."

"Here . . . let me see." She pulled back the lid and peered closely at the eyeball. "There's nothing there now. You keeping anything from me?"

"Like what?"

"The real reason you suddenly rushed out of here. Lazar, if you're in trouble, for God's sake tell me . . . I'm your wife . . ."

He put his arms around her waist and held on tightly. She was his anchor, his support . . . He couldn't let her know what had happened, couldn't expose her to the sordidness. "Katya, I am not in any kind of trouble," he said softly. 'No one's in trouble. Please believe me."

She ran her hands through his white hair, noticing for the first time how streaks of silver were mingling with the blond. She wanted to believe him . . . God, how she wanted to. But she couldn't. Something was terribly wrong and he refused to tell her.

"Walk away from the clubs and the rackets," she whispered, burying her face in his shoulder. "Let someone else have the aggravation."

"Soon," he promised. "As soon as I've done what I have to do."

Aron and David suddenly appeared in the doorway. The sight of his two boys – his sons – was enough to lift Lazar's spirits.

"We're hungry," Aron said. "When are we going to have supper?"

"Mummy's serving it right now," Lazar said. He put a hand on each son's head and led them into the dining room.

"Bigshot!" Jimmy Peters said as he threw open the door of the flat they shared in Hackney. "Big with your mouth is all you are."

"*I* didn't piss myself, did I?" Johnny's face was flushed, he was burning up inside. He almost wished that he had — that would have been a damned sight less embarrassing than being slapped around by Whitey . . . and told off like he was some school kid. And on the ride home, Jimmy had taken up where Lazar had left off.

"From now on you'll keep your big mouth shut and your brain turned off. Let me do the thinking," Jimmy said.

"Okay . . . enough." Johnny couldn't remember the last time he'd fallen out with his twin brother. What made it worse was that he knew Jimmy was right . . . and so was Lazar. They could have shaken that copper off. He would never have been able to identify them. And on top of that, they now owed Lazar five hundred quid.

Jimmy went to a cupboard in the kitchen and pulled out a bottle of Scotch. "You want one?"

"You know better than to ask me that."

"Bigshot . . . can't even take a little drink."

"Lay off me, okay?"

Jimmy poured a drink for himself and felt guilty. Johnny was right. He had no right to make fun of his brother's inability to drink. Johnny suffered from a kidney problem . . . nothing serious as long as he maintained a careful diet that excluded alcohol. And Johnny kept to the diet fanatically, never touched a drop no matter how much he was teased . . .

"You're right," Jimmy finally said. "I'm sorry."

Johnny touched his cheeks and mouth. The skin was still on fire; his lips were swollen. That little white-haired bastard hit his weight, and then some. "What are we going to do now, Jimmy?"

"Absolutely nothing. We stay with Whitey and we do exactly as he tells us to." It was only now, for the first time

270

since he had run out of the bank and seen the constable coming after them, that Jimmy felt confident. Johnny was under his thumb again. But that moment of wildness had cost them dearly. In money and in reputation. They had wanted a top spot in the organization once Lazar expanded. A top spot demanded responsibility, ice-cold judgment – and respect – all of which they'd virtually thrown away today . . . "Whitey told you what to expect if you ever messed up again. I'm telling you the same thing. Flesh and blood doesn't count for anything now." Jimmy swallowed the drink in one gulp. It burned a fire down his throat, warmed him.

"Go splash some cold water on your face," Jimmy said. "It looks like hell. You don't want to go to work looking like you've been on the wrong end of a fifteen-round fight with Joe Louis. You'll get no respect from anyone."

Respect . . . the word echoed inside Johnny's head as he went to clean up. He'd commanded plenty of respect that afternoon, when he'd held the gun in his hand. Even Jimmy had been afraid of him . . .

Johnny swore he'd command respect again.

The window of Superintendent Withers' office at Scotland Yard looked out over the Thames and across to South London. A barge drifted lazily by, navigation lights pinpointing its position on the dark river. Withers gazed longingly at the vessel. A barge captain . . . that was the life, he decided. Up and down the Thames, towing cargo. What kind of responsibility did a barge captain have to bear? Hardly any . . . certainly not the load that Withers was carrying these days, keeping him in the office until midnight. Tonight, he thought sourly as he checked his watch to find it was already past ten, would be no exception.

With every one of the recent bank heists Withers had wondered how long it would take before someone got hurt. Give a bloody Irishman a drink and you'd likely have a fight on your hands. Give him a gun . . . and you had a dead constable.

Withers looked again at the barge, and thought about his own retirement coming soon. Then he'd be off to picturesque

Torquay on the Devon coast, living on the money he'd made from the long association with Joey Taylor. Theirs had been a splendid partnership . . . ample compensation for Withers' failure to rise above superintendent. Maybe it was better this way. Higher up, he might have got bogged down in politics, lost his common touch . . . and gone without the extra income. The partnership had enabled Withers to keep some control over the underworld and at the same time fill his pockets. Until now . . . when these mad Irish bastards were intent on turning London and its neighboring towns into a second . . . Chicago? . . . God help London if it became like that.

A courteous rap sounded on the office door, and a young detective-sergeant came in carrying a manila envelope and a sheet of paper.

"The three bullets that were taken from Constable Jeffries, sir," the sergeant said, passing across the envelope. "Forty-fives. They match the one taken from the ceiling of the bank. And those from the last three raids in London."

"Of course they do," Withers grunted. He hadn't expected it to be any different. In the four raids during the past week and a half only one weapon had been used . . . an American-made Colt forty-five automatic. With the money they were making from the robberies – although today's job had been only three or four hundred quid, according to the bank – how long would it be before they came up with more sophisticated weapons? Since the first raid where the Colt had been used Withers' men had tried to learn if any weapons had been stolen from American bases. They'd had no luck. Bloody Yanks . . . they had no more idea of controlling the spread of arms than the pope had of making love.

Roll on retirement, Withers thought as he studied the bullets. They were so clean that it was difficult to imagine that they had been taken recently from a man's chest. A *policeman's* chest. Gleaming dully, they looked no more lethal than a child's game.

Retirement . . . he should take it easy, play for time. Hand the whole mess over to Special Branch . . . after all, the Irish were involved. But they'd hand it right back to him. At best

272

they'd offer to continue working together. No . . . Withers knew he had to get to the bottom of this by himself. That was the difference between him and the captain of the barge, he decided. Withers was a public servant, had to take whatever came his way . . . and keep right on taking it. Even if he sank to the bottom under the weight . . .

He glanced up, saw the young detective-sergeant still standing in front of the desk. "Have you come up with any more possibilities? Names of suspects?"

"Yes, sir." The sergeant held out a sheet of paper with five names and addresses. "These are the men who spent the war in Dublin and have returned to London in the past couple of months. They've all got records."

Withers ran a knowing eye over the list. All five men lived in the same area, the Kilburn-Willesden-Cricklewood triangle of northwest London. Little Dublin . . . or little Belfast . . . depending on whether you favored the orange or the green. And their records covered everything from breaking and entering to armed robbery.

The dead constable was too much, he decided. It was time to start banging heads . . .

The following night, Saturday, Lazar avoided talking to the Peters twins. He spent an hour at Ruby's, then moved on to Pearl's where he collected money, talked to Goris and Sherman, watched a few games. The twins walked around as if nothing had happened, carrying out their duties. Johnny's lip was still swollen; when anyone asked him what had happened, he said he'd stumbled on a flight of stairs.

Shortly after eleven, Lazar told Sherman he wanted to leave.

"How do you feel?" Sherman asked as they drove away.

"Disgusted. We killed a man who shouldn't have had to die." Lazar still blamed himself. Jimmy and Johnny Peters had merely been his tools.

"Does Katya know?"

"Are you crazy?" He gave Sherman a look, amazed that his friend — his lieutenant — could even ask such a question. "I lead two lives, Harry. You know that."

273

"All right . . . all right," Sherman said, trying to calm Lazar down. "Don't blow up at me."

"I'm sorry." Lazar reached out to touch Sherman on the arm. "I'm just a bit edgy, that's all."

"That's understandable. Do you want to wait a while before we start on Taylor?"

"No." Lazar shook his head. "We said we'd start immediately after the final raid. That policeman being killed won't change it. But at least Withers is going to be even busier than we'd originally planned . . ."

"Tell that to the copper's widow and kids," Sherman said bitterly.

"I know . . . I'm sorry I said that."

They drove to Sherman's flat. From a cupboard in the living room Sherman took out a large-scale map of the West End of London. The map was marked with six circles, three in red ink, three in blue. Each circle had a number next to it. They signified the most profitable clubs protected by Joey Taylor . . . clubs Lazar intended to take over. Those circled in red were drinking clubs; those with blue ink around them were spielers.

Lazar touched his finger to each mark. "The Hi-Lo in Old Compton Street. Benny's in Greek Street. Dominic's in Denman Street."

"That takes care of the drinking clubs," Sherman said, watching Lazar's pointed finger. "Now for the gambling casinos."

"The Casino Club in Archer Street. The Jack Tar in Wardour Street. And . . ." Lazar's finger rested on the blue circle with a heavily penciled number one.

"The plum at the very top of the tree," Sherman finished for him. "Toppers in Regent Street."

Lazar smiled. On the second floor of a building only a hundred yards from the elegant and fashionable Café Royal, Toppers was what every gambling club owner aspired to. Toppers even had strictly enforced dress rules. The big gamblers frequented Toppers; it was nothing for them to win or lose a few hundred . . . even a couple of thousand . . . pounds in one evening.

Lazar knew the man who owned Toppers . . . David Martin, before the war a successful big-time bookmaker who had invested his money in the most exclusive gambling club in all of London. David Martin was one of Joey Taylor's favorites, because with the money he made from Toppers, Martin could afford to pay the most for his protection. Lazar knew he'd have to leave Toppers and David Martin until the very last . . . until he had the other five clubs under his control and Taylor was reeling from the punches.

"Do you still think I can use the Peters twins for this?" Lazar asked Sherman. There was only one way he could take over other clubs – by muscling in on someone else's territory, forcing them to pay *him* for protection. He couldn't afford any bloodshed, though . . . not if he wanted to keep Ivor Davies on his side. Intimidation was his only available weapon . . .

Sherman considered the question carefully. Before the disaster at the bank, Johnny and Jimmy Peters had figured prominently in Lazar's plans. There were other men on the payroll, of course, but none of them had the same amount of guts – sheer, stupid guts – that the twins so obviously had . . . "I think so, Whitey," he said finally, knowing that his own judgment was on the line. "The risks are there . . . but I think Johnny's learned his lesson."

Lazar took another look at the map. "I hope you're right, Harry." He recalled his short conversation with Jimmy about keeping his brother in check. "I certainly hope so."

CHAPTER EIGHTEEN

Shmuel had not felt so nervous since the day he was married. His stomach was in knots, and he couldn't eat the roast beef dinner that Lottie had splurged her meat ration coupons to get. He picked at the food listlessly, finally pushing away the plate. Lottie looked disappointed.

"What's the matter . . . my cooking's not good enough for you anymore?" she asked.

"Your cooking's just fine." He grinned sheepishly across the table at her. "It's my stomach that's not so good."

"Nerves at your age," she chided him gently. "You're a grown man."

"Too grown." He had put on a great deal of weight, in spite of his regular schedule of exercise and activities. He wasn't even certain his tuxedo would fit for tonight's boxing tournament at Clapton Boys' Club. But it was too late to worry about it now. In a couple of hours he'd be climbing into the ring as the master of ceremonies.

"Anyone would think you're an expectant father, the way you're carrying on," Lottie joked.

"Clapton Boys' Club is my baby . . . our baby. We've worked hard for it and I'm still scared something might go wrong." After Lottie had so tragically lost their child, and learned that she could never have another, they had poured all their love and their energy into the boys' club. The boys had, in a great sense, become *their* children . . .

Lottie understood how anxious he was. Everyone would be at the club tonight. The mayor had accepted an invitation. Ivor Davies and Leah were coming. Two hundred tickets had been sold, and Chris Peters had promised that his newspaper would give the event special coverage.

Shmuel left the table and went upstairs to get dressed. He put on the trousers to the tuxedo, breathing in deeply while he did them up, then put on the jacket, studied himself in the mirror. Not bad . . . if it weren't for the damn eyepatch . . . He called out to Lottie that he was ready to leave.

"You look absolutely marvelous," she told him. "As handsome as a prince."

"You don't look too bad yourself." Lottie had bought a new dress for the occasion, pale green velvet, finishing midway down her calves. "Seems a shame that we've got to drive over there in the furniture van when we're all dressed up like this."

Shmuel had been promising himself to buy a secondhand car for ages, but he'd never made enough money to afford one. Or . . . he corrected himself . . . he'd never saved enough money. Any spare cash always went toward the club. Even with the gifts from the lawyer, Shmuel had been forced to dig deeply into his own pocket to pay for all the equipment as well as the rent for the new premises. But after tonight, if everything went well – with donations and the money raised through ticket sales – the club would be self-sufficient. And if it wasn't, he knew that he'd continue to pump money into it. And Lottie would continue to approve.

He pushed Lottie gently toward the door, wanting to be on his way. He couldn't wait to get to the club. To see the work he, Lottie, Chris Peters and other members had put in.

Shmuel swung the ungainly furniture van into the parking lot of the club. As they walked inside he thought about his benefactor, wondered if he would be here tonight to see the results of his philanthropy. The man had requested all newspaper mentions of the club's activities, so he must be interested. Would he be one of the faces around the ring? Would he . . . yes . . . he just might identify himself. Shmuel began to think of words to say that would express his gratitude.

Chris Peters was already inside the club, organizing a group of members in a last-minute clean-up. When he saw Shmuel and Lottie, he came over. Chris was smartly dressed in a dark gray suit and sparkling white shirt. Lottie asked him if the suit was new. He blushed and said yes, and she told him to wear it in good health.

"How do we look?" Chris asked, making a sweeping gesture with his hand as if he owned the place.

"The Albert Hall's got plenty to worry about." Shmuel laughed with delight, taking in every detail. The boxing ring erected in the center of the hall; the lights above it . . . installed at cost; the rows of folding chairs he had borrowed from a nearby church. Alongside one wall a tea bar had been set up, which Lottie would operate with the help of two boys. On the stage at the far end of the hall was a table with the trophies that would be presented by the mayor to the winner of each bout at the end of the evening.

"You're staying at the door, right?" Shmuel said to Chris.

"We've got another hundred or so tickets we can sell. After that . . . we'll charge half-price for standing room only."

Shmuel clapped Chris on the back and walked over to the boys who were putting in the final touches, then went to the dressing rooms at the rear of the stage. Lottie moved in behind the tea bar, setting out crockery and homemade cakes, making sure the enormous tea urn was full. She hoped the spectators would be thirsty . . . each cup of tea they drank would add a little more much-needed money to the club's coffers.

In the dressing room Shmuel found three of the youngsters who would be boxing for the Clapton club. He wished them luck and returned to the main hall. He had trained these boys himself, wanted them to win, of course, but knew that what was more important was that they all enjoy themselves . . .

As he stood by the ring, his hand resting on the ropes, Shmuel's mind began to play tricks . . . his imagination filled the empty hall with people, transformed it into the magnificence of the National Sporting Club. What might have been, he thought . . . what might have been. He touched a finger to his eyepatch, the permanent, painful reminder of that night, and thought about his older brother Lazar.

Did Lazar . . . with all his money, all his men . . . have the same joy that Shmuel did? Could he point to a group of young men and say, *I* gave them pleasure . . . *I* helped them mold their lives . . . made them into better people? No . . . Shmuel was certain of it. Lazar had schemed, and more. His wealth didn't mean a thing. The strongmen who surrounded him were only interested in the money he could pay them. And look at the kind of men they were. Like the Peters twins.

Shmuel looked toward the door, at Chris sitting behind the table, excitement in his eyes as he shared in Shmuel's dream. Shmuel had got Chris away from his brothers, protected him from their influence. With Shmuel's help he was now embarked on a rewarding career. Shmuel felt good about it. He'd cheated Lazar out of Chris . . . cheated the devil out of a soul. That's what Lazar lacked, Shmuel finally decided. A soul. He had a wife, children, money, power. And with all that he still had nothing . . . never stopped wanting something he didn't have, like his big house with enough rooms for a dozen children and all their friends. Lazar would always want more . . . And Shmuel could not help feeling sorry for his brother . . .

At seven thirty, half an hour before they were scheduled to begin, the hall was more than half full. Chris and Lottie both had their hands full selling tickets and tea.

Ivor Davies and Leah arrived five minutes later. After congratulating Shmuel on the tremendous turnout, they pitched in . . . Leah went behind the tea bar to help Lottie, and Davies worked with Chris Peters at the front.

Shmuel watched it all with a huge smile of joy. His dream was coming true. He had worked and struggled to provide the youngsters with a place of their own. Now the local community was accepting it, giving their full-hearted support. He could ask for nothing more.

"Where's Johnny?" Lazar asked Jimmy Peters when the younger twin arrived half an hour late for work at Pearl's.

"He's sick. That's why I'm so late, trying to look after him."

Lazar grumbled to himself. Just tonight Johnny had to be sick, just when he wanted to go over the plans in detail. "What's the matter with him?"

"Something he ate, I guess," Jimmy said. "He was as sick as a dog. I left him in bed."

"Okay. At midnight we're all meeting at Harry's flat in Highbury. On the way over there, drop by and see if Johnny's any better. I want him to get the information firsthand, not through you."

"All right, Whitey. I'll bring him along if I have to carry him."

"And don't forget I'm relying on you to keep him straight." Lazar watched Jimmy walk away to stand by the door with Goris. He could feel his heart pounding. The decision to use the Peters twins as his spearhead had been made. There could be no backing out now. He just hoped Harry Sherman's judgment – and his own – was sound. One wrong move on the twins' part, one piece of unnecessary mayhem and he would have everyone down around his ears. Sure, Joey Taylor was old, nowhere near as sharp as he had once been. And Withers was busy chasing Irish phantoms. But Lazar knew that if something went wrong, if one innocent person was hurt, Ivor Davies would crucify him.

Lazar had once wanted to kill Taylor . . . and Withers. As a fitting act of vengeance for what they had forced him to do to Shmuel. Now he realized he would have to be satisfied with persuading Taylor to step aside. Make him understand that it would be best if he retired and handed over control to someone else . . . to the strongest . . . to Lazar. The same went for Withers. The superintendent was untouchable. Just another candidate for retirement.

Lazar drove to Stoke Newington. He stopped in at Ruby's for five minutes, pleased to see that the club was moderately busy, then drove the short distance to Clapton. The parking lot outside the boys' club was full. Lights shone through the windows. When Lazar stopped, turned off the engine and rolled down the window, he thought he could hear the sound of cheering. "Good luck to you," he muttered. "You deserve it – and so do I," he added as he drove away . . .

Katya was surprised to see Lazar enter the house. "Quiet night?" she asked, wondering what he was doing home so early.

"No, thank God . . . I can't afford quiet nights." He kissed her. "I just thought I'd come back and talk to you." He walked into the living room, made himself comfortable in an armchair. "I drove past Shmuel's club just now. It looked packed."

"It's his big boxing tournament tonight," Katya said. "It must be a success."

"That's what I'm hoping. The club means a lot to him."

"More than the spielers mean to you?"

Lazar was amazed at how well Katya understood him. The spielers made money, would eventually make even more once he expanded and consolidated his position. But what satisfaction was there in it for him? What joy was there in being king of the hill when you had to constantly look over your shoulder to see who was coming up from behind to topple you? He was on a treadmill and knew he could not get off. He had to keep on walking, faster and faster . . . Otherwise the wheel would run over him.

"You think I should go over there?"

"To watch?"

He nodded.

"Shmuel might see you."

"Not if I stood at the back somewhere. He'll probably be in the center of it all."

"Go on then," Katya said. "You know you want to see it. Just look in, that's all." She remembered Harry Sherman suggesting that he and Lazar should go, and she'd been against the idea. She'd said it wasn't time yet for Lazar to try to win back Shmuel. But if Lazar just popped in for a few minutes – and Shmuel didn't see him . . .

Lazar went upstairs, peeked into the boys' room, saw they were both asleep. Aron had the covers back, one arm hanging outside the bed. Lazar tiptoed into the room and pulled the covers up over his older son's shoulders. Just as quietly, he left the room and pulled the door closed. On the way out, he kissed Katya, got into the car and eagerly drove back to Clapton.

He parked twenty yards from the club. Feeling nervous, he walked slowly toward the low building, stood uncertainly in the parking lot while he braced himself to enter. From outside, the cheering and noise was loud. When he opened the door, it hit him like a physical force.

Only the center lights above the ring were on. Lazar peered over the rows of people to the ring where two bantamweights were battling it out, darting around, throwing punches with lightning speed. On the other side of the ring, he could make out Shmuel in a tuxedo, sitting next to the mayor. A flashbulb suddenly popped, freezing the boxers for an instant.

"What are you doing here?" a voice asked quietly.

Lazar spun around to his right, recognized Ivor Davies sitting behind the ticket table. "Thought I'd drop by and have a look. Only for a couple of minutes."

"Cost you a shilling to stand. No more seats left," Davies said.

Lazar pulled out a coin, dropped it onto the table. "I won't let Shmuel see me."

"That's up to you." Davies had somehow expected to see Lazar put in an appearance. Secretively . . . just like he was doing. Shmuel had been more right than he would have guessed about the presence of his unknown benefactor here tonight. Only he would never have guessed who that benefactor was.

What would Shmuel do if he saw Lazar? Davies wondered. What would he do if he learned that Lazar had made this evening — the entire club — possible? . . .

"Where's Leah?" Lazar asked.

"She's at the tea counter."

"How come you're not on duty tonight?" Lazar asked. "Quiet time at the Yard?"

Davies grinned. "I wish. No . . . I called in sick. I wasn't going to miss this evening for anything."

"You're work shy, that's your problem," Lazar teased his brother-in-law. Davies was the second person who'd called in sick that night. At least Johnny Peters was really ill . . . "Things still busy, are they?"

"They've heated up even more since that poor bugger was killed last week," Davies said softly. "Crying shame, that . . ."

"Did you find anyone?"

Davies shook his head. "It's like looking for a needle in a

haystack. It's even harder now because the robberies seem to have stopped, so the gun won't surface."

"I read the police constable's widow got some money."

Davies nodded. "Not from the thugs who did it, though. It was a thousand pounds . . . three times more than was stolen." A bell rang and Davies swung his head toward the ring. "That's the end of this fight. You'd better get going before the lights go back on."

"Thanks. I'll be seeing you." Lazar walked back to his car, feeling cheered by the short visit to Shmuel's club. He could see that his brother was happy . . . It had been a long time since Lazar had seen him like this – not since before the fight with Bomber Billy Harris.

And he'd seen Ivor Davies, had learned that the pace at Scotland Yard had picked up even more. The police thought that the gun used to kill the constable would never surface. Lazar was determined to prove them correct.

He reached the car, got in. As he drove away he saw the shadowy figure of a man approach the club. Another late-comer, he decided. Someone else who'd have to pay a shilling to stand. Davies must be taking money hand over fist for Shmuel tonight.

. . . The man whom Lazar saw did not enter the building, though. Instead, he walked along the side, movements furtive, hat pulled low over his forehead, coat collar up. In the shadow of the wall he stopped and looked around. Protected from view by the cars and by the large furniture van in the parking lot, he felt secure.

He listened to the noise from within, tried to guess what was happening. When he peeked through a window he saw people lining up at the tea bar. He could see the ring was empty. Seats were vacant. It was the break between bouts, he decided. He'd wait until everyone was back in their seats.

Passing close to the window was a face the man recognized. When he saw the eyepatch the man let out a low growl. That was the bastard he really wanted, that one-eyed moron who'd nearly punched him in two that night. He could still feel the power of that punch, the breath being blasted out of his body.

Johnny Peters waited patiently until the lights inside the hall dimmed. When he looked through the window again he saw four figures in the ring. Two young boxers in their teens, the referee, and Shmuel who was announcing the fight. Johnny reached underneath his coat and brought out the gallon can of diesel fuel he was hiding there. He'd chosen diesel because it burned slowly. It didn't explode like gasoline, would give him time to escape safely.

He spilled most of the diesel fuel against the base of the wall, and used the rest to make a narrow trail which ran four or five yards along the concrete. The smell caught in his nostrils and he quickened his pace. He didn't want to hurry, wanted to prolong the moment, take the greatest pleasure from this, his revenge. He couldn't hit directly back at Whitey; he was too scared to try, scared of Whitey and of his own brother. But he could burn out that one-eyed bastard who was Whitey's brother. Kill two birds with one stone, that would. That was clever, he thought. Strike back at Lazar through Shmuel.

As he lit a match and dropped it onto the end of the trail, it occurred to Johnny Peters that his young brother could be inside. But it was too late. The trail of fire was already running steadily toward the building. Chris had no business being in there anyway, Johnny thought. Siding with that one-eyed bastard who'd beaten up his brother. He would just have to take his chances with the rest of them.

The second round of the final bout had just begun. Shmuel settled in his ringside seat, the jacket of his tuxedo open. He dug a finger between his shirt collar and neck, trying to let in the air. The heat around the ring was tremendous, heightened by the seemingly never-ending popping of flashbulbs. Chris had kept his promise. The photographer from the local paper had stayed for the entire evening and had promised a pictorial spread of the evening.

Shmuel glanced at the mayor, sitting to his right in his heavy red robe. How the hell could he stand it? It must be like a steam bath inside that thing.

"You must be very proud of your boys," the mayor said to Shmuel. "They've put on quite a show tonight."

"I'm prouder than any father could be of his own son," Shmuel answered truthfully. He looked around for Chris, saw him talking to the photographer.

The mayor started to say something else, then stopped. "Can you smell something?" he asked Shmuel.

All Shmuel could smell was smoke from cigarettes and pipes. A haze had settled over the center of the hall, streaky clouds picked up by the lights above the ring.

Then, from the side of the hall, a man's voice hoarsely yelled, "Fire!"

The two boxers in the ring broke apart. Shmuel leaped to his feet as the shout was repeated and taken up by other voices. He, too, could smell it now . . . the unmistakable odor of burning wood.

Chaos swept through the hall as spectators struggled to evacuate the area. They tripped over one another in the narrow aisles in a desperate attempt to reach the door. Davies, standing by the door, yelled at them not to panic, but his urgent cries went unheeded.

Shmuel jumped into the ring, clapped his hands loudly, shouted for order. Nothing helped. Men and women who had lived through the blitz five years earlier — endured it with a stoicism that had won admiration throughout the world — now stampeded toward the door in blind, unreasoning panic.

By the tea bar the smell of smoke was strongest, burning the eyes, catching in the throat. Leah shrieked as Lottie pointed toward flames at the base of the wall only a few feet from where they stood. Chris Peters grabbed hold of the two women, pulled them away. Somewhere else, a man smashed a chair through a window; mindless of the broken glass he dove through into the night.

"Take it easy!" Ivor Davies yelled from the door. He plunged into the fray of people struggling to get out, pulled them apart, succeeded in establishing an orderly line.

With a roaring crackle, the wooden inside of the wall began to burn fiercely, strengthening its hold, feeding upon itself.

Chris Peters dragged Leah and Lottie toward the door, handed them over to Davies. Then he looked around for Shmuel.

He spotted him still standing in the ring, a solitary figure in black and white. Shmuel gazed around at the exodus with a feeling of doom in his heart. Only moments earlier he had been enjoying the congratulations of the mayor; now he watched helplessly as all he had worked for went up in flames.

Shmuel's good eye smarted from the smoke. He blinked, looked toward the stage and saw the line of trophies that were to have been souvenirs of this triumphant evening. He jumped out of the ring, pushed aside chairs, determined to save the trophies if nothing else. By the time he reached the stage, the hall was almost empty and the entire wall was on fire. Glass broke with a sharp cracking sound as Shmuel grabbed hold of as many trophies as he could manage. Arms full, he jumped down from the stage and ran toward the door. He was the last one through and turned for a final look as flames took hold of the roof.

A minute later the entire building was burning out of control, watched numbly by the hundreds who had been inside. Cars were started, driven out of the parking lot to safety. Shmuel threw his keys to Chris, told him to move the furniture van. Then he looked around for Lottie. She was with Leah and Davies, fighting back tears as she watched the building being consumed in flames. Shmuel felt like joining her. Lottie had lost as much as he had; they'd both struggled and sacrificed for the club.

"Are you insured?" Ivor Davies asked.

Shmuel nodded. "For the equipment . . . but how can you insure for everything else?" He put an arm around Lottie, tried to comfort her. He himself was close to tears.

In the distance, bells clanged. Headlights from approaching fire engines blinded the crowd. But it was too late to do anything. The building was wrecked.

Four men sat around the small living room of Harry Sherman's flat in Highbury. Sherman, Lazar and two men who worked at Ruby's in Stoke Newington, Mike Malin and

286

Peter Cox. Malin and Cox had been among the first to join Lazar after the war had ended. Malin — a tall, heavy, black-haired Irishman in his early thirties — had been a military policeman in the army. Cox — short and wiry with red hair and pale blue eyes — had been a bomb-aimer in the Royal Air Force, flying Lancasters in the thousand-plane raids that had hammered Germany to its knees. Before the war Malin had been a wrestler, touring the rings in the north of England. Cox had been a barber in the East End of London, acting as a bookmaker's commission agent on the side.

"Where the hell are they?" Lazar grumbled as he checked his watch. "I told Jimmy to be here at midnight. Try them again," he told Sherman.

Sherman dialed the number of the flat where the Peters twins lived. No answer. He looked back to Lazar and shrugged.

There was a double rap on the front door. Mike Malin stood up, ready to answer. "Maybe that's them now," he said. He hoped it was . . .

"Go on then," Lazar told Malin. There was the sound of voices and Malin returned, leading the Peters twins into the living room. Before Lazar could ask Jimmy why he was late for the second time that night, Jimmy spoke.

"Sorry, Whitey . . . but it took a while to get his lordship here ready to come over."

"You feel any better?" Lazar asked Johnny. The older twin's face was white, his eyes looked hollow. "What did you eat that made you so sick?"

"Jellied eels."

"Serves you right." One of the few practices of Lazar's childhood training as a Jew in Germany that still survived was his avoidance of all kinds of shellfish — and he included eels in that category. It was *trayf*, such food . . . unclean, not to be eaten. Even when he was out with Harry Sherman and the bald man polished off a plate of seafood with visible enjoyment, Lazar would feel sick.

"I'll be more careful next time." Johnny sat down on the couch next to Peter Cox and looked around expectantly. Obviously Lazar did not know anything yet about the boys' club burning down. Johnny was pleased. Perhaps while this meeting was going on there would be news, and he'd be able to see for himself how it affected the little white-haired bastard. It had been close, though, Johnny knew. He'd got back from Clapton and thrown himself into bed only minutes before Jimmy had returned from Pearl's to bring him to the meeting at Sherman's flat. While Johnny had dressed he'd noticed the faint odor of diesel fuel on his hands and clothes. He'd washed, but the smell had lingered . . .

Sherman brought out the large-scale map of Central London and spread it across the table. Lazar stood poised over it, index finger pointing to the clubs circled in red and blue. The other men joined him around the table.

"You all know these clubs . . . boozers and spielers. Toppers we leave for the very last, until we've got the others. Now this," he paused to look around the ring of faces, trapping each man in turn, "is the way we're going to do it. Nice at first . . . and I mean *nice*. We only turn them over if we get the push. But get this straight right away. I don't want any customers getting hurt if it comes to trouble. I want property damage only. Okay?"

All the men nodded, and Lazar fixed his eyes on Johnny who stood next to him. "What about you . . . do you understand that?" Lazar's nose wrinkled as he tried to identify the faint but obnoxious smell that seemed to come from Johnny.

"I heard you," Johnny said.

"I hope for your sake you did." He sniffed again, but could not place the smell. He forgot all about it as the telephone rang. Lazar glanced at it with annoyance, while Johnny Peters felt his anticipation build.

"Are you expecting a call?" Lazar asked Sherman.

The bald man shook his head. "Let it ring, Whitey."

Lazar went back to the map, but the continuous ringing interrupted his train of thought. "Better get it," he told Sherman. While he waited for Sherman to answer he gazed at the other men, aware again of the smell.

Sherman walked across to the phone, lifted the receiver and listened. He blinked a couple of times, muttered something

288

into the mouthpiece and then called Lazar over. "It's Katya," he whispered. "There's been trouble at Shmuel's club."

Lazar grabbed the receiver from Sherman's hand. "Katya . . . what is it?"

"There was a fire at Shmuel's club," Katya answered breathlessly. "Ivor just called me."

"Was anyone . . . was anyone hurt?" Why else would she call him? Shmuel . . .

"No," she said, and Lazar felt himself go weak with relief. "But the police are there now. With the fire brigade. The club was burned right down and they think it's arson."

"Arson?" Lazar said it louder than he'd intended. The other men gazed at him curiously. "I'm going over there right now." He dropped the receiver and turned to face the others. "Harry . . . you know the arrangements. Brief everyone. I have to go out."

"Is Shmuel all right?" Sherman asked.

"He's fine. Everyone's fine. But the club's been burned to the ground. Arson."

Johnny watched Lazar leave the room, heard the front door slam. The whole thing was a letdown. Not that Johnny had expected Shmuel to be killed . . . that was too much to hope for. But he'd expected some reaction from Lazar, more than just the rush from the flat. Johnny understood the two brothers were on the outs, but knew Lazar cared about Shmuel, wanted to make it up. Otherwise why would he have come down so hard on Johnny when he'd had the fight with Shmuel?

During the hectic drive to Clapton, Lazar asked himself how it could have happened. The fire officials suspected arson. The question was who. Who were Shmuel's enemies? Lazar thought hard. With the exception of Ben Kosky – a name from ten years before – he could not think of a single soul who would wish Shmuel harm. Anyway, it couldn't be Kosky. The last Lazar had heard, the ex-manager was in Canada . . . Toronto or somewhere.

He arrived at Clapton to see two police cars and a fire engine still at the club. Shmuel was easy to spot, conspicuous in his tuxedo as he talked with Ivor Davies and two uniformed officers. Lazar approached the small group.

"What happened?"

If Shmuel was surprised to see Lazar, he disguised it. He merely nodded toward the rubble. "That's what happened."

"Katya called to tell me," Lazar said as an explanation for his presence. "I'm sorry. Is Lottie all right?"

"Everyone's all right." Shmuel moved a few yards away from his brother and stared at the rubble.

"Where's Leah?" Lazar asked Davies. "She was here earlier. What happened to her?"

"Someone took her home."

"How did you know Leah was here?" Shmuel demanded as he turned back to face Lazar.

Lazar stared at his brother, wondered how to answer. Davies saved him the trouble. "Lazar was here before."

"Here? At the tournament?" Shmuel forgot all about the fire. "What were you doing here?"

"You were having a boxing tournament. I came along to watch for a while."

"You . . . ?" Shmuel looked to Davies for an explanation.

"I took his money," Davies said. "He paid . . . just like anyone else."

"You had no business being here," Shmuel protested.

"Why not?" Lazar demanded. "Is it a crime that I wanted to see how you were getting along? How the club was doing? I was interested enough to come along . . . what's so terrible about that?"

"Interested!" Shmuel stepped right up to his brother, towered over him. "Interested like you were interested in this?" He touched the eyepatch.

"Shmuel . . . maybe you're being a little hasty," Davies said slowly, pushing his way between the two men, thinking that perhaps he could use the confrontation to good purpose.

Lazar guessed what was going through Davies' mind . . . the opportunity to heal the rift between the brothers by revealing the identity of Shmuel's mysterious benefactor. But Shmuel wasn't ready for that yet . . . Lazar knew how to prove it to Davies.

"Shmuel . . . I realize that money alone can't make up for what you've lost tonight. But if you can use this . . ." He pulled out a wad of cash he had taken from Pearl's. ". . . You're welcome to it."

Shmuel stared contemptuously at the money. "Money is still your answer to everything, eh? Don't you ever learn anything about life?" Disgusted, he turned his back and walked away.

"That was for your benefit," Lazar told Davies, embarrassed by the stares of the police officers and firemen who were listening to the exchange. "Before you opened your mouth."

"I know. I'm sorry . . . I just thought it might be a good time to straighten everything out," Davies said, and Lazar put the money back in his pocket.

A constable, holding a large square object, approached Davies. It was a fuel can. "We found this fifty yards away, sir," the constable said to Davies. "Smells like it had diesel in it."

Davies sniffed and made a face. No question that it had been used to start the blaze. Diesel burned steadily but didn't flare up. None of the people inside had heard an explosion or seen a fierce outbreak of fire. Just . . . steady.

"Will you be able to get fingerprints from it?" Lazar asked.

"I doubt it. Whoever set that fire was probably wearing gloves."

Lazar leaned forward to sniff the can as Davies held it out. The smell was foul . . . and alarmingly familiar. Before he could think of anything else a vivid burst of light temporarily blinded him. When his vision cleared he saw a photographer removing a burned-out bulb from his flash. Next to the man stood Chris Peters, writing shorthand notes in a pad as he spoke to the constable who had discovered the can. Lazar hoped he wasn't in the picture.

Shmuel came over to inspect the can. "Someone doesn't like what I'm doing," he said. "And I don't like what they're doing." He looked at Lazar, then motioned for him to move away from the group. "What happened to Chris' brother who worked for you?"

291

"Which one? They're twins. Johnny and Jimmy."

"The one who came after me that night. The one I left on the ground here." He nodded down at the gravel. "Where was he tonight?"

"At the club. At Pearl's," Lazar answered automatically.

"All night?"

Now Lazar knew why that damned smell was so familiar . . . It was the same thing he'd smelled earlier . . . in Sherman's flat when Johnny had stood next to him. Johnny had been sick earlier that evening . . . Johnny had stuffed his face with jellied eels and come down with food poisoning. Like hell he had . . . "All night long," Lazar said slowly, knowing why he had to lie about Johnny. If Shmuel learned that Johnny had been responsible for the fire he'd put at least some of the blame onto Lazar . . . after all, Johnny worked for him. "Both Johnny and Jimmy were at Pearl's the whole time. Why . . . do you think one of them would do it? Especially when their young brother was inside the building?"

Lazar felt his stomach churning, his eyes going blind with anger. That crazy bastard. First he shoots an unarmed constable . . . and now this. What was he hoping to achieve? Kill everyone inside? Even his own brother Chris? Or . . . was there more to it . . . like striking back at Lazar through Shmuel?

"What's the matter?" Shmuel asked, noticing the change that had come over Lazar. "Don't you like what I think of your friends?"

As Lazar opened his mouth to reply, another thought struck him . . . Was Johnny in it alone? Had he fooled his twin brother into believing that he was sick? Or was Jimmy covering for him . . . after Lazar had told Jimmy to keep his wild brother in check? "Shmuel, just because you don't want to take my money . . . and you don't like the men who work for me . . . you don't have to dream up fiction like this. You'd better look elsewhere for whoever is out for you."

"I will," Shmuel promised. He walked away and left Lazar standing alone.

Lazar's thoughts were hopelessly jumbled. He couldn't believe that Jimmy would be involved in this madness. It had to be Johnny, working alone . . .

First . . . Lazar wanted to kill Johnny, to strangle him with his bare hands. Hadn't he warned him what would happen if he so much as looked cross-eyed at Shmuel?

No . . . killing would solve nothing. Right now, Lazar needed everything to be simple and clean. He could not afford complications. Just as he could not afford to turn Johnny over to the police for tonight's work. Never mind about Shmuel blaming Lazar for the fire because Johnny worked for him. Too much was at stake. Johnny knew too much about the firm . . . about Lazar. If he blabbed, they'd all be done. Whether he liked it or not, Lazar and Johnny were stuck with each other.

For the time being.

Suddenly, Lazar felt like a chess player with a pawn advantage as he approaches a crucial juncture of the game. A good chess player used a pawn advantage cleverly, shielded the man until he was ready to sacrifice it to gain position . . .

Running a firm was just like a game of chess, Lazar decided as he watched the firemen poke among the ruins of the building. Johnny was the extra pawn on Lazar's board. Lazar would use him until his value had diminished. And then he'd sacrifice him . . . give a body away.

Only, when he gave away the body of Johnny Peters, it would be very cold . . . unable to talk about anything to anyone.

CHAPTER NINETEEN

From the very beginning, the Peters twins had figured prominently in Lazar's plans to take over Joey Taylor's most lucrative clubs. He could not change his mind now, not if he didn't want awkward questions. Especially from Johnny. To fire the older twin now would undoubtedly tip him off about Lazar's true feelings toward him . . . and Lazar wasn't ready for Johnny to find those out just yet.

First, Lazar decided to visit the drinking clubs, those premises circled in red on Harry Sherman's map of Central London, all within a shout of each other.

Lazar selected the Hi-Lo on Old Compton Street to open his campaign. At nine thirty on a Saturday night he drove to Soho with the Peters twins and Sherman, parked the car near the Hi-Lo and got out. Rather than walk straight into the drinking club which was located above an Italian restaurant, he instead strolled around . . . up and down the narrow roads which joined Old Compton Street to Soho Square. Sherman was at his side; the twins lagged a couple of yards behind.

Sherman understood why Lazar was making this walking tour of Soho, just as he understood so many other things about the younger, white-haired man who had become his closest friend. Lazar was taking a gigantic step, and he was nervous . . .

People out walking parted to give the four men undisputed possession of the sidewalk. A couple of heavily made-up prostitutes eyed the small group with interest. Only for a moment. When the streetwise women recognized them for what they were they turned the other way, looked elsewhere for customers.

"Are you ready?" Sherman asked quietly as they walked

along Frith Street. Ahead was the Pied Piper public house where they had trapped Davey Vanetti that night when Lazar had taken over. Already they had passed the narrow courtyard and Lazar hadn't given it a second glance.

"Are you?" Lazar raised a hand and quickened his pace. The men with him picked up speed.

Back in Old Compton Street they stopped outside the Italian restaurant. "Up there," Sherman said, pointing to the side entrance, the flight of stairs that ran up to offices on higher floors . . . and the Hi-Lo.

Lazar pushed back the door, took the stairs two at a time. A door on the second floor was ajar. Light shone through the crack. From inside came the sound of men talking, a quiet hum of conversation. Lazar elbowed the door aside and walked into the Hi-Lo, waited for the others to join him. The club was full . . . Saturday night business was good, much better than at Pearl's or Ruby's . . . this was the West End.

A burly man in a well-pressed suit approached the group of newcomers, recognized Lazar and smiled faintly. "How are you, Whitey?"

"Okay. The boss around?"

"In the back."

"Thanks." Lazar walked past the doorman, followed closely by the other three men. He moved between tables, past the bar, not looking at anyone seated there. By the side of the bar was a door leading to the office. He knocked once and entered. Inside was a gray-haired, swarthy man sitting at a table.

Alex Kerbeykian had opened the Hi-Lo shortly after the beginning of the war and had made a fortune from the business that foreign troops had brought. Before that, Kerbeykian had been a legitimate publican in nearby Lisle Street. There was more money in illegal boozers than there was in a pub, though, even if the risks and expenses were greater. At least once a month the Hi-Lo was raided by police. Anyone caught on the premises was bound over for a year in the sum of five or ten pounds; the worst that could happen if they were found again was that they would forfeit their bond.

Even with the money he paid over to Joey Taylor, Kerbeykian was realistic enough to know that he had to suffer the inconvenience of an occasional raid. The police were entitled to look as if they knew what they were doing.

Kerbeykian was going over the books when Lazar entered with Sherman and the twins. The Armenian knew something was wrong. Like other drinking clubs, the Hi-Lo was a meeting place used by everyone. No enmities, no squabbles were indulged; it was neutral ground. So when four men representing another club marched unannounced into his office, Kerbeykian knew he had trouble on his hands.

"Hello, Alex," Lazar said. "Glad to see you're doing so well."

"What is it, Whitey?" Kerbeykian got up from the table and came forward. He was a big man, well over six feet, with a stomach that tried to push its way past his shirt buttons.

Lazar offered his right hand, but was refused. "I need a favor, Alex."

"What?" Kerbeykian glanced from Lazar to Sherman, placed him. Then to the twins, whom he could not identify.

"I've got a couple of boys, just come out of the army," Lazar looked over to the twins. "Johnny and Jimmy Peters. They're good kids – war heroes – but I'm too small to use them. Can you help them out with a job?"

Kerbeykian glanced at the telephone on the table. What would Lazar do if he lifted the receiver and dialed Joey Taylor's number right now . . . called in some of the insurance he'd been paying for over the years? Or yelled for help from outside . . . from the bar? He had three men out there on duty. But no . . . he decided against it when he noticed how Jimmy Peters had parked himself directly in front of the door. No one was going through it . . . "I've got all the help I need, Whitey. Sorry."

"A small favor," Lazar said, in a friendly tone of voice as if he had not heard Kerbeykian's rejection. "You can afford it, Alex. You must be doing bundles out there."

"What kind of a job?" Kerbeykian asked cautiously. Maybe he shouldn't slam the door on Lazar just yet.

"Out front. They'll keep your place as quiet and respectable

296

as Buckingham Palace. They were commandos, you know. Loads of medals."

Kerbeykian understood why Lazar had tossed in that final remark. Just to make sure the Armenian knew how tough the twins were. "I don't think I need any of what you're selling, Whitey," he said. "I've already got it."

"Alex . . . I'm asking a tiny favor of you, that's all. Just to help out a couple of good men. Anyway . . . when have a couple of extra men ever gone to waste? Who knows what's going to come through your door . . . one . . . day?"

The threat had been made, the gauntlet flung down. Kerbeykian had to decide whether or not to pick it up. Rumors had been flying around for months that Lazar had been taking on men, seeking to expand. Now the rumors had hardened into fact. Kerbeykian knew he could pick a fight with Lazar . . . one he himself would probably lose with the mere handful of men he employed. Or he could accept the intrusion . . . for the moment. Until he had time to complain to Joey Taylor. "How much?"

"Fifty pounds a week for each of them. There . . ." Lazar added soothingly, ". . . that's not unreasonable, is it?" He needed Kerbeykian to say yes and give him his first firm footing, his beachhead. If Kerbeykian said no, Lazar would be faced with a fight immediately, a struggle he would have to win convincingly if he were to show other club owners that he meant business. An early fight would be at best inconvenient. At worst . . . a messy disaster. He didn't need it. The only fight he *wanted* was with Joey Taylor . . . "For that kind of money, Alex, they'll stand out there like . . . like two guardsmen."

"Okay," Kerbeykian said grudgingly. "But that's it . . . that's all I can afford." He motioned to the twins, carrying the charade to the full. "You two can start on Monday night . . . eight o'clock."

"Monday night?" Lazar asked. "What's wrong with tonight?"

"All right. Tonight."

Lazar made a show of turning to Johnny and Jimmy. "You've got your orders from your new boss. Don't let him

297

down. Thanks, Alex," he added, turning back to the Armenian. "I owe you a favor."

"Sure you do." Kerbeykian made up his mind to call Taylor the instant his visitors left . . . he had no doubt that the twins would be leaving with Lazar and Sherman. That was the way it worked . . . you hired them but you hardly ever saw them. Only on paydays when they came to pick up the protection money. And the occasional surprise visit to check on whether you were doing enough business to warrant an increase.

The four men walked out of the Hi-Lo, down to the street. Lazar glanced up at the club's windows, guessed that at this moment the Armenian was telephoning his protector. Before the night was through Joey Taylor's phone would be ringing continuously. Too bad if the old man liked to go to bed early. Tonight he'd be out of luck.

By midnight, Lazar had persuaded all three drinking club owners to hire the Peters twins at fifty pounds each a week. The following night he'd visit two of the spielers he'd selected . . . and persuade the owners to take on two more boys fresh out of the army . . . Mike Malin and Peter Cox.

Toppers — the best spieler of all — he would leave until the very last. When everyone would be able to see which way the wind was blowing.

"How did it go?" Katya asked when Lazar returned home shortly after three o'clock in the morning. She had waited up for him, half-dozing in an armchair in the living room.

"Just like Harry and I planned it," Lazar answered easily. He'd told her beforehand what he planned to do. He knew there was no way he could keep something of this importance — declaring war on Taylor — from her. But he'd made it sound like the simplest thing in the world.

He sat down, smiled in appreciation when Katya offered to make him a cup of tea. "No trouble?" she asked.

"From the club owners? No . . . of course not. But I'm waiting for that to start ringing." He pointed at the telephone.

"Do you think it will?"

"Not for a while. Joey Taylor will want to know exactly

298

what's happening before he presses the panic button. He'll talk with everyone first." And that was the trouble with Taylor, Lazar decided. All he could do was talk. The man was too old for action . . . The owners of the three clubs Lazar had moved into that night understood that perfectly. They knew Lazar was locking horns with Taylor, challenging his authority. And they were willing to sit on the fence, pay off both sides until one man emerged victorious.

"What if someone starts trouble at your clubs now?" Katya asked. "Aren't you spread a bit thin, having all those men working at other clubs?"

Lazar chuckled at her concern. "The twins will put in an hour or so at each club . . . maybe two nights a week. The same goes for Peter Cox and Mike Malin. The others will still be watching my places."

But Katya wasn't easily fooled. "Lazar . . . tell me the truth . . . what will Joey Taylor do?"

"He'll be realistic." Lazar hoped so, at least. "Realistic enough to know that he can't handle it anymore. He'll step down. And at the same time he'll still have enough sense of responsibility that he'll want to avoid a war. So he'll name a successor . . . Me."

Over the next couple of days Taylor received calls of complaint from the five clubs that Lazar had visited. Whitey was walking in, the owners said . . . Trying to take over. What did Taylor intend to do about it?

Taylor closed his eyes in anger. Lazar was blatantly disobeying his orders . . . just like Manny Goodman had done. Taking everything into his own hands because he was too ambitious. And . . . fool that he was! Taylor cursed himself . . . he'd allowed Lazar to become strong enough to do it. Goodman had only blackmailed him, a touch of extortion saved until the very end as a last-gasp measure to cheat the hangman's noose. But Lazar was intent on taking over his business . . .

He had to act. The club owners were watching him . . . those already affected and those whose turn would come if he did nothing. They all wanted to know . . . was he still strong or was he tottering? And was Lazar, in fact, taking what was rightfully his?

Taylor called Lazar to The Bishop's Avenue.

There was no courteous offer of a drink when Lazar arrived with his ever-present shadow, Harry Sherman. Outside, standing by the car, the Peters twins waited, awed by their first visit to Taylor's magnificent home.

"Whitey . . . you're stepping way out of line. I will not tolerate it."

Lazar listened politely, surprised that Withers was not there. He didn't know that Withers had told Taylor to handle the crisis by himself, bluff Lazar back into obedience. Withers was too busy with his police work at the moment to spare the time.

"I want your men out of those clubs. They don't belong there. And you . . ." He pointed a bony, accusing finger at Lazar. ". . . do not belong in the West End."

"Are you threatening me, Mr. Taylor?" Lazar glanced at Sherman, saw the calm expression on his face. He realized now there had been no need to bring the twins. Taylor just wanted to talk. Because that was all he was fit for . . . talking. "I'm not scared of you, Mr. Taylor. I don't have to be scared of you anymore, not when I've got an army of my own."

Taylor's eyes narrowed. No man had ever spoken to him like this in his own home. "You might have men, Whitey. But I've still got the firepower. The big guns are on my side."

The big guns . . . Lazar almost laughed out loud at the words. Taylor had men, certainly. But they were only as loyal as their next paycheck. And he also had Withers . . . where the hell was he anyway? . . . But big guns didn't win wars, Lazar wanted to tell Taylor. The army with the most motivation won them. And, by God, Lazar had motivation . . . The memory of Shmuel being hammered brutally in the ring by Withers' nephew was motivation enough to win a thousand wars. And against forces ten times larger than his own.

"Then I'd suggest you oil those big guns, Mr. Taylor. Because you're going to need them . . . every single one of them." He stood up, walked to the hat rack and took down

300

the steel-lined bowler hat with the vee-shaped dent. "You might need this also. You can use it as a chamber pot . . . in case your stomach can't stand all the excitement."

He signaled to Sherman and both men left. Taylor continued to sit, clutching the steel-lined bowler hat like a trophy.

Ivor Davies was checking through reports when his telephone rang. It was Withers, telling Davies to come up to his office for a meeting. When Davies asked what files he should bring, Withers gruffly told him to bring nothing except himself.

"Sit down," Withers commanded. He himself continued to stand, looking through the window at the Thames. "Your brother-in-law's getting too big for his boots, Davies. You'd better have a word with him."

"Oh . . . what about?" Davies feigned total ignorance although he knew damned well what about. Lazar had kept him completely informed of every move he made. He was doing it cleverly, Davies had to admit that. Nudging Taylor . . . not shoving him outright into a war. Just pushing him and waiting to see what happened.

"Are you really as stupid as you're trying to sound?" Withers turned back from the window, caught Davies in an icy glare. "Your precious white-haired brother-in-law is making waves, disturbing the status quo. He's barging his way into territory where he has no business."

"I wouldn't know about that, sir," Davies replied with contrived courtesy. "We each lead our own lives. And just as long as he doesn't rub our noses in it, I'm prepared to let that arrangement continue."

Withers exploded. "He's putting his men into boozers and spielers that are protected by someone else. He's trying to take them over. What do you call that?"

"I'm sorry, sir . . . I don't understand. What do you mean . . . protected by someone else?"

"You know bloody well what I mean!" Withers roared, enraged by Davies' obvious play-acting. "Joey Taylor looks after them. He keeps the peace for us . . . makes it easier for us."

Davies was taking enormous pleasure in the spectacle of

301

Withers admitting the subtle cooperation that went on between police and villains. Too bad some of the boys from Fleet Street weren't here, he thought. The *News of the World* would have had a field day. "These clubs you're talking about, sir . . . they're not licensed, are they? Therefore, as far as we're concerned they don't exist."

Withers ignored the jibe. "Maybe you think you can protect him, Davies. But you're wrong. If I decide to squash him, there's nothing you'll be able to do for him. So you tell him from me to lay off. Otherwise I'll come down on him . . . hard."

Davies had an idea why Withers was so irritable, and it was not because of what Lazar was doing to Taylor. Withers was catching hell from the very top for being unable to come up with any leads on the bank raids and the murdered constable. "Is that all you want me for, sir?"

"Yes. Get out of here."

Davies picked himself up from the chair and left Withers' office. On the way down to his own office he began to think. Withers was worried. Taylor was worried. Lazar had chosen his moment well. If Lazar pushed just a little bit harder, they might both come tumbling down.

And if that happened, who knew what upward changes there would be within the department?

Lazar decided to wait before taking his next step. Right now he had Taylor backed into a corner. He wanted to see what Taylor would do once he learned that his instruction to remove the men from the five clubs was being disobeyed. Lazar hoped he would have the brains to recognize the inevitable . . . and step down.

With five hundred pounds a week coming in from those clubs Lazar had money to throw around again. He supposed he could send another contribution through the lawyer to help rebuild Clapton Boys' Club. But this time he wanted Shmuel to witness his generosity from close up. Not like when he had offered money outside the burned-out club. That had been a tactless gesture . . . deliberately so, to keep Ivor Davies from blabbing about the anonymous contributions.

This time, Lazar wanted to do something with style . . . He had earned it.

He told Katya of his idea and she was thrilled by it. Together, they went out to look at banquet halls. When Lazar found one he liked he put a deposit on it for a Saturday night six weeks ahead. Then he hired a caterer. And a band. And entertainers for a cabaret.

Finally, when he had made all the arrangements, he entered the offices of the local newspaper where Chris Peters worked, asked for the young man. Chris came out from the back, shirt sleeves rolled up, a pencil balanced behind his ear. When he recognized Lazar his expression of curiosity turned to one of coolness.

"I've got a story for you," Lazar said.

"What kind of a story?"

"About a big charity function in six weeks. Dinner . . . dancing . . . a show. The works. All for a good cause."

"What kind of good cause? One of your own?" Chris held the same opinion of Lazar that Shmuel did, an opinion that included his twin brothers as well. Not that they ever came by the house anymore; both his mother and he had made it quite plain that they were not welcome. "You can take out an advertisement for that," he said, and turned to walk away.

Lazar forced himself to persist. "It's a benefit for Clapton Boys' Club," he said quietly.

"You've got nerve. What are you paying with . . . guilt money . . . for what you did to the building?"

"Wait a minute —"

"If it wasn't you it was one of my lousy brothers. Johnny had that fight with Shmuel, and he's not one to let something like that go by without getting his own back."

"He was in Pearl's the night it happened." Lazar hated himself for the lie; loathed himself for having to protect that piece of garbage. "The entire evening."

"Yeah . . . sure. That's what you say." Chris started to walk away again. Lazar grabbed him by the arm, pulled him back.

"You just listen to me, Chris. I'm going to tell you something which had better not go any further. Because if it

303

does . . . it'll upset Shmuel a damned sight more than it'll upset me."

"A secret, is it? I'll bet you've got a ton of those locked away."

"Only this one. If you doubt my motives, just ask yourself why I should have sent hundreds of pounds through my lawyer to help Shmuel in the past?"

"You?" Chris was speechless for several seconds. Finally he managed to ask, "But why?"

"Because I wanted to. Do I need any more of a reason than that?" Lazar watched the young man carefully. "Are you going to tell him now? If you do, it'll shatter him."

"No. Only one person can tell him that. You."

"That's right. Now what about getting this story in your paper?"

"Give me the details. I'll get it in." Chris pulled the pencil down from behind his ear, found a notepad. "But you've got a tough job ahead of you . . . getting Shmuel to go along with it."

"He won't be able to back out," Lazar said with certainty. "I'll be doing something publicly for the club. Once it's in black and white he wouldn't dare turn his back on it."

"Perhaps." While he took down the details, Chris found himself beginning to like Lazar. He was seeing a different side of the man, and he liked what he saw.

But how could anyone, Chris asked himself, with the smallest streak of decency in him put up with his twin brothers?

Shmuel was confused when Chris told him what was going on. Why was his brother making this . . . this gesture of benevolence? Shmuel knew that this time he had little choice but to accept his brother's help with good grace.

"All the proceeds are to go to the club, is that it?" Lottie asked Shmuel and Chris as they sat in the flat above the furniture shop. "Every single penny?"

"That's right," Chris said enthusiastically. They'd have enough money now to buy so many things they needed.

"A dinner-dance . . . a cabaret . . . for more than a hundred couples," Shmuel murmured. Even at a minimum of three pounds a couple, more than three hundred pounds would be raised for the club. They could sure as hell use that. The insurance had covered less than sixty·percent of the equipment that had been lost in the fire. It was only after Chris' editor had threatened to print something in the newspaper about the company's hesitance to honor the policy they had paid anything at all.

"Why are you so enthusiastic about this?" Shmuel asked Chris. "How did he persuade you to support him?"

"I thought he was sincere about the whole thing. And he did turn up that night of the fire. He was really concerned."

"And the fire started half an hour later. I still think it had something to do with one of your brothers."

"Maybe whoever set fire to the club was trying to get Lazar as well as you," Lottie suggested. "Or . . . maybe they were just after Lazar and didn't realize he'd already left."

Shmuel was shaken by what Lottie had said . . . Had the arsonist been after Lazar? Suddenly, Shmuel felt full of compassion for Lazar. What was the use of all the money in the world if you had to keep looking out for someone who wanted to do you in?

"I'm going to see him," Shmuel decided. "Do you want to come with me?" he asked Lottie.

She shook her head. "This is something you have to do by yourself. You've got to go on your own . . . and do whatever you think is best."

Katya opened the front door, sucked in her breath in surprise when she saw Shmuel standing outside. Behind him, she could see the old furniture van he used for his business. "Hello, Katya. Is Lazar at home?"

"No . . . he's working. Do you want to come in?" she asked. "I can call him at Pearl's, have him come right over."

"Thank you." He entered the house where he had once lived, looked around and saw how it had all changed in ten years. At the foot of the stairs he spotted children's toys that had not been put away. "Are the boys still awake?"

"Probably. Do you want to go up there while I call Lazar?" She went into the living room. As she lifted the receiver to dial Pearl's she heard Shmuel's slow footsteps on the stairs. She told herself she shouldn't have been surprised to see him. She'd known it wouldn't be long before he found out about what Lazar was doing. Still she'd been shocked to see him.

"Lazar . . . Shmuel's here. In the house. He wants to see you."

"I'll be home in a few minutes."

Shmuel was sitting in the living room with Katya when Lazar arrived. There was a brief moment of uncertainty as each brother opened his mouth to speak. Finally Shmuel said, "Chris told me about what you were planning."

"And?"

"I'm curious. I want to know why you'd do something like this. What are you going to get out of it?"

"Lazar doesn't expect to get anything out of it," Katya said. "If anything, the opposite is true. It's costing him a fortune."

Shmuel knew that already. But he couldn't help himself . . . "Are you looking for an interest in my boys' club, Lazar? Muscling in . . . isn't that what you call it?"

"Don't be so bloody stupid!" Lazar shot back. "I'm doing it because I want to help you. You had a rotten piece of luck with that fire." He didn't mention that the eyepatch Shmuel wore was another rotten piece of luck. "I'd like to do what I can to help you out."

"Why?"

Lazar wondered what would happen if he tried to throw Shmuel out of the house. He'd probably go . . . just like that. And Lazar would be no nearer compensating Shmuel for what Johnny Peters had done. "Shmuel, the story will be in the newspaper . . . so will the advertisement. I'll be able to sell fifty tickets at least. What are you going to do? Make a fool of both of us by refusing to accept the money on behalf of the club?"

Shmuel thought it over. Lazar had him trapped, and he knew it. He had to accept. But he didn't have to give his brother the satisfaction of knowing how much he really needed his help . . . Not now. Not yet. But when, Shmuel wondered, would this nonsense ever end? . . .

"Lazar . . . this doesn't change anything. This doesn't give you any part of me . . . of the club. It gives you nothing."

"I never thought it would," Lazar said. "But then again, I wasn't looking for anything in return . . . *if* you can manage to believe that."

CHAPTER TWENTY

Withers was glad to get away from the Yard, even if it was only to pay a call on Joey Taylor, to help him out with his problems. The superintendent's telephone had been ringing constantly, his desk was overflowing with memos − grumbles of disapproval from above . . . from government level even . . . about his inability to apprehend the thugs who'd butchered that poor bastard during the bank raid in Bedfordshire. Withers knew he was no closer to solving the case than he had been when the young detective-sergeant had brought in the three bullets. It bothered him. In spite of the harassment aimed at the Irish Republicans − as well as anyone even remotely connected with them − he was getting nowhere fast. Looming over his head now was the rather uncomfortable prospect of retiring with the murder of a police officer unsolved. Someone else would pick up the pieces, make the eventual arrest. And everyone at the Yard would say: "Ah, yes . . . this was the one Withers couldn't figure out."

And on top of all that, Withers had to contend with a panic-stricken Joey Taylor, who was losing control . . .

The superintendent could not help feeling a grudging admiration for Lazar. He had chosen his moment well . . . when Taylor was old and weak and Withers was occupied elsewhere. He was using brains . . . just like he'd done to get rid of Manny Goodman and take over the firm in the first place; not to mention getting his sister free of that madman. Lazar wasn't one of your run-of-the-mill crooks, Withers decided regretfully. He was smart. And because of that, he'd be a damn sight harder to jump on.

"Has he got a weak spot?" Withers asked Taylor as they sat

together in the study of the house in The Bishop's Avenue.

"Manny Goodman," Taylor answered, and Withers' eyebrows lifted in question. "Whitey's got Manny on the brain ... scared that one day he might return. Whitey's got a lot to lose if that should ever happen."

"How do you know about Goodman?"

"I hear things," Taylor said. "Whitey's been trying to find out where Manny is through those Yanks he once worked with."

"Not much chance of that, is there?"

Taylor shook his head. "It's enough that I know where he is." And *who* he is, Taylor added silently. You don't exile a man — after almost having him hanged — without keeping an eye on him. It wasn't only Lazar who had a lot to lose if Manny ever returned ... he'd come looking for Taylor too. Manny had done well with his new life, used the contacts Taylor had given him as part of their bargain, worked his way up in the loanshark racket to become one of the most feared collectors of bad debts. His violence had found a more appreciative market in New York than in London.

"What else?" Withers asked. "Whitey must have some weakness."

Taylor thought about Lazar's wife and sons. No ... nothing there to use. "Maybe his brother. I know Whitey sends him money. For some youth club or other."

"His brother, eh?" Withers remembered Shmuel — another poor bastard. Stupid too ... he'd thought he could beat the system ... punch his way out of a drugged stupor. Shmuel had once been Sammy Brooks ... well, all fighters had something to hide. They were all in a crooked racket. Yes ... maybe he'd find something there to use against Lazar. "Leave it with me, Joey. I'll check around, see what I can find out."

"How long will that take?"

Withers noticed Taylor was becoming more nervous by the minute. "As long as it takes. I've got other work to do ... remember?"

"Whitey needs to be taught a lesson," Taylor said. "His men are still in those five clubs. Every day they stay there ...

milking the owners . . . I lose respect because I'm doing nothing about it."

"Just keep it that way," Withers told him. "We can't afford any wars." He decided the meeting had dragged on for long enough. Taylor had no suggestions to offer other than using force. He . . . Withers . . . was the power of their partnership, the brains. He always had been. Because he had influence where it counted the most – within the police establishment.

Over the next couple of days, Withers farmed out official work while he concentrated on Shmuel. He checked him out with as much care as he would use in the most difficult police case. He learned about the shop, how much he made, how much he owed, how good his credit was. He checked on Lottie, the school where she taught, how long she'd been there. And he learned about Clapton Boys' Club . . . and how it had burned down. Shmuel was planning to reopen it, though, with money that would be raised through a charity function . . . organized by his brother. So Taylor was right – Shmuel *was* Lazar's weak spot. But there was nothing about the former heavyweight boxer that Withers could use against Lazar. He was as clean as they came.

Withers became intrigued, though, by two words that appeared on the police report dealing with the destruction of the clubhouse. "Suspected arson." Maybe that was something he could get his teeth into. Just because the local police had been unable to find out who'd done it didn't mean that Withers would fail too.

He dug deeper, studied all the reports, talked with the investigating officers, went over every word of every statement with a fine-toothed comb. And he forgot all about using Shmuel against Lazar . . . because there in the reports was the name of a man much closer to Lazar. The one man whom Shmuel believed held enough of a grudge against him to start the fire. Johnny Peters. The police hadn't been able to pin anything on Johnny. They'd interviewed him four times but his alibi – provided by Lazar – was unshakable. Withers decided it was worth looking into. Hard. If he could connect Johnny with the club fire, he could hold it over his head like a sword of Damocles, force him to work against his governor. Against Lazar.

It didn't take Withers long to come up with the history of Johnny and his twin brother Jimmy. Their honorable military records . . . and their less than honorable but far more interesting criminal records.

It was time, Withers decided, feeling extraordinarily pleased with himself, to make the acquaintance of Johnny Peters . . .

Johnny had put in a couple of hours at the Hi-Lo on Old Compton Street, long enough to show his face and pick up the hundred pounds in weekly wages for himself and his twin. Just like Jimmy was doing at one of the other clubs. And Mike Malin and Peter Cox, too. Saturday night they always dropped in, judged if business was enough to merit a bigger cut, passed on the information to Lazar.

Looking at the hundred pounds in his hands, Johnny decided it was the easiest money he'd ever earned. A damn shame it had to go to Whitey, though. Still . . . Johnny consoled himself by thinking that there would come a time when he'd get to keep all the money. When he'd be strong enough to push Lazar aside. He couldn't try anything now, that was for sure. Lazar had too much on him . . . just like Johnny himself had the goods on Lazar. For better or worse, they had to put up with each other for a while.

As he reached the street a car pulled up alongside him. Johnny's stomach lurched as he recognized the ominous-looking plain black Wolseley. The Yard.

"Get in, Johnny," Withers said through the open window. "I'll give you a lift."

"I don't need one. My car's over there." Johnny didn't know the man with the moustache, but the threat was evident.

"I don't care whether you need a lift or not. I'm telling you to get in."

"Who are you?"

"I'm Superintendent Withers from C.I.D. And I'm telling you for the last time to get in."

Johnny looked closer, saw that no one else was in the car

and felt a bit better. If it was an arrest there would be a carful, not just one. He climbed in, pulled the door closed and sat back as Withers sped away.

"What do you want with me?"

"Have you ever heard my name before?"

"Should I have?"

"Depends on your guilty conscience."

"Guilty conscience for what?" Johnny was starting to sweat.

"Don't fool around with me, son," Withers said coldly. "I know you did it. I know all about it . . ."

Johnny tried to put down his rising fear. How the hell could the law have found out? Who'd talked? Only two other people – no, three – knew about him shooting that cop. Whitey. Jimmy. And Harry Sherman. Which one of them had put the finger on him? And why? They were all as much tied in as he was.

". . . But I'm willing to give you a chance . . ."

A chance? To walk away from a murder? And the murder of a constable at that? Johnny couldn't understand it. No matter how big a bunch of crooks the police were they always hung together when one of their own was done in. "I don't know what you're talking about," he finally managed to get out.

"Of course you don't, just like you never knew that boys' club up in Clapton was run by your governor's brother . . . right?"

"Boys' club?"

"That's right . . . Clapton Boys' Club. Place you put a match to." Withers suddenly swiveled in the seat, took his eyes off the road long enough to look at Johnny's face.

Johnny licked his lips nervously. "I was working that night, I've got witnesses. I've got an alibi—"

"Sure . . . and all your alibis are liars like you are." That was something Withers could not figure out. Why in God's name would Lazar one minute be pouring money into his brother's club . . . and the next minute be protecting the man who had burned it out? It didn't make any sense –

Nor did Johnny's fear. What the hell had made him sweat like this? An arson job? Well . . . they could get him for attempted murder as well. Maybe that was why he was so edgy . . . Not only would he get the book thrown at him . . . he'd probably get the cat in the bargain. Most men would take any amount of time so as not to get flogged . . . "Believe me, son. If I want I can send you up so fast your head'll spin. Even if you're innocent as a baby — which you're not."

"What do you want from me?"

"That's better." Withers pulled the car into the curb and switched off the engine. Johnny noticed they were parked in Golden Square. It was deathly quiet here. The buildings surrounding the square were dark, closed for the weekend. Gas lights stood far apart, hardly lifting the gloom. "What can you tell me about Whitey?"

"Like what?"

"Like something I can nail him on."

There was only one thing . . . and Johnny wouldn't tell Withers about that. Lazar would only be an accessory. He and Jimmy would carry the full rap. And this was what only moments earlier Johnny had thought Withers had on him . . . "I can't tell you anything."

"Are you sure?"

"Yes."

"Did you ever see him threaten any of the club owners when he walked in?"

"No," Johnny lied. He was still more frightened of Lazar than he was of Withers. The superintendent thought he could send him down for arson and attempted murder. Lazar had the goods on him for a whole lot more.

"I still don't think you're being very cooperative, son. Remember what I told you before. I can break any alibi. How nice is your back going to look with stripes? Be a long time before you go swimming again on a public beach after the cat leaves its mark on you."

Johnny paled at the idea . . . his fear shifted focus dramatically. "What do you want me to do?"

"I want you to keep your eyes open. I want you to report back to me anything I can use against your governor. Understand?"

"Yeah . . . I do. You want me to deliver Whitey to you."

313

"That's right . . . clever boy." Withers gave a satisfied smile. He'd read Johnny Peters perfectly, a man who'd sell out anyone to save his own skin. "Where do you want me to drop you?"

"Take me back to where you picked me up. My car's there."

"Sure. I'm always ready to oblige a citizen who helps the police." But Withers was still bothered by that earlier question. What had Johnny been thinking about before, when Withers had taunted him? Was it the punishment he'd face for burning down the clubhouse . . . or was it some other caper he was worried about? Not that it really mattered. Withers had all he needed on Johnny . . . and he was going to use it to nail Lazar.

He drove the short distance back to Old Compton Street. Johnny pointed out his car and Withers pulled in behind it. "I'll be expecting to hear from you."

"You bet," Johnny said. He got out of the car, swore quietly as he watched it drive away toward Wardour Street. He'd made a lousy bargain . . . turned squealer with no advantage to himself. Withers had bluffed him, all because he'd worked himself up into a sweat over nothing. He had his alibi for that evening. Withers had made a fool out of him . . .

As he searched for his car keys Johnny began to think of it in another light. Withers wanted Lazar out of the way. There was nothing but good in that for Johnny. And then . . . he asked the same question that Withers had asked himself. Why had Lazar given him an alibi for that night? Lazar had believed he was sick in bed, yet he had still sworn that he'd been at the club. And his twin brother, Jimmy, had been puzzled by the same thing. Not that Jimmy had the least suspicion that Johnny had been responsible for the blaze.

And then the answer became clear to Johnny. Lazar was scared . . . of *him*. He'd supplied the alibi because he knew what Johnny could say about him. Even as an accessory for the murder in Bedfordshire, Lazar would get life. Johnny began to feel much better . . .

He found the car keys, stepped up to the driver's door. From the dark shadows of a shop doorway a figure materialized and

314

Johnny's heart skipped a beat.

"Hey, Johnny . . . I thought you were never going to turn up."

"Pete . . . what are you doing here?" Johnny managed to ask, fighting down his surprise at the sudden appearance of Peter Cox.

"I was at the Casino Club in Archer Street, picking up the takings. I saw your car so I thought I'd get a lift back to Pearl's."

"Sure. Get in." Johnny started to sweat again. Had Peter Cox seen him getting out of the Wolseley? Had he seen the driver? Did he recognize him? Did he even know who Withers was?

Peter Cox didn't know who Withers was. He just knew enough to realize that anyone driving a black Wolseley wasn't to be trusted. A cop's car was like his shoes . . . it stood out for miles whether it had a sign on it or not.

Cox was a very single-minded man. He was never confused by conflicting loyalties . . . he always remembered that his loyalty lay with the man who put food on his table. Before the war, when he'd earned extra money as a bookie's commission agent, he had never once thought of cheating the bookmaker. He wasn't afraid of the bookie . . . he was just loyal to him. Same was true when he was a bomb-aimer in the Lancaster. Cox's loyalty had been to his fellow crew members.

Now, his loyalty was still to one man. Lazar. When he arrived at the club Cox did not hesitate to tell Lazar that he had to speak with him. About Johnny. Lazar invented some pretense for Johnny to leave the spieler, sent him on an errand to Ruby's in Stoke Newington. Then, with Harry Sherman, he listened to what Cox had to say about Johnny getting out of the black Wolseley. It took little time for both Lazar and Sherman to identify the man Cox described with the red face and the moustache.

"Thanks, Pete. You'd better go back outside now. I'll look after it from here." He liked the way Cox just left. Didn't ask any questions; just walked out of the back office and resumed his duties outside.

"What do you make of it?" Lazar asked Sherman.

"I'd say Joey Taylor's started to fight back. He's trying to get at you through Johnny Peters."

"No . . . not Taylor. Withers is more like it. He's the snake." Lazar remembered clearly the superintendent when he'd broached the deal to do away with Manny and Vanetti. "He's Taylor's boss. Taylor's gone running to him and now Withers has found the time to handle it. He's trying to fix me from the inside, turn my own men against me."

"What about Johnny?"

"We should have got rid of him before . . . long before." Lazar told Sherman about the fire, a secret he'd kept until now, and explained how he'd viewed Johnny as an expendable pawn. "I was willing to wait for a while. But not now . . . he's become too big a liability."

Sherman sighed. "I'll take care of it for you."

Lazar shook his head. "No, this is my problem. Johnny and Withers. I don't want anyone else involved." He thought of how both of them — the young punk and the police superintendent — had each hurt Shmuel, how each had robbed his brother . . . of his eye, and of his club. Lazar's awareness of his own part in both events only hardened his determination to exact revenge. For Shmuel . . .

"Whitey . . ." Sherman's voice was gentle. ". . . Only Withers is your problem. Johnny's mine. I introduced him to you, recommended him."

Lazar understood why the offer was made. Not because Sherman had brought Johnny into the firm . . . but because the bald man loved Lazar like a brother. To refuse his offer would be to reject the man's affection. "What about Jimmy?" Lazar asked. Jimmy hadn't done anything wrong, and Lazar didn't want to see him harmed . . . he still felt a bond there because the younger twin had been unable to pull the trigger.

"Jimmy won't ever have to know, will he?" Sherman said. "Not if it's done cleverly. Not if we make it look like a convincing accident."

Yes . . . an accident. Lazar was all for that. Johnny would meet with an unfortunate accident.

And then Lazar thought about Shmuel's young friend, Chris, and he wondered how his brother Johnny's accident would affect him.

Lazar's revelation that he had been the mysterious benefactor of the Clapton Boys' Club had a strong effect on Chris Peters. What struck Chris was that Lazar had donated the money secretly . . . he'd not tried to make a big production out of it. There were two reasons for that, Chris knew. Shmuel would probably have refused the help, for one thing. But the second reason was more important . . . by doing it quietly, Lazar had proved that he genuinely wanted to help his brother realize his dream; he wasn't trying to buy his way back into Shmuel's affections.

Chris looked up from his coffee and after-dinner liqueur, glanced at the dais table where Shmuel sat with Lottie, Leah and Ivor Davies, Lazar and Katya, and a couple of local dignitaries. All the men were wearing tuxedos this time, not just Shmuel.

It was the biggest function Chris had ever attended, and what pleased him most was that this one wasn't just a part of his job as a reporter . . . he was here because he belonged.

He turned back to his own table, locked eyes with the bald, tubby figure of Harry Sherman who sat next to him. The other people at the table were friends of Lazar's . . . a singer who played the West End dance halls and appeared on radio, a bookmaker and a jockey, all with their wives. Only Chris and Sherman were alone.

"Why aren't my brothers here?"

"You want them here that much?" Sherman asked. He puffed lazily on a huge cigar; tendrils of gray smoke drifted from the corners of his mouth. "They've got to work." Sherman studied the young man, amazed at the difference between him and the twins.

"Where are they working? At Pearl's?"

Sherman nodded. It was close enough to the truth. They'd all be back at Pearl's later that night, after they had made the token appearances at the West End clubs, collected the money to help pay for this evening's festivities. "You don't think very much of them, do you?"

"What I think of my brothers isn't your business," Chris shot back, and instantly regretted the outburst. "Sorry . . . I didn't mean it to come out like that."

"Don't worry about it, son. I don't mind being told off sometimes." He turned toward the dais table as the red-coated toastmaster banged his gavel for attention. Sherman felt slightly more comfortable that Chris didn't have any time for his brothers . . . he wouldn't be so upset when Johnny disappeared. Tonight, in fact. Along with his newfound friend Withers.

Sherman folded his hands across his stomach, left the cigar sticking out of his mouth as he listened to the toastmaster introduce Shmuel.

Shmuel stood up, coughed nervously, glanced down at Lottie for support. Half the faces out there he didn't even know. Friends of Lazar's, and well-meaning members of the local community who had bought tickets after seeing the advertisement and story in the newspaper. They'd all come to see him . . . all come to wish him luck. It scared the hell out of him.

"Ladies and gentlemen . . . a few of us" – he singled out Chris with his eyes while he laid a hand on Lottie's shoulder – "have put a lot of time and effort into Clapton Boys' Club. When we had the fire we almost lost heart. But now, looking at you all tonight, realizing what your support means, I'm glad we didn't."

A thunderous burst of applause greeted the statement and for an instant Shmuel could almost believe he was back in the ring . . . While he waited for the applause to die, he wondered what to say next. He'd said enough already. But there was still one more thing he knew he had to mention.

"Tonight . . . and all it stands for . . . would not have been possible without the help of one man, my older brother Lazar." He wondered how many people out there knew he and Lazar hadn't spoken to each other for ten years. Shmuel had never even thought the day would come when he'd stand

318

up in front of a hall full of people and say what he was saying.

Without rising from his seat Lazar gave a modest bow of the head. More applause. He looked at Katya on his left, who was smiling as she gazed up at Shmuel. Then he looked out into the hall, sweeping his eyes across those faces familiar to him. His eyes met with Harry Sherman's, and the bald man stared back, acknowledging the pact that joined the two men inseparably.

Lazar thought about the times he and Sherman had followed Johnny Peters. Twice they'd been lucky and had seen him with Withers. Early one morning after Pearl's had closed, Johnny had driven to Covent Garden, almost losing his tail in the frantic bustle of the fruit market. At the last moment, Lazar and Sherman had spotted Johnny's car pulling to a stop outside an all-night café . . . and the portly figure of Withers had climbed in quickly. Another time, Sherman had followed Johnny to a Saturday afternoon soccer game. Johnny hadn't been interested in the game . . . because next to him, in the reserved seats, was Withers.

Two wasted trips, Lazar recalled. Because Johnny could have had nothing to tell Withers. But Withers was willing to be patient. Tonight, that patience would come to an end.

From somewhere in the hall a man's voice yelled, "Speech!" The shout was taken up by all the people Lazar had invited to the dinner and his face reddened. This was Shmuel's night and Lazar didn't want to do anything that might spoil it. He held up a hand to dismiss the requests. But the crowd didn't let up and, finally, the toastmaster took over. He rapped his gavel on the table and called out Lazar's name. Lazar stood up uncertainly. Katya reached out to squeeze his hand.

"Whatever I might have done tonight . . . and believe me it was very little . . . was nothing compared with what my brother and his wife have been doing for the past few years. All the credit . . . everything belongs to Shmuel and Lottie, and to those who have worked with them." He looked at Shmuel, but his brother's face was impassive. Lazar dropped into his seat, wishing he knew what his brother was thinking.

319

Had the evening made a chip in the wall that stood between the two men?

During the dancing that followed dinner, Shmuel took Leah out onto the floor. She asked him how he was enjoying the evening. He seemed so somber. Finally he said, "I don't know . . . Lazar seems to be enjoying himself . . ."

"Shmuel . . . you've got to stop making yourself believe that what happened" — Leah indicated his eyepatch — "was entirely Lazar's fault. It was and it wasn't. And believe me, he never intended it to happen. It's haunted him for years."

"Is that why you and Ivor are so friendly with him? Because you don't feel it was his fault?"

"No . . . as it happens we both think a lot of him."

Shmuel laughed. "That's funny. Your Ivor is a policeman and he's a friend of my brother."

"Lazar's never knowingly broken the law." Except for that one time, she thought. And if ever the law was broken as an act of mercy, that was it.

"Leah, he's trapped me into too many things in the past. I'm still wondering why he put this dinner and ball together, laid out all the money. I don't really trust him."

"He did it because he wanted to help you," Leah answered instantly. She did not know the real cause of the fire . . .

"We'll see," Shmuel said, unconvinced.

Harry Sherman asked Katya for a dance, Lazar nodded approval. On the floor, she noticed that Sherman was perspiring heavily. She asked him why . . . was dancing such a strenuous exertion?

He managed to smile at the question. Should he tell her that he was scared out of his wits because he and Lazar were launching a plan of action that would cancel out the debt that had cost Shmuel his eye . . . and his club. "This suit," he finally grumbled. "It fits like a straitjacket."

"I think you look very handsome in it," Katya complimented him. "Are you going to wear it when you go to Pearl's later tonight?" She had no doubt that both Lazar and Sherman would go to the spieler in Dalston after the dance was over. Business, after all, was still business.

Sherman hadn't considered that. Nor had he considered something else. Two men wearing tuxedos would stand out late at night . . . and the work he and Lazar had to do that night required total anonymity. "I think I'll change," he said to Katya. "And I'd better tell Lazar, otherwise he's going to be the odd man out." He looked around for Lazar, froze as he saw him standing next to Lottie.

Katya followed Sherman's gaze. Was Lazar going to ask Lottie to dance? Was this how he would try to break the ice?

Lazar had spotted his opportunity when Shmuel took Leah onto the floor and Sherman waltzed off with Katya. "May I?" he asked quietly.

Lottie looked up. She'd seen Lazar approaching, had hoped he was not going to ask her to dance. Now that he had asked, she couldn't very well say no . . . not after all he'd done that evening. While she walked onto the dance floor, she tried to reconcile the gesture of holding the ball with the Lazar she knew. What was he . . . schizophrenic?

"A penny for them," Lazar said when he saw Lottie deep in thought.

"I was trying to make some sense out of you . . . understand you." She wanted to be candid. "Like tonight, for instance. Taking such an interest in Shmuel all of a sudden."

"I've always had an interest in my brother."

"Yes? Then you've certainly had some very funny ways of demonstrating it. That night you made him go with you and that despicable Manny Goodman . . . And that other night at the National Sporting Club . . ."

"How . . ." Lazar's mouth dropped as he remembered Shmuel in a hospital bed, saying he was too ashamed of his brother to even tell Lottie what had really happened.

"It was years before Shmuel would tell me the truth about that night," Lottie said. "All because you had to pay back a favor. And what about the night you came around to the club with Harry Sherman and Chris' twin brothers . . . and one of them tried to start a fight with Shmuel?"

Some fight, Lazar recalled . . . one punch and Johnny was down on his knees. "I just wanted to look at the new clubhouse, that was all. I didn't know Chris . . . didn't know it was his brothers who worked for me."

"And what nice work," Lottie said sarcastically. "What lovely people you employ for your lovely work."

They bumped into another couple. Lazar turned around to recognize Shmuel and Leah and murmured an apology. Shmuel gave a tight smile, took Lottie in his arms and continued to dance.

"I guess that leaves the two of us," Lazar said to Leah. His face was burning with embarrassment; he felt that everyone in the hall was staring at him. He knew also that he was no closer than he had ever been to making up with his brother.

The ball finished shortly before midnight. Everyone stood at attention while the band played "God Save the King," then began to drift toward the doors. Lazar whispered to Sherman that he'd call for him at the flat in Highbury.

"Say goodnight to Shmuel and Lottie," Katya whispered.

"I'd have thought they'd come over to me."

"Lazar . . . maybe tonight helped Shmuel's club. It didn't help you. Just accept it and make the best of it."

Holding Katya's arm, Lazar joined the line of well-wishers. When he stood in front of Shmuel he held out his hand awkwardly. Shmuel took it, held on for an instant.

"Thank you for your help, Lazar." He resisted the impulse to say anything more.

"You're welcome, Shmuel." Lazar broke the handshake, took Katya's arm again and led her outside to the car.

CHAPTER TWENTY-ONE

Harry Sherman was waiting in the street outside the block of flats when Lazar drove up at a quarter to one. He climbed into the passenger seat, unbuttoned his coat. They had both changed into everyday suits.

"How did it go?" Sherman asked.

"With Shmuel? Nothing's changed." Lazar's voice was filled with regret. "When he saw me dancing with Lottie, he grabbed her away quick."

"So at least you tried."

"And I paid him back a little bit for what Johnny did to him."

"Yeah . . . and now we're going to pay off the rest." Sherman pointed out a public telephone and Lazar stopped. Sherman got out, dialed the home number of Superintendent Withers in the northwest London suburb of Maida Vale. While the phone rang he placed a handkerchief over the mouthpiece.

After half a dozen rings, a man's sleepy voice answered. Sherman spoke in a rough voice. "Mr. Withers . . . it's Johnny. I've got to see you. Now."

Withers tried to shake the sleep from his brain. "What do you want?"

"I've got news. It's important."

"What?" Withers asked sharply.

"I can't tell you over the phone. Whitey did a couple of things tonight . . . big things. Meet me somewhere. I'll pick you up."

Withers forced himself to think. It was a bad line, crackly, but the voice on the phone sounded urgent. "Can you be outside my house in thirty minutes?"

"Yeah . . . no trouble. I told Whitey before, I didn't feel

well. I'm at home now."

"Good . . . I'll see you in half an hour. And this had better be important."

"Oh, it is, Mr. Withers. It is." Sherman replaced the receiver and returned to the car. Lazar had moved into the back of the car. Sherman got behind the wheel. "Half an hour in front of his house."

"Where's the gun?"

Sherman dug inside his coat pocket and handed the Colt to Lazar. Thank God they hadn't got rid of that gun, Lazar thought . . . hadn't thrown it away after Johnny shot that constable up in Bedfordshire. Sherman had hidden it in his flat behind the fireplace. It was going to come in useful tonight . . . And then they'd get rid of it forever.

Withers told his wife he had to go out on a case. From downstairs he dialed the number of the twins' flat in Hackney. Just to be sure. The telephone rang unanswered for fully two minutes. Johnny must have left already.

Waiting downstairs, Withers wondered what the important news could be. Since muscling in on the five West End clubs, Lazar had been quiet. Too quiet. As if he were waiting to see what Taylor would do. That wasn't the way you took over from another man . . . a man like Joey Taylor. You went in, hit him hard and kept on hitting him until he went down. And then you put the boot in to make sure he didn't get up again. Never give anyone a second chance . . . no matter which side of the law you were on. Lazar hadn't done any of these things. He seemed to be content taking a hundred pounds a week from each of the five clubs he'd invaded. That wouldn't last for much longer . . . not if Johnny Peters' news was as important as it sounded.

Withers sat in the living room waiting, smoking his pipe as he looked through the front window. A car came slowly along the street and Withers stood up. The car moved past and he sat down again. A minute later another car rolled by, went past, stopped. With a whining protest from its transmission it reversed to a halt outside the house. In the darkness, Withers could make out one figure in the car, the driver. He got up from his chair, went out the front door and approached.

When he was a couple of yards away he stopped, suspicious. It wasn't Johnny behind the wheel. It was Harry Sherman.

But before he could do anything the rear door swung open. Lazar, who had been crouched out of sight, pointed the gun straight at Withers' chest.

"Get in!" he hissed.

Withers froze at the sight of the gun. Lazar jumped out of the car, shoved the gun into Withers' back, pushed him into the rear of the car and climbed in after him. Sherman put the car in gear and drove away.

"Thought it was Johnny Peters, didn't you?" Lazar said. "All ready to squeal on me?" He kept the gun pressed into Withers' side, the hammer cocked.

"What are you going to do?"

"Take you for a ride." Lazar glanced toward the front, saw that Sherman was heading north along the Edgware Road toward the Irish section of Kilburn only a mile away. "You're the lowest, you know that, Withers? The biggest crooks don't come close to scum like you!"

"Wait a minute . . . !" Withers was scared now. "I can help you . . . can do things for you. You don't know how much I can help you."

"You can't do a thing for me." There was a barely controlled anger in Lazar's voice as he stared with contempt at the superintendent.

"I can help you get Taylor. You want his position, his power . . . I can get it for you."

"I want my brother's eye back . . . can you get that for me as well?" Lazar asked savagely. "You remember that night, don't you? Your nephew?" If Shmuel had spoken to Lazar tonight – had in some way forgiven him for that tragedy – Lazar might have just settled for Johnny Peters . . . But it was clear that Shmuel did not forgive him. And that hardened Lazar's resolve.

"You're . . . you're going to kill me?"

Lazar didn't bother to answer.

325

"You'll never get away with it, you know that. You kill a man of my rank and every copper will be looking for you. Every mobster as well. Sooner or later you'll slip up and everyone'll be waiting like a pack of jackals, ready to tear you apart. And you'll hang . . . just like your brother-in-law should have done." A smile flickered across Withers' face. "You're forgetting that favor, aren't you? How we got your sister away from that sadistic little bastard —"

"Shut up or I'll let you have it right now. In the stomach. And you can die slowly and painfully."

Withers' face tightened.

"You think I won't get away with it?" Lazar couldn't resist bragging. "You know what this gun was used for the last time? Johnny Peters used it . . . to kill that constable up in Bedfordshire. During the bank raid."

For an instant Withers forgot all about his own danger. "What? That was the Irish . . . the IRA. The bullets matched up to other raids they'd done." And then Withers remembered his first meeting with Johnny . . . the panic the older twin had been in. Withers had thought it was fear of being nailed for arson and attempted murder. And all the time Johnny had thought he was being picked up for murdering a policeman . . .

"That's what we wanted you to think," Lazar said. "To get you running around in circles while we plotted against Taylor."

"You cunning bastard."

"Am I? Or does the title fit you better? You're the one who uses a cop killer as an informant, not me. I'm getting rid of him."

"But I can tell you things about Johnny," Withers blurted out.

"What things?"

"He . . . burned down your brother's club in Clapton."

"I know," Lazar said coldly. Withers had lost his last card . . .

"We're here," Sherman said from the front. He turned off the engine. Lazar looked at the bombsite where Sherman had stopped. The nearest houses were a hundred yards away. It was a perfect spot.

"Get out. Slowly." Sherman opened the rear door, stepped aside quickly as Lazar backed out, keeping the gun trained on Withers. "Out."

Withers emerged, arms raised. Determined to rob the superintendent of even the hope that they'd be caught, Lazar said, "I told you what this gun was used for. When they dig a bullet out of you and match it up, they're going to be looking for a gang of Irish bank robbers . . . who don't even exist." He motioned with the gun toward the deepest shadows of the bombsite, picked his way carefully over bricks and rubble as he followed Withers. From behind, Lazar could hear Harry Sherman's feet slipping on the bricks.

"This is far enough."

Withers turned around slowly. Lazar held the gun in his right hand, the muzzle pointing at the superintendent's stomach. For a moment it remained steady, then the barrel began to waver slightly. Withers' eyes narrowed; his muscles tensed.

"Get on with it, Whitey," Sherman muttered, looking nervously over his shoulder. They needed to get out of here fast.

Lazar gripped the gun tighter, lifted it to point at Withers' face. Still the wavering motion continued . . . I can't do it! . . . a voice screamed deep inside Lazar. I hate this man more than any other. For what he's done to my brother. For what he's trying to do now to me. And still I can't pull this damned trigger . . .

Withers saw it too. He lunged forward, hit Lazar full in the chest, knocked the gun away. It skidded over rubble and Lazar fell to the ground, chest crushed beneath Withers' weight.

"You little bastard!" Withers hissed. "Who the hell do you think you are that you could kill me?" His hands were on Lazar's throat. Lazar couldn't breathe. He swung his arms wildly, futilely.

Withers removed his right hand, felt around on the ground for a brick, found one, clutched it. Withers' mouth spread into a grin as he lifted the brick high in the air, ready to smash it down onto Lazar's face –

A gunshot sounded. The brick dropped from Withers' hand, crashed down alongside Lazar's head. The remaining hand on Lazar's throat fell away and Withers' body sagged. His head lolled forward, his chest collapsed. Lazar looked up and saw Sherman standing only two yards away, the gun held tightly in both hands.

Then Lazar looked over to Withers. Above the right ear, where the heavy-caliber bullet had exited, was a gaping jagged hole.

"You all right?" Sherman's voice was shaking.

Lazar swallowed hard as he tried to get his breath. He'd thought about Shmuel losing the eye; he'd thought about the Brownshirt in Aachen. And still he had been unable to pull the damned trigger . . . If Sherman hadn't been there, he would have been killed by Withers.

Sherman stuffed the gun back into his pocket, helped Lazar to the car. Only when they were half a mile away from the bombsite did he slow down, turn in his seat to look at his passenger. Lazar's face was shining with sweat, his eyes wide, vacant. "Get hold of yourself, for Christ's sake," Sherman whispered urgently. "We aren't finished yet."

"I know." Lazar wiped his face, rolled down the window to let in air. "Thanks . . . for what you did back there." He replayed the events in his mind, demanded of himself why he hadn't been able to fire the pistol. Because he couldn't shoot a defenseless man? *Execute* him? The other times he'd killed – the Brownshirt in Aachen, Vanetti – he'd acted out of desperation, or provocation. On the bombsite it had been too cut and dried. Withers standing, waiting to be shot. And he just hadn't been able to do it . . .

"It's all right. I wanted that bastard just as badly as you did," Sherman said. He drove in silence for half a minute, then asked, "What do we do about the gun?"

"Ditch it later on. After we take care of Johnny."

"Are you sure you're up to it?"

"Don't worry about me. It was just . . ."

"Just what?"

"I couldn't kill a man in cold blood." Lazar swiveled on the seat. "If that's being weak, tell me. You don't have to work for a man you think is weak."

"Whitey . . . it's not a weakness . . . it's a blessing. It puts you one up on the kind of bastard we left back there."

Lazar found the comfort he'd needed to hear in Sherman's words. And he was surprised that Sherman had been able to point the gun and squeeze the trigger so calmly. No . . . he hadn't been calm . . . he'd been shaking. But he'd fired to protect Lazar, to save his life. "How long do you think it'll take to find him?"

"Who knows . . . ? Maybe today. Someone's going to report him missing. He's too big a fish not to notice."

By the time they reached Pearl's it was a little after two thirty. Lazar had recovered his composure. He met with the teams that had collected from the West End clubs, took the money from them. Then, as the card tables emptied, he told his men to go home. Goris went. So did Peter Cox and Mike Malin. Soon, only the Peters twins were left.

"Jimmy . . . do me a favor," Lazar said to the younger twin. "Shoot up to Stoke Newington, pick up the money from Ruby's."

"Sure." Jimmy took his coat, went outside to his car and drove away. Sherman walked over to the one remaining table, quietly told the players and the bookmaker running the game that the spieler was closing up. They finished the hand, settled up and left.

"How about a drink, Harry?" Lazar called as the bald man locked the door from the inside.

"Why not?"

"How about you, Johnny? What do you want?"

Johnny looked uncertainly around the now empty spieler. The floor was littered with the debris of the evening, crushed cigarettes, empty packs, scraps of paper that had once held scores, crumbs from sandwiches.

"Well?" Lazar prompted.

"I'll take some lemonade," Johnny said, risking the derision of Lazar and Sherman. To his relief, they didn't laugh.

"I'll get it," Sherman offered. He took a bottle of lemonade from the tea bar and went into the back office. When Lazar and Johnny followed, Sherman had poured the drinks . . . Scotch for himself and Lazar and a tall glass of sparkling lemonade for Johnny.

"Your health," Sherman said, and emptied his glass.

"How did the dinner and ball go?" Johnny asked casually.

"Pretty good." Lazar sipped his own drink thoughtfully, his eyes fixed steadily on Johnny. He waited for several seconds and then said, "It made enough money to open another club for you to burn down."

Johnny's face dropped.

"Finish your lemonade," Sherman ordered before Johnny could say anything.

Johnny swung around and saw the gun in Sherman's hand. Sherman might have trembled after shooting Withers, but he was as steady as a rock now.

"Finish your lemonade."

Johnny rubbed his tongue across the roof of his mouth. The lemonade had a distinct bite to it. He hadn't noticed it at first, now he could taste the bitterness. "What's in it?"

"Nothing for you to worry about."

"Whitey . . ." Johnny swung back to Lazar. "Why?"

"Are you going to beg? Just like your friend did?"

"My friend?"

"Withers. We left him on a bombsite in Kilburn half an hour ago. Now it's your turn."

"Whitey . . . !"

"Finish your lemonade," Sherman ordered a third time.

Johnny didn't know what was in the drink − poison or just a knockout drop. Already his head was beginning to feel light, his legs weak. He blinked rapidly and looked again at Sherman. The bald man swayed in his vision. The gun grew larger as Sherman came closer, rammed the muzzle behind Johnny's ear. Johnny emptied the glass.

Almost at the moment he swallowed the remaining lemonade the glass dropped from his fingers. Lazar stretched forward to catch it, just as Sherman grabbed Johnny's body with one arm, stuffing the gun back into his pocket with his free hand.

"Get him out to his car and take it around to the next street," Lazar ordered. "I don't want Jimmy seeing it when he gets back."

"Okay, Whitey." Sherman picked up the unconscious

Johnny, hoisted him over his shoulder. He walked carefully through the narrow alleyway and dropped Johnny to the ground. Going through his pockets, he found the car keys. Then he walked to Johnny's car, reversed it as close as possible to the mouth of the alleyway. When he got out he stole a quick look toward the blue light over the door of the police station only a hundred yards away. No one was in sight. He grasped Johnny under the arms, dragged him to the car, tumbled him into the back seat. Finally, he drove the car to the next street and locked it before returning to Pearl's.

"All ready?" Lazar asked.

Sherman jangled Johnny's car keys for reply.

"How long is that stuff good for?"

"Three or four hours. Depends on his constitution. There was enough in that glass, though, to sink a battleship."

"Good. We'll wait for Jimmy to get back."

Jimmy Peters returned fifteen minutes later. After he handed Lazar the money from Ruby's in Stoke Newington, he looked around, mystified. "Where is everyone?"

"The games ended so we sent the boys home."

"Johnny too?"

"He left maybe fifteen minutes ago."

"Did he say where he was going?"

Sherman answered. "He mentioned something about driving to the West End. Maybe he's gone for a drink."

Jimmy gave Sherman a fleeting, peculiar look, started to say something but thought better of it. "He's probably gone home," he finally said. "I'll see him there. Goodnight."

"Goodnight, Jimmy," Lazar watched Sherman hold open the door, then returned to the office and stuffed the bottle of Scotch into his pocket. They waited for ten minutes before they closed up. Outside, there was no sign of Jimmy's car. Lazar drove his own car to the next street and waited behind Johnny's motor while Sherman got into it. Then they drove for the second time that night to northwest London.

Between Hendon Central and Colindale, the Northern Line underground branch ran at surface level. The two cars stopped on a poorly lit road with easy access to the line. Lazar

went to Johnny's car, helped Sherman carry the still unconscious man over a fence, down a grassy bank to the track.
Lazar stared anxiously at the metal rails . . . two low rails for
the wheels, two raised on insulators that carried the electricity.
Sherman had said the power was off this time of night . . .
and stayed off until around five o'clock, just before the first
trains rolled out of the sidings.

"I'll show you," Sherman said. He dropped Johnny's legs
and walked over the track. Lazar winced and tried to close his
eyes as Sherman's foot hovered over a live rail. "Safe as
houses, see?" Sherman tapped the live rail with his foot, and
then bent down and placed the palm of his hand on the shining
metal. He returned to Lazar, grabbed Johnny's legs and
carried him down to the track.

For the second time that night, Lazar hesitated . . . By the
edge of the track, he pulled back on Johnny's arms, held
Sherman up. Sherman stopped. He knew what was going on
in Lazar's mind. And he knew also that since his family had
been destroyed, Lazar — his boss and his best friend — was
also the only family he had . . .

"I'll take him, Whitey," he whispered.

"No." Lazar straightened his back and picked up Johnny's
arms again. They carried Johnny onto the track, set him
down gently across one of the live rails. Lazar took out the
bottle of Scotch from his pocket, splashed liquor over Johnny's
face and shirt, poured some into his mouth. He wiped his
own fingerprints from the bottle, pressed it against Johnny's.

"One more thing," Sherman said. He squatted down beside
Johnny, took the man's right foot and jammed it underneath
the live rail, against the wooden sleeper. He tugged at
Johnny's ' ..xed the foot tighter. "Just to make sure,"
Sherman said.

On the way back to Lazar's car, they stopped just long
enough to put the empty bottle of Scotch in the glove
compartment of Johnny's car . . . where the police would
undoubtedly find it.

Sherman and Lazar drove away. They had one more stop
to make. In the middle of Tower Bridge, right over the

separation point and surrounded by comforting darkness, Lazar wiped the gun clean of fingerprints. Then he dropped it into the murky water of the Thames.

He glanced at his watch . . . four thirty. Withers would still be lying in the bombed-out building in Kilburn. And Johnny was stretched across the live rail at Colindale. Soon, the power would be turned on. And when that happened, Lazar's revenge would be complete . . . Two men who had hurt his family would be no more.

The drug wore off. Johnny's eyes opened to stare upward at the slowly lightening sky. Stars shone weakly; the quarter moon had lost its brilliance.

Where was he? What position was he in that could be so painful, so uncomfortably awkward? His mouth felt like concrete and his limbs ached. His head throbbed, and he could remember nothing.

No . . . wait . . . a scene was replaying itself. A drink in Pearl's. Lemonade. And a gun in Harry Sherman's hands . . .

He moved. His hands scraped sharp stones, smooth metal. He forced his aching eyes to focus. Long, shining strips of metal ran off into the distance, never-ending. Rails . . . live rails! He was on the underground track somewhere . . . and he couldn't move . . .

Sheer terror cleared the remaining effects of the drug from Johnny's brain. His foot was jammed, stuck underneath — Jesus Christ! — a live rail! He pulled at his foot, pushed, tugged and grappled. But he couldn't free it.

What time did the power come on? He almost wished he had a saw, an ax, anything so he could free himself.

He screamed for help. The noise echoed back as mocking laughter from a line of elm trees a hundred yards away. There were no buildings within half a mile.

He tried to stand, pulling against his trapped foot, lungeing with all his weight, with all his strength against the rail that held him prisoner. A searing, agonizing spasm shot up his leg as bones snapped in his desperate effort to be free.

A surge of triumph gave him energy as his mangled foot

moved, started to slide free. Thoughts of vengeance spurred him on. What he'd do to Whitey . . . to Sherman . . . to that one-eyed moron, who were all responsible for this. There . . . his foot was almost free. Another twist, another pull — and damn the pain — he'd be free . . .

And then . . . Johnny's hair began to rise, to stand on end. Pain like he'd never dreamed was possible ripped through him . . . He was dead in an instant.

The power had been turned on.

CHAPTER TWENTY-TWO

Three days later they buried Johnny Peters in the rain. Hard-driving rain that swept across the cemetery, soaking the small group who stood somberly around the open grave. Lazar pulled his umbrella closer. Across the other side of the open grave he could see Johnny's brothers . . . Jimmy and Chris . . . together for once. Just as he was . . . standing next to Shmuel who was attending the funeral out of respect for his young friend Chris.

Johnny's mother was there as well . . . a small, tired-looking woman with straggly gray hair. Her eyes were sunken, red-rimmed with crying. No matter what she had thought of her oldest boy, she was still a mother . . .

Lazar looked around some more. Sherman and all the men from Pearl's and Ruby's were present . . . their mark of respect. Too bad he'd gone out drinking, everyone said . . . although God alone knew what he was doing wandering across the underground track. In Colindale of all places . . . there was nothing up there but the airfield and the police college. Must have tripped on the live rail, caught his foot. Been trying to free himself when the power came on. Even the police couldn't figure out what he was doing there. His car was parked nearby. And he'd been drinking heavily. Maybe he'd seen something that had attracted his attention. The inquest would record it as death not through accident, but by misadventure . . . because Johnny Peters had had no business being on the track.

The minister made a few comments, speeded up in deference to the foul weather. The casket was lowered into the earth. Lazar turned to Shmuel. The last funeral they had attended together had been for the boxer Shmuel had killed . . . Tim Fredericks.

"You don't look very unhappy for a funeral," Lazar whispered. He felt he had to say something to his brother . . . and at the same time take his mind off who lay in the casket.

Shmuel stared straight ahead, across the grave to the family. "If I grieve for anyone it's for Chris. Certainly not for his brother. As far as I'm concerned, there's no one in that box."

"You still think it was Johnny who burned you out? Even though I said he was working for me at Pearl's during the time it happened."

"It doesn't matter anymore, does it?"

"I suppose not." Lazar paid attention to the service for a few seconds, but his mind wandered . . . What would Shmuel say . . . how would he react . . . if he knew that Johnny had not died by accident? If he knew who had killed him — and why? "Have you thought about what you're going to do with the money from the gala night?"

"Look for a new site, I suppose. Once Chris gets over this." Shmuel sensed that Lazar was trying too hard to be sociable; it embarrassed him. He had come to the funeral out of respect for Chris. Shmuel turned around to look at his brother. The angle of his umbrella changed and water dripped onto the shoulder of Lazar's coat. "I meant what I said the other night, Lazar. When I thanked you. You did something decent and I appreciated it."

Lazar started to say something but Shmuel went on before he could. "We live in two different worlds, Lazar. They don't mix. I'm sorry."

The service finished. Shmuel made his way over to the family. Ignoring Jimmy completely, he shook hands with Chris and his mother. Lazar followed, shook hands with all three mourners. Had his own mother's eyes looked like this when she learned what he had done in Aachen? he wondered. He felt pity for the woman, even a moment of shame that he was responsible for her grief. But if she knew what her son had been like . . . maybe she did know . . . and being a mother, maybe it didn't matter . . .

"Whitey . . ." Jimmy's voice made Lazar turn. "I . . . I'm taking off a day or two, all right?"

"Take as long as you want. And if there's anything you need" – he included all three members of the family – "just let me know. Anything." He hurried away to join Sherman who was waiting for him. He looked for Shmuel, but his brother had already gone.

Lazar went with Sherman to Stoke Newington where Katya made a meal ready for them. "Was Shmuel there?" she asked.

"He stood next to me," Lazar answered.

"Did you speak to him?"

"I tried."

"I see." Katya fell silent as she served the two men. She understood Lazar's disappointment . . . even the gala benefit hadn't helped him restore his brother's affection. What would it take, she wondered, to break through Shmuel's stern resolve . . . to see the brothers united once again . . . ?

The telephone rang. Katya went to answer it, then called Lazar. "It's Ivor."

"Hello?"

"How was your funeral?" Davies asked.

"It rained."

"Always does on funerals. British weather's very good like that . . . gets everyone in the proper mood."

"Is this why you called?" Lazar asked. His heart quickened . . . had he slipped up? Left a clue somewhere that showed the police that Johnny had met his death through foul play?

"No. I called because I need a favor."

"A favor?"

"I want you to keep your eyes and ears open – the same goes for your men – because we want whoever killed Withers."

"What?" Only at the last instant did Lazar remember to display the surprise he'd rehearsed for the moment this call came through. What with Johnny's funeral and seeing Shmuel again today, he had almost forgotten about the superintendent. Three days had passed since Withers had been killed and there had been no mention of it. Until now. "Withers is dead?"

"His body was found this morning on a bombsite in Kilburn. Shot once through the head. Been there a few days, according to the examiner."

"You've no motive . . . no clues?"

"Not yet." Davies decided Lazar didn't have the least idea of how complicated police work really was. "His wife . . . widow . . . says he got a phone call late Saturday night. Went out and never came back. She put in a report that he was missing. It wasn't until this morning that a gang of kids playing on the bombsite found the body."

Damn . . . Lazar thought. There was always someone left behind to grieve. He recalled Johnny's mother at the funeral. Now there was Withers' widow. Even someone like the corrupt superintendent was missed by somebody . . .

"I suppose I should say I'm sorry, but I'm not."

"That's what I figured. You'd better be careful you don't brand yourself a suspect. Christ knows . . . we're looking for one."

"What do you mean?"

"With Withers gone Joey Taylor's lost his protection. You want to move in . . . to some people that might be a motive. Better than any we've got now."

"That's a ridiculous theory," Lazar broke in. "You were with me on Saturday night at Shmuel's party. And after that I went to Pearl's." Where the hell was that bullet? The bullet that would tie Withers' death into the bank raids . . . into the IRA. That was the whole damned reason they had used that gun. He hung up and returned to Sherman and Katya. They asked him what the call concerned and with a forced calm he told them that Superintendent Alan Withers had been found murdered.

By the next day, Lazar was off the hook. An extensive search of the murder area had turned up the bullet that had killed Withers. It was scratched and lightly battered from where it had hit concrete after exiting Withers' head, but police technicians were still able to match the grooves under a comparison microscope with the bullets taken from the dead constable in Bedfordshire, and with those used in previous bank raids.

Jimmy Peters returned to work at Pearl's. He was unusually silent; Lazar figured it was the continuing shock of losing his twin brother. If he felt sorry for anyone it was for Jimmy. The younger twin had always shown more brains, more heart, than Johnny . . .

Lazar held a meeting with Sherman, Jimmy, Mike Malin and Peter Cox. Joey Taylor's umbrella of protection had collapsed. It was time to move in . . . to finish off the job. "This Sunday night we're going to Toppers in Regent Street. If the other five clubs have failed to shake Taylor, when we take a piece of Toppers he'll have to act. Or step aside." He looked at the other men, finally focused on Jimmy. "Do you feel up to it?"

"Sure I do." Jimmy looked distracted and Lazar wondered whether to include him or not. Maybe it would be better if he were not exposed to the action just yet . . .

"Look, Jimmy, if you want some more time off, say so. No one's going to think any worse of you for it." There was a chorus of assent from the other men and Jimmy smiled wanly.

"I'm all right, I tell you." When Lazar looked away, Jimmy's smile disappeared. He was puzzled by something and no matter how hard he tried he could not figure out why Lazar . . . or maybe Sherman . . . one of them for certain . . . had killed this superintendent whose murder was being blamed on the Irish. Lazar had overlooked one point . . . Jimmy knew all about the history of the gun that had killed Withers. He had once held it himself . . .

Jimmy didn't know — didn't care really — why Withers had been bumped off. But it tied him in even tighter with Lazar. Maybe it was information he could use one day. At the moment, though, something else was bothering him. Something far more important than why Lazar had killed some superintendent . . .

Harry Sherman's voice interrupted Jimmy's thoughts. He was warning Lazar that he could be in for a real fight at Toppers. "David Martin won't take it lying down, Whitey..."

Sherman was saying. ". . . You walking in there just like that and wanting a piece of his profits. Maybe the others did, because they wanted to see which way the wind was blowing, but not him."

"No?" Lazar smiled grimly as he thought about the tough ex-bookmaker who enjoyed such a strong position in Taylor's affections. They'd find out how tough he really was on Sunday. "He's got a choice, hasn't he, Harry? Either he can pay up like everyone else . . . or he can let me have the entire show."

Lazar's confidence was riding a supreme high.

Withers' death had shaken Taylor. When the superintendent had been alive Taylor had taken him for granted. Now that he was gone Taylor realized how exposed he was, vulnerable to any attack . . . like the one Lazar was making on him.

Somehow Taylor couldn't believe that his partner was really dead. Murdered by a bunch of Irish thugs . . . for God's sake . . . and so close to retirement. Perhaps there was a message for Taylor in Withers' death. That he, too, should retire while he still could. Not hang on one day too long, take one chance too many like Withers must have done. Taylor had his retirement home already. A small house in Cowes, on the Isle of Wight. A very genteel area, where boat races were held. Rose bushes in the front garden. A view of the water from the back.

But he couldn't retire just yet. He had one mission to accomplish before he walked away from London, closed the books on his long career of controlling the firms. He had to put Lazar in his place . . . show that little upstart who was still the boss. Taylor owed it to everyone else. Let one horse take the bit between his teeth and the rest of the team would follow suit. They'd be back where they were twenty years earlier . . . spending more time and effort fighting each other instead of making money. Even without Withers, Taylor would take care of Lazar. Not only that . . . but he'd do it *for* Withers, for his memory.

He called David Martin to the house in The Bishop's Avenue. Martin was his favorite among the club owners who paid protection. Martin's cut had never diminished . . . not like Lazar, who complained all the time that he couldn't give more because his own takings were down. Martin would help . . . especially if he was offered the seat of power once Taylor decided to step down. Martin was ready for that kind of power. He already had respect . . . everyone looked up to the kind of club he ran.

Yes . . . Martin would help Taylor teach that white-haired bastard a lesson . . .

Lazar spent most of Sunday at home. In the morning he took his two sons over to the park, played ball with them, ran until his legs ached and his lungs threatened to burst. But the strenuous exertion took his mind off what had been done . . . and what remained to be done.

He spared a moment to think about Johnny Peters and Withers. Both dead . . . and both deservedly so. In different ways, both men had sought to harm Shmuel and himself. A similar fate, he swore, would await any who chose to harm his family. Even if it meant risking his own life.

But . . . he wondered . . . would Shmuel, who wouldn't even speak civilly to him, react with the same burning loyalty if Lazar himself was threatened?

That evening, five men crowded into Lazar's car at Dalston and set off for the West End. In front with Lazar was Jimmy Peters. In the back were three other men who worked for Lazar.

Every so often Lazar checked the rear-view mirror. At first, casually. Then, when he didn't see what he was looking for, he became agitated. He pulled in for a minute, looked over his shoulder, past the three men in the back. Jimmy asked why he'd stopped. Lazar said nothing, too distracted with something else. Finally, he shook his head and drove on, not wanting to wait.

He parked in Regent Street and the five men walked single-file up the staircase leading to Toppers. On the landing, Jimmy muttered a curse and knelt down to tie up a loose shoe-lace. The men behind him went on ahead. His shoelace tied,

Jimmy stood up to follow them, now bringing up the rear.

Lazar was first through the door. And once inside he stopped uncertainly. The fifteen card tables that dotted the expensively carpeted floor were empty; normally, those tables would be full . . . crowded with players in high-stakes games. The two roulette tables were also empty, their wheels still and silent. There wasn't a gambler in the club. All Lazar could see was the tall, stocky figure of David Martin standing in the center of the floor, hands on his hips. And around the walls, waiting, were another half-dozen men. Lazar looked up at one who was slowly fitting a set of brass knuckles to the fingers of his right hand. Others were dangling heavy lengths of chain, swinging them back and forth. One man had an open razor, running his thumb lightly across the blade.

"Hello, Whitey . . . boys," Martin greeted his visitors. "We've been expecting you."

Lazar heard another sound, glanced over his shoulder. Behind Jimmy, on the landing, another four men had appeared. They moved into the club, closed the door to seal off escape.

"I had to close the club for a night, Whitey," Martin said. "And Sunday's my best night. That costs me money . . . and makes me very upset." He came closer, stopped only two yards from Lazar. Lazar could smell the brilliantine that Martin used so heavily on his carefully combed gray hair. "Did you come all the way over here from Dalston to offer me a couple of your boys as doormen? I don't need any, do I? See . . . ?" He indicated the men spread around the walls. "I've got plenty of protection."

Even in that moment Lazar wasn't afraid. All he felt was anger . . . at having been betrayed. David Martin had known he was coming, had waited for him to show up . . .

A door at the rear of the club opened. A familiar figure emerged, elderly, smartly dressed. "You need a lesson, Whitey," Joey Taylor said. "A big lesson . . . in the worst possible way."

"These men are yours?" Lazar asked calmly. So . . . he hadn't been betrayed after all. He'd been outfoxed. By Taylor . . . who had guessed that Lazar would make his move

342

once Withers' death was public knowledge.

Taylor smiled, pleased with himself. "I told you I had the big guns," he said. "But you wouldn't listen to me, would you? You thought I was too old, didn't you? Thought I'd have no power, nothing, with poor Mr. Withers gone."

"You don't have any power at all, Taylor."

Lazar's insolence stung Taylor. His top lip quivered, his eyes gleamed with fury. "You're going to regret those words, Whitey. You're going to regret that you ever decided to go up against me . . . that you were ever born." He came alongside Martin, held out a hand. The club owner passed across a folded razor. Taylor opened it, glanced at the blade. "I'm going to mark you myself, Whitey. It's been a long time since I marked a man . . . but you're going to help me remember what a pleasure it can be."

At the sight of the razor, Lazar stiffened. "Hold him!" Martin barked. Instantly, the men around the walls closed in. Jimmy Peters and the three other men who had come from Pearl's were shoved off to the side.

Lazar felt strong hands grip his arms. He lashed out with his legs, felt satisfaction as his left foot caught Taylor squarely on the shin. The elderly man cried out in pain, then cut off the sound immediately as though scared of showing weakness. His face turned crimson with rage and the hand holding the razor started to shake.

"Hold him still," he ordered. "On his knees."

A shoe crashed into the back of Lazar's legs. His knees buckled and he collapsed. Hands held him down. Above, he could see Taylor's face come closer . . . could see the razor in his hand . . .

"You shouldn't have done that, Whitey. You shouldn't have kicked me like that," Taylor hissed. "I was going to go easy on you . . . mark you where the scars wouldn't show as distinguishing features on a police file."

Lazar understood what he meant . . . When you marked a man you either carved his face − which might one day help the police to identify him − or you carved his buttocks. Which was just as painful, infinitely more embarrassing, but of no assistance at all to the police . . . And the police were the ultimate enemy . . .

"But now I'm going to cut up your face so bad that Frankenstein's monster will look pretty next to you. You're going to get a lesson you'll never forget."

Lazar's eyes stayed riveted on the shining blade . . . Where the hell were Harry Sherman and the rest of them?

Sherman was out of breath, furious with himself . . . and with Lazar. The three cars following Lazar had got caught behind a truck within half a mile of starting out from Pearl's. Then at lights. Sherman had confidently expected to see Lazar when he'd got clear of the tangle. But that stupid bastard had gone on by himself . . . damn him! He was so keyed up he couldn't wait. Sherman prayed he hadn't walked into a whole pile of trouble. Martin was too tough to be taken with just a handful of men.

With Peter Cox, Mike Malin, Goris and another half-dozen men following, Sherman ran from the convoy to the doorway leading up to Toppers. The other men crowded close behind, feeling in their pockets for weapons.

The door to Toppers was closed and Sherman halted, suddenly even more afraid for his friend's safety. On a normal business night there would be some sound coming from within. And the door would be open, a man on duty. This was too quiet. He called Cox over, asked him what he made of it.

"Straight in," Cox said without hesitation. Not even bothering to check whether the door was locked or just pulled closed, Cox lifted his right leg and hammered at the handle with his foot. The door flew back. Sherman's men poured through the opening. And then they stopped, stunned by the sight that met them. Jimmy Peters and the men from Pearl's were off to one side, under guard. More men stood in a semicircle in the middle of the club. At their center, Lazar was held prisoner by two men. One gripped his arms, forcing him down; the other held his head underneath the razor balanced in Joey Taylor's still-shaking hand.

"Get 'em!" Sherman roared, and lunged toward the two

344

men who held Lazar on the floor.

Cox threw himself feet first through the air, kicked the razor out of Taylor's hand. The others spread out, squared off with Taylor's men.

Lazar sprang free as Sherman slammed into the two men holding him. He was up on his feet instantly, grabbing for the nearest weapon . . . a chair . . . which he swung high into the air and smashed down over the head of the man next to him. Only when his victim fell to the carpeted floor, his head bleeding profusely, did Lazar recognize David Martin. So much for the tough ex-bookie. Make book on *that* . . .

Still holding the chair in both hands, Lazar surveyed the room. The weapons, thank God, had been discarded as if by mutual agreement. Instead, the men were all using fists, feet and heads. As Lazar watched, Mike Malin, the former wrestler, grabbed someone by the jacket lapels and brought his forehead crashing down across the bridge of the man's nose. Then he hoisted him up and tossed him over the bar.

Lazar spotted Cox in trouble, defending himself against two opponents, both larger than himself. Instantly he dove into the fray. The chair shattered over the head of one man. The other, turning to see where it had come from, never saw the punch Cox launched. It caught him flush on the jaw and dropped him unconscious.

From somewhere else came the sound of shattering glass as a heavy metal ashtray missed its target and sailed through a window. Lazar barely heard the noise. All he could think of now was Taylor. Where the hell was he? He swung his head around, checked each flurry of action. He couldn't see the controller anywhere . . . and more than anyone else he wanted *him*. He raced into the office. Empty. But at the far side was another door. A back entrance. And it was open.

Taylor had run. At the first sign of trouble he'd turned tail and taken off. He'd been a hard man when he'd held the razor, secure in the knowledge that it was ten against one. But when Sherman and the rest had arrived, Taylor had turned yellow . . . acted just like the old man he was. And in that moment Lazar was certain of his right to challenge the man. If you couldn't stay to fight it out, you had no business being in power.

He returned to the main area of the club. Outnumbering the opposition, his men were now getting the better of the fight. Two of Taylor's men lay unconscious on the carpet. The rest were making a last-ditch attempt to fight . . .

Above the noise came an urgent shout from a man positioned by a window which overlooked Regent Street. "Police!"

Everyone froze. Then Lazar's men began to break off, retreat. They went down the stairs quickly, quietly, split up as soon as they reached the street. Two constables ran along Regent Street, blowing their whistles to summon assistance. The men pouring out of Toppers turned their heads away to hide any wounds.

Lazar reached his car, waited for Jimmy Peters and the three others who had traveled from Dalston with him. When the car was full they sped away.

Back at Pearl's, the entire team regrouped. Forgetting how close he had come to being marked for life, Lazar – and all the others – were jubilant. Taylor's reign was over. All that was needed now was for the crown prince to decide when the coronation would take place . . .

And now Lazar knew that he could even keep the promise he had once made in jest to Katya. He would open a nightclub. A super-respectable establishment that would be featured in every guide to London. He even knew where it would be. At Toppers . . . the only spieler to fight him. And what a location. On Regent Street, close to the Café Royal. With that kind of address it couldn't go wrong.

When the butler opened the door of the house in The Bishop's Avenue later that night, he didn't seem in the least surprised to see Lazar with Sherman and Jimmy.

"Is he at home?" Lazar asked.

"In the study, sir."

"Alone?"

"No, sir."

"Thank you." Lazar led the way, pushed back the study

door and walked in. Taylor was sitting behind the desk, still dressed in the same suit he had been wearing at Toppers; his hand, where Cox had kicked him, was bandaged. Three men whom Lazar recognized from Toppers kept Taylor company. One of them had a rapidly swelling black eye; another was gashed on the cheek. They looked at Lazar and his men like well-trained guard dogs only waiting for the command to rip the intruders to pieces.

"You're either very brave or very foolish, Whitey," Taylor said quietly.

"What would a man who runs away from a fight know about bravery?" Lazar asked in return.

Taylor got up from behind the desk. "Bravery should have a constant companion . . . wisdom. A wise man would not enter a lion's den like you have . . . with only two men." He indicated Sherman and Jimmy who stood behind Lazar.

"Two men?" Lazar smiled, made a quick motion with his right hand. Before any of Taylor's men could move, Sherman walked quickly to the windows. He pulled back one drape. On the other side of the window was the unmistakable grin of Goris. He pulled back another drape . . . and Peter Cox stared in. And another . . . to let Mike Malin see inside the study.

"Shall I carry on?" Sherman asked.

"That's up to you," Lazar told Taylor. "Have you seen enough yet?"

Taylor looked from one uncovered window to the next. "How many men do you have out there?"

"Two dozen."

"Two dozen . . . an army." Taylor resumed his seat behind the desk. His face was composed but the slight sag of his shoulders indicated his defeat. "What do you want from me?"

"Two things. I want your retirement . . ."

"And?"

". . . Your blessing."

"My blessing?"

"I want you to nominate me as your heir."

Taylor slid open a desk drawer. Instantly Sherman was at his side, his hand covering Taylor's. The drawer held only a

347

box of cigars. Taylor put one in his mouth. At Lazar's bidding, Jimmy stepped forward with a light. Taylor looked up absently, nodded. "Why should I nominate you?"

Lazar motioned to the three men who had been in the study with Taylor to leave. They walked toward the door, instantly obedient to the man they saw as their new leader. They had come to the house loyal to Taylor. Now they realized there would be no more paychecks from him. Only from Lazar.

"I want to avoid bloodshed, Mr. Taylor." Lazar was being polite again. "I'm offering you the opportunity to leave here and enjoy your retirement."

Taylor swung his eyes back to the windows, saw the faces there. "Where would you like me to go?"

"The choice is yours."

Taylor thought about it . . . "I have a house on the Isle of Wight," he said after a moment. "In Cowes. I go there sometimes."

"I also want this house, Mr. Taylor. I'm prepared to make you a fair offer for the property."

That surprised Taylor. He looked at Lazar as if discovering a new facet to his personality. "It's a long way from Stoke Newington to Bishop's Avenue, Whitey. I wonder if you realize that."

"I made the trip a long time ago," Lazar told him. "It was just a question of waiting for the right house to come on the market." He walked across the study, closed the drapes. There was no longer any need for the threatening faces. Taylor had conceded. The brief war was over. Now it was time for diplomacy, the drawing up of a treaty. "By the way, Mr. Taylor . . . do you know where Manny is?"

Taylor smiled, remembering telling Withers how Manny was Lazar's weak spot. How much would Lazar give to learn Manny's whereabouts, his new name? "Is the skeleton in your cupboard making you a little nervous?" Taylor glanced at Jimmy, wondered if he knew about Manny. It had been before his time, of course. But stories like that had a habit of persisting . . . "I don't know where he is."

348

"I think you're lying."

"Your thoughts are your business. But I wouldn't worry about it. Manny would never come back to England as long as *I'm* still alive." Taylor's eyes flicked to Jimmy again, saw the spark of interest.

Lazar returned Taylor's smile with a tight grin of his own. "You're right . . . I wouldn't worry if he did come back," he said, determined to have the final word. "You'll be hearing from my solicitor about my offer on the house." He turned to leave. Sherman followed, but Jimmy hesitated, threw a look at Taylor before accompanying the two other men.

As the door closed behind the three men, Taylor relaxed. The charade was over and so was his reign. But he'd been allowed to walk away. He supposed he should be grateful for that. Only a few hours earlier he'd been ready to carve up Lazar's face. Didn't Lazar hold a grudge?

He walked to the hat stand, took down the steel-lined bowler hat with the vee-shaped dent. He tried it on, wondered how he could ever have walked around with such a weight on his head. He'd been younger then, of course. Stronger. And it had saved his life. Just as yielding to Lazar's demands had saved his life this time.

Katya instantly fell in love with the house on The Bishop's Avenue. Perhaps there weren't really enough rooms for a dozen children and all their friends but she didn't care. She had the two sons she wanted . . . and for them there was room to spare.

The children were crazy about the garden, spacious rolling lawns that contrasted so dramatically with the small, cramped patch of grass they'd had in Stoke Newington. Lazar felt tears begin to well up in his eyes as he watched the boys romp around. He'd waited for this moment for so long.

He remembered the time he had taken them over to the park, played ball with them before he'd led the assault on Toppers. That outing had been an all too infrequent occasion. Now he would have more time to spend with his sons. He wouldn't need to work until the small hours every night; others could do it for him. He'd start taking the boys out more often. They liked to kick a ball around . . . good, he'd take them to soccer matches on Saturday afternoons, buy season tickets. It would do him good as well. He'd be able to relax, to enjoy the life he'd fought so hard to create for his family.

But at the back of his mind one thing still haunted him. One which he knew would never diminish, never disappear. He had got where he wanted − the house, the money, the power − but the price had been huge. There was no pride in the memory of the men he had put down. No matter how much they deserved it. But worst of all was the agonizing thought . . . that even if the hardest men in London respected him, his own brother did not.

As he looked out over the lawns to where his sons played, at the house itself where Katya was busy deciding what she would change − he'd told her to do whatever she liked as long as she didn't touch the study − Lazar decided that he would give it all away, go back to his beginnings . . . yes, even back to coming off the boat in the East End of London . . . if he could once more have Shmuel as a friend. A brother.

1951

CHAPTER TWENTY-THREE

Lazar kept the promise he had made to himself. He spent more time with his sons, took them to soccer games. And when the team the boys loved – Tottenham – won the championship in 1951, Lazar held a huge party in the house on The Bishop's Avenue . . . as much for himself as for his sons.

But late at night, when most of the guests had departed, a final visitor arrived. Detective Superintendent Ivor Davies. And the news he had for Lazar quickly destroyed the party spirit. He showed Lazar a police report: "Joey Taylor was found dead at his home in Cowes, on the Isle of Wight. He has been murdered . . . strangled."

Lazar was stunned. Once a terror, he had become an old, harmless man. Who would want to kill him? . . . "When did it happen?"

"About five days ago," Davies said. "He lived alone, never saw anyone. The woman who cleaned the house once a week found him."

"What was it . . . a robbery?"

Davies shook his head. "Nothing was taken so far as the local police can figure out. Except there was an address book lying on the table, next to where he was found. One page had been torn out."

"Any particular page?"

"The one with the letter *G* on it."

Lazar forgot all about the victory party. A cold sweat broke out all over him.

"I've got to get back to the Yard," Davies said. "I'm on duty. But I thought you'd want to know."

"Thanks, Ivor." Lazar saw Davies to the front door, then

sought out Harry Sherman. "Someone just killed Joey Taylor . . . and ripped the *G* page from his address book."

Sherman swore. "So he did know all along where Manny Goodman was . . ."

"More important, where is he *now*? And who killed Taylor and tore out the page? Get hold of our people . . . find out where they've been the past week. *Everyone*."

"I'll get onto it right away."

Lazar went into the paneled study, locked the door. The first thought to surface was that the late Joey Taylor had once sat behind this desk . . . in this very room.

Lazar sat alone in the paneled study for a long time after the last guests had departed, his mind full of disquieting questions. He could hear Katya upstairs preparing for bed, could recognize the familiar sounds of her nightly routine . . . There were footsteps which Lazar knew meant that she had gone to peek into their younger son David's room. She hadn't looked into Aron's room for more than a year now, ever since her older son had started to close his door at night . . .

Lazar got up from behind the desk, left the study and walked around the first floor of the house . . . The trappings of his victory party were still in evidence. Navy blue and white streamers hung motionless from the ceilings. He pulled them down. The taste of triumph over his team's success had turned sour.

All because of Joey Taylor's death.

Lazar couldn't find it in himself to feel sorry for the old man. After all, he'd had his part in Shmuel's losing his eye. But Lazar could know some regret . . . it did mean a piece of his life had passed forever. In the Isle of Wight, Taylor could never do any harm . . . he was finished and he knew it. The old man was just grateful to be allowed to live out the days remaining to him. But while he was there Lazar felt that time was standing still. With Taylor dead, the clock was moving again. Too quickly.

Face it . . . it wasn't only that Taylor was dead . . . he'd been murdered. By someone who had torn out the *G* page from an address book. Lazar wondered if he was assuming too much — was he seeing ghosts of his own making? — by believing that the missing page meant Manny Goodman, showed where he was . . . ? Or was it a coincidence? The address book . . . the missing page . . . had nothing to do with Taylor's murder at all . . . ? Wishful thinking. Ivor Davies didn't think it was a coincidence. If Davies didn't believe it was so important he would have just telephoned Lazar to pass on the information. He wouldn't have made a special visit, rushed in and out again to Scotland Yard.

According to Davies someone had gone to Taylor's home on the Isle of Wight to locate Manny. That the address book had been next to Taylor's body told Lazar that the old man had willingly provided the information. And whoever it was given to had strangled Taylor. Why? Why commit murder when you've already got what you want, when there's nothing to be gained by killing a man time would soon take, and who was apparently not a threat . . . ?

The telephone rang — Lazar jumped at its shrill noise, grabbed the receiver before it could wake anyone. It was Harry Sherman to tell Lazar that he had already spoken to more than a dozen men on the payroll . . . and all could account for their movements over the past week.

"That's the problem," Lazar said. "Anyone could have shot down to the Isle of Wight, caught the train to Portsmouth and then the ferry across without being missed."

"Why are you so sure it's one of our people?" Sherman asked.

"I'm not, Harry. I'm not sure about anything. I'm just starting at the easiest place."

"Whitey . . . even if it were one of ours, why the hell would they want to know where Manny was? Other than you, me and Goris, who even knows about Manny?"

"I don't know that either. But Ivor Davies is worried about Leah. And I'm nervous too. Did you talk to Goris?"

"He was the first . . . and he can account for every minute of every day."

"That's not why I asked. Was he worried . . . about Manny?"

"Didn't show it, but then he never shows very much

355

of anything."

Lazar agreed. Of the three men who had participated in setting Manny up for the double-murder charge Goris was the only one who'd never lost any sleep over it.

"Did you tell Katya why Ivor was over at the house?" Sherman asked.

"No. What's the point in getting her worried? I just want some of our people here all the time. They can take shifts." Katya would want to know why he had men in the house, he realized. He'd have to tell her something . . . "And, Harry, I want a watch kept on Shmuel's place . . . the shop and the flat above. Without him knowing."

"How will we do that?"

"Find out if any shops in that area are vacant. Lease one and put in a couple of men. You stay there with them . . . at least you know what Manny looks like." Again Lazar wondered if he were overreacting. Manny faced a hangman's noose as soon as he stepped back onto British soil. Would he risk that? Of course, the risk might not be so great anymore. He'd been provided with a new identity when he'd been sprung from prison. And fifteen years had passed . . . not to mention a war that had changed the face of the whole world. No, there was only one threat that had kept Manny away . . . and that was Joey Taylor's promise to kill him if he ever came back. And now Taylor was dead . . . so Manny might figure he was safe . . .

Whoever had strangled Taylor knew of the deal. Taylor had to be killed, or the keys to the Bank of England vault wouldn't have tempted Manny to return. Taylor was the one man who scared him . . . from conditioning way back . . .

"Why don't you call Shmuel and tell him?" Sherman's question cut into Lazar's thoughts.

"He's not too responsive to help from me . . ." His mind was still exploring the last thought about motive . . . Who else, other than Sherman, Goris and himself, knew about the deal between Manny and Taylor? A deal as old as Manny's escape from the death cell?

"Maybe he'll be scared enough for Lottie's sake so he'll listen to you —"

"Just do it the way I'm asking, please, Harry." Lazar was concerned about everyone, but did he really have any reason to worry about Shmuel and Lottie? Shmuel had never done Manny any harm. Manny wouldn't come looking for Shmuel . . . he'd come looking for Lazar, and Sherman and Goris . . . And Leah and Katya too . . . because their testimony had helped a British judge and jury pass a death sentence on Manny.

And then Lazar thought of something more chilling than any possibility so far. *Maybe* it was Manny himself . . . had he somehow come back already, confident that Taylor would be too old to keep his promise of years earlier? Had Taylor's death been the first step of Manny's long-waited-for revenge. And was he even now making his way toward London? Was he already in the city? Under a different name . . . untraceable? Lazar had told Sherman to watch out for Shmuel because the bald man knew what Manny looked like. But did he? How changed would Manny be? Would *any* of them be able to recognize him . . . before it was too late? Lazar thought of Katya . . . and Leah . . . and of his sons sleeping peacefully upstairs . . . If it was Manny . . . writing the first chapter of his revenge . . . this one against Taylor, the man who'd ordered his frame-up . . . why had he torn the pages from the address book? Obviously to leave his signature . . . announce he was back . . . It was just the way his twisted mind would work . . . psychological as well as physical terror . . .

Suddenly from the ceiling, from the walls, from the floor, there seemed to come a familiar, terrifying sound . . . the awful giggle that Lazar remembered so well, the laugh he would always associate with Manny when he'd held the dead prostitute's severed ear . . . when he'd humiliated Davey Vanetti in the Soho courtyard . . .

The laughter was coming from everywhere, and Lazar clasped his hands over his ears. The receiver dropped from his hand, clattered to the floor. And Lazar did something he had not done since his childhood in Cologne. He closed his eyes . . . and prayed to God for help.

CHAPTER TWENTY-FOUR

By Monday morning Lazar had forgotten all about the party. He got up late, still remembering the terror of when he'd imagined Manny's crazy laughter bubbling out from the walls of the house.

Over breakfast, he told Katya that he was having three men posted permanently at the house. She asked why.

"Because" – Lazar looked at her across the table, looked deep into her green eyes – "because we might have a problem." He had to tell her, knew that he could not keep something like this from her, no matter how much he wanted to spare her the anxiety that went with it . . .

"What kind of a problem?" Katya forced out the question, not wanting to hear something that might shatter the peace and security of their lives now.

"When Ivor came in last night, he told me something . . ."

Katya's interest – and her anxiety – increased. She had wondered what Davies wanted with Lazar so late at night. "Go on."

"He had a police report for me to see. About Joey Taylor. He'd been found strangled at his home on the Isle of Wight."

Katya gasped. "Who would want to kill him?" she asked. Lazar told Katya about the address book that had been found beside Taylor's body. And the missing pages . . . the "G" page.

"Manny Goodman's address?" Katya said. "Oh, my God . . ."

"For all we know, it *might* have been Manny who strangled Taylor. You remember what he was like as well as I do. He wouldn't think twice about killing Taylor."

Katya remembered what her father had said about Manny.

He'd been right . . . they should have listened to him. "You honestly believe he'll come here?"

"Where else would he come, Katya?"

"But nobody's certain it's Manny," she protested. "He could have been dead for ten years . . . your friends in America could never find him . . . and Joey Taylor might have been murdered for some totally unrelated reason."

"The address book, you're forgetting about that, aren't you?"

"Why would Manny tear out the page showing his own address . . . in case he got lost?" Katya could feel herself becoming angry. All right . . . perhaps she did accept now what Lazar was telling her. But she would not permit her home to be turned into a fortress. Those days were finished. At least . . . at last . . . Lazar was respectable now. The feuding, the bloodletting happened somewhere else . . . "And why would he leave the book there?" she demanded. "With the page missing . . . just like the police found it? To warn us?" She meant it sarcastically.

"That's right," Lazar said quietly. "To warn us. And at the same time to frighten us, to let us know that he's come back. That's just the way his mind would work." He could see it clearly, Manny giggling as he tore out the page and left the mutilated address book next to Taylor's still-warm body.

"Lazar . . . I still think you could be assuming too much."

"No, and neither is Ivor. He's arranging police protection for Leah and Adele. And I'm having Shmuel watched around the clock." Then, with abrupt determination, he added, "You can do either of two things, Katya. Accept the men I'm moving in here. Or go away. Take the boys with you. Go to a hotel on the coast until it's over."

"I will *not* leave this house," Katya said.

"Then please accept what I'm doing."

Katya bit her lips while she debated the choice. She didn't want strange men − even if they worked for Lazar − moving into her house.

"You won't even know they're here," Lazar said. "They'll work in shifts, patrol the house, watch the grounds. No one will be able to get near or go by." Katya was still hesitant.

359

"Katya . . ." In spite of himself his voice became harsh. "I want a decision right now. Either those men move in . . . or you take the boys, and move out, right now."

Katya knew she had to make an immediate choice. Lazar was adamant. When it came to protecting his family he was like an oak tree . . . he bent for no one. Finally, she nodded.

Only afterward, when Lazar had left the house, did Katya begin to allow herself the fear she had tried to deny.

Harry Sherman found a vacant store diagonally opposite Shmuel's furniture shop on Stamford Hill. Once it had sold clothing. Now it was empty, just painted walls and a bare wooden floor. Sherman arranged to rent the shop by the month. Glad to lease the site – even if only on a monthly basis – the real-estate agent didn't bother to ask any questions.

Late that night a small van drove up outside the shop. Out of it came collapsible furniture – tables, chairs, cots. Once they had made themselves comfortable, Sherman turned on a radio and got out a pack of cards. While one of the men scanned the street from behind the screen of bedsheets they had put up, Sherman and the other men played rummy.

As he felt the cards fitting snugly into his hand, arranged them into sets and suits, it seemed to Sherman as if nothing had really changed at all. He was more at home playing cards in these temporary surroundings than he was in the luxury of Toppers. He didn't mind this duty at all.

Leah tucked her daughter into bed, kissing her goodnight and then went to her own bedroom. She peeked through the window and saw the police car outside. While Davies was on duty, the house would be under permanent watch.

The sight of the police car brought little comfort to Leah. Like Lazar, she had no doubt that if Manny had really returned he would visit those who had conspired to set him up. She was especially frightened for her daughter's sake. Manny was mad, viciously so. She knew well that he wouldn't think twice even about hurting a child.

She moved away from the window, sat down at the dressing

360

table, rested her head on her arms and began to cry.

Lazar's plan to protect his brother and sister-in-law stayed a secret for less than two days. It wasn't Shmuel or Lottie who noticed the unusual goings-on in the newly leased shop on the other side of the street. Of the three men stationed there, Harry Sherman was the only one they knew by sight; and Sherman always made certain to come and go only after he had checked the area carefully.

Instead it was Chris Peters who became suspicious when he visited the flat one evening after work to meet with Shmuel. After cycling over from his mother's house in Clapton, Chris chained his bicycle to a lamppost outside Shmuel's shop. As he removed the bicycle clips from his trousers and straightened up, he looked across the street, saw a car pull up. A heavy, vaguely familiar figure got out wearing a hat, slammed the car door and walked quickly toward the shop. The door swung open and Chris could see inside. Intrigued by the sight of cots, tables and chairs in the shop he continued to stare. Before the door closed, the man who had got out of the car removed his hat to expose an all-too-familiar bald head.

Chris ran up the stairs to Shmuel's flat, breathlessly led Shmuel and Lottie to the window. "How long has that shop been taken?" He pointed across the street to where light filtered through bedsheets covering the shop's windows.

"A couple of days," Shmuel replied. "Why?"

Chris ignored the question. "What are they doing there this time of night?"

Shmuel shrugged. "How do I know? Maybe they're fixing up the place."

"I've never seen anyone going in there," Lottie said.

"There are three men inside. They've got beds, tables, chairs, just like they're living there. And I think one of the men is Harry Sherman. I just saw him get out of that car." Chris pointed to the car parked in front of the shop. "I think they're watching you."

"Watching me?" Shmuel became angry. "What about your

361

brother? Is he there with them?"

"Jimmy? I didn't see him." Chris wasn't certain when the last time was they had met . . . at Johnny's funeral five years earlier? Jimmy didn't come by the house at all anymore.

"I'm going over there right now." Shmuel didn't like Lazar suddenly taking such an interest in his life, wanted to find out the reason for it.

"I'll come with you," Chris offered.

"You stay here with Lottie."

"No . . ." Lottie said. "Take him with you. I'll be all right until you get back."

Shmuel threw on a jacket, ran down the stairs and across the street. Outside the door to the shop he stopped, waited for Chris to catch up.

Before Shmuel could knock, the door swung open and Harry Sherman stood in the entrance, looking like any man relaxing at home after a hard day's work. "Hello, Shmuel . . . Chris. What do you want?"

"I want an explanation." Shmuel pushed past Sherman. The other two men, sitting at the table eating fish and chips out of greasy newspaper, looked up. One started to get up but Sherman waved at him to be still.

"Just what the hell is going on here?" Shmuel demanded. "Why am I . . . under watch like this?"

"Don't ask me. I'm just following orders."

"My brother's? Why?"

"You'd better ask him. I can't tell you anything." It was obvious to Shmuel that Sherman wasn't about to say anything.

"I will ask him," Shmuel said. "But in the meantime you and your friends had better leave this shop. Otherwise I'm calling the police."

Sherman swung his eyes to Chris. "We're not going any-where, Shmuel. We've paid a month's rent for this place and we're staying right here." Sherman was at the moment more afraid of disobeying Lazar's instructions than he was of Shmuel . . . He did not want to betray the trust Lazar had placed in him.

"You're not leaving?" Shmuel took a step forward. "We'll

362

see about that."

Chris stepped forward quickly, placed himself between the two men and pushed Shmuel back. He remembered Lazar's telling him about secretly funding the club, and knew there had to be a reason for what Lazar was doing now. "Why don't you talk to your brother first?" Chris said, still holding Shmuel back. "Find out what he's got to say before you do anything."

Sherman was relieved.

"Where? At his house?" Shmuel didn't seem too pleased with the prospect.

"Why not?" Sherman checked his watch. Lazar wouldn't be leaving for Toppers for at least another hour. He was surprised that he was going at all, but he knew Lazar was determined to keep up his routine. His wife and two sons, he had said, would be safe with three of his men in the house.

For the second time that evening, Chris offered to accompany Shmuel. "What about Lottie?" Shmuel wanted to know. He didn't like this at all; Lazar should be the one coming to *him* to explain.

"We'll stay here . . ." Sherman said. "Keep an eye on things for you."

"You . . . and these two?" Shmuel pointed to the men sitting at the table.

"Believe me, Shmuel, you should be bloody grateful we're here."

Shmuel could see that there was only one way to find out what was going on, and that was to visit Lazar . . . He went back to the flat, told Lottie to lock the door and to let no one in until he returned. Then he and Chris drove to Hampstead Garden suburb.

Shmuel had never even driven past the house on The Bishop's Avenue where Lazar now lived. But he could not help being impressed when he pulled into the semicircular driveway, saw the white house, the spacious, floodlit grounds, the fountain. Lazar had done all right for himself, he thought. Yes, Lazar had done all right.

Two figures appeared from the front of the house and walked briskly across the floodlit area. Both men carried clubs. "Are you Shmuel?" Peter Cox asked as he opened the driver's door and stepped back. He didn't have to wait for an answer . . . the eyepatch was identification enough. On the other side of the van, Mike Malin opened Chris' door.

"Where is my brother?" Shmuel asked.

"Inside. He's waiting for you." Cox led the way into the house. Shmuel looked around, expecting to see Katya. He saw only Jimmy Peters seated in the wide entrance hall. Jimmy stood up when he recognized Chris, held out a hand. Chris ignored his brother completely.

Cox led Shmuel and Chris to the study, where Lazar was sitting behind the desk. Shmuel was struck instantly at how silver his brother's hair had become . . . how lined his face was, gaunt even. The price of success, Shmuel thought sadly . . .

"You saw Harry and the others, eh?" Lazar said. "What a shame." Sherman had telephoned from a public telephone the moment Shmuel had left.

"Why is it a shame to know I'm being spied on?" Shmuel looked out through the open windows at the illuminated grounds, and thought of how the boys in his club would enjoy all this . . . if they only could . . .

"Shmuel . . . Chris . . . will you sit down?" Lazar indicated for Cox to leave. "I'm going to have to ask you to be patient with me for a little while. Someone else is coming . . . Ivor. He'll be able to explain everything far better than I can."

Shmuel forced himself to sit down and wait. To learn that Davies was involved brought some measure of reassurance.

"How is Lottie?" Lazar asked.

"She's all right. How long before Ivor gets here?"

"I called him after I heard you were on your way over here. It shouldn't be long. Would you like anything while you're waiting?"

"No, thank you," Shmuel said. Chris shook his head. "Where's Katya?"

"Upstairs. Would you like to see her?"

Before Shmuel could answer there was a knock on the study door. Ivor Davies walked in, and for a moment Lazar was reminded of the first time he had visited this house . . . with

364

Manny . . . and how he and Manny had been kept waiting by Taylor for the arrival of another man. A high-ranking police officer . . . just like Davies was now . . .

"Ivor!" Shmuel burst out. "He has men watching my home, my shop. I want to know why."

"For the same reason I've got the local police watching my home in Ilford," Davies replied calmly. "For protection."

"Protection?" Shmuel looked at Davies. "Why do I need protection . . . Lazar's protection?"

"We've reason to believe that Manny Goodman has come back," Davies said. "One man is already dead. I think he could be coming after the rest of us. It's safer to take these precautions."

"He has no reason to harm me . . ." Shmuel said. Or had he? . . . After all, Shmuel had fired Manny as manager in favor of Ben Kosky.

"When did Manny ever need a reason for anything he did?" Lazar demanded.

"But why do I need protection from you? Why can't I have police protection?"

"Because Lazar can spare more men," Davies answered. "And he can do a more thorough job than we can." Davies wished he had Lazar's men at his home in Ilford instead of the police. Only it obviously wouldn't do for a detective-superintendent to take that approach. It was bad enough asking for police protection. It had opened old wounds, made people remember that Leah was the former Mrs. Manny Goodman, the wife of a convicted murderer . . .

"Look . . ." Lazar said to Shmuel, "Harry and the others are staying put whether you like it or not. Right now I don't care what you say, but until the police catch Manny, and I'm sure we're all safe, those men are staying. Just like my men are staying here."

Shmuel swung around and marched from the study, through the hall, past Jimmy and out into the night air with Chris right after him. Jimmy followed, watched them climb into the heavy furniture van and drive away. Then he walked to the street, stayed there even after the van's taillights had disappeared.

"Are you coming back in, Jimmy?" Mike Malin called from the doorway of the house. "There's a pot of tea brewing." Malin guessed that Jimmy was thinking about his young brother . . . they hadn't spoken a word to each other.

"In a minute," Jimmy called back. He stayed out in the street, arms folded across his chest. He was thinking, all right, but not about his brother Chris . . . he was thinking about Lazar . . . how worried he was. They all were . . . all of them dead scared. They all thought that Manny had come back. He had haunted them for years, and now they saw Manny behind every tree . . . in every shadowy corner.

And all because Joey Taylor had been strangled. And a page had been ripped out of an address book . . . by him, Jimmy . . .

Taylor had been so frail, Jimmy recalled . . . his neck little more than bone and windpipe. Jimmy figured he could have strangled the old man with just one hand . . . A walking skeleton, he'd been. Cancer did that to a man . . . Jimmy had seen it happen once before, to his own father. Yes . . . he'd done Taylor a favor by strangling him. Saved him the agony of living out those final weeks or months . . . or whatever was left to him.

Jimmy had been extremely patient. Five years had passed since his twin brother's death on a railway line. Five years in which his one and only aim had been to work his way into Lazar's deepest trust and confidence. Only one man was closer to Lazar than Jimmy. And that was Sherman. So close that he must have helped Lazar to kill Johnny that night. They'd been together in Pearl's . . . just the two of them . . . and together they'd said that Johnny had left, gone drinking in the West End. And that had been their mistake, Jimmy thought bitterly. With the kidney problem — and his fanatical obedience to the diet — there was no way that Johnny could have gotten drunk enough that night to stumble on a live rail . . .

Even five years later Jimmy didn't understand why Lazar had wanted Johnny dead. But he didn't really care anymore. Only one thing concerned him now . . . revenge. He wanted

Lazar and Sherman . . .

Sure, Johnny had been an idiot at times, hotheaded beyond reason. Christ knew how often Jimmy had wanted to throttle his brother for some craziness . . . like that time when he'd shot the copper. But Johnny had been his twin . . . his identical twin. Not just flesh and blood, but two halves of the same seed from their mother's womb. When Johnny had been killed, a little piece of Jimmy had died along with him. And the only way that Jimmy knew of to recapture that piece of himself was by killing those responsible for Johnny's death.

And now that Jimmy finally understood the riddle of Manny Goodman, he knew how to take Lazar and Sherman . . . He'd tried to take Lazar once before, when he'd warned Taylor about the planned assault on Toppers. Only he hadn't known that Lazar would be taking an army with him.

Jimmy often thought about that conversation between Lazar and Taylor the night Lazar had taken over. Taylor had planted a seed in his mind. But he'd forced himself to wait five years before seeing Taylor, to make sure there wasn't any doubt about his loyalty to Lazar . . .

He had caught an early morning train to Portsmouth, taken the ferry across to the Isle of Wight. Taylor hadn't been at all surprised to see him. Sooner or later he knew Jimmy would come. Jimmy had tried to betray Lazar once before. He'd try again.

Jimmy had been shocked by Taylor's appearance. The old man was barely able to move around the house. All his shopping was done for him by the woman who cleaned house once a week. He had refused a nurse or a daily help, just like he had snorted at the idea of being moved to an old-age home . . . his pride dictated that he be left alone.

"You took a chance waiting so long," Taylor had said to Jimmy. "I might have been dead already from this bloody worm inside of me." He took Jimmy into the living room, told him what had happened that night in Davey Vanetti's flat. How Manny had been fitted up for the double murder . . . with the invaluable help of Withers. Jimmy had listened intently; never once had he thought of telling Taylor at whose hand Withers had really died.

When he had told Jimmy everything, pausing every so often to regain his breath and strength, Taylor fumbled in a drawer until he found an old, worn address book. On the "G" page was an address in New York which bore the name of Edwin Green. He ripped out the page, handed it to Jimmy. Jimmy had turned to leave, eager to return to London and the next step in his revenge. But then he had remembered something Taylor had said on the night of his abdication five years earlier.

"What was that you once said about Manny never coming back while you were still alive?"

Taylor's eyes had widened at the sight of Jimmy's strong hands as they spread themselves into a menacing circle. Taylor knew he was dying anyway . . . but he didn't want to die just yet. And certainly not like this. He wanted to see Whitey get taken first. "It meant nothing. I was just covering myself with Whitey."

"I don't believe you. Manny needs to know of your death . . . needs to be certain of it."

Taylor had fought, beating futilely at Jimmy's face with bony fists. And all the while Jimmy's hands had tightened their grip. Until suddenly the blows ceased. Taylor's body went limp. Unable to cope with the furious activity, his weakened heart had surrendered the fight. It had taken Jimmy several seconds to realize what had happened. For an instant he felt ashamed. Then, as if he were handling a baby or an expensive piece of china, he'd set Taylor gently down in the chair and left the address book on the table next to him. A nice little touch . . . one that would sow the seeds of terror in Lazar's mind . . .

Jimmy began to smile to himself. Lazar was certain that Manny was already back . . . that Taylor's death had been by Manny's hand. Good. Whitey was frightened. Jimmy could see it in the way he looked, the way he acted. Filling the house with guards. Having Sherman keep a permanent watch on Shmuel's home. Being a witness to Lazar's fear would heighten Jimmy's revenge, make it that much sweeter. And he wouldn't even have to lift a finger to make that revenge happen.

Lazar's anticipation, his terror, would reach breaking point during the next three weeks . . . that was how long it would be until Manny Goodman arrived back in England. Only the previous morning had news of Taylor's death reached the newspapers. Jimmy had cut out stories from the *Daily Mirror* and the *Express*, sent them air mail to the address of Edwin Green in New York.

Manny would reach England like a primed artillery shell.

CHAPTER TWENTY-FIVE

Manny Goodman got out of the taxi, paid the driver and walked quickly toward the lobby of an apartment hotel on East Sixty-third Street between Park and Madison avenues in New York City. The expensive leather attaché case he carried in his right hand swung back and forth as he walked. Along with the Brooks Brothers gray suit, he looked like any one of a million businessmen returning early from the office.

"Good afternoon, Mr. Green," the doorman called out cheerfully as Manny entered the building. "How you doing?"

Manny acknowledged the man with a slight inclination of his head. He went to the mailbox, took out three letters addressed to Edwin Green, then headed for the elevator and his apartment on the eighth floor. On the way up he glanced at the three letters he had taken from the box. Two from New York . . . and one with an English stamp and a London postmark. He frowned, debated whether to open the envelope while in the elevator, finally decided to wait until he reached the privacy of his own apartment.

The apartment had been cleaned while he'd been out — fresh linen, the bed turned back. Manny threw his attaché case and the letters onto the bed, then walked to the bathroom. While he washed up, he thought about the letter from London. Who could that be from? No one in England knew of Edwin Green. Except Joey Taylor, of course . . . and he wouldn't write . . . he was just happy as long as he knew where Manny Goodman was . . .

Manny studied his reflection in the bathroom mirror. No one from England would recognize him now, anyway — thanks to Taylor's insurance policy . . . money enough for a new start that included surgery to change the shape of his face. The chin was much squarer, the nose smaller, turned up at the end instead of being long and straight. The years had themselves changed his hair . . . thinner in the center and the front, streaked generously with gray at the sides. Only the eyes had not changed. They were still the same vibrant blue. And the tic beneath the left eye that jumped into life whenever he was agitated. Neither time nor plastic surgery could change either of them.

He decided to leave the letter for a few minutes, went back into the bedroom and opened the attaché case, shook the contents onto the bed. Although he might have looked like a successful businessman, the case contained nothing that any ordinary businessman would carry around. A set of brass knuckles, a four-pound hammer, a pair of fine leather gloves and a thick, dog-eared notebook. Manny opened the notebook, crossed out a name with red ink. Some debts, he reasoned, had to be written off when it was obvious that they were beyond redemption. But this particular debtor wouldn't boast about having beaten Manny . . . at least, not until he was out of the hospital. And that could be from up to two months with the broken legs and fractured ribs he'd received today.

Even so, Manny didn't like writing off bad debts. He worked as the chief collection agent for the biggest loanshark in the city, keeping a percentage of what he recovered. When a debt was written off he was out his share. No matter how much he made an example of the debtor, how much he enjoyed it, it nevertheless didn't pay him.

When Manny had first arrived in New York — a stranger who didn't even know his way around the streets — he'd started small by working as a collector for a small-time bookmaker. Showing no reluctance to use violence he'd spread terror among gamblers who were delinquent in their payments. His returns had quickly become the largest. Soon his successful methods were noticed by more powerful men as intrigued by his Cockney accent and no-nonsense approach to the problems of bad debts as he had once been taken with Lazar's platinum-blond hair. Over the years the Cockney accent had virtually disappeared, but he could revive it whenever he chose. It was his party piece, guaranteed to bring appreciative chuckles from his friends whenever he chose to play the clown.

Finally he directed his attention to the day's mail. One letter was from the owners of the building to inform him of an increase in rent. He tossed it aside. The second contained an invitation to a Beethoven concert. He checked his diary and decided to accept. It was all part of the image he had created for himself in New York — a cultured, worldly man . . . who had no compunction about breaking a man's leg to compensate for a hundred-dollar usurious loan that had gone bad.

He turned to the third letter, the one that bore the London postmark. He slit open the envelope with his fingernail, pulled out several pieces of paper. One was the letter itself, scrawled in an almost illegible hand on cheap lined white paper. The other pieces were newspaper clippings. Manny spread them out . . . and he recognized photographs of Joey Taylor. He looked at the headlines. "GANGSTER POPE STRANGLED IN ISLE OF WIGHT," read one. The other was kinder . . . "GANG PEACEMAKER FOUND MURDERED."

He began to read the letter, glancing first at the signature. Who was Jimmy Peters? And how did he get my address? Manage to tie me in with Manny Goodman? As he read, the answers became clear. Joey Taylor had given out the information. And now Taylor was dead, which made it very safe for him to return to England. But did he really want to go back to England? He had nothing there anymore. His life was in the United States . . . he'd never had it as good in England a s
he did here.

And then he stopped kidding himself. Of course he damned well wanted to go back. Just once. Because this Jimmy Peters . . . this letter writer . . . wanted to help him work his revenge on those who'd set him up.

Manny read the letter again, then a third time. He made a note of the return address before he tore the letter to shreds, set fire to it in a glass ashtray. He went to the telephone, called his boss, asked politely for a month's vacation time. Then he called steamship lines, inquired about the earliest sailings to England.

As he left the apartment and took a taxi to the Cunard Line offices, he started to think it was a pretty good day. Sure, he'd lost out on a debt. But he'd put a man in hospital for a couple of months – which would make twenty other wavering debtors somehow find the money to square their accounts. And to top it off . . . he was going back to England for a very important visit . . .

At Cunard, he booked a first-class passage on the *Queen Mary* to Southampton. He'd wire Jimmy Peters his arrival time. He'd return to England in the style befitting the kind of man he now was.

The morning mist was just clearing when the *Queen Mary* docked at Southampton. Manny leaned over the varnished rail and stared down at the pier, remembering the last time he had sailed into Southampton from New York. That time he had been returning from his honeymoon . . . returning to fall straight into Lazar's trap.

The sight of English soil made him nervous, made him remember how close he had come to death . . . only days away from having a rope dragged around his neck, a trapdoor dropped open beneath his feet. And for a crime he hadn't committed. He laughed to himself. The insurance he'd taken out against Joey Taylor – the details of every transaction left in the safe hands of a trusted lawyer – had paid off handsomely.

Now he was returning again. As a successful man known as Edwin Green . . . all ready to cancel out the debts that had been run up against a man once called Manny Goodman.

He wondered what Jimmy Peters would be like, the man who had contacted him. He'd be young . . . the ambitious ones always were. And shrewd. He'd have to be that to get Taylor to cough up the address in New York. But why was he so intent on opening old wounds – what reason did he have? That question intrigued Manny the most. All this Jimmy had mentioned in the letter was that he, too, had a score to settle with Lazar. Maybe you have, Manny thought. But it's nowhere near as urgent as mine.

Far below on the dock Manny spotted a policeman's uniform. He stiffened, and almost as quickly relaxed. He had nothing to fear in this country. No police in England would be looking for him now. He'd gone. Disappeared. Vanished forever. The law had written him off as an uncollectable debt, he thought wryly.

He watched while the stately liner was moored to the dock, then went down to his first-class compartment. The steward was there, waiting for his tip. Manny didn't disappoint the man and tipped him extravagantly. That was one of the first lessons he'd learned about his adopted country. Yanks always tipped well . . . too well . . . and he was one them now, wasn't he? Yes, he was an American. He idly wondered what accent to use when he contacted Lazar. Whitey . . . the little traitor. Should he threaten him with a New York accent? Confuse him? Or should he just rise like a ghost with the old familiar Cockney slang? Trying to decide which course to take gave Manny enormous pleasure . . .

He passed through immigration without difficulty, showed his United States passport, said he was staying for a couple of weeks on vacation, displayed his return ticket on the *Queen Mary*, smiled when the official stamped the passport. He collected his baggage, went through customs and waited. At the far side of the customs hall he spotted a young man with curly hair and blue eyes . . . and a half-opened red rose in the buttonhole of his blue suit. Manny directed the porter to wait with his baggage while he approached the man.

"Jimmy?"

"Mr. Green?"

They shook hands formally. Manny called over the porter, followed Jimmy to the car that waited outside. The porter loaded the baggage and Manny tipped extravagantly again, enjoying himself as he pretended to be confused by the currency.

"Did you have a good trip?" Jimmy asked, driving away from the docks.

"Not bad. A couple of rough days, that was all." Manny looked at Peters with interest. "Tell me something about yourself, Jimmy. And the others. I've been away a long time." It didn't seem like it, though, now that he was back. Manny felt like he could step straight into the action again, as if he'd never been away.

For the rest of the ninety-minute drive Jimmy filled Manny in on what had happened since he had joined the firm in 1946, right up to the protective measures that had been taken by Lazar following the death of Taylor. Every so often, Manny would ask for something to be repeated as he tried to organize everything in his head.

"If you're guarding Whitey's house, how come you could meet me?" Manny asked when Jimmy had finished.

"We're alternating. Otherwise Whitey figures we'll get sick of the sight of each other."

"That makes sense." Manny looked at his driver, noticed he'd discarded the red rose that had been agreed upon as a means of identification. "So . . . you killed Joey Taylor, eh?"

"He was dying anyway. Cancer. I just helped him along."

Manny laughed. "Thoughtful of you."

"I'm puzzled why he had your address . . . after what I heard had happened."

Manny turned serious, bitter. "That cunning old bastard had contacts the world over. Maybe he was scared to touch me — because of what the lawyer was holding — but it sure made him happier to know where I was." Then he laughed again. "His pal's dead as well, eh? Withers? And Whitey done it?" That news had surprised him. Lazar had more guts than Manny had given him credit for. And brains. To take Withers out of the game on a wild goose chase while he plotted against Taylor was sheer genius. But then Lazar had been the man who had suggested making Davey Vanetti eat the ear. Perhaps he shouldn't be so surprised after all.

"Where do they all live then?" he asked Jimmy.

Jimmy reeled off addresses. Ilford . . . that suited Leah and Davies. Manny wasn't surprised about Leah marrying that cop. Manny had to admit, though, that he'd come up . . . detective-superintendent. And Shmuel . . . he'd never made anything of himself because he was too damned upright, too stupid to ever take anything that wasn't one hundred and ten percent honest. And finally, Lazar . . . lording it up by living in Taylor's old house. Now that was style. Gone respectable as well, with a thriving nightclub. Used it as a cover for all the strong-arm stuff that kept everyone else in line. Yes . . . Lazar was a worthy successor to Taylor. Too bad he had just a short time left to enjoy it . . .

"What do you hope to get out of all this?" Manny asked casually. "Just revenge for what happened to your brother?" Some fool he must have been, Manny decided . . . blowing away a constable just like that.

"Maybe I can move into the space Whitey leaves."

"Maybe you can at that," Manny agreed. But not from me, sonny . . .

"Do you want to look around town or should I take you straight to the Dorchester?" Jimmy asked when they reached the outskirts of London.

"Take me to the Dorchester. I'll look around later." That was a nice touch, Manny thought. He and Leah had stayed at the Dorchester on their wedding night. And instead of making love to her like any other enthusiastic groom would have done, he'd slapped her around because she'd looked so happy. He hadn't been exactly thrilled to get married. But it was the only way he had seen of keeping tabs on Lazar . . .

"Don't come into the Dorchester with me," Manny said. "Just drop me off. I'll arrange to meet you later." He didn't want to be seen in the company of Jimmy.

"Sure, Manny. Sure."

"Who?" A spark flashed dangerously in Manny's blue eyes.

"Eddie . . . Mr. Green."

"That's better," Manny said, his eyes as cold as ice. "And don't you ever forget it."

Late that afternoon, Jimmy chauffeured Manny around town. First they drove to the East End. Jimmy waited patiently while, with hands clasped behind his back, Manny walked around, noticing the bombsites, the new buildings going up. London had caught it good and proper, he thought. He walked along Booth Street, stopped in front of the greengrocer's shop. It had changed hands, of course. Leah must have sold it before marrying Davies.

Then he walked along Wentworth Street . . . to Petticoat Lane market. Everything had changed and yet nothing had changed. Here he was . . . a new man with a new country . . . and the same people were still selling the same merchandise from the same stalls. They were older, perhaps, but their manner, their style, had not been changed by the years. Manny stopped to look at a middle-aged man who worked with his son selling china. They had a routine, an act to attract the customers. The son played the fool to the father's straight man. Manny remembered the act from twenty years earlier; only then the father had been the son, and he'd been playing the clown to his own father's straight man. Manny stood in front of the stall for a full minute . . . and the middle-aged man stared straight through him as though he'd never seen him before.

"Where do you want to go now?" Jimmy asked when Manny returned to the car. He wasn't sure what to make of the man he'd picked up at Southampton that morning. From what he'd heard, Manny had been a holy terror. Except for the spark of anger when he'd been called by the wrong name, the man sitting next to Jimmy seemed like a quiet, successful businessman. Even given to sentimentality, the way he'd strolled around the old neighborhood. Had Jimmy made a mistake by bringing him back?

"Show me where Harry Sherman lives," Manny said. "And Goris."

"What about Whitey's house?"

"I know it. That's one address I don't need pointed out to me."

Manny sat back in the passenger seat, silently working out the task that lay ahead. It had all seemed so simple on the ship . . . even before, when he'd first been contacted by Jimmy. He'd known then exactly what had to be done . . . Wipe out everyone even remotely connected with the frame-up that had almost sent him to the hangman's noose. Now he realized that was too big a job. He just wanted the three men who had set him up that night. Leah and Katya would get theirs through Lazar's death. Even Shmuel would mourn for him, though Manny knew that the two brothers hadn't spoken civilly to each other since before the war. There would be no one to mourn for Sherman . . . or Goris. They both lived alone. Pity.

And then, before Manny returned to New York and resumed the life of Edwin Green, there would of course be Jimmy Peters to take care of. Manny could understand Jimmy's sought-after revenge, sympathize with his desire for a piece of Lazar's empire once Lazar was out of the way. But who the hell did he think he was that he could use Manny Goodman as his own tool?

Three weeks had passed since Taylor's death, and Leah's initial gratitude for the police protection had vanished. She had become sick of the black police car parked outside the house whenever Davies was absent. Each time she saw it — with the two uniformed constables inside — she was reminded that her violent ex-husband might have returned . . .

But had he? Even Davies' once-concrete suspicions were now waning. When Taylor had been found murdered, the page torn out, Davies had jumped immediately to the conclusion that Manny had been responsible. But since then? Nothing. The world had continued as normal. Except for the police car parked outside the house.

"Ivor . . . that car has to go," Leah told him when he returned home. "It's been three weeks, for God's sake! I can't stand it anymore."

He understood what she meant. But something highly visible was needed . . . to scare Manny off in case he did surface. "Another two weeks," Davies promised. "Just to make sure. It can't do any more harm to have the car there for another couple of weeks."

"I don't know if I can stand it."

"You can," he told her gently, although he did not know himself what could possibly turn up in two weeks that hadn't turned up yet. He had men looking everywhere. So did Lazar.

378

But they hadn't been able to come up with anything leading to Manny. That's if he was in London to begin with, Davies thought sourly.

He picked up the telephone to call Lazar, and Katya answered. Davies asked how she was bearing up under the strain and like Leah she asked how much longer she was expected to take it. "Until we unearth him," Davies answered. He wondered what happened when they did find him. Would it all be legal, would they drag him back to jail and make him serve out his sentence . . . at the end of a rope? Or would they do it the way Lazar wanted? . . . an accident . . . a quiet grave somewhere. Death of a man unknown? That couldn't be done if the police got to him first. But if one of Lazar's men found him . . . Davies found himself wishing it would happen that way.

He asked Katya to put Lazar on the phone. "Anything new?"

"Not since I spoke to you this morning. What about your side of things?"

"Nothing. And Shmuel?"

"Harry and the boys are still in the shop." Davies' concern had somehow persuaded Shmuel and Lottie to allow themselves to be protected by Lazar's men. "Ivor, I'm all for calling this entire thing off. Katya's becoming paranoid about it. Every time there's a knock at the door or the phone rings she goes crazy. We can't go on living like this. She and the boys are prisoners." He kept to his normal routine, but whenever Katya went shopping, or when the boys went to school, they were escorted door-to-door.

"Leah, too," Davies admitted. "I told her another couple of weeks, then we'll call the whole thing off. Admit we made a mistake."

"Some mistake," Lazar said, knowing how Leah was going through hell because her entire neighborhood now knew about her past. Then a bizarre thought struck him. What if Taylor had engineered the whole thing himself? He was terminally ill anyway. What if he had paid someone to put him out of his misery? And deliberately left the address book with a page missing . . . a page that had nothing of importance on it? For the simple purpose of creating confusion and terror? God . . . what a brilliant act of vengeance that would be, he thought. Masterful.

He hung up, then dialed the number of the vacant shop on Stamford Hill. Harry Sherman answered; he had nothing to report.

"Leave the others, Harry, and come by the house for dinner. Then we'll go to Toppers. You can do with a night away from that place."

The offer sounded good to Sherman. A good meal would go down well. He arrived at the house thirty-five minutes later. Peter Cox opened the door for him, asked how the stake-out was going. Sherman grimaced and Cox nodded understandingly. At least the men working shifts in the house had comfort, he thought; sitting in that damned shop for twelve hours on end must be hell.

After dinner Lazar and Sherman drove to Regent Street. "We're going to call this whole thing off in another couple of weeks or so," Lazar said. "I think we might have panicked."

"Better to panic than to be sorry. Believe me, Whitey, I didn't mind sitting in the shop all this time."

"I know you didn't." Sherman would never admit it even if he did mind, Lazar knew. "What about the others?"

"No . . . they didn't mind either." At the beginning of the second week, one of the men in the shop had complained. Sherman had dragged him into the back, forced his head into the toilet bowl and promised that if he moaned once more he'd jam his head into the bowl and flush it until he drowned. There had been no complaints after that. "What about the boys you've got in the house?"

"They're all right. I wish I could let you just work shifts like the rest of them, Harry, but I need you there all the time. You know what he looks like. And I can't send Goris to the shop . . . he's getting too old."

"Don't worry about it. Anyway . . . it's not much longer, is it?"

They parked, went upstairs. Even for midweek the club was busy. Sherman checked over the menu. It was good, but what Katya had cooked that evening was better. He was glad he'd been invited to eat at the house and not at the club.

Jimmy Peters was on duty. So was Goris. The sight of the two men pleased Sherman. He hadn't seen them together since before Taylor's death had prompted the alarm. Maybe things were getting back to normal now . . . He went over to talk to the two men. They discussed the precautions that were being taken. Sherman was pleased to see there was no griping from Jimmy . . . he understood the urgency of the situation as well as anyone, had put in his shifts at the house without a word of complaint. Like a loyal soldier he was prepared to put up with looking after Katya and the boys. Maybe Johnny hadn't worked out, Sherman thought, but his brother more than made up for him.

In the flat above the furniture shop, Shmuel pulled back a curtain and stared across the street. Light shone through the bedsheets covering the windows of the vacant shop; the shadow of a man moved in and out of the light. Shmuel was surprised that the police hadn't been to investigate yet. But then he supposed that either Lazar or more likely Davies had a contact with the local police. They probably knew what was going on over there, and were happy to leave it alone.

"Do you think I should go over and offer them something to eat?" Lottie asked. She was washing up after dinner, while Chris Peters dried.

"I'll take something over if you like," Chris offered. He knew his brother wasn't there.

"Leave them alone," Shmuel said. "They can look after themselves." He turned away from the window and sat down. He knew he was grateful that Lazar cared enough to post a guard. But if it hadn't been for Lazar there would have been no need for it in the first place.

At eight thirty, the door to Toppers opened and a couple walked in. The smartly dressed man went to the reception desk and announced he had a dinner reservation. "Green. For two," he said with a distinct American accent, flicking his blue eyes down the list.

"Yes, sir. Would you like to leave your coat in the cloakroom?"

Manny returned to the attractive blonde who was with him and helped her off with her coat, then followed the waiter to his table. He saw Jimmy Peters . . . and just as he sat down, he spotted Lazar standing by the side of the bar, talking to Sherman and Goris. The long years of waiting . . . hoping . . . praying for a chance to avenge himself . . . suddenly dissolved as Manny fixed a burning gaze on the three men who had tried to destroy him.

"What is it?" the woman with Manny asked.

He turned around, looked across the small table for a moment, unable to identify the blonde who had asked the question. Then he remembered. She was a fellow guest at the Dorchester, a new divorcée from Philadelphia who was celebrating her independence by touring Europe. Manny had met her in the hotel bar the previous night, asked her out. Not because he was attracted to her . . . but because he needed an escort if he was to visit Toppers and see for himself what Lazar had achieved. Alone, he might have stood out; with a woman he was just one of many couples. "Just looking around," he finally said. "Nice place."

"Anything's nice compared to Philadelphia," the woman said and Manny smiled. "But I don't think *he's* much of an advertisement for a top night spot." She pointed a finger at Goris. "A face like that . . . it's enough to give me nightmares for a week. I hope he doesn't come over here while we're eating. I'll never be able to finish."

"Don't look at him," Manny whispered. "He probably got it during the war . . . they must have had one hell of a time over here."

After dinner they danced until midnight. Several times Manny guided his partner close to where Lazar stood by the bar, and with each pass Manny grew more confident. If Lazar couldn't recognize him, then no one would. Including Sherman and Goris. Once, Goris stared right into Manny's face from a distance of two yards. Manny smiled, and Goris returned it with a travesty of his own. Manny knew he'd be able to pick off his targets with ease . . . No one knew what he looked like.

"I'll take you back to the hotel now," Manny told the woman, who seemed disappointed. Manny smiled apologetically, claiming he was tired . . . touring the city had worn him out. But he'd like to have a nightcap with her back at the Dorchester. He retrieved their coats, left the cloakroom attendant a pound, which opened the man's eyes wide. At the exit, Jimmy Peters stepped forward to open the door. As Manny slipped past, Jimmy whispered, "Two o'clock."

They caught a taxi back to the Dorchester, arriving at twelve thirty. In the woman's room there was a bottle of Scotch, and she rang down for ice. Manny sat on the edge of the bed, seemingly relaxed. Inside his head, though, a clock was ticking off every second.

Half an hour later, the blonde divorcée was both frustrated and confused. Her escort for the evening had seemed a personable, dynamic sort of man. But in the bedroom he'd been a disaster. She'd waited for him to make a move. And when he'd done nothing but sip his Scotch slowly, she'd taken the initiative. Even under her tantalizing caress, he'd been as unresponsive as a piece of furniture; his mind was so obviously somewhere else.

"Don't you find me attractive?"

"Sure I do. But I told you earlier on . . . . I'm worn out." The last thing he needed was to make love to this woman. It would interfere with the first part of his mission and nothing could be allowed to do that. Now was the perfect time to start . . . when Lazar and the others were beginning to relax. He had to act tonight. "Maybe tomorrow night," he promised the woman.

She looked at him. "Don't be so damned sure of yourself."

Manny just smiled. He couldn't care one way or the other. Women had always come easily to him; this trollop, busting free after her divorce, wasn't going to make him lose any sleep. He blew her a kiss from the doorway and walked out into the corridor.

Back in his own room he changed from his suit into a dark

pair of trousers and a raincoat. He went to one of his cases and felt inside for the razor he'd bought the previous day, at a hairdresser's supplier in Soho. He removed the razor from its box, ran his thumb lovingly across the blade . . . The sharpness brought back memories . . . Closing the razor he lifted it to his lips, kissed it. Tonight was the time to begin putting those memories to their final rest.

Toppers closed at two o'clock in the morning. Sherman drove back with Lazar to The Bishop's Avenue. Lazar invited him to spend the night in the house but the bald man said he'd return to Stamford Hill, the vacant shop and the watch on Shmuel and Lottie . . .

Jimmy Peters went straight to his own flat in Hackney. He lay down on the bed but was unable to fall asleep. After a while he got up, lit a cigarette, poured himself a drink and stared out of the window. He'd be glad when it was morning . . .

Goris also went home, to the flat in Shoreditch where he'd lived since long before the war . . . long before he'd ever met Lazar. Goris had never wanted to move to a better neighborhood in spite of his now respectable salary. Shoreditch suited his simple needs, made him feel secure. His only investment was to buy the small block of eight flats where he lived and let the rent from the other seven pay the mortgage. He'd probably stay there until he died, surrounded by the same furniture he'd first bought when he'd moved in. Goris knew he was worth more money than he'd ever thought was possible, and he had no idea whom he'd eventually leave it to when he died. But he refused to worry about that . . .

He parked the car a dozen yards from the entrance to the dingy block of flats, made sure the doors were locked, then started to walk toward the entrance. Something was different; it took him a couple of seconds to realize what it was. The damn streetlight outside the building entrance was out.

A figure materialized, wraithlike, from the shadows of the building entrance. "Hey, buddy . . . can you give me directions to Liverpool Street Station? I'm lost."

Goris stopped, startled. Lost was right. What on earth was

a Yank doing in Shoreditch this time of night? Or any time of the night for that matter? "You go to the end of the street and turn right. Keep on walking . . ." The words died in his throat as he looked harder at the man in the poor light. "You . . . you were in Toppers tonight."

"That's right, Goris." The American accent was replaced by a Cockney tone. "And the dame I was with thought your face was enough to give her nightmares for a week. What do you think about that?"

"Ma . . . Manny?" Goris couldn't take his eyes off the razor in Manny's hand . . . the blade gleamed dully. "Your . . . your face. It's different."

"Yeah, it is . . . isn't it? Different enough to fool you and Whitey and Sherman before. Thought I'd take a little look at what Whitey had made for himself . . . with what he stole from me." He moved closer, toying with the razor. "You've done pretty well for yourself also. A landlord. When you never used to have the bloody brains to come in out of the rain."

"What do you want, Manny?" Goris prayed that his reflexes, his nerves, would react as swiftly as they had before. Or was he too old and too fat now?

"What do you think I want?" Without warning, Manny lashed out with the razor, the blade completely open. Goris jumped back but wasn't quick enough. The blade was sharp . . . he felt nothing more than a quick, fleeting pain as it slashed across his right cheek. He raised a hand to defend himself, and Manny swung again . . . wildly, blindly. The blade hacked across Goris' hands like an ax. Then a foot drove itself into his groin.

Goris gasped, clutched himself with his bloody hands. A cry started from his throat and Manny's hand snaked out again. The once shining blade, now marred with dripping blood, danced horizontally across Goris' mouth. The old wound opened, the flesh around his mouth flapped grotesquely. His tongue burned with agony and he started to choke on the blood that flowed down his throat.

One final time the blade moved in Manny's hand . . . He stepped behind Goris, grabbed the stricken man by the hair, pulled back, stretched the neck tight. Then Manny drew the blade slowly across Goris' throat. Blood spurted, pumped with arterial force, and Manny leaped back. A giggle broke the silence of the night.

He wiped the razor clean, placed it leisurely in his coat pocket while he watched Goris slowly and silently bleed to death on the concrete. Then he walked away, stopping just once to look back at the huddled figure before the darkness swallowed it . . .

Perhaps that blonde divorcée from Philadelphia would still be awake. He could use her now . . . now that he'd worked up an appetite.

CHAPTER TWENTY-SIX

Any doubt that Lazar might have had about Manny's return – or whether Taylor's death had merely been a macabre practical joke – disappeared the moment he viewed Goris' mutilated body in the morgue at London Hospital. Only one man could willingly do that kind of damage to another human being. Lazar had no doubt that Manny Goodman was somewhere in London.

Lazar turned away from the corpse, looked at Ivor Davies, who had called him to the hospital to identify the body. Goris had no family, no close friends. As his employer, Lazar was needed to make formal identification. "Where was he found?"

"Outside the block of flats where he lived," Davies replied. "At three thirty-five this morning. By some drunk. He sobered up damn quick, I can tell you."

Before the morgue attendant could cover the body, Lazar looked down again. Goris' face was so mutilated that Lazar could not even make out the original scar across the mouth. Poor bastard, he thought . . . poor, poor bastard. To die like that, with your blood leaking away into the road. To madman Goodman's giggle accompaniment.

"I'll take you home," Davies offered.

"Haven't I got to sign some papers first? I'm like his next of kin."

"We can arrange to do all that tomorrow." Davies led Lazar from the hospital. For half a minute they stood by Davies' car while Lazar breathed in deeply, tried to control his raging stomach and blot from his mind what he had just seen. When Davies opened the car door, Lazar shook his head.

"Thanks, but I can see myself home. You get back to Ilford

and look after Leah,"

"The locals are still watching the place," Davies said. "I'm going back to the Yard."

"Why? What do you think you can do there?"

Davies shrugged. Lazar's question was unanswerable. They hadn't managed to do anything yet . . .

"You won't catch him," Lazar said. "No one'll catch him. The only thing we can do is wait . . . until he comes after me."

"How can we nab him then?" Lazar's remark worried Davies. What was Lazar planning to do . . . set himself up as bait? "Look what he did to Goris."

"Goris didn't have the protection I do." Lazar felt sick about the man's death. He'd let him go home by himself, continue living by himself . . . when he'd arranged protection for everyone else. But how was he to have known that Manny was aware of the part Goris had played in that night's work?

"Ivor . . ." Lazar said quietly, reaching a decision, ". . . get rid of the local police at your house. They're worse than useless."

"What?"

"Move Leah and Adele in with Katya and the boys. My house is like a fortress right now. Nothing can get in without being spotted."

Davies wasn't sure he liked the idea. "Why don't I just send Leah and Adele away? The same goes for Katya and the boys?"

"Katya won't go. I asked her a long time ago, right after you told me about Taylor's death. Anyway . . . I want my family where I can keep them guarded. You'd be doing yourself a favor by moving your family in there too."

Davies thought it over, had to agree it made sense. And it would take that damned police car away from the front of his house. "I'll bring them over this afternoon."

"Good. And I'll call Shmuel. Maybe I can persuade him and Lottie to move in too."

"That's a big maybe."

"I know. But it's a better bet than trying to keep them under surveillance from the shop across the road."

When Lazar arrived home Jimmy Peters and two other men were on duty at the house. Lazar took Katya into the study, told her exactly what he had seen. There was no question about it now. Manny was back . . . and he was exacting a terrible revenge. Katya turned white, felt her stomach rebel as Lazar described — sparing the worst — Goris' horrible death. "He must be sick to do something like that to another man."

"We know that already. Katya, do me a favor. Speak to Lottie. Tell her that she and Shmuel have to move in here until it's all over. She might listen to you more than if I spoke to Shmuel."

Katya dialed the number, gave Lazar a quick, worried smile when Lottie answered. "Lottie, it's Katya. Please listen very carefully to what I have to say . . . believe me, it's for your own benefit." Speaking quickly, she told Lottie about Goris' death.

Lottie gasped. Shmuel, who was sitting close to her in the living room, looked up from the newspaper he was reading. "What is it? What's the matter?"

She waved a hand at him to be silent. "Are they sure it's Manny?" Lottie asked Katya.

"Katya?" Shmuel repeated. Now what was going on? Wasn't it bad enough they had to put up with being watched from across the street? He took the phone away from Lottie. "Who is this?"

"It's Katya."

"What do you want?"

"I . . . Lazar . . . we want you to move in with us."

"Why?"

"Because another man's been killed. Do you remember Goris?"

"From Pearl's?" Shmuel couldn't remember meeting the man but knew the name.

"He's dead. Manny killed him. Do you need any more of a reason than that?"

Shmuel glanced at Lottie. "I don't understand," he said, bewildered. "Why . . . if it's Manny . . . would he kill Goris? The poor man just worked for him, that's all."

Katya held a hand over the mouthpiece. "Lazar . . ." she whispered. "Shmuel wants to know why Manny would kill

Goris. I can't tell him."

Lazar took the phone from her. So much, he thought, for Katya speaking to Lottie. "Shmuel, pack some clothes, shut up your shop for a while and come over here . . . if you don't want any harm to come to you and Lottie."

"Why was Goris killed?" Shmuel demanded. "Until I hear the answer to that question I'm not doing anything."

"I can't tell you over the phone, can't you understand that?" Lazar shouted, and Shmuel recognized fear in his brother's voice. Lazar was genuinely terrified . . . not only for himself but for all the family. "All I know is I can protect you here. You'll be safe as long as you're here."

"Tell him that Leah and Adele are moving in," Katya whispered, tugging at Lazar's arm. He did and waited for Shmuel's response.

"You really do think we're all in danger, don't you?" Shmuel said.

"More than any of us have ever been in before."

"And from one man . . . one crazy man. All right," he decided. "I'll come over this afternoon. I'll listen to what you've got to say."

"But . . . but what about bringing Lottie?"

"I'll decide about that only after I've heard the truth. And you'd better tell it to me."

"I will," Lazar promised. "I will."

Ivor Davies brought his family over to the house shortly after two o'clock. The maid showed Leah and Adele upstairs to a room she had prepared for them, while Davies joined Lazar in the study.

"You're going to tell Shmuel all about that night, are you?"

"I've got to . . . so I can protect him and Lottie. Are you going to stay with me?"

"What good do you think that'll do? My being here won't make what you did — even if it *was* Manny Goodman — any more respectable in Shmuel's eyes. Anyway . . . I'd rather it wasn't public knowledge that I was aware of all of it. Especially if he ever decides to tell his young friend

Chris about it."

Lazar hadn't thought about that. "The kid could make some kind of name for himself with that information, couldn't he?"

"You're bloody right he could," Davies said grimly. "*If* he could prove any of it."

There were a damn many other things that he could make a name on, Lazar thought. Like Withers . . . and Johnny. Christ, he'd have a heyday — not to mention destroying Lazar's empire. Davies' too; he would never be able to survive a scandal like that . . .

Shmuel arrived at four thirty, after Davies had gone. Lazar led his brother into the study, offered him a seat. But Shmuel remained standing, his face set.

"I'm waiting to hear what you have to say."

Lazar took a deep breath. "Manny Goodman never murdered anyone. Goris, Harry Sherman and I killed Davey Vanetti and his lieutenant. And then we left evidence pointing to Manny."

Shmuel had long ago decided that whatever his brother did could not shock him anymore. He'd done too much already. But he was wrong. Learning about how he had been drugged . . . made to lose an eye to further Lazar's ambition . . . was nothing compared with finding out that his brother had committed two murders and thrown the blame on an innocent man. No wonder Manny had come back, was avenging himself against those who had framed him. "On top of everything else, you're a murderer as well, eh? And you had to drag Leah and Katya into it? Make them lie to serve your purposes?"

"What would you have done, Shmuel, if you'd learned that Manny was mistreating Leah?" He saw Shmuel falter and felt a tiny spark of hope. "When she came back from her honeymoon she was a mass of bruises. He beat her, terrorized her."

"Lazar . . ." Shmuel's voice was ominously quiet. "Are you lying to me? Because if you are you won't have to wait for Manny to find you. I'll break you in two right here and now."

"Would you believe it if you heard it from Leah?"

"I don't know what to believe anymore where you're concerned."

"I'll get her, and you can make up your own mind." He walked past Shmuel, opened the study door, called Leah. She was in the living room with Katya and the children.

"Leah, please tell Shmuel what happened during your . . . marriage . . . to Manny."

She looked at Shmuel, fixed him with a steady gaze. "He beat me up. Almost every night." She was amazed that she could talk so calmly about those days . . . especially now that Manny was back. "A couple of times he almost killed me."

Shmuel took his eyes away from his sister's face, looked again at Lazar. "But why Vanetti and the other man? Why not just Manny?"

"It was all part of the same deal," Lazar said, tired now.

"Deal? With whom? The man who lived here?"

"And others. To avoid a gang war that Manny was precipitating."

"A deal . . . everything's a deal with you, isn't it?" Shmuel sighed, his body sagged. "I think Lottie and I would rather take our own chances. I'm not sure I like the way you've suddenly become so interested in our welfare." He turned around and walked out of the study.

Lazar followed him, watched him climb into the van and start the engine. He knew it was time to play his trump card.

Chris Peters was proofreading a story he'd just written when the telephone rang. He picked it up, listened and then replaced the receiver. He told his editor that he had to go out.

He cycled to Stamford Hill, noticed that the furniture van was absent. After a few minutes Shmuel drove up. "Don't go in," Chris said. "I've got to speak to you."

"What's the matter, Chris? Why were you waiting out here?"

"Your brother just called me."

"Lazar? Oh . . . he thinks he can use you to make me change my mind, does he? Don't get yourself involved, Chris. Don't make the mistake of sticking up for him because he once did us a favor with that gala night. That was out of guilt — "

"One favor?" Chris asked. "Only one?"

"What do you mean?"

"Who the hell do you think sent you all those anonymous contributions through the solicitor?" Chris burst out, suddenly angry with Shmuel. "Well? Who do you think did it . . . someone with nothing better to do with their money?"

"Lazar did? How do you know?"

"Because he told me. When he came to me with his idea for the gala night."

"And you believed him?"

"I had to . . . because he couldn't have known about that money from anyone else. Just we knew . . . you, me and Lottie. And the solicitor and the person who was sending the money." Chris thought of something else. "He didn't want to tell me, either. Only when he saw that I didn't trust him . . . didn't trust his motives for organizing the gala night . . . did he say anything. And then he swore me to secrecy, said I was never to tell you. But I'm telling you now so you'll stop hating your brother and do the right bloody thing . . ."

Shmuel looked down, embarrassed by Chris' outburst. Once, when the money had first started to arrive, he'd considered the possibility that Lazar might be responsible. But Shmuel hadn't let himself believe it . . . He *wanted* to hate Lazar, to continue blaming his brother for the loss of his eye, wanted to hold him responsible until he went to his grave. Above all, he wanted to hurt Lazar like he had been hurt. And the way to do it was to keep ignoring Lazar's passionate desire to make amends.

"Go across the street," Shmuel told Chris. "Tell the men in the shop that their services aren't needed anymore. I'll go to my brother's."

The guard on the house in The Bishop's Avenue changed shifts at six that evening. Jimmy Peters and the two men on duty with him went off. Three other men came on, checked around the grounds carefully. Harry Sherman also moved in, the stakeout at the furniture shop finished. Lazar wanted the bald man with him. With everyone under the same roof, Manny would have to come to them.

Well after midnight, when most of the house was asleep,

Lazar sat up in the paneled study with Sherman. Neither of them would be able to sleep. They played rummy across the desk, drank tea when one of the guards brought it in. At one thirty the telephone rang. Lazar let it ring a couple of times. Then Sherman grabbed the receiver. "You expecting a call?" he asked, a fat hand over the mouthpiece.

Lazar shook his head, took the receiver. "Yes?"

"Whitey . . . did I wake you up?" And then came a familiar high-pitched giggle.

Lazar's eyes showed his undeniable terror as he looked across the desk at Sherman. There was no need for the bald man to ask the identity of the caller. He quietly opened the study door, went outside to the hall and picked up the extension.

"Whitey, are you there? It's been a long time since we talked. I think we're overdue for this little chat."

"Manny . . ." Lazar forced the name past suddenly parched lips. "Where are you?"

"Wouldn't you like to know?"

"You're crazy, Manny. Everyone's out looking for you. My men, the law, everyone. They're going to catch you."

"No, they're not. No one's ever going to catch me. Goris didn't recognize me, did he? Not until it was too late." In the narrow confines of the telephone booth Manny glanced sideways at Jimmy Peters, who was crushed up against him. "You don't know what I look like anymore, Whitey. You don't even know my name these days, do you? So how are you going to catch me? You're a blind man, Whitey, tapping your way around in the dark with your little white stick. Tap . . . tap . . . tap . . ."

"What do you want, Manny?"

"What do I want?" Manny started to laugh at the question; it changed immediately to the giggle which sent shivers into Lazar's spine. "I want everything that's mine, Whitey. I want you. I want Harry Sherman. I want Leah. I want *all* of you . . . and I'm going to get . . . I'm going to do to you . . . every single one of you . . . what I did to Goris. Did you see what Goris looked like when I finished with him? Do you think Katya will look pretty like that? And Leah?" Before Lazar could answer, Manny replaced the receiver. He was breathing heavily, his forehead covered with sweat.

When he could control himself he pushed his way out of the phone booth, turned to Jimmy. "Your governor's a very frightened man just now."

"How long are you going to keep this up?"

"As long as I'm enjoying it."

"And then . . . ?"

"And then I'm going to cut their throats like so many chickens."

"Did you mean what you said . . . about the women?"

"Maybe." He slapped Jimmy on the shoulder. "What's the matter with you . . . getting a bit squeamish all of a sudden, are you?"

Jimmy didn't answer. It had all seemed so simple when he's got Manny's address from Taylor. But now his fear of Manny was starting to override his hatred for Lazar and Sherman. He'd opened a bottle . . . rubbed an oil lamp . . . and released a genie. And Jimmy wasn't certain that he had any control over that genie at all.

Sherman returned to the study to find Lazar pacing the room, hands clasped behind his back. Lazar didn't hear the bald man enter. All he could think of was Manny. He *was* after everyone, was determined to wipe out the family completely. And he'd been right that Lazar was groping in the dark. How did you fight an enemy you couldn't see, couldn't recognize even if you did see him?

"You want to look around the house?" Sherman suggested. He knew that he would feel safer if he could see for himself that everything was secure.

"Let's go." Lazar led the way from the study, padded quietly through all the ground-floor rooms. Then upstairs. He looked into Katya's room, the boys' rooms, the room where Leah and Adele slept, all the spare rooms. The door to the room where Shmuel and Lottie slept was closed. He didn't open it.

"Let's go outside," Lazar said. Sherman followed him

through the front door. Almost immediately they were challenged by the guard and Lazar began to feel the slightest bit safer. At least the guards were alert.

"It's okay. It's me . . . Whitey."

The guard relaxed, turned away to continue his patrol.

"What are you going to do?" Sherman asked.

Lazar didn't know. Would Manny be at all open to a trade-off? Was he really after those men who had set him up? Or was he so hell-bent on destroying the entire family that he wouldn't even care?

CHAPTER TWENTY-SEVEN

Manny decided to give Lazar the weekend, knowing the waiting would play on Lazar's nerves, devastate his ability to think or act with logic or decisiveness. He didn't call the house again until the following Monday night, again at one thirty.

Sitting in the study with Sherman, Lazar grabbed the phone. "*Yes?*" The single curt word echoed his fear.

"What's the matter?" Manny crooned. "Are you scared?"

"I'm not scared of a lunatic like you," Lazar looked up as Sherman left the study, headed for the extension in the hall.

"Not scared? I think different. I think you're shitting yourself right now. You're trying to imagine what I look like, aren't you? Where I am . . . what I'm called . . . and when I'm coming to get you. But you don't need much imagination to know what I'll do to you . . . do you? What the razor in my hand looks like? And how Leah and Katya will look when I've finished with them?"

Why the hell was it so damned impossible to find one man? Lazar asked himself. With the forces that he and Davies had they should have come up with something long before this.

In the phone booth Manny glanced at Jimmy. Clever little bastard that Whitey was . . . moving everyone into the house where he could protect them. Even with Jimmy's help, Manny wasn't certain he'd be able to get inside. And he certainly wouldn't be able to get out again.

"Manny . . . do you want just me or do you want everyone?" Lazar asked.

"I want you and Harry," Manny answered. "My two old

Solo-playing mates from Shaffzics. Remember those nights, do you, Whitey? I taught you how to play . . . and like everything I taught you, you learned too bloody well." He could sense that Lazar was offering an exchange, and was glad. Time was no longer on his side. Right now he was on top of everything. He'd killed Goris and was laughing at Whitey's terror. But the longer he left it the more chance there was of something going wrong. Jimmy Peters, for one thing. No matter how much he claimed to hate Lazar and Sherman, Manny decided he wasn't to be trusted. He might let something slip . . . or Lazar might find reason to suspect that there was a spy inside his camp. Manny had to finish it off. Kill Lazar and Sherman . . . and then rid himself of the only witness. He'd get back on the boat. Go back home . . . yes, the U.S. was his home now. He'd be able to continue his life with no more memories to haunt him . . .

"I'm willing to make an exchange, Whitey," Manny said. "You come to me. You and Harry, face-to-face. And I promise I won't touch your women or the kids."

"Where are you?" Lazar asked.

"In a minute, Whitey. In a minute. I want to get something straight with you right away. If I see more than you and Harry, then you won't find me. You'll never find me. But I'll find everyone else . . . believe me, I will. And I'll do to them what I did to Goris."

"Just me and Harry." Lazar knew Sherman was listening in, hoped he understood.

"Good. Just keep remembering Goris."

"And Joey Taylor," Lazar murmured.

"No . . . I didn't kill Taylor. Someone else did that . . . someone who hates you just as much as I do." The giggling again. "With all the people who hate your guts, Whitey, it's a bloody marvel you can sleep at nights."

Lazar looked around the study. Someone else? Which meant that Manny was not working alone — "Where will you be?"

Manny had considered that carefully. He wanted somewhere large. A place where he could see if he was being double-crossed. And a place that would be empty at this time of night.

"Remember where we used to go sometimes on Saturday afternoons?"

"Tottenham?"

"That's right. I'll leave a gate open for you. The first turnstile at the Paxton Road end. I'll give you half an hour . . . and if you're not there, I'll be coming over to your house."

"I'll be there." Lazar memorized what Manny had told him. He hadn't thought he'd be going back to the stadium until summer's end, when the new season started. Now he was returning early . . . to either kill or be killed.

"You make sure you are." Manny hung up the phone. He came out of the phone booth, stood with Jimmy in Paxton Road and looked up at the stadium. Then he started to walk toward the first turnstile, turning up his coat collar against the rain that was beginning to fall. The door was easy to force. Once inside, he pushed the door closed and he and Jimmy vaulted over the turnstile. All they had to do now was wait.

Moments after he hung up, the study door swung open and Lazar jumped in fright. He only caught his breath when he saw Sherman standing there. The bald man had on his jacket, ready to go out.

"Did you hear?" Lazar asked.

"I'm ready." Sherman reached into his pocket, tossed a narrow object across the study for Lazar to catch. It was a razor. "No second thoughts tonight, Whitey. When you see the chance, you use that. And you keep on using it until you're bloody sure he's dead."

"I will." Lazar threw his mind back seventeen years. To Aachen, the teahouse . . . He pictured the Brownshirt, the flourishing red moustache, and knew he'd have no trouble using the razor tonight.

They left the house, and immediately were challenged by Peter Cox. Lazar questioned his decision to go. With this kind of security Manny would never get near the place. They could let him hang on forever. Until he lost all control of himself and made a mistake. Or would he? There was never any way of knowing how his crazed mind would react. And he was sure there was an informer . . . No . . . Lazar decided . . . this was the best way. For the first time since he had returned they knew where he was. Maybe *they* could finish it . . . and not Manny.

"Where are you going?" Cox asked.

"We're going out. To settle it. He just called again."

"I'll come with you."

Lazar shook his head. "Just me and Harry."

Cox looked at Lazar like he was crazy. "You'll walk straight into a trap, going to him like that."

"That's a chance we'll take."

"For Christ's sake, Whitey! At least tell us where you're going to meet him."

"Keep your voice down, you fool!" Lazar dropped his own to an urgent hiss. "If I tell you, you've got to swear that you won't follow us. It's got to be between him and us."

Cox swallowed hard. "All right."

"He's waiting for us at the Spurs ground. There's a gate open, at the Paxton Road end. He's inside."

Cox nodded. "Good luck." He held out a hand but Lazar didn't see it as he hurried away toward his car. Sherman climbed into the passenger seat, pulled the door closed quietly. "Let's go," Sherman said and sat back, resigned to whatever would happen over the next half-hour.

Katya had heard the telephone ring. The burst of movement from downstairs, the loud, then whispered, conversation from the front of the house, and finally the sound of a car moving off. She slipped on a dressing gown and ran downstairs. The ground floor was empty. She opened the front door and called out for Peter Cox.

"Where's Lazar?" she asked, seeing that his car was missing. "And Harry?"

"They've gone out."

"Where?" The phone call . . . it had something to do with the phone call. "Who called?"

Cox fidgeted uncomfortably, his loyalty split between what he had promised Lazar and fear for his governor's life. The fear finally won over. "They've gone to meet Manny."

"Oh . . . my God! Where?"

Cox told her, Katya rushed back into the house. Should she call Davies? Where was he . . . at home alone in Ilford while his wife and daughter slept upstairs? Or was he at the office? Suddenly she remembered Shmuel. She ran upstairs, banged on the door of the room where Shmuel and Lottie slept. Nothing. She hammered again, threw open the door, turned on the light. Shmuel sat up in bed groggily. Next to him lay Lottie, slowly waking up.

"What is it?" Shmuel asked.

Katya gasped when she saw him for the first time without the eyepatch. An empty socket – with puckered skin half drawn over the space – stared back at her.

"What's the matter?" Shmuel asked. "What is it, Katya?"

"It's Lazar!" Katya quickly forgot about Shmuel's eye. "He's gone out to meet Manny . . . to settle it."

"What?" Shmuel swung himself out of bed. "He's crazy."

"Where are you going?" Lottie asked, reaching out to hold him back. He shook her hands away, walked quickly to the chair where his clothes were lying. While Katya watched, Shmuel pulled trousers and jacket over his pajamas, did up his belt, thrust his feet into his shoes.

"Where is he meeting Manny?"

Katya repeated what Cox had told her, about the entrance to the stadium in Paxton Road.

"Shmuel . . . come *back*, you'll be killed yourself . . ."

Shmuel didn't answer. He went past Katya, ran down the stairs and pulled open the front door. In his hurry he had forgotten to put on the eyepatch. The moment he cleared the front door, Peter Cox grabbed him by the arm.

"Where do you think you're going?"

"Out of my way," and Shmuel threw him off, ran toward the nearest car. Sherman's. He looked through the window. No keys. Cox grabbed him again. Another of the guards joined in.

"No one's to follow him, those were his orders," Cox shouted, suddenly regretting he had told Katya where Lazar and Sherman were going. He should never have broken his word . . .

"Lazar doesn't give *me* orders . . ." Shmuel threw both men off, gripped Cox by the shoulders. "Give me the keys to your car."

"Find them yourself – "

Shmuel raised a fist and Cox struggled to escape. Anyone else and he'd have dived in with both feet. But Shmuel was Lazar's brother. "I can't help you . . . don't you understand that?" Cox told him. "I made him a promise."

Shmuel lowered his hands, turned around and ran toward the furniture van. It wasn't fast but it still might get him there in time. He jumped into it, started the engine, lurched out of the driveway. Cox yelled at the other two guards to stop him. They leaped into another car, gunned the engine, started off after the van. Cox ran into the house to find Katya on the telephone, speaking to Davies.

"Who are you calling?"

"It doesn't matter," she said.

Cox felt useless. He could not be loyal to Lazar unless he turned against Lazar's family. An impossible situation.

No lights glowed in the vast, empty stadium. But the full moon showed from time to time through broken clouds to illuminate the playing field. The moon did not reach into the rear of the covered stands, though, and Manny and Jimmy Peters stood securely in the deep shadows, looking down toward the single unlocked door. Soon . . .

Manny turned his back on Jimmy and looked out over the field. He closed his eyes . . . could almost believe that he was living again in London, coming here regularly as he had done with Lazar. Before Lazar had betrayed him . . . It was fitting that he should meet with that little white-haired Judas in this place. Jimmy had told Manny about Lazar bringing the boys here, and the party they had thrown at the house on The Bishop's Avenue. The next gathering there would not be to celebrate . . . but to mourn.

"You get Sherman as soon as he comes in," Manny whispered. He didn't know why he was talking so quietly. In a stadium that could hold sixty thousand, he and Jimmy were the only two people. "And then leave Whitey to me." He brought out the razor, opened it. Jimmy produced his own weapon, a slim, double-edged commando knife.

Jimmy thought about Sherman. The bald man had been his mentor, had got him the job with Lazar in the first place. He'd got jobs for both twins. And now Jimmy was going to finish him off. It wouldn't be hard at all, Jimmy kept telling himself, just as long as he remembered his brother after that live rail had gone through him.

Shmuel drove as fast as the old furniture van could go. He knew he was being followed, had seen the lights come out of the driveway and knew they wanted to stop him because of their misguided loyalty to Lazar.

What loyalty did *he* have? he suddenly questioned. Why was he chasing off like this? It wasn't only Lazar anymore, though he knew he had to go to his brother no matter what. It was also because of Leah. If he'd known that Manny had beaten his sister, he would have killed the little spiv long before Lazar and Sherman had set him up, would have broken him in two with his bare hands . . .

He glanced in the mirror. Lazar's men in the car behind him were gaining, trying to overtake on the outside. Shmuel pulled out. The car behind braked violently, skidded and righted itself. Shmuel smiled grimly. They shouldn't mess around with a determined man driving a furniture van. He raced through a set of lights just as they changed to red, but to his dismay saw that the car had also got through. He kept to the outside, hogging the road.

The car closed the gap again, tried to sneak through on the inside, its driver intent on cutting in front of the van once he had the lead, forcing Shmuel to stop. Shmuel watched him carefully. It was too late now to change lanes and push them back. They were level with the rear of the van. If he pulled over now, he'd send them off the road.

The wheel twitched in his hands. Before he realized what he

was doing, he'd slammed on the brakes, yanked the wheel over, skidded on the wet road surface back into the inside lane. There was a grinding of metal, a loud bang as the car caromed off the curb, a smashing of glass as it mounted the sidewalk, spun out of control and crashed into a shop front. Shmuel looked just once in the mirror. Doors were opening. The two men in the car were getting out, unhurt. He felt better.

He was going to help Lazar, to help him . . . and he would allow nothing on earth to stop him. And in that moment Shmuel realized that after all these years he loved his older brother.

Lazar parked in the shadow of the Paxton Road end of the stadium and got out. Sherman joined him and they both looked up at the letters above the many entrances. Then they walked slowly toward the first door. Sherman pushed at it with his foot. The door swung back, creaked a little. He motioned to Lazar and both men moved silently through. Lazar climbed over the turnstile with ease. Sherman followed, puffing and panting as he hoisted his bulk over. Then they stood inside the stadium, looking around nervously, expecting an attack but not knowing where it would come from.

Davies sat behind the wheel of the police car as the siren screamed through the darkened streets. It was raining heavily now. Goddamn them all! he cursed silently. Stupid bastards! Not only Lazar and Sherman, but Shmuel as well. They'd all be killed facing that madman on a battleground he'd chosen. If only he could get there in time. He might be able to stop the carnage and catch Manny. But if he got away this time God knew they'd never catch him. And Leah . . . though she might escape from this night, she'd never be able to relax again. Knowing that Manny might still be out there somewhere, carrying out his insane vengeance.

A street-cleaning truck blocked the road up ahead. But Davies didn't think twice. He jerked the wheel to the left, roared across the sidewalk and back onto the road. He didn't have the time to be cautious . . . or frightened.

He saw that the rain had let up and turned off the wipers. It was the first thing that had gone right since Katya had called him. He prayed that it was a good omen.

"Oy, Whitey! Up here!"

Manny's voice rang down to ground level where Lazar and Sherman stood. Both men lifted their heads, saw on one of the terraces a figure silhouetted against the moon. Then just as suddenly it disappeared.

Sherman started up the steep flight of stairs, but Lazar pulled him back, offered to take the lead. Too often Sherman had taken his place. This was one time when he had to go first.

Shmuel barely noticed his own shop as he barreled the van down Stamford Hill toward Tottenham. Just another couple of miles and he'd be there. Another couple of miles. Please God, he thought . . . don't let me be too late!

Davies was making the same prayer as he sped through Clapton at sixty miles an hour, becoming more tense as he neared his destination.

Another few minutes . . . that was all. Another few minutes and it would all be over. He'd finally have Manny . . . and Lazar would be saved. He hoped.

Lazar emerged from the stairs midway up the terraces, looked down across the moonlit field, spun around. Shadows on the terraces mocked his futile efforts to spot Manny. He could see only the wide steel supports running up to the roof, the crash bars that prevented the crowds from rushing down, and Sherman gasping his way up the steps. "Manny! Where are you?" Lazar screamed. "Are you too chicken to face me?"

Sherman reached the terraces, looked around with bewilderment as well. Like a magician, Manny had disappeared. Then Sherman screamed in terror . . . an arm was wrapped around his throat . . . and the sharp, double-edged blade of a commando knife was shoved between his ribs.

"You!" Lazar gasped when he recognized Jimmy Peters, hiding behind the entrance of the stairway. "It was you!"

"That's right, Whitey," Jimmy said quietly as he let Sherman's body drop onto the cold concrete. It hadn't been difficult at all. Just one quick movement and the point of the knife had slipped between Sherman's ribs, plunged into his heart. Just the way they'd taught him at commando school.

"Why don't you ask him why, Whitey?" Manny's voice came from Lazar's right and he appeared from behind the steel support which had hidden him. In his hand the razor gleamed.

"My brother Johnny didn't drink," Jimmy said. "You didn't know that, did you?"

"What?" Lazar felt in his pocket for the razor Sherman had given him, pulled it free, clicked it open.

"Johnny didn't drink. He couldn't have gotten drunk enough to stumble over some live rail, Whitey. You killed him . . . Why?"

"Answer the man," Manny prompted. "He's got a right to know why his brother died."

Lazar's reply was a sudden lunge with the razor. Jimmy jumped back with ease, laughed contemptuously at the attempt.

"Me, first, Whitey," Manny said. "I've got the older grudge to settle." Manny advanced slowly, the razor held out. Like he'd once done in the flat above the greengrocer's shop on Booth Street. Lazar backed away, down the wide steps that led down to the playing surface. Only Manny's voice told him who it was; he hadn't recognized his face at all. That's why Goris had been killed so easily, he thought. Manny must have walked right up to him.

The low wall which separated the terraces from the playing area pressed against Lazar's back, and he stopped.

"Why don't you tell Jimmy why you killed his brother?" Manny taunted as he followed Lazar down the steps. He stopped a couple of yards away, looking into Lazar's eyes. "Come on, Whitey . . . you can tell us. We were your friends once."

Lazar looked past Manny to where the body of Harry Sherman lay . . . All the times Harry had fought for him, stood alongside him. And now he was dead . . . all because of *him* . . . Lazar lashed out with the razor but it cut thin air as Manny ducked. Lazar closed his eyes, expecting to feel Manny's blade slicing through his own face. Nothing happened. When he looked again, Manny's taunting face was still two yards away. "Jimmy still wants to know why you killed his brother, Whitey."

"Because he turned into a squealer," Lazar spat out. "That's why."

"Johnny?" Jimmy couldn't believe it.

"That's right. He was working hand-in-hand with Withers from C.I.D. to fit me up for something because I was going against Taylor . . . just like Withers did to you," he added for Manny's benefit. "Come on, Manny," he coaxed, holding up the razor. "You want me . . . you come and get me." As his imagination replaced Manny's face with the Brownshirt's in Aachen, his grip on the razor grew tighter, more confident.

Manny moved in, feinted. But Lazar vaulted backward, over the low wall, onto the running track, then onto the field. Here it was bright, open. There were no shadows for Manny and Jimmy to hide in.

Manny's voice followed him. "You can't go anywhere, Whitey. There's nowhere for you to hide." He climbed the wall, dropped down onto the other side. Jimmy jumped over the wall a few yards to the right, moved out to cut Lazar off. Lazar saw the maneuver, changed his own direction, wanting to keep both men in sight. He felt something at his back, turned and realized he was against the goalpost. Manny darted forward a couple of yards, froze when Lazar swung around in time to see him.

Lazar felt behind him, wiped the sweat from his hand on the goal netting. Jimmy moved around the other way, approached from his left. Too late Lazar realized he was as trapped here as he had been on the terraces. Jimmy was much younger; could outrun him with ease, keep pushing him into Manny's arms . . . and onto his blade.

Lazar thought a final time of the Brownshirt in Aachen . . . reaching down for the knife that lay on the table . . . picking it up . . . thrusting it into the man's stomach. He lunged

407

forward, carving a huge semicircle in front of him with the razor. The sound of Manny's surprised scream as the blade bit through his coat, into his left arm, was like adrenalin to Lazar. He swung again . . . with all his strength . . . with every ounce of concentration he possessed . . . aiming this time for the throat. Manny weaved away, in pain from the cut on his arm. And Lazar − trying desperately to maintain the swing − slipped on the wet grass and fell to the ground.

Before he could move, a shoe hammered his wrist. He cried out as his hand was viciously kicked open, the razor knocked away. Then Manny was down on top of him, dripping blood from his arm onto Lazar, his eyes blazing. Beneath his left eye, the tic was jumping . . .

Manny had no more time for jokes, no time for taunting. Now he had a job to do. He pressed the blade against Lazar's windpipe, felt it move up and down as Lazar breathed heavily. His eyes met Lazar's . . . and a small, triumphant grin etched itself across Manny's face.

Shmuel reached the stadium, drove around until he spotted Lazar's car. He jumped out of the furniture van, ran heavily toward the nearest door to the stadium. It was locked. Shmuel backed up two paces and threw himself at the door. The lock gave and the door bounced back. Faced by a turnstile, Shmuel heaved himself over it and began running for the closest stretch of light . . . one of the entrances to the terraces where the moon shone through.

"Good riddance, Whitey."

Manny pressed down, drew his hand across Lazar's throat. At the last moment Lazar struggled, gagged as blood and air filled his throat and lungs, felt the cold steel burning its way through his flesh. He tried to scream but couldn't. All he could do was watch as Manny stood up. Finally he lay still.

Manny stared down at the gaping wound in Lazar's throat, at the blood and rain mixing on the grass. Then he turned away, began walking toward the Paxton Road stand. His arm didn't hurt anymore . . . Vengeance had dulled all pain. He didn't think the cut was that deep anyway; his coat sleeve had protected him somewhat. He couldn't go to the hospital to get it stitched; he'd have to do the job himself, pinch it closed, hold it together with tape. He knew he wouldn't get an infection. The people who made razors used too good a grade of steel.

Jimmy hurried to join him. He looked back at Lazar's body just once, offered up a silent prayer that his dead twin brother could see that justice had been done. Manny slowed down, waited for Jimmy to catch up with him. Then, in a comradely gesture he put his arm around Jimmy's shoulder. "Give me a hand," Manny said. "Bastard cut me . . . I feel weak."

"Sure," Jimmy moved into the embrace, anxious to help Manny, anxious to be away from this damned place. He didn't see the folded razor in the hand that Manny placed on his shoulder, never heard a sound as it slid open.

Shmuel burst onto the terraces and looked straight out onto the field. Two figures were walking toward him, oblivious to his presence. Behind, they were leaving a third figure . . . a white-haired man on his back, arms and legs outstretched. Shmuel started to run down the steps. In the moonlight he could now recognize Jimmy Peters. He seemed to be helping the other man to walk. It had to be Manny . . .

As Shmuel watched, Manny's hand on Jimmy's shoulder suddenly came alive. Jimmy sensed the danger too late. He tried to move but Manny had the razor pressed against his jugular vein. One quick sweep — before Jimmy could even wonder why — and his throat was slit.

"Manny!" Shmuel roared as he reached the bottom of the terraces and hauled himself over the wall. "Manny!"

Manny stepped back, let Jimmy's body slide to the wet grass. He looked toward the Paxton Road stand, saw Shmuel charging at him, fists punching the air. The sight of the one-eyed man racing toward him unnerved Manny. He faltered; feeling the pain shoot up his arm, he felt light-headed. In a desperate attempt at defense he held up the razor. One more body wouldn't make any difference now.

Five yards away, Shmuel crouched and dived. A flailing arm knocked the razor aside. Then his hands were on Manny's throat, thumbs gouging his windpipe. Manny's feet came off the ground as Shmuel's immense strength lifted him high into the air. A scream started . . . and died as the air was choked from his body. His eyes started to bulge, his skin turned blue.

And then, as if realizing at last what he was doing, Shmuel opened his hands, let the semiconscious body fall to the ground. He stood over Manny, chest heaving. He turned, walked to the body of Jimmy Peters, knelt down alongside it and felt pity . . . for his young friend Chris who would have to attend another funeral. From Jimmy, he walked to Lazar, again knelt down, let the tears flow as he gazed at the body of his brother. Shmuel lifted Lazar up, cradled him in his arms.

The sight of his brother's horrible mutilation snapped something deep within Shmuel's mind, and a sudden determination blossomed . . . He laid his brother's body gently on the grass, stood up, walked slowly to where Manny lay, now beginning to revive. Shmuel undid his wide leather belt, tugged it free from the loops. Manny opened his eyes, felt his neck, breathed in hoarsely. He focused on Shmuel, saw the belt stretched between both hands, and recognized the determination in his eyes.

"What . . . what are you going to do?" Manny croaked.

Shmuel never said a word. He reached down, yanked Manny to his feet. When Manny struggled, Shmuel slammed a fist into his stomach, doubling him over. Then he looped the belt around Manny's neck, pulled it as tight as it would go until the buckle was pressing hard into his windpipe. Manny clawed at the belt, tried to loosen it as Shmuel dragged him toward the goal at the Paxton Road end of the ground. Shmuel looked at the square wooden crossbar, wondered if it would take Manny's weight. Choosing a section where the bar met the post, he pulled on it. The wood was firm.

Manny's weakening, desperate blows pummeled Shmuel's head, but he didn't feel them. He threw the free end of the belt over the crossbar, pulled down on it, somehow managed to tie a simple knot. There was no slack here as there would be in a proper hangman's noose. No trapdoor to open. No sudden jerk that would snap the neck. Here, when Shmuel stepped back and released his hold, Manny's body would just swing from the crossbar.

Shmuel stepped back. Released his hold. And from six yards away, arms folded impassively across his chest, he watched Manny Goodman choke to death.

Ivor Davies spotted Shmuel's furniture van parked near Lazar's car, saw the open gate that Shmuel had smashed his way through. He rushed in, straight up the stairs onto the terraces, and almost stumbled over Sherman's body. He straightened up, looked outward, not able to believe the scene on the field.

Bodies seemed to be everywhere. A man was hanging from the crossbar of the nearest goal. And Shmuel was standing, statue-like, while he watched Manny Goodman swing.

Davies went down the steps carefully, over the low wall. He looked at Jimmy Peters' body . . . Lazar's. Then he moved toward Shmuel, stood next to him watching Manny. Davies realized Manny was still alive . . . barely. He wondered whether he should help him, cut him down. He could face a real hangman's noose as he should have years ago. No, he decided . . . it was better this way. Davies put a hand on Shmuel's shoulder and watched with him.

Justice was being executed. And, most importantly, some-one was seeing it done.

CHAPTER TWENTY-EIGHT

It always seemed to rain on funerals, Shmuel thought, as he stood by the graveside listening to the service. He looked at the coffin, still not able to believe that his brother Lazar was inside.

There were going to be a lot of funerals . . . Lazar, Sherman, Jimmy. And Manny himself. But no one would be attending Manny's. Ivor Davies had said it would take place in a prison, quoting that section of the death sentence where the judge said, ". . . And that your body be afterwards buried within the precincts of the prison in which you shall have been confined before your execution . . ." They were keeping to that. Perhaps Manny had not been hanged according to the letter of the law, but no one was prepared to make a big fuss about it.

Shmuel looked at Davies. Only the two of them knew how Manny had really died. Before Davies had gone back to his car to radio for help, he'd taken Manny down, removed the belt and left him lying on the grass with the others. The death had been recorded as strangulation – in self-defense, by Shmuel after he had been attacked.

The service was over. Shmuel stepped forward to shovel earth onto the casket, jammed the shovel back into the pile of dirt and stepped aside. The period of mourning would take place at the house in The Bishop's Avenue. He'd stay there with Lottie for the entire week. So would Leah. He wished it was over already. Watching Katya and Leah . . . and Lazar's two sons . . . for a week would be harder than that time on the playing field. But he knew he had to be with them. They were family, as dear to him . . . he realized now . . . as Lottie was.

On the ride back to Hampstead Garden, Shmuel shared the back seat of the first car with Davies. "Going to be a rough week," Davies said quietly. "How do you feel?"

"I don't really know, Ivor. Somehow I always knew deep down that it would end like this. That Lazar, one day, would have to pay back for all he did. But so many men . . . so many dead."

"Yeah, I suppose you're right." Davies had known it as well. Lazar had fought to become respectable, looked up to. But the havoc he'd created along the way would never rest, would haunt him and would come back finally to kill him.

Only one thing continued to puzzle Davies . . . Jimmy's motive. Why had he sided with Manny? He supposed he'd never know for sure now . . . everyone who could tell him was dead . . .

The procession of cars pulled up outside Lazar's house. Doors opened, somberly dressed men got out and went inside. Shmuel kissed Leah and Katya, held onto them tightly as if he were trying to absorb their grief, take some of it from them. "Where are the boys?"

"At a friend's home. They'll be back later," Katya answered. She had refused to let either of them attend the funeral; it would be bad enough for them to be around the house all through the week of mourning.

Davies followed Shmuel into the living room where small wooden chairs had been set out for the immediate family. Shmuel looked at them, remembering that he had never sat in mourning for his parents. Because of the rush there had been no time. Because of Lazar. He felt someone's hand on his shoulder and turned around.

"Shmuel . . . I want to ask you something," Davies said. "Something I don't understand."

"Go ahead."

"The night it happened. You were staying here . . . all right, I understand that. But you and Lazar hadn't got on since . . . since that." He nodded toward the eyepatch. "Why did you go off after him like that? Risk your own life to try to save his?"

Shmuel shook his head. He'd thought about it . . . he'd wondered about it all the time he had been driving to Tottenham. Even when he'd forced the car with Lazar's men off the road. And it was only when he'd looped his belt over the crossbar of the goal to make a British judge's death sentence finally come true that he'd realized exactly why he had done it.

"You didn't owe him anything," Davies said. "Why?"

A thousand memories started to unfold in front of Shmuel. The flight from Cologne . . . the East End . . . meeting Lottie at the Maziche Adas . . . the fight with Bomber Billy Harris and the awful knowledge that his own brother had sacrificed him . . . and finally facing up to the fact that Lazar had supported the boys' club all this time, funded it secretly so he could help his brother . . . a brother who was too proud and too bitter to acknowledge that help, to allow his older brother to crawl out from under his terrible burden of guilt.

But one memory overrode all the others. No matter what else Lazar had done, one act would always redeem him.

"Ivor," Shmuel said softly. "He waited for Leah and me in Maastricht. What else could I have done?"

THE END

EAGLES
by Lewis Orde

Son of a Catholic mother and a Jewish father, Roland Eagles is orphaned at fifteen when a German bomber destroys his family. Scarred by the horrors of Bergen-Belsen, he survives by instinct alone.

Using his business and gambling skills to build a financial empire, he elopes with the beautiful daughter of a diplomat—only to lose his wife in childbirth.

From the innocent passions of his first love, to the tight embrace of money and power, from the war-torn miseries of Europe to the lavish opulence of Manhattan society, this is the story of a street-wise boy whose remarkable life was ruled by ambition and power, tragedy and triumph.

0 552 12669 1   £2.95

A SELECTED LIST OF FINE NOVELS
AVAILABLE FROM CORGI BOOKS

WHILE EVERY EFFORT IS MADE TO KEEP PRICES LOW, IT IS SOME-
TIMES NECESSARY TO INCREASE PRICES AT SHORT NOTICE. CORGI
BOOKS RESERVE THE RIGHT TO SHOW NEW RETAIL PRICES ON
COVERS WHICH MAY DIFFER FROM THOSE PREVIOUSLY ADVERTISED
IN THE TEXT OR ELSEWHERE.

THE PRICES SHOWN BELOW WERE CORRECT AT THE TIME OF GOING
TO PRESS (MAY '86).

☐	12281 5	JADE	Pat Barr	£2.95
☐	12142 8	A WOMAN OF TWO CONTINENTS	Pixie Burger	£2.50
☐	12637 3	PROUD MARY	Iris Gower	£2.50
☐	12387 0	COPPER KINGDOM	Iris Gower	£1.95
☐	12503 2	THREE GIRLS	Frances Paige	£1.95
☐	12641 1	THE SUMMER OF THE BARSHINSKEYS	Diane Pearson	£2.95
☐	10375 6	CSARDAS	Diane Pearson	£2.95
☐	09140 5	SARAH WHITMAN	Diane Pearson	£2.50
☐	10271 7	THE MARIGOLD FIELD	Diane Pearson	£2.50
☐	10249 0	BRIDE OF TANCRED	Diane Pearson	£1.75
☐	12689 6	IN THE SHADOW OF THE CASTLE	Erin Pizzey	£2.50
☐	12462 1	THE WATERSHED	Erin Pizzey	£2.95
☐	11596 7	FEET IN CHAINS	Kate Roberts	£1.95
☐	11685 8	THE LIVING SLEEP	Kate Roberts	£2.50
☐	12607 1	DOCTOR ROSE	Elvi Rhodes	£1.95
☐	12375 7	A SCATTERING OF DAISIES	Susan Sallis	£2.50
☐	12579 2	THE DAFFODILS OF NEWENT	Susan Sallis	£1.75
☐	12118 5	THE DEBUTANTES	June Flaum Singer	£2.50
☐	12609 8	STAR DREAMS	June Flaum Singer	£2.50
☐	12636 5	THE MOVIE SET	June Flaum Singer	£2.95
☐	12700 0	LIGHT AND DARK	Margaret Thomson Davis	£2.95
☐	11575 4	A NECESSARY WOMAN	Helen Van Slyke	£2.50
☐	12240 8	PUBLIC SMILES, PRIVATE TEARS	Helen Van Slyke	£2.50
☐	11321 2	SISTERS AND STRANGERS	Helen Van Slyke	£2.50
☐	11779 X	NO LOVE LOST	Helen Van Slyke	£2.50
☐	12676 4	GRACE PENSILVA	Michael Weston	£2.95

*All these books are available at your book shop or newsagent, or can be ordered direct from the
publisher. Just tick the titles you want and fill in the form below.*

CORGI BOOKS, Cash Sales Department, P.O. Box 11, Falmouth, Cornwall.

Please send cheque or postal order, no currency.

Please allow cost of book(s) plus the following for postage and packing:

U.K. Customers—Allow 55p for the first book, 22p for the second book and 14p for
each additional book ordered, to a maximum charge of £1.75.

B.F.P.O. and Eire—Allow 55p for the first book, 22p for the second book plus 14p per
copy for the next seven books, thereafter 8p per book.

Overseas Customers—Allow £1.00 for the first book and 25p per copy for each
additional book.

NAME (Block Letters) . . . .

ADDRESS . . . .

. . . .